Praise for Linda Green

'Emotionally moving. A thought-provoking page turner
with a poignant three-generational link'
Jane Corry, author of *The Dead Ex*, the *Sunday Times* bestseller

'Linda Green gets better and better and this book is
as absorbing as any a tale you will read this year.
A masterclass in crime woven with authentic feeling
and experience. We're in the hands of an expert'
Jo Spain, author of *The Confession*

'Linda Green is bloody brilliant!'
Amanda Prowse, bestselling author of *My Husband's Wife*

'Clever and compelling' Dorothy Koomson

'Witty and funny' *Company*

'Enjoyable, original and intriguing'
B A Paris, bestselling author of *Behind Closed Doors*

'Brilliantly plotted' Emily Barr

About the Author

Linda Green is a novelist and award-winning journalist who has written for the *Guardian*, the *Independent on Sunday* and the *Big Issue*. Linda lives in West Yorkshire. Her book *While My Eyes Were Closed* was a paperback bestseller and *After I've Gone* was a top five Amazon Kindle bestseller. Visit Linda on Twitter @LindaGreenisms and on Facebook at Author Linda Green.

Also by Linda Green

After I've Gone
While My Eyes Were Closed
The Marriage Mender
The Mummyfesto
And Then It Happened
Things I Wish I'd Known
Ten Reasons Not to Fall in Love
I Did a Bad Thing

the last thing she told me

Linda Green

Quercus

First published in Great Britain in 2018
This edition published in 2019 by

Quercus Editions Ltd
Carmelite House
50 Victoria Embankment
London EC4Y 0DZ

An Hachette UK company

A CIP catalogue record for this book is available
from the British Library

PB ISBN 978 1 78648 373 7
EBOOK ISBN 978 1 78648 374 4

10 9 8 7 6 5 4 3 2 1

Typeset by CC Book Production

Printed and bound in Great Britain by Clays Ltd, Elcograf S.p.A.

For all the women and girls
who have been made to feel shame

It was the shame, you see. The shame I brought on my family. Sometimes it is easier not to believe than to accept something so awful could have happened. That is why people bury things far beneath the surface. Deep down, out of sight and out of mind. Though not out of my mind. I carry the shame with me always. The shame and the guilt. They do not go away. If anything, they weigh heavier on me now than they did back then. Dragging me down, clawing at my insides. And when people say that what's buried in the past should stay there, they mean they don't want to have to deal with it. They're scared of the power of secrets to destroy lives. But keeping secrets can destroy you from the inside. Believe me, I know. And even the best-kept secrets have a habit of forcing their way to the surface.

1

The house appeared to know that its owner was about to die, shrouded, as it was, in early-morning mist, the downstairs curtains closed in respect, the gate squeaking mournfully as I opened it.

If there was such a thing as a nice house in which to end your days, this certainly wasn't it. It was cold, dark and draughty, perched high on the edge of the village, as if it didn't really want to be part of it but was too polite to say so. Behind it, the fields – criss-crossed by dry-stone walls – stretched out into the distance. Beyond them, the unrelenting bleakness of the moors.

I shivered as I hurried up the path and let myself in.

'Grandma, it's me.' The first thing I thought when I didn't hear a response was that maybe I was too late. She'd been weak, drifting in and out of sleep when I'd left the previous night. Perhaps she hadn't made it through till morning.

But when I entered the front room – in which she'd lived, eaten and slept for the past year – she turned her face to give me the faintest of smiles.

'Morning,' I said. 'Did you manage to get some sleep?'

She nodded.

'It's not too late to change your mind, you know. We could get you to hospital, or the hospice said we could call them at any time.'

She shook her head. She'd remained adamant she would leave the house only in a coffin. She'd also refused medication to relieve the pain. It was as if she thought she somehow had a duty to suffer.

'Well, at least let me stay over tonight. I hate the thought of you being on your own.'

'I won't be here tonight.' Her words were faint and difficult to understand. She'd taken her teeth out several weeks previously and refused to put them back in since.

'Come on. You've been saying that for weeks.'

'I'm tired. It's time to go now.'

There was something about the look in her eye as she said it that told me she meant it. I sat down on the end of her bed and took her hand. Her skin was paper-thin, revealing the bones and blue veins beneath it. She'd once said she liked me coming to visit because I was the only one who let her talk about death without getting upset or pretending it wasn't going to happen.

'Is there anything I can get to make you more comfortable?'

She shook her head again. We sat there for a while saying nothing, listening to the ticking of the clock and her shallow breaths. I tried to imagine what it must be like knowing you are about to die. I would want my family around me, I knew that.

'Do you want me to give Mum a call?' I asked. She managed to raise her eyebrows at me. It was as near as I'd get to a telling off at this point. She had always been very accepting of their distant relationship. It was me who struggled with it.

'I could ask James to bring the girls over.'

She shook her head again and whispered, 'I don't want to upset them. They're good girls. Anyway, I've got them with me.'

She gestured towards the mantelpiece. Every school photo they'd ever had – Ruby on her own at first, all toothy grin and straggly hair, then, a few years later, with Maisie's elfin face of delicate features and porcelain skin, next to hers – until last year, when Ruby had started secondary school and they'd had separate photos. Ruby's grin was now replaced with a self-conscious upturn of closed lips. It was as if someone had adjusted her brightness control. The contrast with Maisie's confidence and burgeoning beauty was obvious to see and unspoken by all. Except Grandma, who had said it was a shame you couldn't show the size of someone's heart in a photo. And had remarked how much Ruby looked like me in her uniform.

My own school photos were still up there on the cabinet. And Justin's, poking out from behind them. I suspected I had arranged them like that myself years ago, without her ever realising it. Rows of little frames covered with dust. In a way, she was surrounded by her family, a cardboard cut-out version.

'Justin sends his love,' I said. That was a lie. I'd texted yesterday to tell him she didn't have much longer, and his response had been to ask me to give him as much notice as possible about the funeral so he could book a flight to come over.

I wondered if it bothered Grandma and she was good at hiding it, or if she'd simply never had high expectations of her loved ones. Maybe coming of age in the war had something to do with it. Perhaps it taught you not to take anything for granted.

I passed her the glass of water and she managed to take a tiny sip through the straw. I put it back on the bedside table, glancing at the wedding photo of her and Grandad, as I did so. 'Does it help to think he'll be there for you?' I asked.

'He'll have given up waiting and gone off down pub,' she replied.

I smiled. Grandad had never been big on patience. He'd never been big on shows of emotion, either. The wedding photo was the only time I'd ever seen them holding hands. I wondered if Grandma had minded, but concluded that now wasn't the time to ask. She was quiet again, her breaths shallower still. I squeezed her hand. 'I'll be here with you until the end,' I said. 'I'm not going anywhere.'

She looked up at me. 'I'm leaving you the house.'

I frowned at her. 'But what about Mum?'

'She doesn't want it.'

'Has she told you that?'

'She doesn't have to.'

I felt somewhat unworthy of such a huge bequest. 'Well, Justin, then.'

'He doesn't need it.'

It was true, though it felt wrong to acknowledge it.

'Thank you,' I said, barely able to speak. 'It'll make such a difference.'

'I know,' she said. 'The girls can have their own rooms. And you always wanted a garden.'

It suddenly occurred to me that she thought we were going to live here. That this would be our home. I didn't want that. It was such a bleak house. The obvious thing was to sell it, so we could afford somewhere bigger than our little two-bedroom terrace in town. Maybe even with a garden. But I didn't want to tell her that. I didn't want to say anything to worry or upset her at this late stage. I smiled and nodded, patting her hand.

'Leave it to Ruby when you go,' she added. 'It belongs in the family.'

I opened my mouth to say something but nothing came out. I couldn't start arguing with her. It wasn't right to pick a fight with someone on their deathbed. If those were her final wishes, I owed it to her to listen graciously and go along with everything she said.

She shut her eyes. I wondered if this was it. I'd never been with a person when they'd died. I didn't know what to expect. I wasn't even sure what to do or who to call afterwards. I swallowed, glad at least that I was with her. That she hadn't died on her own. Ninety was a good age. That was what people would say. And she'd lived a good life, been free from any major health problems until the last couple of years. But it still seemed empty somehow, her slipping away in this house with only me for company.

I looked down. Her eyes remained shut, but I could see her chest rising and falling ever so slightly. She was still with me, but surely not for much longer. I slid my hand away, tiptoed out of the room and shut the door behind me, then took out my mobile. I didn't think she could hear me, but it still seemed wrong to speak within earshot. I went through to the kitchen. It was a strange collection of assorted relics from past decades. An old-fashioned kettle on the hob, which she'd refused to get rid of. A seventies breakfast-bar stool, which was now positively retro. None of it matched, none of it fitted but, as with the rest of the house, it was all unmistakably Grandma's.

I called Mum. She took her time to answer. When she did, it seemed from her tone that she was expecting the worst. She didn't say anything more than hello, waiting instead for me to break the news.

'I don't think she's got long.'

'Right. Is she in pain?'

'She's doing a good job of covering it up if she is. She said it was time to go.'

There was a pause at the other end. I thought for a moment that Mum might change her mind and say she was on her way. She didn't though.

'OK. Well, let me know any news.'

'That's it?'

'Come on, Nicola, don't make this any harder than it already is.'

'She's about to die without her only child being there.'

'We've gone through all this. It's not that simple.'

'Well, whatever it is between you two that needs saying, now's your last chance to say it.'

'I'm not about to upset her on her deathbed.'

'Maybe she's waiting for you to say something. Maybe that's why she's hung on so long. And you'll regret it if you don't. It'll be like that bloody Mike and the Mechanics song.'

'I don't think so. It's best this way. I know you don't believe me, but it is.'

'Best for who?'

'Look, I'm thinking of you, all right? And I'm grateful you're there with her but I can't come over.' Her voice broke and she hung up. I put my phone back in my pocket and blew out slowly. At least Justin had the excuse of being in Ireland. Mum was only a few miles up the road in Halifax. All I could think was how I'd feel if Ruby and Maisie weren't with me at the end. If they couldn't be bothered to bury the hatchet with me and come to me on my deathbed.

I went back into the front room. For a second, I thought she'd gone while I'd been on the phone, but her chest was still rising and falling. I sat down next to her and put my head in my hands. I had been sitting there for quite some time, maybe twenty minutes or so, before I heard her voice.

'There are babies.'

I looked up. I hadn't expected to hear another word out of her. I took her hand again. Her eyelids flickered open.

'Babies? Where?' I asked.

'At bottom of garden.'

I frowned at her. She'd been coherent all the way through. Maybe this was a sign that she was at the end now. Then something clicked, and I realised what she was talking about.

'No, Grandma. Fairies,' I said. 'You've got fairy statues at the bottom of the garden. The ones I used to dance around when I was little.'

There wasn't a pause on her part.

'Not fairies, babies,' she said firmly. 'Look after my babies for me.'

'What do you mean?' I asked. 'What babies?' It was too late. Her eyes shut again and a second later she was gone. It was as if those words had taken the last breath out of her. I felt for her pulse, just to make sure, but there was nothing. I screwed up my eyes and let my head drop, feeling the tears coming but wanting to stave them off and gather myself. Aware that I was the responsible adult in the house now, no longer the little girl dancing around the fairy statues in the garden while Grandma cooked tea for me. I gulped as the tears arrived in a rush. A life snuffed out. The memories, experiences and stories gone with her. Our family reduced to three generations, not four. And all I could think of as I sat there and sobbed was the last thing she told me. I had no idea what she meant. Maybe she hadn't been with it. Perhaps she'd even been dreaming. She might not have been talking to me at all. But she had sounded so certain of what she had said. what she had asked me to do.

I realised I should call someone. Her GP to start with. Presumably they'd be able to tell me what I needed to do. I stood up, my legs a little shaky. I'd always thought that when someone died they'd look different in some way. But Grandma seemed pretty much the same. Though maybe there was something about her face. Maybe something had lifted. Because she finally did seem at peace.

A few hours later I stood on the front step of Mum's house, waiting for her to come to the door. The freshly signed death certificate was in my bag, the image of Grandma's body being taken away still fresh in my mind. I wanted to go home to James and the girls, but I also knew that, despite everything, it was right to tell Mum in person. Maybe I was hoping to see an emotional reaction, one I might have missed on the phone. But when she opened the door and saw me there, she just nodded, her face expressionless. I stepped inside and shut the door behind me.

'I'm sorry,' I said.

'Did she go peacefully?' Mum asked.

'Yeah. She was talking, on and off, and then she was gone.'

'Where is she now?'

'The undertaker's. Dr Atkinson came over, signed the death certificate and got it all sorted.'

'She's a nice doctor, I've always said that.'

I shook my head.

'What?' asked Mum.

'Are you not even in the slightest bit upset?'

'We all knew it were coming.'

'Yeah. I've still bawled my eyes out, though.'

Mum shrugged. 'It'll probably hit me later. When I'm on my own.'

'Or maybe you're not that bothered.'

'Nicola, please don't start.'

'It's not me who's starting, though, is it? It's you not behaving like a normal daughter.'

'Come on. That's not fair. Everyone has their own way of dealing with these things.'

'These things? You mean the death of your mother?'

Mum looked away. 'It's more complicated than you realise.'

'So you keep saying. What would be more helpful is if you actually explained what went on between you.'

Mum started to walk away down the hall.

'I take it that's a no.'

'You should get back to your girls,' she said, stopping and turning to face me. 'Give them a hug from me.'

Mum's eyes were glistening. Sometimes the wall she'd built came perilously close to falling down. If I pushed at a brick, it might topple.

'She said something just before she died. Something I didn't understand.'

'What?'

'She said there were babies at the bottom of the garden. She asked me to look after her babies.'

For the first time I saw Mum's face crack. Her eyes widened, and her bottom lip trembled. 'I wouldn't take any notice of her. She were probably losing her mind by then.'

'She wasn't, though. I asked her if she meant her fairy statues, but she was adamant they were babies.'

'She were probably thinking about angels. She used to believe in angels, you know. She told me once her angels would be waiting for her at the end.'

I stepped outside. Maybe Mum was right. It made more sense than anything I could come up with. It was only after I'd shut the door behind me and heard the anguished sob from the other side that I wondered if she might not be able to tell me the truth, even if she wanted to.

Dear Betty,

I knew the first time I saw you that you were the girl for me. I didn't say anything, but I watched you all the time. I couldn't take my eyes off you. I could see you weren't like the other girls. You were younger, obviously, and so fresh-faced and pure — a proper English rose.

And, like all roses, you don't have to shout about your beauty. There is nothing brash about you. In fact, you're a little shy. But you are also so full of life, of joy. Sometimes I think you might actually burst, you seem so happy. I like that in a girl. Life is so short, we are all aware of that, and I don't see the point of living it miserably.

Your smile is pretty much the brightest damn thing I have ever seen. It lights up not only your face but all those around you. That's why I smiled at you when you walked past me, your hair swishing back and forth, looking pretty as a picture. I couldn't help it, you see. That's the effect you have on me. And for the rest of the day I carried the light of your smile around with me. Secretly letting it warm me from the inside.

You are the girl who makes everything worthwhile, the one I think about from the moment I wake up to the moment I go to sleep. Which is why I decided to write to you to let you know how I feel. Because maybe I'm a little shy too but I want you to know this. That, whatever the future holds for both of us, I will always be grateful for your smile. And I will carry it with me forever.

Yours,

William

2

When I got home, James greeted me at the door with a hug. There was nothing more guaranteed to get my tears started again.

'I'm sorry,' he said, 'I know how special she was to you.'

'It hasn't really sunk in yet. I can't believe she's actually gone. I kind of thought she'd hang on forever.'

James hugged me harder and brushed the tears from my eyes.

'What have you said to the girls?' I asked.

'Just that you'd be gone for a long time because Great-grandma was very poorly.'

I nodded. I'd wanted to tell them myself. I still remembered Mum making such a pig's ear of telling me that Grandad had died when I was thirteen that I'd thought it was Grandma who'd gone. Not that I imagined James would make a hash of it – he'd probably do a better job than me – but I suspected Ruby would take it badly and I wanted to be there for her.

'Where are they?' I asked.

'In the front room. Maisie's watching *The Worst Witch* again. Do you want me to come in with you?'

'Just give us a few minutes,' I said. He nodded and kissed my forehead.

I think Ruby guessed the second I walked into the room. She clocked my red-rimmed eyes, then started fiddling with the zip on her hoody. Maisie carried on staring at the screen, seemingly oblivious to my arrival and what it might mean. I had to reach over for the TV remote control and turn it off.

'Mummy, I was watching that,' Maisie protested. I resisted the temptation to point out that she'd already watched the episode at least four times and it would still be there whenever she wanted to carry on.

'I know,' I said, adopting my best breaking-news-of-a-death voice as I sat down on the sofa next to them, 'but I need to talk to you. As you know, Great-grandma was very old and poorly and I'm afraid she died this morning, while I was with her.'

Ruby burst into tears. I put my arm around her. 'It was very peaceful,' I went on. 'One minute she was talking and the next she was gone.'

'What was she talking about?' asked Maisie. I hesitated. Telling them the truth wasn't such a good idea just now.

'One of the last things she said was how much she loved you two. She pointed to the photos of you, said it was like having you there with her.'

'Why didn't you let us go with you?' asked Ruby.

'I did ask but she didn't want to upset you.'

'But I'm upset anyway,' sobbed Ruby.

'I know, love. But it's extra sad being with a person when they die.'

'Did she go blue?' asked Maisie.

'No. People don't go blue when they die.'

'Not even a little bit?' I shook my head. Maisie seemed disappointed. 'Where is she now?'

'The undertaker came to take her to a funeral parlour.'

'Is it like an ice-cream parlour but with dead people and no sprinkles?'

'Sort of,' I said, managing a smile for the first time since Grandma had died.

'It's not funny, Mum. Tell her it's not funny,' said Ruby.

I sighed and stroked Ruby's hair. It was at times like this that I wished I could split myself in half to be the two different mums my girls needed.

'It's OK, love. Great-grandma would still want us to smile. It's fine to cry but it's OK to smile too.'

'What will happen to her body now?' asked Maisie, unperturbed.

'Well, it will stay in a special cold-storage place until the funeral.'

'Will she be frozen like an ice pop?'

'No, just kept nice and cool.'

'When's the funeral?' asked Ruby.

'I don't know yet. About a week or so, I expect.'

'Will I get a day off school?' asked Maisie.

Ruby shot her a look before I had the chance to say anything.

'We'll talk about whether you want to go to the funeral when it's all arranged. You don't have to. It's completely up to you. Sometimes children like to come and say goodbye and sometimes they'd rather not. We can take you to visit the grave afterwards, if you'd prefer.'

'I want to come,' said Ruby.

'I do too,' said Maisie.

'Well, like I said, let's talk about it more in a couple of days.'

James came in carrying a tray of mugs. 'I thought it might be a hot-chocolate moment,' he said, putting them down on the coffee-table.

Maisie's eyes lit up. 'Do you always get hot chocolate when someone dies?' she asked.

'Maisie,' said Ruby, sharply. 'Mum, tell her.'

'It's OK,' I replied, brushing a damp strand of Ruby's hair from her face. 'We're still allowed hot chocolate, you know.'

'Yeah, but she's being disrespectful.'

'She doesn't mean to be,' I said quietly. 'It's because she's young.'

'Why does she always get away with stuff because of her age?' asked Ruby.

'She doesn't. You just forget what it's like to be eight.'

'I was never like that when I was eight,' said Ruby.

That was true. Ruby had always seemed much more mature than other girls her age. She had recently turned thirteen but it felt as if we'd had a teenager in the house for some time. She didn't look like one yet, though, for which I was grateful.

James squeezed onto the sofa between Maisie and Ruby and kissed each in turn on the top of their heads. Ruby burst into a fresh round of tears.

'I know it's sad she died,' said James, stroking her hair. 'But it might help if you try to remember all the happy times you had with her. You were her first great-grandchild, you know. That's pretty special.'

'Yes, but she's gone now, so I don't have any great-grand-parents left.'

'Do I have any great-grandparents left?' asked Maisie.

'No, love,' I said. 'But you've both got Grandma, haven't you? And, er, Grandad.'

'But he's in pain,' said Maisie.

'Who told you that?' I asked, wondering if Mum had said something to the girls, not that she had anything to do with Dad, either, but she heard things second-hand via Facebook.

'No, Maisie,' said Ruby, 'I told you Grandad's in Spain.'

James started laughing before I did.

'Stop it,' said Ruby, scowling at us, 'stop laughing.'

'We can't help it,' I said. 'She does say funny things sometimes.'

'Yeah, well, she shouldn't. Not when someone's just died.'

I picked up Ruby's mug and handed it to her, hoping the hot chocolate might have a more soothing effect on her than I did.

'And I've still got Nanna and Grandpa in Scotland too,' piped up Maisie.

I rolled my eyes. I was quite sure she didn't intend to be so insensitive, but she really did pick her moments. 'You both have,' I said. We'd always told Ruby she could call them Nanna and Grandpa too, but she'd refused. She was a stickler for the truth, Ruby. Always had been.

'Maybe we could get up to see them soon,' said James. 'Or

they might come down at Christmas to visit.' We knew that was unlikely. They'd moved to Scotland to be near James's sister and her three young children, presumably having given up on James ever providing them with a grandchild. They weren't to know he was about to meet a woman with a ready-made one.

'Was Grandma there when Great-grandma died?' asked Ruby, having taken a few sips of her hot chocolate.

'No,' I said.

'Why not?'

'She didn't want to be. Some people find these things difficult.'

'But she was her daughter. I'd be there if you were going to die.'

'Thank you,' I said, ruffling her hair. 'That's good to know.'

'Will I get hot chocolate when you die too?' asked Maisie, looking up at me.

After I'd turned out the light, I sat on Ruby's bed for a long time. Maisie had fallen asleep within minutes. She had breezed through Grandma's death the way she breezed through everything in life, a casual observer, giving a cursory glance and nod in that direction, then moving on to wherever she was heading next.

Ruby clearly wasn't finding it so easy. She lay there, her eyes still moist with tears, staring at the ceiling. I held her hand, not wanting her to cry herself to sleep without me.

'Why wasn't Grandma there, really?' she whispered.

'I told you, love. Some people don't like the thought of being with someone when they die.'

'But she hardly ever went to Great-grandma's house when she was alive.'

Nothing got past Ruby. I leant over and stroked her head. 'They just weren't that close. Not all mothers and daughters are like us.'

'Had they had an argument?'

'Well, we all have arguments, don't we?'

'I mean a big one.'

'I don't know. They were like that for as long as I can remember.'

'But I loved Great-grandma and I love Grandma. I don't understand why they didn't love each other.'

'Oh, I'm sure they loved each other. But you can still find it difficult to get on with someone you love.'

'Will Grandma go to the funeral?'

It was a fair question, one I'd been pondering myself, but, unfortunately, I didn't know the answer.

'I don't know. I hope so.'

'So do I,' said Ruby.

'How is she?' asked James, when I finally made it downstairs to the kitchen.

'Troubled, as ever.'

'She'll be fine,' he said, putting his arms around me. 'Although she'll find the funeral tough. It's a tricky one at her age.'

'I know, but I don't think we've got much choice – you know what she's like. She's just been asking whether Mum will go.'

'What did you say?'

'That I hoped so.'

'Do you think she will?'

'I honestly don't know. I rang her when it was clear Grandma didn't have long left. She still wouldn't come.'

'How was she when you told her?'

'Pretty detached. She didn't cry or anything. Well, not until I'd shut the door.'

'What do you mean?'

I sighed and sat down at the kitchen table. James sat opposite and pushed the mug of tea he'd made towards me. I picked it up and warmed my hands around it. 'Just before Grandma died, she said a weird thing. She said there were babies at the bottom of her garden.'

James frowned. 'Sounds like she'd lost the plot.'

'She hadn't, though, that's the thing. I told her she was getting confused with the fairy statues, but she was adamant there were babies there. She asked me to look after her babies and that was the last thing she ever said.'

'Maybe she was talking about the girls.'

'When I told Mum she said Grandma believed in angels, that she was probably talking about angels, but after she shut the door, I heard her start crying.'

'She doesn't like getting upset in front of people, you know that,' said James.

'None of it makes sense. But it was obviously important to Grandma. She wouldn't have said it otherwise.' I wiped my nose on my sleeve. 'Grandma said something else before she died too. She said she had left the house to us.'

James looked at me. 'Really? Wow, that's incredible.'

'I know.'

'It must be worth a fair whack. I mean, we could get somewhere really decent in Hebden with the money it'll make.'

I pulled a face.

'Sorry,' groaned James. 'That probably sounded awful.'

'No, it's not that. She didn't want me to sell it. She said she wanted us to live there.'

It was James's turn to make a face. 'Oh, God. You wouldn't want to, would you? It's so dark and grim and it blows a fucking gale up there.'

I couldn't help but smile. James had grown up in Leeds. There was only so much rural he was prepared to put up with. 'I know. It wasn't exactly what I had in mind either but the trouble is, now she's said it, I'd feel awful going against her wishes.'

'Right.' James slumped in his chair. I knew it bothered him that we couldn't afford anywhere bigger. Somewhere with a garden and a room each for the girls. As much as I loved Maisie, I was damn sure I wouldn't have wanted to share a room with her when I was a teenager.

'Look, let's wait until I've seen the will and we know for sure what the situation is. I've got to go back to the house tomorrow to get all the paperwork I need to register her death.'

'Shouldn't your mum be doing all of that?'

'Probably. But she won't go to the house. I'll let her know when I've made the appointment at the register office. It's up to her if she turns up.'

I lay in bed later that night, James's arm still draped over me, though he had long fallen asleep. I couldn't see much prospect of that for myself. It wasn't what we were going to do about the house that was keeping me awake, though. It was Grandma's final words echoing back through the darkness.

Look after my babies.

For a long time, he didn't seem to notice me. Not in that way. I was just a kid to him. An awkward teenager with wonky teeth and legs that were out of proportion to my body. There were plenty of older, more sophisticated women around. The sort of women who wore perfect cherry-red lipstick and laughed as they tossed their perfect hair. Why would he even look at me? But the day I had my hair cut, he did look. I saw him do a double-take as I walked past him. The shoulder-length cut made me look older, I knew that. The hairdresser had said so. Even my mum said so. My hair swished as I walked. It had never done that before. And because it swished I found myself swishing with it. He looked at me like he was seeing me for the first time and smiled. The sort of smile men give women, not little girls.

My cheeks flushed. I wasn't quite sure what to say or do, so I kept on walking, aware of his eyes still on me as I passed him. Trying to let my hair swish just that little bit more.

You always remember it, the first time a man looks at you like that. I felt as if something had changed inside me, a switch had been flicked, and everything was different now. I was entering a whole new world. A world in which I didn't know the rules, let alone understand them. It was scary but exciting too. Because when you've been a little girl for so long, the idea that you might have become a woman is overwhelming. I smiled to myself and somewhere inside me a tune was playing. A grown-up tune, not a little girl's one.

3

'Bye, love. Hope you have a good day.'

I wasn't allowed to kiss Ruby in public any longer so, as much as I wanted to, I didn't attempt to. Ruby didn't bother replying. She walked off up the street, looking forlorn, her rucksack drooping off her back in sympathy. I hadn't wanted to suggest a day off school because I knew it would cause problems if I took a day off work. It would be bad enough having time out for the funeral. It was a small school and there was no cover for a teaching assistant, which meant even more work for Fiona.

Besides, I was sure Ruby would feel better once she was at school and had something to take her mind off Grandma. Moping at home would do her no good. I sighed as I realised I sounded like a mother – my own mother.

Maisie tugged at my hand. 'Come on, Mummy. You mustn't be late, or you'll get in trouble with Mrs Stimpson.'

I smiled down at her and started walking. At that moment I wanted to rewind eighteen months to the point where we were all at the same school. People had often asked me if it was weird, working at the school my children attended. And I'd always said, no, it wasn't. It seemed entirely normal to me. I'd loved having Ruby in the classroom with me for her last year at primary school. But it had meant that her starting secondary school had hit me hard. Other parents had let go long ago. I never had.

Maisie chatted away as we walked through the town. It was a bright day, the autumn sun already over the hills and inching down one side of the valley. I loved living there. Loved that you could look up and see exactly where you were in the calendar at any time of year. I'd have hated living somewhere so grey and out of touch with nature that I'd have had to check my phone to see what month I was in.

Maisie was telling me about the new range of smelly stationery Emily had got. I said, 'Oh,' and 'Right,' and nodded intermittently but my mind was elsewhere. Tearing back and forth between whether Ruby would manage to keep herself together at school, whether Mum would turn up later at the registrar's and what Grandma had meant about the babies.

I wondered if she'd had a couple of miscarriages. Mum was an only child: perhaps there had been other babies who hadn't made it. Grandma had never spoken about it, but that didn't mean it hadn't happened. If she'd had a miscarriage at home, she could have buried the little she had been left with in the garden. Her way of remembering. Maybe Grandad hadn't known about it. They'd never seen each other in their underwear before they'd got married, Grandma had told me that much. She might not have felt able to tell him about a miscarriage early in their marriage.

'Emily!' Maisie let go of my hand as we reached the playground and ran towards her best friend. Fortunately Emily was always at breakfast club too, so Maisie didn't mind having to come to school early. She ran back to give me a hug, then disappeared inside with Emily in a blur of ponytails and excited giggling.

I arrived in the staffroom just as Fiona had put the kettle on.

'Morning. Good timing as ever.' She said with a smile.

I smiled back but I'd forgotten that Fiona had a built-in putting-a-brave-face-on-it detector.

'Your grandma?'

'She went yesterday. Peacefully. I was there.'

'Oh, Nic, I am sorry,' she said, giving me a hug.

Andrew, the year-five teacher, glanced at us but I didn't feel like making a staffroom announcement. It was only Fiona who had known she was dying.

'I'll need some time off for the funeral. I don't know yet when it will be. I'll try to make it the afternoon so I can be in for the morning if possible.'

'Don't be daft. You need to take the whole day off. I'll sort the kids out with something to keep them quiet. How have the girls taken it?'

'Maisie's fine and Ruby's being Ruby.'

'Oh dear,' said Fiona, handing me a mug of coffee. 'It's always hard for the sensitive ones. Is she going to the funeral?'

'I don't think I could stop her if I wanted to.'

'It's probably a good thing. Give her a chance to say goodbye and all that. Was your mum there?'

'No,' I replied.

Fiona raised an eyebrow. 'But she'll be at the funeral?'

'We'll have to wait and see.'

Fiona nodded, knowing not to push it. 'Did your grandma have any other family? Brothers or sisters?'

'Two older brothers and an older sister, apparently. She'd lost touch with them years ago, though. Some big family fall-out. I imagine they're all dead by now, so it doesn't really matter.'

'Is your brother helping?'

'What do you think?'

'Families, eh?' said Fiona. 'Lucky you're bloody brilliant at holding everything together.'

I smiled at her, not wanting to admit that most of the time I struggled to hold myself together, let alone anyone else.

It was weird, driving back to Grandma's house knowing she wasn't there. Ruby had wanted to come but I'd told her it would be boring for her and she was better off staying at home with James and Maisie. As I pulled up outside I felt tears prick and had to sit in the car for a few minutes to compose myself. The house would feel so empty without her, even though she'd only been a tiny shrivelled figure lying on the bed in the front room for the past few months.

I got out of the car, walked up the path and let myself in, 'Hi, Grandma, it's me,' stuck somewhere in my throat. I shut the door behind me and stood for a moment, the silence echoing back at me. There was an envelope on the mat with my name on it. I tore it open: a sympathy card from Andrea next door. She must have seen the body being taken away yesterday. She'd been good to Grandma, always checking on her to see if she needed anything from the shops. I should probably knock and thank her but I wasn't sure I was up to it. I shut my eyes for a minute. Took a deep breath.

The house still smelt of Grandma. Old and soapy with a hint of Yorkshire tea (two sugars, of course). I ran my fingers over the flock wallpaper in the hall – maybe her smell had impregnated it. I imagined Maisie doing a scratch and sniff test to find out.

I walked into the front room. It was, of course, just as I had left it yesterday. I'd pulled the blankets up (Grandma had never taken to duvets) over the pillow as if I was hiding something underneath. I was. It was the indentation of her head that I didn't want to see. I swallowed and looked around the room. The table was a mess of knick-knacks, assorted cups and saucers, and a half-eaten packet of Jacob's crackers, which I knew I should throw away, but I couldn't face it. I was trying to ignore the fact that the house was now unlived-in and unloved. No one except Grandma had ever liked it.

I remembered Grandad complaining frequently about the room being too gloomy to read the sports pages without the light on. Not to mention the noise of the wind against the bedroom window at night. And Mum never visited if she could help it. Family Christmases had always been at her house, and on Grandma's birthday Mum would ask Dad, and later me or

Justin, to fetch her for tea at ours. When I'd asked her why we never went to Grandma's, she'd always said it was too cold and damp. Even in the middle of summer.

Grandma was probably right: no one else would have wanted the house. Not to keep, anyway. But I still felt uneasy at the idea of us selling it when I knew that wasn't what she'd wanted.

I glanced down at the floral carpet, worn in places and held together with tape at the edges to stop it fraying. It was, like the rest of the house, a relic from a bygone era. In many ways it should have died with her. Perhaps it would be kinder to put the whole house to sleep than to sell it. Whoever bought it would get rid of the carpet and probably strip the floorboards underneath, exposing them to the light for the first time in years.

I sighed and steeled myself for the task at hand. Grandma had a briefcase for important papers. I presumed it used to belong to Grandad, as she'd never needed one for work. I couldn't remember seeing it in the front room, but with all the clutter it was hard to know. I guessed it was still upstairs in Grandma's old bedroom.

Every creak on the stairs sounded louder than usual. When I got to Grandma's room I hesitated outside the door. It felt wrong, entering when she wasn't there, wasn't even present in this world any more. The idea of people going through my stuff when I was gone filled me with horror. I made a mental note to get rid of anything I wouldn't want people to see, long before my time was up.

I pushed the door. Everything was as I remembered. The double bed was still there. James and I had carried the single from the spare bedroom downstairs when Grandma had moved into the front room. It was presumably Mum's old bed. I couldn't imagine that it had ever been replaced.

There was still a nightie hanging up behind the door, an assortment of creams and half-empty tubes and bottles on the dressing-table. I ran my fingers over the candlewick bedspread. It would probably go to the charity shop, though I couldn't imagine there was much demand for bedspreads, these days. I suspected it would stay there for months and I would see it when I went in some time next spring and bought it back because I couldn't bear to think of a piece of her life being left there forever.

I opened the wardrobe and rummaged around at the bottom. The briefcase was in the corner at the back. I took it out and put it on the bed. It was even more battered than I remembered: the leather was worn away at the corners and the handle was coming off at one side. The jumble of papers inside didn't surprise me. Grandma had never had an efficient filing system. I tipped the contents out on the bed and started sorting through the various envelopes, putting all the documents I'd been told I needed to register the death in a separate pile.

The white A4 envelope marked 'Will' in shaky capital letters was the last I came to. I opened it to find a piece of A4 paper with the letterhead of a solicitors' firm in Halifax, informing her that her will would be securely stored with them, as per her instructions. I slipped the letter back into the envelope. I would ring them tomorrow. At least we wouldn't have to wait long to find out the situation with the house. I picked up the papers I needed and popped them into my bag, then put the briefcase back into the wardrobe.

I stopped to have a look through the things hanging from the rail. There were dresses I had never seen her wear. Things from the fifties and sixties. I had no idea what we'd do with them. A vintage shop, perhaps? I spotted a yellow polka-dot dress I remembered from an old photograph of her and Grandad on their honeymoon. They'd been standing on the front at Bridlington, Grandma every inch the English rose. She'd been such a beautiful young woman. Beautiful in a very natural, innocent sense. Grandad's frown seemed out of place. She'd told me that the sun was in his eyes but, to be honest, Grandad had always seemed to be frowning. I put the dress at the end of the rail, knowing I couldn't possibly get rid of it. Maybe Ruby would like it. It would be nice to give the girls something that had belonged to their great-grandma. She would have liked that too. She was always one for keeping things in the family.

I went downstairs and looked around the kitchen. It was hard to know where to start, there was so much to get rid of. I opened the fridge. It was the weirdest thing, seeing half-finished packets of ham and cheese that had outlasted the person who was eating them. I wondered for a second about taking the contents of the fridge home, but it felt wrong somehow, even though Grandma had hated waste. I was pretty sure I wouldn't be able to stomach eating it, anyway. I began emptying everything into the bin, trying not to think of what Grandma would say.

When I'd finished, I took the kitchen bin out of the back door and dumped the contents in the wheelie bin. It was starting to get dark and the wind was developing a chill, I glanced down the garden and my gaze fell on the two fairy statues in the far corner. Something twisted inside me as I recalled Grandma's words. I walked down the path towards them. I couldn't remember a time when they hadn't been there, yet I'd never studied them in detail. They looked like they were made of cast iron, although they had been coated in something which was now a dirty alabaster colour and chipped in places, to reveal the iron underneath.

The nearest figure to me was of a fairy sitting on a toadstool, her bare legs tucked underneath, her wings outstretched behind. The second statue, set back slightly from the first, was of a fairy kneeling, one hand on the ground, the other outstretched, a butterfly resting on her fingertips. Her eyes were closed. I'd once asked Grandma if she was making a wish for the butterfly to stay there always. She'd smiled and told me that was exactly what she was doing.

I'd talked to them when I was little. I'd even given them names, although I couldn't remember them now. I'd often asked Mum if we could visit the fairies at Grandma's. Mostly, she had found a reason to say no: too busy, too late, too wet, too cold. But on the rare occasions we had gone, the first thing I'd done was to run down the garden to say hello to them.

Grandma had been talking about them at the end, I was sure. All those memories she must have had of the times we'd gone down the garden together to see them. The way we had both lingered over our goodbyes. It was the statues she'd wanted me to look after. Maybe that was why she'd left me the house.

Perhaps that was all that was needed. For me to take care of her fairies.

The next day, when I arrived at the registrar's office in Halifax after school, Mum was sitting on a chair clutching the worn straps of her navy handbag. She looked up at me, the dark circles under her eyes more visible than usual.

'Hi,' I said, managing a smile. 'I wasn't sure if you'd be able to make it.'

'Tricia swapped shifts so I could do an early.' I sat down next to her. 'Thanks for sorting everything out,' she said. 'I know it should be my job.'

'It's OK,' I replied, feeling bad for being angry with her now. 'How are the girls?'

'Ruby's pretty upset. She's desperate to come to the funeral.'

'Then let her.' My eyebrows rose. I had expected Mum to be against the idea. 'Give her the chance to say goodbye,' she said.

'What about Maisie?'

'Maisie too. It's important.'

Before I had the chance to say anything more, a young man emerged from a door at the back of the room. He was dressed in a brown suit and his face sported an expression straight out of the compassionate-sympathy training manual.

'Mrs Hallstead and Miss Hallstead?'

We nodded and stood up at the same time. 'I'm so sorry for your loss,' he continued, shaking our hands in turn. 'Please do come through.'

I followed him into the office. It was decorated in neutral colours and was entirely functional, apart from a box of tissues on the desk. When I turned to check on Mum, she was biting her bottom lip, seemingly trying hard not to be the first to need one.

When we left the registrar, I didn't tell Mum I was going to pick up a copy of the will. Maybe because I thought it would be too much for her. Maybe because I suspected she hadn't been left anything and it would be too awkward.

I sat in my car, waited for her to leave first, then turned right out of the car park, instead of left for home.

When I got to the solicitors', they had the sealed envelope ready for me.

'If you'd like to open it now, have a read-through and ask any questions, you've very welcome to do so,' said the young woman, once I'd shown her my ID and the death certificate. 'Otherwise, take it home, read it in your own time and feel free to contact us if there's anything you don't understand.'

As desperate as I was to read it, it didn't seem right to do so in public. Grandma had always been of the don't-wash-your-dirty-linen-in-public persuasion so I'd read her final wishes in private. 'Thanks,' I said. 'I'll take it home.'

She handed me a leaflet about understanding wills. Then I got straight back into the car and drove home. When I let myself in, James was cooking dinner.

'How did it go?' he asked.

'OK. I haven't read it yet. Where are the girls?'

'Maisie's watching TV in the front room. Ruby's in her bedroom.'

'Right. I'll do it now, then.'

I went upstairs, shut the door, peeled open the envelope and took out the will. It felt intrusive, like opening Grandma's head and peering inside. The first thing I saw was my name, as executor of the will. I turned the page and saw straight away that I was the sole beneficiary of the estate. There was no stipulation in the will that the house should be passed to Ruby but Grandma had said so and I couldn't delete it from my mind.

James looked up as I returned to the kitchen.

'Well?' he asked.

'The house is mine.'

'Great. Does it say anything about you not being able to sell it?'

'No, but it doesn't make any difference, does it? She made it very clear what she wanted. She asked me to leave it to Ruby. I can hardly go against her final wishes, can I?'

'No,' said James, deflating in front of me. 'I guess not.'

12 May 1944

Dear Betty,

I meant what I said, you are as pretty as a picture. And now I know you have the voice of an angel too. I couldn't go any longer without speaking to you. I had to know if the owner of that smile felt the same way about me. And Betty, your voice is the sweetest thing I swear I have ever heard.

I know you're shy. I get the impression you're not used to being around men. Maybe your mother has warned you off them. But Betty, I tell you, I'm not like the men she has told you about. All I care about is treating you right. Making you feel like the special girl you are. I want you to be my special girl, Betty. I want your smile to be just for me. And the other boys can keep their Rita Hayworths and Betty Grables because I have you. An apple pie and ice-cream girl, that's what my mother would say about you. And one day Betty, I want to take you home to meet her and the rest of my family because I know they'd love you. And then you'd know how serious I am about you.

One day this war will be over. I know many guys aren't going to make it through to the end but I'm a born optimist (that's another thing my mother says) and I know I'll be one of the lucky ones who survive. I can see a time when all this is over and we can build a new life together, you and I. We can start a family of our own, and I know it might sound like I'm running away with myself but if there's one thing this war has taught me, it's that life is short and we need to grab happiness while we can. These are the dreams which keep me going when it gets really bad, when I don't know if we're going to make it back. I think of you and my future life with you, Betty, and that's what gets me through.

The best way to stay optimistic is to think about the future. Not tomorrow or next week, because they're scary too, but way into the future. And however far I look, it's you I see standing next to me, Betty. You I want to spend the rest of my life with. I hope that ain't scaring you because I don't mean to scare you. I just want to show you how serious I am. You can trust me, Betty. Because I'm going to take real good care of you.

Yours always,
William

4

The girls were standing by the front door, ready to go, when I arrived downstairs. I'd told them children didn't have to wear black to funerals, it really wasn't expected, but Ruby had insisted. And even though she was wearing the same parka, black trousers and shoes she wore for school, it was the knowledge that today it was funeral uniform that got to me.

I'd never been more grateful for the splash of colour Maisie provided. Her royal blue school anorak and the blue bow in her hair provided a welcome contrast to the black the rest of us were wearing.

'Ruby said I should have black on like everyone else,' she said.

I shook my head. 'Blue was Great-grandma's favourite colour. She'd be very happy you were wearing it to say goodbye to her.'

Maisie still looked unsure. 'Will everybody be crying?' she asked.

I crouched next to her. 'Some people will but not everybody. People have different ways of showing they're sad.'

'Do we have to be sad all day?' she asked.

I smiled and gave her a hug. 'No. You can think of all the special memories you have of being with Great-grandma. That might make you feel happy.'

I caught Ruby giving me a sideways look as I stood up. 'You OK, love?' She nodded and looked away again.

James came back in. I'd asked him to clear out the car while I was getting ready. I didn't want to turn up outside Grandma's house with an assortment of My Little Pony merchandise in the rear window and leftover Haribos stuck to my coat.

'Right. Are we ready?' he asked.

I took Maisie's hand and led the way down the path.

'I thought we were going in a big black car,' said Maisie.

'That's from Great-grandma's house to the church.'

'Why don't we walk to the church because it's next to school and we walk to school?'

'I know,' I said, 'but we're going to get Great-grandma first and come back with her.'

'Can I sit on the coffin?' asked Maisie.

'Mum, tell her,' said Ruby.

I sighed as I opened the car door. It was going to be a difficult day. 'No, Maisie. You can sit nicely next to Ruby and me.'

James gave my shoulder a squeeze. 'Are you all right?' he asked.

'Yeah,' I replied. Even though I wasn't.

We pulled up outside Grandma's house. The sun had come out and was doing its best to brighten things up.

James helped Maisie out while I opened the door for Ruby.

She didn't have to say anything for me to know what she was feeling.

'It'll be fine,' I whispered to her, and led the way up the path to the front door. I'd visited a couple more times since I'd collected the documents and it should have been getting easier, but I still felt the same shiver as I stepped into the hall. The same emptiness and silence everywhere.

'Where's the coffin?' asked Maisie.

'The undertakers are bringing it in the hearse. When that arrives, we'll be following behind in the big black car I told you about.'

'What do we do while we wait?'

'Well, we could talk about our memories of Great-grandma, if you like?'

Maisie shook her head. 'Can we go and see the fairies?'

'Not now, love. Grandma and Uncle Justin will be here soon.'

'And then can I go and see them?'

'No, because we'll be leaving then. We'll see them when we come back later.'

'Why are we coming back?'

'There's a lot left to sort out, love, with all of Great-grandma's things.'

Maisie nodded. 'Is someone else going to live in her house?'

I glanced across at James. 'We're not sure yet. We'll get everything sorted after the funeral.'

I saw Mum's car pull up outside. She stayed in the driver's seat while Justin got out and headed up the path. I went to the front door to meet him.

'Hi, sis,' he said, as I opened it. He never looked any older, which annoyed me. I always hoped that at some point his work-hard, play-hard lifestyle would catch up with him. He bent to give me a kiss. 'She had a good innings, didn't she?'

'I guess so. Is Mum not coming in?'

Justin shook his head. 'Said it'll only upset her.'

We walked through to the front room. The girls saw Justin just once a year when he came over at Christmas, but I knew I could rely on Maisie to muster the required enthusiasm.

'Uncle Justin!' she squealed, running to give him a hug. 'Great-grandma's dead and my friend Emily has got a new strawberry-scented pencil case.'

To be fair to Justin, he didn't balk at the idea that these two things carried equal weight in her life. 'And you've grown at least six inches since I saw you last,' he said, then looked across to Ruby. 'So have you, Rubes. Quite the teenager, aren't you?'

She hated him calling her 'Rubes' but summoned a half-smile and let him plant a kiss on her cheek.

'Good to see you,' said James, his hand held out for Justin to shake. He didn't like my brother and I presumed the feeling was mutual, but they were both polite enough to go through the motions on occasions such as this.

'Where's Grandma?' asked Maisie.

'She's waiting in the car,' I said. 'She just wants a few moments on her own.'

'Is the coffin here yet?' Maisie asked.

'It is now,' replied Justin, looking out of the window.

My body went cold as I saw the hearse pull up outside. All I could think was how much Grandma had loved this house. How all the images of her inside my head were of her here, making tea in the kitchen or pottering about in the garden. And now she was about to begin her final journey from it. It wasn't even hers any more. It was mine. Mine and then Ruby's.

I saw Ruby's bottom lip start to tremble and took her hand. She didn't offer any resistance. Momentarily, she was my little girl again. James took Maisie's and we followed Justin out of the house. Several neighbours were standing in their front gardens.

'What are they doing?' whispered Ruby, wiping her eyes.

'Just paying their respects to Great-grandma.'

'Being nosy, more like,' she said. 'If they want to pay their respects, they should come to the church.'

I stifled a smile. As James had often said, Ruby was her mother's daughter. 'Some of them are coming to the church,' I replied. 'Andrea said she'd be there. But people like to do this too.'

One of the undertakers opened the door of the funeral car. I turned to see Mum walking over. She bent to hug Maisie. When she stood up, she had tears in her eyes.

'Right then,' said Justin. 'Let's see if we can all fit in.'

Justin and James sat on the two pull-down seats behind the driver. Mum and I sat on the back seat with the girls between us. Ruby started crying as soon as she saw the hearse set off in front of us. I put my arm around her, battling hard to keep my own tears in check, as I knew it would only make things worse. Even Maisie was quiet, as if the reality of what had happened had finally started to sink in.

'There's my school,' Maisie said to Justin, as we drove past slowly. He smiled and nodded. I think we were all glad of any distraction from Ruby's crying.

We pulled up outside the church. I rummaged in my bag and handed Ruby a tissue. 'Take your time,' I said. 'There's no rush.' She wiped her eyes and blew her nose. 'Deep breaths,' I said. 'We'll do this together.'

We got out of the car. The vicar, or Rev Kev as he was known to all at our school, came straight over and shook hands with me. 'Hello again, Miss Hallstead, and welcome to you all,' he said, looking at each of us in turn. 'Being able to support members of our extended school family at such a difficult time is a real privilege for me.'

He crouched to Maisie's level. 'I know from speaking to your mummy what a lovely lady your great-grandma was, so we're going to say some special goodbyes to her in the church today.'

Maisie fiddled with the blue bow in her hair as she clung to me with the other hand.

'Right,' he continued, straightening. 'I'd better go inside. Do take a few moments, and I'll be there to support you throughout.'

'Where did you find him?' whispered Justin.

'Leave it,' I replied.

We stood at the entrance to the church and watched as the undertakers opened the rear of the hearse.

'Oh, look! There's our flowers,' said Maisie, pointing excitedly at the heart of white daisies with a blue ribbon they had chosen. 'And there's a fairy on top too. Whose is the fairy?'

'It's from me,' said Mum, her voice barely above a whisper. 'Only it's supposed to be an angel.'

I stood at the graveside, watching them lower the coffin. Maisie's head was buried in my coat: she had decided she didn't want to watch. She'd started crying during the service. I think it was the solemnity of the occasion that had got to her, despite Rev Kev's best efforts to make it a 'celebration of Betty's fascinating life'. It was weird, hearing him talk about her as if he'd known her, when all the information had come from me and Mum. About how she'd served in the Land Army in North Yorkshire during the war and had later worked as a sewing machinist in a clothing factory. I hadn't been interested when she'd first told me about it. You aren't interested in anyone but yourself when you're a teenager. And yet, hearing about it in the church, I had so many questions I wanted to ask her. It was too late, of course. She was about to be covered with earth. But it didn't stop me wishing I'd asked much more. Because all I could think of, as I heard the first dull thud of soil on wood, was that it wasn't just Grandma's body that was being buried: all the secrets of her life were being buried with her.

It wasn't until I turned around that I saw Mum. I'd been so busy comforting Maisie and keeping an eye on Ruby, who was with James, I hadn't really thought about her. I suppose

I'd presumed she'd be fine. She wasn't, though. She was crouching, her face contorted in pain, her mouth emitting a silent scream. Justin was standing next to her, looking helpless, one hand under her armpit, trying to prevent her sinking to her knees.

I took hold of her other arm and helped to pull her up. 'We've got you now. We've got you.'

I didn't plan to stay long at the pub. The term 'wake' was rather grand for a dozen people picking at some sandwiches that no one had the appetite for. Ruby was giving me I-don't-want-to-be-here looks and I didn't either.

Andrea came over to me. 'Sorry again for your loss, I shall miss Betty.'

'Thanks,' I said. 'And thanks for all you did for her. It gave me peace of mind, knowing you were looking out for her.'

'Least I could do for such a lovely lady. We used to have some good chats.'

I wondered if Grandma might have said something to her that would help me understand what she'd been talking about when she'd asked me to look after her babies.

'Did she talk to you about when she was younger?' I asked. 'What it was like when she first moved in.'

'Not really,' Andrea replied. 'More about what your girls had been getting up to. She didn't seem to be one to dwell on the past.'

'No,' I said. 'I wish I'd asked her more about it when I had the chance.'

'Sometimes they don't like talking about it, though, do they? It was tough for their generation. They lived through a lot.'

'Yeah,' I replied. 'I guess they did.'

When the last neighbour had left and we'd assured the pub staff we really didn't want the leftover sandwiches, we headed back up the hill to Grandma's house.

I was waiting for Mum to make an excuse about why she didn't want to come in, but Justin saved her the trouble. 'I'd better be going,' he said. 'I've got a flight booked from Leeds Bradford.'

'You aren't going to come in? There's some stuff I've been sorting through. I was going to ask if you wanted any of it.'

'No, you're all right,' Justin said. 'Just do with it whatever you think best.'

I was right. He really didn't give a toss.

Maisie was tugging on my hand. 'Can I go and see the fairies now?' she asked. 'You promised I could see them when we got back.'

'I did, didn't I? Just say goodbye to Grandma and Uncle Justin, then Daddy will take you.'

Maisie gave them the quickest hugs on record. Ruby followed with pecks on the cheek. James said his goodbyes, then followed the girls down the side alley.

I turned back to Mum and Justin. 'There's something I need to tell you both,' I said. 'I got the will from the solicitor. I'm named as the executor, and, I'm really sorry, but she's left the house to me.'

Mum said nothing.

Justin raised his eyebrows. 'Presumably you're going to sell it?' he asked.

'She asked me not to. She wants me to leave it to Ruby.'

'You can't do that,' said Mum.

'Why not?' I asked.

'You don't want to live there.'

'I don't think we've got much choice. That's what she wanted.'

'Well, rather you than me,' replied Justin.

I turned to Mum. She was looking pale and shaky again. 'I'm going to start going through all her things soon. Come over and have a look. You can take whatever you'd like.'

'No, thanks,' said Mum. 'You keep what you want. There's nothing for me here.'

'Right,' I said. 'Well, take care. I'll see you soon,' I kissed her cheek. Her body was stiff and unforgiving. The hurt from the graveyard had been covered up. Papered over, I guessed, so it wouldn't show. It was still there, though.

I said goodbye to Justin and waited to wave as they drove off, then went back into the house.

I was glad of a moment alone, after what already felt like a long day. I walked through to the kitchen, filled the kettle and put it on the hob. I glanced out of the window and saw Maisie beside the fairy statues, playing with a stick she must have found. James and Ruby were standing together talking, a little further away. I turned to get the milk I'd bought out of the fridge.

A few moments later, the back door burst open and Maisie ran in, gripping something in her outstretched hand. 'Mummy, look what I've found!' she said.

'What is it?' I asked.

She opened her fingers to reveal a tiny off-white object, an inch or so long and partially covered with soil.

'A fairy bone,' she replied, beaming.

He played a little game with me. I would walk past him and he would look in my direction, his eyes lingering a little longer each time. I noticed and he knew I'd noticed, but he still didn't say anything. I think it was all part of the game.

Then one day he said, 'Morning, sweetie pie,' as I walked past. I smiled at him, not knowing what to say or do in reply.

'Cat got your tongue?' he asked.

The colour was rushing to my cheeks again, so I said the first thing that came into my head. 'Nice morning.'

It was a stupid thing to say but he smiled anyway. A funny sort of smile this time. I wasn't sure if it was a good smile or not.

'That it is. Did you catch sunrise?'

I shook my head.

'Well, you missed a good 'un. That's best thing about having to get up early. There's a great view from ridge on tops, you know. I could take you sometime, if you like.'

I didn't know what to say. He wanted me to go somewhere with him. Alone. To watch the sunrise. It sounded like a romantic thing to do.

'Maybe,' I said.

'Come on! It's not like you need your beauty sleep. Or are you worried you won't be allowed?'

My jaw tightened. I hated him thinking I'd need permission to go anywhere with him. Even though it was true. 'I can do whatever I want with whoever I want,' I replied.

'Is that so?' He whistled. 'How about tomorrow, then?'

'I'll have to see.'

'You mean you do need to ask someone's permission?'

'Tomorrow will be fine. What time?'

'Five. That should give us a chance to get to top of ridge for sunrise. I'll meet you at bottom gate,' he said, pointing to the field at the far end of the road.

I nodded, back to being unable to speak. He walked off whistling. My insides started running around bumping into things. I had no idea how I was going to get out and back again without waking anyone. All I did know was that as no one had ever asked to take me to watch a sunrise before, I had to find a way.

I didn't sleep much that night, waking almost every hour on the dot. I got up at half four and tiptoed to the bathroom for a quick wash. It felt exhilarating, being up at that time, trying not to wake anyone else, having somewhere secret to go with a man. A man much older than me. A man with a twinkle in his eye. A man I knew I should not be seeing on my own. That was what made it all so exciting.

I managed to shut the back door with the gentlest of clicks. I pulled my jacket across my front. I had dressed for April but not April at four thirty in the morning. I curled my fingers back inside my sleeves, straining my eyes in the gloom to see if I could make out a figure at the gate. I couldn't. I hurried on, following the curve of the dry-stone wall out of the village. There was just enough light spreading across the sky to enable me to see where I was going. The birds were starting to herald the new morning, their excitement matching mine. As I drew nearer to the gate I could see he was already there. Standing in the field and leaning on it from the other side, an easy smile on his face.

'You made it, then,' he said, as I stopped in front of him.

'I said I would.'

'Bit nippy for you, is it?'

I uncrossed my arms. 'I'm fine, thanks.'

'You can have my jacket if you want.'

I shook my head.

'Right then. Are you coming over? Only we need to get a move on.'

I started to climb over the gate. My boot got stuck on the second bar and he reached out his hand. I took it to steady myself. It felt wrong and right at the same time. When I swung my top leg over he took hold of my hips and lifted me down before I'd realised what was happening.

'Thanks,' I said.

'It's all right. Nothing of you, is there?' He smiled as he said it, but I wasn't sure if it was a good thing or not. Whether he meant I was still just a kid. That I didn't have proper hips or a chest you could stick out.

He led the way up the field. It wasn't muddy, so I could manage to keep up with him. He didn't say anything, so I didn't either. When we got to the top of the field he leapt over the gate so fast I couldn't even work out how he'd done it. He turned back to watch me.

'You ought to be able to jump over it too with legs like that,' he said, as I started to climb. I'd always felt a bit embarrassed about my long legs. The other kids at school used to say I looked like a flamingo. I didn't know what to say so I concentrated on climbing down safely. He didn't try to lift me this time. I wasn't sure if I was disappointed or not.

When I got down he was halfway along the ridge. I ran to catch up with him, not wanting to miss the sunrise, having got that far. We made it to the top just as the sun peeped over the horizon. I watched as the colours rose and spread across the sky, changing every second and filling the world, or our little bit of it, with light and life and colour like I'd never seen before.

'There,' he said, smiling as he put his arm around my waist and gave it a squeeze. 'I told you it'd be worth it.'

5

'Where did you find it?' I asked Maisie, trying to keep my voice calm.

'Under the fairy statue. That's where the fairy bones are,' she said, very matter-of-fact.

'And was it just there or did you dig for it?'

'I had to dig for it. I poked the stick a long way down and made a big hole and stuck my arm down it. I was looking for fairy treasure, but I found a fairy bone instead.'

I noticed the soil on the sleeve of her school anorak, which was pulled halfway up her forearm.

'Can I hold it, please?'

Maisie handed it to me. I'd been hoping it would be heavy, like a piece of pottery or clay, but it wasn't. It was light and brittle. I tried to ignore the sense of unease growing inside me.

'Have you shown Daddy?' I asked.

'Yes. He said it was pretty, but Ruby said I was making it up. I'm not though, am I, Mummy? It is a fairy bone, isn't it?'

I looked at her face. It had already been a tough day for her. 'Maybe,' I said. 'I don't really know.'

'Can I keep it?' she asked.

'Erm, I'm not sure. Do you think the fairies might miss it?'

'No, they don't mind.'

'Well, I suppose you can, then.'

'Yay, I've got a fairy bone,' she said, running back out to the garden. I caught James's eye and beckoned him over.

'Well, she seems to have cheered up a bit,' he said.

'Have you seen it?'

'What?'

'The thing she says is a fairy bone.'

'Only briefly. I wasn't really paying attention.'

'Go and have a proper look. It feels like a bone.'

James's expression changed as he saw what I was getting at. 'Oh, come on. It's probably part of one a dog buried years ago.'

'Grandma never had a dog.'

'Well, before her, then.'

'Go and have a look.'

James went to Maisie. I watched as she handed it to him and James examined it, holding it up to what was left of the daylight. He smiled and gave it back to Maisie, then returned to me. 'I think it's just an animal bone. Maybe she buried a pet under there. She had cats once, didn't she?'

I nodded.

'Well, there you go.'

'Yeah,' I said, still not convinced. 'You're probably right.'

'I'm always right, you know that.'

He pulled a face at me as he said it. 'Come on, let's get the girls home. It's been a long day.'

The following morning when James woke, I was already up and showered. He squinted at me as I got dressed. 'I thought it was Saturday?'

'It is.'

'So why are we getting up before a small person jumps on our bed?'

'Can Ruby go with you when you take Maisie to her swimming lesson this morning?'

'Of course. Are you OK?'

I sat down on the edge of the bed. 'I need to go back to Grandma's house. I can't stop thinking about it.'

'What?'

'The bone, of course.'

James groaned and sat up in bed. 'You could dig down in any garden and find something like that.'

'It isn't any garden, though, is it? It was Grandma's garden and the last thing she told me was that there were babies at the bottom of it.'

'Nic, I know it's been a tough couple of weeks, but I think you're reading too much into this.'

'So let me go and put my mind at rest. If I find nothing there, fine. I'll leave it at that.'

'You're seriously going to dig?'

'Well, I won't find anything by gazing at the surface with my X-ray vision eyes, will I?'

'No.' James said with a smile. 'I guess not.'

'Tell the girls I've got boring stuff to sort out at Grandma's house but I'll be back for lunch and to help Ruby with her homework this afternoon.'

'OK. I'll see you later. Happy digging.'

When I arrived, I went straight to the tool shed. Grandma had taken on a gardener when the upkeep had got too much for her. Alan, his name was. He'd come up to me after the service at the church yesterday, said what a lovely lady she'd been and how knowledgeable she was about what would survive in such an exposed spot. I liked him. He'd been reliable and fastidiously tidy, so the shed was neatly organised, the tools still gleaming with the oil he'd put on when he'd stored them at the end of the season a few weeks ago.

I took the spade from the corner and marched over to the fairy statues. I could see the hole Maisie had left and started to dig to one side of it, my heart beating quicker with every spadeful of soil I removed. I had no idea what I'd do if I found anything. I was hoping to be proved wrong, hoping James was right and I'd go home feeling stupid for having dug a hole two feet deep for no good reason.

But I also knew I had to do this. It was the only way I was going to get Grandma's words out of my head and convince myself there must have been a perfectly innocent explanation for what she'd said.

The pile of earth I'd dug out was half as high as the fairy statue when I first saw two off-white objects in the soil. I turned the spade around and scraped some more earth off. The noise of metal against bone made my stomach turn. I removed some more earth to reveal a longer bone. It looked like part of an arm. A tiny human arm, although it might have been a cat's leg. I shut my eyes and tried to slow my rapid breaths. I didn't know what to do. If I went home now and told James, he'd still say I couldn't be sure what I'd seen. I had to ensure there was no doubt left in my mind.

I resumed digging. I wanted to keep my eyes shut but I was worried I might damage whatever I was uncovering. I dug further towards the base of the fairy statue. There was another bone, slightly larger and longer than the previous ones. I made a whimpering sound. My heart quickened. I carried on digging, unable to stop. I couldn't go any further without moving the statue. I put the spade down, stepped over the hole and stood with my feet either side of the fairy. I had no idea how heavy it would be, but the soil was soft after all the rain we'd had, and the base of the statue wasn't set far down. I dragged it a few inches to one side and took up the spade again. I think I knew what I would find but, although I felt sick, I was compelled to finish what I had started, to make absolutely sure.

It didn't take long to get to what appeared to be a shoulder bone. My legs went weak and tears ran down my cheeks. I kept digging, though, until I got to it. The thing I was sure was there. A tiny skull. Not a cat or dog's. An unmistakable human skull.

I let go of a cry and sank to my knees, sobbing. Grandma had known exactly what she was saying because it was true.

There were babies at the bottom of the garden. Well, one, anyway. And if there was one, the likelihood was there would be another. I looked at the second fairy statue but couldn't find the strength to get up and start digging again. Couldn't face what I was sure I would find. They weren't statues at all. They were gravestones. It was a burial site I had danced around as a child. A burial site that Maisie had been digging in yesterday. Exactly how those babies had come to be buried there, I didn't know. But I did know that I couldn't simply put the earth back, cover it up and forget about it. I had to find out the truth.

Having said that, it didn't seem respectful to leave the bones exposed. But I wanted to be able to show James the evidence. To prove to him beyond all doubt. I felt in my jacket pocket for my phone. I'd take a photo. My hands were shaking so much I had to take half a dozen shots before I got one that wasn't blurred. I stared at it on the screen. The bones before me. Denied a proper burial, presumably because someone had had something to hide. Had it been Grandma's baby? And, if so, how did it die? Did she kill it? Would she have been capable of doing that? I knew post-natal depression could be bad, but killing her own baby? And if there was another baby, had she killed that one too? Had my grandmother been some kind of monster?

I put the phone back into my pocket and picked up the spade again. I would sprinkle some of the earth back, so you couldn't see the bones. I wasn't covering it up, simply being respectful. When I had finished, I put the spade back in the tool shed and stood there for a moment, trying to get my head around what had just happened. I took my phone out again and called James.

'Hi, you,' he answered. 'Discovered Richard the Third's body yet?'

I couldn't speak for a second. When I did, the words came out slowly and shakily. 'I've found a baby's bones.' There was silence, so I continued: 'Under one of the fairy statues. It definitely wasn't a cat or dog. There was a tiny human skull.'

'Fucking hell,' said James. 'Are you OK?'

'No. Not really.'

'God, I'm sorry for joking about it. I should have taken it seriously.'

'I didn't really believe it until I saw it. But there was something about Grandma's voice when she told me about the babies. She knew exactly what she was saying.'

'What are you going to do?'

'I've got to report it, haven't I? I can't pretend I never saw it.'

'Are you absolutely sure they're human bones?'

'I took a photo. I'll send it to you now. Call me back when you've seen it.'

I sent the photo and stood in the garden, staring at the statues, unable to look at them now without also visualising what lay underneath. My phone rang. It was James.

'Jesus,' he said. 'I can't believe that's been there all these years.'

'I reckon there's another under the other statue.'

'Do you think they were your grandma's babies?'

'Probably. How else would she have known about them?'

'And you're definitely going to call the police?'

'Well, I can't not report it.'

'What if you don't like what they find? It could be a whole can of worms.'

'I'll have to deal with it. I can't pretend I never saw it. It would eat away at me forever.'

'What about your mum?'

'I'll go to see her now. I want to find out if she knew about it. Maybe that's what this whole rift with Grandma was about. Perhaps Grandma confessed to her years ago.'

'Surely your mum would have told someone, though.'

'I don't know. What if she was only Ruby's age when Grandma told her? You're not going to grass on your own mum, are you?'

'I guess not.'

'Well, let's see what she says. I'll go to the police straight afterwards. It's up to her if she wants to come with me or not.'

'Good luck. Give me a call when you're done.'

I put the phone back into my pocket and took a final look at the statues. All I could think of was the times I'd sat and talked to them as a girl. The songs and games I'd made up as I played around them. And Grandma had watched me, knowing what lay beneath them, but hadn't breathed a word.

Mum looked surprised to see me when she opened the door. She was wearing the old pair of jeans and baggy sweatshirt that I knew were her cleaning clothes. She cleaned the whole house on Saturday morning before she did anything else. Always had done.

'Is everything all right?' she asked.

I shook my head and stepped inside. 'After you left yesterday, Maisie found a bone in Grandma's back garden. Under one of the fairy statues.'

Mum frowned. 'What sort of bone?'

'We weren't sure. It was tiny. That's why I went back there this morning. I dug down underneath the statue. There were other bones. Little human bones. And a tiny human skull.'

Mum stared at me, the colour drained from her face. 'Oh, God, no,' she said, her hand going to her mouth.

'I think Grandma was telling the truth. I think it is a baby. I think there might be another.'

'No,' she said.

'It can't be anything else, Mum. I saw it – I took a photo if you want to see for yourself.'

'No!' She virtually shouted it this time.

I hesitated, not wanting to upset her any further, but I couldn't let it go without asking. 'Did you know about it?' I asked. 'Did she tell you?'

Mum shook her head. Her whole body was shaking.

'I'd understand if she did and you hadn't felt able to tell me. I just need to know.'

'She never told me owt. Not a word. You know what she were like.'

'I thought maybe it was because of this that you two—'

'No,' she cut in firmly.

'Right. I wanted to check before I took it any further.'

'What do you mean?'

'Well, I've got to tell the police, obviously.'

Mum's eyes widened. 'You can't do that.'

'Why not? I've just found what appears to be the remains of a baby in the garden of the house Grandma has left me. I can't cover it up and pretend it never happened.'

Mum started crying. Silent tears streamed down her cheeks. 'You could do,' she said quietly. 'No one else would ever know.'

'Well, I've told James for a start.'

'He's not going to tell anyone, is he? Not if we all agree to keep it to ourselves.'

'And why would we do that?'

'Because it's not anyone else's business, is it? It's our family it affects. Raking up things from past isn't going to help anyone. It'll simply cause more pain, and I think our family's suffered enough.'

'What do you mean by that?'

Mum looked at the floor. I saw her swallow hard. 'Exactly what I said. Mum were only buried yesterday. We're all still grieving. We don't need police digging around for dirt. Mum wouldn't have wanted that.'

'So why did she tell me about the babies? Whatever happened, she must have wanted me to know.'

'You don't have to tell the police, though, do you?'

'Of course I do. It was a baby, Mum. You can't hide something like that.'

Mum sat down heavily on the stairs, her head in her hands.

I went over to her and put my hand on her shoulder. When she looked up at me her face was contorted in a way I had never seen before. 'Leave it alone, Nicola. You don't know what you're dealing with.'

'You know something, don't you? Something you're not telling me.'

She shook her head slowly. 'I'm as much in the dark as you are but I don't see need to go meddling in past.'

'So what do you want me to do?'

She hesitated, then said, 'You never saw it. You put the earth back, delete the photo and none of us ever speaks of it again.'

'Jesus, Mum. What sort of solution is that? It would be a crime not to report what I've found. You're seriously saying you want me to commit a crime?'

'No one would ever know.'

'But it's awful, harbouring a secret like that. And what about when I die and the house gets passed on to Ruby? I leave her to deal with it, do I?'

'You don't need to pass it to Ruby. You don't need to live in it. By the time it's all cleared out you can sell it. Someone local will want it – you won't even need to put it on market.'

'And what if they find the bones?'

'They won't. People don't go looking for bones in their back gardens. You put the statue back and that's end of.'

I threw up my hands in the air and took a few steps backwards. 'I don't believe I'm hearing this. You want me to break the law and go against Grandma's final wishes. What kind of mother are you?'

She started crying again but I had lost all sympathy with her. 'Look, I don't know what this is all about, but I have no choice. You need to understand that.'

'We all have choices, Nicola. But we don't always realise it at the time.'

I walked out of the door, shutting it behind me, angry that she would put so much pressure on me. I got into my car, pulled my belt across and sat there, aware that my hands were shaking. The thing I was most scared of was that she was right and this would turn out to be a terrible mistake. What if the police uncovered something so horrible that our family never recovered from it? But I had already started the process. The genie would not go back into the bottle. And the idea that I should return to Grandma's, fill in the hole and forget about it was ridiculous. It would eat away at me. Far better to get to the bottom of it now than let it fester away and leave Ruby to deal with it one day when I was gone.

No. Whatever this was about, Mum's issues with Grandma were getting in the way. And I was not going to let them stop me doing what was right. Grandma had told me about the babies. She wanted the truth to be known.

I pulled off and, at the end of the road, turned in the direction of the police station.

23 May 1944

Dear Betty,

Spending time with you today meant so much to me. I know it's difficult trying to snatch moments when other people aren't around, but a minute with you can live forever in my heart. And to touch you, Betty, to put my hands around your waist, I can still feel the tingle in my fingers. It felt like you were light as air when I lifted you up. It's the joy in your heart that makes you seem as if you will rise up into the sky and float away if I don't keep hold of your hand.

We may not be able to grab many moments together but we will make every second count. Part of me wants to tell the world that you are my special girl but I know I can't do that at the moment. The last thing I want is for you to get into trouble. But there's nothing stopping me telling you that you're my special girl, Betty.

When I'm not with you, I think of you every moment, dream of you every night. And when I see you from afar

I can't help but smile to myself because that's what you do to me.

But I live for the moments we can be alone together. Before the world is up and watching us. When we have only the birds for company. Sometimes I think they are singing about our happiness. When they soar up into the sky, it is some kind of celebration of our love. I'm glad the birds know. No one else will realize they are singing about us. But one day Betty, when you are older and this war is over, everyone will know. I will shout it from the rooftops for the whole world to hear. I will go down to Buckingham Palace and tell the King and Queen. But for now, I must be patient.

There is something kind of sweet about keeping it to ourselves. The way we can smile at each other and no one else knows what is passing between us in that smile. Only we know that it is so much more than a friendly greeting. I think of you night and day Betty. I hear your laughter on the breeze. I see you in everything I do. And I dream my life away waiting for that next snatched encounter. Those precious few minutes when we can be together and you are my girl and I can touch you and smell you and look at you and breathe you in.

Yours always,

William

6

I pulled up outside Grandma's house, the police car behind me. When you had a photo of a human skull on your phone, it was very difficult for them to ignore you. I got out and went over to the two officers who had followed me, aware that the neighbours might well be looking out and wondering what was going on. I couldn't imagine the police had much of a presence in Pecket Well.

'We'll go down the side entrance,' I said to PC Hyde, who had taken my statement. 'It leads straight to the back garden.'

I felt a pang of guilt when I saw the fairy statues. Whatever was under them had lain there undisturbed for so long, it seemed wrong to intrude on their peace now. Perhaps Mum had been right, and this would serve no purpose whatsoever, apart from upsetting my whole family. There was no turning back now, though. I told myself Grandma had initiated this, not me. And she must have had her reasons.

'It's the closest one I dug under,' I said, walking down the path.

PC Hyde stopped next to me and surveyed the scene. His

colleague, a woman in her twenties called PC Cole, came around to the other side. 'And you say these statues have been here for as long as you can remember?' PC Hyde asked.

'Yes, as long as my mum can remember too. My grandma lived here from when she got married, about sixty years ago.'

'Where's the spade you used?'

'In the tool shed.'

I fetched it, handed it to PC Hyde, and watched as he made his way, somewhat cautiously, back to the fairy statue and started to scrape away the freshly dug soil I had covered the bones with. I wondered if he thought this might be some kind of wind-up. It did have the ring of a pub dare about it. I could have got the photo on my phone from anywhere. I guessed that was why he'd chosen to come out and see for himself before he called in Forensics.

It didn't take him long to uncover the bones. I watched his face change as he realised this was for real. His female colleague stepped back a couple of paces and lowered her head, as if in silent respect. A few moments later, PC Hyde walked to the other side of the garden and started speaking into his radio. That was the moment it hit me. That whatever I had uncovered now had a momentum of its own. The outcome was out of my hands. I was merely the person who had discovered it.

PC Cole looked at me – she was young and seemed uncertain as to what to say.

'It's so sad,' I said, staring at the statue. 'Whatever happened, she took it to her grave.'

She offered a supportive smile.

PC Hyde came back. 'Scenes of crime officers are on their way,' he said. 'I'm afraid this will have to be treated as a crime scene now. It's very difficult to do these things in a low-key way. You may want to go and have a word with your neighbours so they don't worry unnecessarily. Unless you'd rather we did it?'

'No, it's fine. I will,' I said, although I had no idea what I would say. Yesterday some of them had attended Grandma's funeral. Today I was going to tell them there was a body buried at the bottom of her garden. I didn't know what they'd make of it. To be honest, I didn't know what to make of it. And while I was hoping there would be an innocent explanation, I was well aware that others might jump to a rather different conclusion.

I went to see Andrea and Paul next door first. Proper neighbours, Grandma used to call them, like in the old days. All I could think of as I stood on the step was the lovely things Andrea had said to me about Grandma after the service and whether her view of the sweet old lady next door was about to change.

She came to the door in jeans and a hoodie, with a chilled-out Saturday-afternoon expression on her face. I could hear music coming from one of her children's rooms upstairs.

'Hi,' I said, 'thanks again for coming to the service yesterday. I'm, er, just letting you know that the police are on their way to search Grandma's garden.'

She looked at me blankly.

'I found some bones while I was digging yesterday. They look like human bones. They're very old, mind. I've got no idea why they're there, but I thought I'd better tell the police.'

Andrea looked past me to the police car parked outside. Her eyes widened. 'There's a body in her garden?' Her voice was more high-pitched than usual.

'No, not a body, just some old bones. I wanted to put your mind at rest, before you saw the police arrive, that's all.'

'Goodness, that must have come as quite a shock,' she said.

I wasn't sure whether to tell her what Grandma had said. She might be able to shed some light on it. Although, as they'd only lived there about ten years, I doubted it.

'Grandma mentioned something about what was in the garden right at the end. It didn't really make sense, to be honest. I take it she never said anything to you about it.'

'Well, no. I'd remember it if she had. It's not the sort of conversation you expect to have with an elderly lady. Do you know how long the police are going to be there?'

'No,' I replied. 'But maybe we can get it all sorted out quickly.'

'Let's hope so,' she said, frowning. 'It's not the sort of thing anyone will want going on in the village.'

As she shut the door and I turned to walk slowly away, I imagined her going back to Paul and relating what I had told her. That would be the starting point of the conversation, at least. No doubt they would go on to discuss all the possibilities of who the bones had belonged to and how they'd got there. The same things that had been flying around in my head. And at some point they would probably discuss whether the old lady whose path they'd cleared of snow had used the same spade to bury a body in her back garden.

I'd only managed to catch a handful of other neighbours by the time Forensics arrived. It was seeing the first guy emerge from their van in one of those white suits that really did it for me. I felt like I'd stepped on to the set of *Happy Valley*. PC Hyde had a word with him, then two other men got out of the van carrying a large piece of rolled-up white material and long poles.

PC Cole came over to me. 'They're going to put the tent up over the area,' she said. 'Standard procedure in this type of case. Helps protect the crime scene and stops the neighbours getting too nosy.' She gave a little smile.

I didn't respond. My brain was still trying to process the fact that Grandma's garden was now a crime scene.

'There's really not much else you can do here now,' she went on. 'If you want to get home, we'll keep you informed of any developments.'

I knew she was right. It would be dark soon, and I wanted to get back to the girls after a long day, but it still felt wrong, leaving the bones there with the police. I had a weird maternal feeling that I should watch over a baby that might have been Grandma's. I had to remind myself that there was nothing I could do to help it now, other than to ensure the truth came out.

'Right. You've got my number if you need anything.'

'Yeah,' she replied. 'Try not to worry. It might turn out to be nothing.'

I smiled and nodded. Even though I knew that wasn't going to be the case.

'Mummy,' said Maisie, rushing out to me, 'Ruby says I'm not allowed to sing because it's annoying her, and Daddy says he's too busy helping Ruby with her homework to play with me, and he didn't even plait my hair for swimming because of his plumber's fingers.'

Usually, I'd have been exasperated to arrive home and be bombarded with ongoing family disputes before I'd even got in the door, but I actually found it quite comforting to know that normality still existed in our house, even if events outside were far from normal.

'OK,' I said, slipping off my boots on the mat. 'I can take over homework duty now and Daddy can play with you, but you do need to go somewhere you won't disturb Ruby.'

'What about my hair?'

'Well, I declare this a crazy messy-hair day and it will do just fine.'

Maisie laughed. 'What are plumber's fingers?' she asked.

'I think Daddy meant his fingers are better at fastening washers than doing fiddly plaits.'

'Can he put some washers in my hair?'

I pulled a face at her. 'No. Now, where's your sister?'

'In the kitchen.'

'Right, how about you go up to your room to play and I'll send Daddy up in a few minutes?'

She shot up the stairs. James poked his head around the

kitchen door. I gestured at him to come out and shut it behind him.

'How are you?' he said, giving me a kiss.

'Pretty numb, to be honest. I can't quite get my head around what's happening. The police have set up one of those big white tents in Grandma's back garden.'

James blew out and shook his head. 'Jeez, that sounds serious. What did your mum say?'

'She didn't want me to report it. Said we should keep shtum and no one need ever know.'

'That doesn't surprise me.'

'What do you mean?'

'You know what that generation are like. Wanting to keep a lid on everything. Always obsessed with what other people will think of them.'

'Well, I told her I didn't have a choice. This thing would eat away at me if I didn't tell them. Grandma wanted the truth to come out and that's what we're doing.'

James winced. 'You might not like the truth when it does come out.'

'I know. But I'd rather I have to deal with it than leave it to Ruby when I'm gone.'

'I guess so.' James didn't sound convinced.

'You think I've made a mistake, don't you?'

'No. You did the right thing to report it. I'm just worried about you having to deal with all this on top of your grandma dying.'

'So am I,' I said quietly, keen that the girls shouldn't hear.

'What if they find the bones of another baby? People are going to think she murdered them.'

'Hey, let's not jump too far ahead,' said James, pulling me into him and giving me a hug. 'No one's talking about murder. I'm sure there's some totally innocent explanation.'

Before I could reply, the kitchen door opened and Ruby came out. She looked at us suspiciously, obviously aware of the sudden silence. 'I'm stuck on simultaneous equations.'

I mustered a smile for her. 'Bit of luck for you that's my specialist subject.'

'Are you coming to see *Paddington 2* with us?' asked Maisie, the following morning, between mouthfuls of marmalade on toast.

'Sorry, love. I've still got things to sort out at Great-grandma's house.'

'Emily said it's very funny.'

'I'm sure it is. You enjoy it and I'll watch it with you when it comes out on DVD.'

I looked at Ruby, who was chasing the last of her Shreddies around the bowl. 'You really enjoyed the first film, didn't you?'

She shrugged. I glanced at James, who shrugged too.

'Well, have fun and save me some popcorn.'

'No chance,' said Maisie. 'I'm going to have all of mine before the film starts.'

'And I bet you'll still try to pinch some of mine later,' said James.

'Yep,' she replied.

James had told me that last time they'd gone to the cinema he'd had to sit between them to stop her stealing Ruby's too.

'Right, see you later,' I said, finishing my tea and standing up. 'Don't forget your hat.'

'What hat?' asked Maisie.

'The one you keep your marmalade sandwich under, of course.'

I didn't go straight to the house. I headed towards Mum's instead. I wasn't exactly relishing the prospect of another confrontation, but I knew I had to tell her about the police search before she heard about it from someone else. I was also hoping she'd mellowed since yesterday. One look at her face as she answered the door suggested that wasn't the case.

'Morning,' I said, stepping inside without being invited.

'You told them, didn't you?' said Mum.

'I didn't have any choice.'

'Of course you did.' She sighed and walked away a couple of paces.

'It's a criminal offence, concealing a body,' I said.

'No one would ever have known about it, if you'd kept quiet.'

'Mum, I couldn't have lived with myself if I'd done that.'

'So now we've all got to live with consequences, whatever they may be.'

'Nothing's going to happen to us, is it?'

Mum raised her eyebrows. 'You don't know that. You've got no idea what you might be getting us into.'

'Well, feel free to enlighten me, if you do.'

Mum looked at the floor. I still couldn't help feeling she knew more about this than she was letting on. Even if Grandma had never told her about the babies directly, she might have said or done something that had made her suspicious.

'I don't know any more than you,' Mum said. 'But I'll never forgive you for opening this up. Whatever happens, whatever they find, just you remember that you're responsible for all of this, and you're the one who's going to deal with it.' She jabbed her finger at me, as if I was an evil daughter who had deliberately brought shame on the family.

'Great, thanks. And I hope you remember everything I did for Grandma, all the times I dropped by to see her, did jobs around the house, got her shopping in, kept her company when you didn't even bother to go and visit.'

'You don't understand,' shouted Mum.

'Then make me understand. Tell me something I don't know. Because, right now, none of this makes sense, least of all your reaction.' I braced myself for the lecture about how I'd always been headstrong, always thought I'd known best yet had still been stupid enough to get myself knocked up at university.

It didn't come, though. She simply stared at me and spoke quietly but firmly: 'You'd better go now.'

'Fine. I came here to tell you that the police have put up a tent in the garden and started digging, and to warn you they might get in contact with you at some point, but if you don't want to know anything more about it, that's fine.'

Mum's face crumpled. 'I want nothing more to do with this, or with you, do you understand?'

'You're not serious?'

'I am. I told you not to meddle and you went ahead anyway. You're on your own now.'

I stared at her, unable to believe what I was hearing. 'What about the girls?' I asked.

'You should have thought about them before you told the police, shouldn't you?'

Her words stabbed me in the stomach. I struggled to breathe because of the pain. 'You can't do this. You can't cut them off to punish me for something Grandma did.'

She looked at me, and I thought for a second she was going to say something. Change her mind. Break down in tears. She didn't. She stood silently. The pain was etched into her face but she'd meant it. Meant every word. 'Go,' she shouted.

I turned and left the house.

My phone rang as I was pulling up outside Grandma's. The caller introduced himself as DI Freeman from CID.

'Hi,' I said. 'I've just arrived outside, actually.'

'Great,' he replied. 'I'll come out and speak to you in person.'

It was only as I got out of the car that I noticed PC Cole standing outside the side entrance. There was police tape across it. In the background I could see several officers in white overalls in the garden. This wouldn't go away, that much was clear.

A middle-aged man with windswept sandy hair came out

of the side entrance. We shook hands. The first spots of the promised rain started to fall.

'Do you want to come inside a minute?' I asked, gesturing towards Grandma's kitchen.

'Yeah, thanks,' he replied.

I got out my key and opened the back door. The kitchen still smelt of Grandma. I saw him take a look around. 'She was a bit of a hoarder,' I said. 'It's like something out of another era.'

'My nan was the same,' he said. 'People didn't used to move around in those days. Maybe that's why they kept hold of so much stuff.' He looked at me and came straight out with it. 'We've found a second set of bones under the other statue.'

'Right,' I said, as if it was a perfectly normal thing to be told.

'They're very similar in size to the first set. We've sent them both off for analysis now. We'll be able to tell you more when we've got the results back. In the meantime, we need to do a search of the house. It's not that we're expecting to find anything in here, but we need to rule it out as part of our procedures.'

The thought of them taking the house apart, as if Grandma had been a mass-murderer with bodies lined up under the floorboards, jarred with me. 'I know you've got to do your job, but I really don't think you'll find anything in here. As I said when I made my statement, Grandma was very specific about where the babies were.'

'I understand that. Hopefully that will prove to be the case and we'll be out of there as soon as we can be.'

He wasn't going to be budged on the issue, but I still felt uneasy about letting them do it. 'You won't, you know, tear anything up or knock anything down inside, will you? Only my grandma wouldn't have liked that.'

He gave me what I imagined was supposed to be a reassuring smile. 'We'll be as careful as we can. You can rest assured that everything will be put back as it was when we've finished, and any damage caused will be put right.'

'Any idea how long it will take? Only I've got lots of my grandma's belongings to sort through and I need to get started on some of the paperwork to do with the will.'

'I'm hoping we'll have it all done within a couple of days. That's assuming we don't find anything that warrants further investigation, of course.'

'You won't,' I replied.

'The other thing,' he said, 'was that you mentioned in your statement your daughter found a bit of bone. We'll need that too.'

'Oh,' I said, picturing Maisie's face when I told her. 'It was only a tiny thing.'

'I appreciate that, but in order for our forensics team to be able to piece everything together, we'll need it as soon as possible.'

'Right. Can I go home and tell my daughter first? Only she doesn't know about any of this yet. She thinks it's a fairy bone.' I wondered for a moment if he was starting to think I'd lost the plot.

'OK,' he said. 'I shouldn't really do this but as it's a Sunday – I've got a little girl myself so I know what it's like – I'll send someone round for it first thing in the morning.'

'Thanks,' I said, feeling as if he was on my side. 'I really appreciate it.' We stepped outside and I locked the back door. I was about to put the key back in my bag when I remembered. 'You'd better have this,' I said, handing it to him. 'I've got a spare at home.'

'Thank you,' he replied. 'The other thing you need to be aware of is that our media team took a call from *Look North* earlier. We're expecting them to turn up at any time.'

'Oh. Right.'

'Can't help it, I'm afraid.'

'They won't name her, will they?'

'Probably. She was on the electoral register, nothing to stop them, really.'

'But what will they say?'

'They'll say what's happened. That two sets of bones, believed to be human, have been found in the back garden. What people make of that is up to them.'

He wasn't on my side at all. He was being nice to me but he still probably thought Grandma was a murderer. I said goodbye and headed back to my car, not wanting to be there when the media turned up. Maybe Mum was right. Maybe I didn't have a clue what I'd unleashed. And maybe I was going to regret it.

It became a regular thing after that. I met him at the gate early every Tuesday morning and we'd walk up to the ridge together to watch the sunrise. It was our thing. I don't know why. There was no one around to see us at that time. I guessed that was important to him although I didn't really see why. We weren't doing anything, just walking and talking. Some days he didn't even talk much. He looked at me, though. He was always looking at me. It was like he was sizing me up, trying to work out if I'd grown since the previous week. It made me think of that thing in Hansel and Gretel where the witch keeps checking to see if Hansel is fat enough to eat.

It was 21 June, the day he decided I was ready. The longest day of the year. He told me it was a special day as we walked up to the ridge. I thought he meant because of the summer solstice: it was the earliest I'd ever got up to see the sunrise. I didn't think there was another reason.

The sky was clear, the ground under our feet firm after a rare dry spell. He sat down at the top of the ridge and patted the ground next to him. We never sat down, always stood, but I did what I was told. He put his arm around me, his hand resting on my shoulder. Like he was protecting me. Like it was all perfectly normal. That we did this stuff all the time. I kept staring straight ahead at the horizon, scared to look at him in case he asked me something and I said the wrong thing in reply. He waited until the second the sun popped up and then he turned and kissed me, properly, on the lips. He had his hand at the back of my head, so I couldn't pull away. I don't know if I would have done if I could. All I knew was that I couldn't.

His lips were warm and dry against mine. His moustache prickled my face. He smelt of men. Grown-up men. The sort I shouldn't have been sitting on top of a ridge with at four thirty in the morning. Maybe that was why it didn't feel romantic, just wrong. When at last he pulled away he had a smile on his lips. His eyes bored into me, watching me closely. Waiting to see what my reaction would be.

Behind him the sky was ablaze with orange. All I could think of was to keep staring at the sunrise. Make it look as if this kind of thing happened to me every day. More than anything, I didn't want him to know that I had never been kissed before. Not even by a boy, let alone a man. I wondered if he'd been able to tell that. If I'd done it all wrong. Maybe he was laughing at me inside. I said nothing. I got up and started walking back down the ridge. There was a moment when I didn't think he was going to follow me. But a few seconds later I heard his footsteps behind mine.

'What's wrong with you?' he asked.

'Nothing.'

'Don't go all coy on me now. You've been wanting this for a long time.'

Had I? I wasn't sure any more what I wanted. What I thought this whole thing was about. I said nothing and carried on walking, trying desperately to stop the tears that were gathering at the corners of my eyes. I should have felt happy. A man had kissed me. I should have felt grown-up. I didn't understand what was wrong with me. Why I felt like that.

When we got to the gate he let me go on ahead. He always did. I suppose it was so nobody saw us together, though I'd never actually asked. I usually said goodbye then, but I was scared of opening my mouth in case my voice came out all wrong.

'I know you're playing hard to get but you'll be back for more,' he called, from behind me.

7

I made sure the girls were busy upstairs before I turned on the local evening news. I'd been warned. I knew it was coming. And yet I still felt physically sick as I watched the footage of a reporter outside Grandma's house come up on the screen, saw the shot zoom down the side entrance to the white tent in the garden. I heard the words the reporter said but they didn't feel connected to me. She was talking about police digging in the back garden of a house in Pecket Well that had belonged to a recently deceased ninety-year-old lady, Betty Pilling. She was not talking about Grandma. And when she said the investigation had commenced after the discovery of what were believed to be human remains, she was not talking about the fairy bone Maisie had found. Or the tiny skull, the photo of which I still had on my phone. She was talking about something else entirely. Something unconnected with me.

'Hey,' said James, coming into the room and seeing the tears streaming down my face.

'Look what I've done,' I said, pointing at the screen. 'I've fucked up big-time. Everyone's going to be talking about it, asking questions. The girls are going to get all kinds of grief at school.'

'Come on, we knew this could happen,' said James.

'Did we? I don't think I did. I had this stupid idea that the police would come and say it was nothing to worry about, put them back in the ground and thank me for doing my public duty.'

'You still did the right thing.'

'I think I've been incredibly stupid. I may regret this for the rest of my life. We don't know where it's going to end, do we? What if they say she murdered them? We can't prove them wrong.'

James sighed and stroked my arm. 'Nic, she's dead. They can't bring charges.'

'It doesn't matter, though, does it? It's her reputation, that's what will be in tatters. Our whole family's reputation. This is what Mum warned me would happen and she was probably right. And now she never wants to see me or the girls again and the whole thing's a fucking mess.'

James let me bury my head against his chest. I was a tangled mass of hair and tears and regret. Nothing had changed, really. Maybe nothing would ever change. I used to think that becoming a mother must somehow endow you with wisdom and common sense but clearly that was not the case. I was still as capable of screwing up now as I had been at nineteen.

'Does she still want to see me, then?' asked James.

'What?'

'Your mum. You said she doesn't want to see you or the girls again. Does that mean I still have to see her?'

'Piss off,' I said, digging him in the ribs.

'At least it got a smile out of you.'

'It's still a complete mess, though,' I said, wiping my eyes and pushing my hair back behind my ears. 'I'm going to have to talk to the girls. I can't have them going into school tomorrow not knowing what's happening. I'll be there to support Maisie but Ruby will be on her own.'

'I'll do it if you don't feel up to it.'

'No. I got us into this mess, I need to get us through it.'

I waited until just before bedtime. Sunday evenings at this time of year were usually cosy affairs, involving baths, onesies and catching up on crap TV. They were occasionally punctuated by a wail of 'I can't find my PE kit' or 'I've forgotten my homework' and a resulting chaotic interlude but they usually ended with everyone in a suitably content Sunday stupor. Now I was about to throw a hand-grenade into that. Somehow I needed to find the strength to cope with the fallout.

Ruby was already in bed, her head buried inside the latest Katherine Rundell. It was one of the things I missed, reading to her. It had disappeared when she started high school, along with handholding and calling me 'Mummy'.

Maisie would no doubt follow suit at some point, but for now I could still enjoy bedtime reading with her – even if she did interrupt at least three times a minute.

I sat down on the end of Maisie's bed. She was snuggled

with her usual menagerie of soft toys. Her long, dark-brown hair was still damp at the ends but that was the least of my worries tonight.

'I need to talk to you both about something,' I said. Ruby immediately looked up from her book, her expression hovering between three and four on the worried scale.

'Maisie, you know when you found that fairy bone in Great-grandma's garden?'

'This one?' she asked, picking it up off her bedside table where it was displayed on a piece of pink tissue paper.

I nodded. 'Well, it made me wonder if there were any more bits of bone under there. So I did a bit of digging myself yesterday and I did find some more. The thing is, though, they're not actually fairy bones.'

'Are they a cat or dog's bones?' asked Maisie. 'Daddy said Great-grandma might have buried a pet in her garden.'

I could feel Ruby's intense gaze on me. I had to be truthful, as difficult as it was going to be. 'We don't think they're animal bones either. It looks like they could be little human bones from a very long time ago.'

Maisie frowned at me, looked at the bone fragment in her hand and immediately put it down. 'Like cavemen bones?'

I was making a hash of this. Ruby's gaze still hadn't left me. She was now at six on the worried scale. 'Not from that long ago, no. But from before Daddy or I were born.'

'Why were they buried in Great-grandma's garden?'

'We don't know,' I said, glancing at Ruby. 'That's why we've asked the police to investigate.'

'The police?' said Ruby, dropping her book on the bed. 'Why are the police involved?'

'Because you have to tell them if you find human bones. They should really be properly buried in a graveyard.'

'Couldn't we just put them in with Great-grandma?' asked Maisie. 'I'm sure she wouldn't mind. We could poke them down to her.'

'It doesn't work like that, love.' I smiled. 'We have to let the police investigate.'

'Are they there now?' asked Ruby. 'At Great-grandma's house?'

'Yes – well, they might have stopped for the night, but they've been digging there today. And the other thing you need to know is that, because people don't find human bones in back gardens very often, some journalists came to film a story about it for the local TV news.'

Ruby fixed me with a hard stare. 'Is Great-grandma in trouble with the police?' she asked.

I was grateful that she was being careful about what she said in front of Maisie. 'No, but the police have a duty to try to find out how those bones got there and who they might have belonged to.'

'My bone still belongs to me, though, doesn't it?' asked Maisie.

I sighed and shuffled up the bed a bit so I could hold her hand. 'The policeman in charge asked me if he could have a look at the bone you found. It might help them with the investigation.'

Maisie burst into tears. 'But it's my special fairy bone. I don't want to give it back.'

I leant over and hugged her to me, stroking her hair. 'I'm sorry, sweetheart. The policeman is going to take very good care of it for you. He said he's got a daughter too.'

'Is he going to give my fairy bone to her?'

'No. They're going to examine it properly and put it with the others.'

'Will I get it back?'

I shut my eyes, wishing I was anywhere but having this conversation. 'I don't know. We'll have to wait and see.'

It took a few minutes for Maisie's sobs to subside. Ruby was still staring at me from her bed. I could almost see the questions going around in her head. Questions she couldn't ask in front of Maisie.

'Tell you what,' I said to Maisie. 'How about you go downstairs and ask Daddy to make you some warm milk?'

'Can I drink it in bed?' she asked, her face immediately brightening.

'Just this once.'

Maisie leapt out of bed, put her slippers on and left the room. I went over to Ruby's bed and sat down next to her. 'Thanks,' I said. 'I know it's hard when Maisie's here.'

She hesitated before she spoke. Her voice was quiet and shaky. 'Do the police think Great-grandma killed someone?'

I sighed and stroked her hair. 'They've found two little sets of bones,' I said. 'They look like they might have belonged to babies. We don't know why they were in Great-grandma's garden, but the police are trying to find out.'

Ruby frowned, obviously struggling to take it in. 'Do they think Great-grandma killed the babies?'

'I don't know what they think, love. They're simply doing their job. But I don't think Great-grandma would ever have harmed a baby, let alone killed it, do you?'

Ruby swallowed and shook her head.

'I want you to remember that, OK? Sometimes, when things like this happen, people gossip but they didn't know Great-grandma, did they? So, we shouldn't take any notice of what other people say.'

Ruby went quiet. She was struggling to cope with the social side of school as it was and now I'd given her a whole new reason to be worried about it.

'And if anyone does say anything nasty, you tell a teacher or tell me when you get home and I'll deal with it.'

She nodded. 'No one's going to prison, are they?'

'No,' I said. 'Nothing like that. There'll probably turn out to be a completely innocent explanation. Sometimes, in the old days, people lost babies and they were very sad about it and didn't want other people to know.'

'Do you think that's what happened to Great-grandma's babies?'

I wondered whether to tell her what Grandma had said to me before she died, but decided I'd already given her enough information to keep her awake. 'Yeah,' I said, taking her hand and giving it a squeeze. 'I think I do.'

*

The police officer came for Maisie's bone while she was brushing her teeth before school. I handed him the envelope I'd popped it into and shut the door, relieved to have got away without a big scene on a Monday morning.

Ruby saw it all, though. She saw it all and said nothing. Which was far worse than asking lots of questions. She was always quiet when she was worried.

'It'll be fine,' I said to her, forcing a smile onto my face.

'Don't treat me like I'm eight years old,' she replied. 'I'm not a kid any more.'

I sighed as I watched her put on her parka. She was right. I wasn't handling this well. Not well at all. 'If anyone says anything today, tell them that, whatever happened, it took place years ago. Before you were born, before I was born. It's got nothing to do with you.'

She raised her eyebrows at me, picked up her backpack and opened the door.

'Hope it goes OK,' I called after her. She didn't reply.

When I arrived at school I went straight to the year-six classroom. I wasn't sure if any of the other staff would have seen the evening news bulletin or heard about it on the radio that morning, but I didn't want to take the risk of someone talking about it without knowing my connection. Fiona had a strong coffee waiting for me on her desk. She'd texted last night, asking if I was all right. I'd told her what Grandma had said before she died. Fiona very rarely swore in texts – something to do with being a teacher, I guessed – but she had made an exception for this.

She looked up at me from the pile of books she'd been going through and stood to give me a hug. 'How are you?' she asked.

'Been better,' I replied. 'I can't get my head around hearing people talk about Grandma on the news.'

'Have you told the girls?'

'Had to, really. Couldn't risk them coming into school and kids saying something and them not knowing anything about it. I don't think Maisie understands how serious it is – she was more concerned about having to give back the bit of bone she found. Ruby gets it, though. I think she's pretty freaked out by it, to be honest.'

'I'm not surprised. What about you?'

I shrugged. 'I started the whole thing. Whatever they find, whatever turns out to have happened, I'm the one who set it all in motion.'

Fiona handed me my mug. 'Hey, come on. You did the right thing.'

'I'm not so sure. Mum's disowned me, Ruby's freaked out and Maisie's mad at me for taking her bone. It isn't exactly working out well for us.' I took a sip of my coffee.

'What do you think happened?' Fiona asked

'I don't know. I'm hoping they were stillborn and she buried them in the garden. Maybe she had them before Mum . . . Maybe she tried for another baby afterwards but it never happened. That's the better option.'

'You don't think she could have—'

'No,' I said. 'I don't think she had it in her to hurt anything.'

Fiona sighed. 'It just makes you think,' she said. 'All the secrets that must have been kept by that generation. All the terrible things that must have been hushed up.'

'I know. Whatever happened, she had to live with that. I don't expect she breathed a word about it. Not until her final breath anyway.'

The door burst open and Luke from our class came in, gasping for breath and with his jacket hanging off one arm. 'Miss, Noah just shoved me in the back for no reason and now he's saying I'm a grass for telling on him.'

'Come on, then,' said Fiona, standing up. 'Let's go and sort it out.'

I found the message from DI Freeman when I checked my phone at afternoon break. As there was no such thing as a quiet corner of the staffroom, I went back to the classroom to return his call.

'Miss Hallstead, thanks for calling back. Couple of things I need to update you with and some questions.'

'Go on,' I said, bracing myself for the possibility of them having found another body.

'We've completed our scans of the garden and the search inside the house and we're satisfied that there are no further human remains there.'

The taut piece of elastic that had been running the length of my body snapped, allowing my body to sag in relief.

'As I said before, the bones we've recovered have been sent away for testing, which will include DNA extraction. It would be really helpful for us now to get DNA samples from yourself and other members of your family, which will help us to establish the identities of the deceased.'

I wondered if he was not using the word 'babies' on purpose, in an effort not to upset me, or if it was simply police-speak.

'Right,' I said. 'I'm happy to do it. What do you need? Only I'm not very good with blood tests – they can never find my veins.'

'It's just a saliva swab,' he said. 'We scrape something that looks like a cotton bud across the inside of your cheek. Completely painless. One of my officers can come to your house to collect it. It should only take a few minutes.'

'That's fine. Any time after four.'

'Great. Thank you. Do you think your mother would be willing to give a DNA sample too? It's entirely voluntary but it would help us with the investigation.'

I groan inwardly. 'Er, I don't know. She doesn't want to be involved. She's finding it all very upsetting, but I'll ask her for you.'

'If you could, that would be helpful.'

'You won't have to, you know, exhume Grandma's body, or anything, will you?'

'No, that won't be necessary. We've taken her hairbrush and toothbrush. That's all we need.'

'Oh, right, good.'

'Well, thanks for your cooperation. We'll be finished inside your grandma's house by the end of tomorrow and we should be done in the garden by then too.'

'Great. Are the media there again today?'

'They were first thing. They've gone now. I've told them we don't expect to find anything else of interest at the site.'

'So we just wait for the DNA results now?'

'Yeah. I'll let you know as soon as we have them.'

I thanked him and put the phone back into my pocket, thinking how strange it was to be feeling relieved that there were only two dead babies in Grandma's back garden.

The first thing Maisie did when we got home was run to her room to see if the bone was still there.

'It's gone,' she called, then ran back downstairs. 'Did the policeman come to take it away?'

'Yes, this morning, while you were getting ready for school.'

'But I didn't hear the siren.'

'It was a detective. They don't have sirens or flashing lights on their cars and they don't wear police uniform.'

'What do they do, then?'

'Look for clues.'

'Clues to what?'

'Well,' I said, trying to choose my words carefully, 'in this case, they're trying to find out who the bones in Great-grandma's garden belonged to.'

Maisie was quiet for a moment, presumably thinking. 'Was it one of my ancestors?'

'They're not sure yet, love. That's why they're going to do

some special tests. They're coming here soon to take some saliva from my mouth. They want to test it to see if I'm related to the person whose bones they found.'

I waited, fearing Maisie would come back with another question that was even tougher to answer. I needn't have worried, though.

'Will you have to spit? Only you always say it's rude to spit.'

'No,' I said, managing a smile. 'They just get it from inside my cheek with a sort of cotton bud.'

'Good,' replied Maisie.

Ruby arrived home twenty minutes later. Maisie had gone up to their bedroom.

'How was school?' I asked.

'Fine,' she replied, dumping her backpack on the kitchen floor.

'Did any of the kids say anything?'

'Only a couple. Most of them don't know yet that it was my great-grandma. It'll probably be all over school by tomorrow.'

'Do you want me to go and see your head of year? Or I could email her, make sure she knows to look out for any problems?'

'What's the point? It's not going to change anything, is it? The kids aren't stupid – they won't say anything in front of teachers. They'll be talking about it on Snapchat and stuff.'

'Well, I'm going to email her anyway, just so she's aware of the situation.'

'Whatever,' replied Ruby.

A few minutes later the detective knocked on the front door before I'd had a chance to explain anything to Ruby.

Maisie came running downstairs. 'Is that the policeman?' she asked.

'I think it's a police lady, actually,' I said, looking through the glass panel of the front door, then turning to Ruby. 'She's come to take a DNA sample from me. To see if they can link it to the DNA they get from the bones.'

'Whatever. I'm going upstairs.'

I opened the door to reveal a tall, willowy woman in plain-clothes. 'Miss Hallstead? I'm DC Bowyer,' she said, in a broad Yorkshire accent, flashing an ID card.

'Hi,' I said, 'come in. This is Maisie, my youngest.'

'Hello, Maisie,' she said. 'Was it you who found the first bit of bone?'

'Yes,' she replied, visibly puffing out her chest. 'I thought it was a fairy bone but now Mummy said it might be one of my ancestors.'

'Right,' said DC Bowyer, exchanging a glance with me. 'Well, thanks for your detective work.' She turned back to me. 'Are you ready?'

A few minutes later I was sitting having my mouth swabbed, feeling for all the world as if I was the one on trial. And beginning to understand why Grandma had kept her secret for so long.

7 June 1944

Dear Betty,

I kissed you, Betty Braithwaite. I kissed you on the lips, just like I always dreamed I would. I think I took you by surprise and I hope you didn't mind but I couldn't stop myself. That is what you do to me. I know folks say not to rush things but that's easy if you've got all the time in the world. It's not like that for us. We both know this could come to an end at any time. And I didn't want to die wishing I'd kissed you when I'd had the chance, which is why I did what I did yesterday.

You tasted sweet, Betty. The sweetest lips I have ever tasted. I can still smell your hair against my face. See the shy smile when you looked up at me afterwards. Were you smiling because my moustache tickled or simply because you were happy? I don't know if you've even been kissed before but you're my girl now, Betty. And now I've kissed you once, I don't want to stop there. Next week feels like such a long time to wait to be with you again. I see you walking past and I ache knowing I can't touch you until then. It's torture just to hear you laughing with the other girls because I want to be with you so much. I want to kiss those lips of yours again, to put my arms around your waist and hold you tight. I want to do a whole lot more than that too, but I understand you want to take things slow. I know you're scared but you can trust me. You're not a little girl any more. You're growing up real fast into a beautiful young woman. And I don't want anyone else to think they can muscle in on my girl. I want to tell them all, you know. Tell them not to even look at you because you're taken. One day soon, I'll do that, Betty. One day we can be together properly. And it won't be long now. That's what the guys are saying. And as soon as it's over, I'm going to whisk you away from here to a new life, Betty Braithwaite. Because you'll always be my girl.

Ever yours,
William

8

At break-time the staffroom was awash with doom and gloom, the head having revealed the extent of the budget cuts we were facing. Things were already so bad we'd introduced a 'One, two, save the glue' song for the kids, in an effort to make the glue sticks last longer. There was nothing left to cut. Which meant jobs were on the line.

'If they start getting rid of teachers or TAs, well, there's no point left,' said Fiona, slumped over her coffee on the seat opposite.

I checked my phone for what must have been the sixth time that morning. Still no reply from Mum to the text I'd sent her. As she wouldn't take my calls, it was the only way I could ask about the DNA test. I hadn't expected her to say yes, but I had expected a curt *No*. It was the continued radio silence that was troubling me.

'You OK?' asked Fiona, frowning, as I slipped the phone back into my bag. 'Only you seem a bit distracted.'

'Mum's still not talking to me. I'm doing a pretty good job of trying to alienate my entire family, to be honest.'

'Why does she blame you?'

'I wish I knew. Classic case of shooting the messenger, I suppose.'

'Unless it's more than that,' said Fiona. 'Maybe she knows something she's not letting on. Maybe she's trying to protect your grandma.'

'You've been watching too many Scandi crime dramas.'

'It makes sense, though, doesn't it? I bet the girls would do the same for you if you asked them to keep a secret.'

'I'm not sure,' I said, putting down my coffee mug. 'I don't know what went on between Mum and Grandma but they certainly weren't close.'

'Are you sure there's no one else still alive who might know something?'

'Her sister and brothers were all older but she lost touch with them years ago, after the war, I think, so we know nothing about them. When I asked Mum before the funeral, she said she didn't even know their names, let alone where they'd lived. They're probably all dead now, anyway. Mum seemed to think Grandma was the youngest by some way.'

'One of those late surprises women had in those days?'

'Maybe.'

'Still, might be worth digging around among your grandma's stuff – you never know what you might find.'

I shrugged.

'You don't seem too keen.'

'I'm starting to realise,' I said, 'that the trouble with digging is exactly that.'

*

I had to go anyway. That was what I told myself when I set off for Grandma's house after tea the following evening. There were still bank details and things I needed to find for the will, practical matters that needed sorting out, which no one else would do. They weren't the only reasons I was going, though. Despite everything, I wanted to dig. Not so much dig, perhaps, as rummage. Not the way people rummaged through a bargain tub of clothes in a charity shop, grabbing, poking and looking for defects: I wanted to rummage gently and lovingly in the remnants of Grandma's life. To touch, to stroke, to feel connected with her again. And maybe to find out a few things that might help me to make sense of what was happening.

I pulled up outside, relieved to find there was no longer a police officer stationed at the top of the side entrance and the media had departed. Maybe they had been disappointed that there was no Fred West-style story to tell. That once the police had confirmed it was just the two babies' bones they had found, they had moved on to other things. It was a sad story, not a bad story. Or, if it was a bad story, the likely perpetrator was six feet under and hardly in a position to stand trial. A tiny part of me felt offended that they weren't actually interested in my grandmother's life, only in whether she had committed a criminal act.

I got out of the car and walked up the side entrance. The white tent was gone from the garden. It was dark, and hard to see if the fairy statues had been put back in the same places. I turned on the torch on my phone and walked down the path to the far corner. The statues had been put back, although not in exactly the same places. The one with her wings open was further back than she had been before, and the other fairy had been angled differently, the outstretched hand now pointing towards next door's fence. A crushing sadness washed over me. The ground beneath them had been emptied of its secrets. They had nothing to stand guard over now. Nothing to protect. And I had no doubt that that had been their role all these years. If they could have cried, they would be crying now. I wished, not for the first time, that they could speak. As a little girl, I'd wanted to be their friend, wanted them to call my name and ask me to play with them. Tonight, I simply wished they could whisper their secrets to me, tell the story that remained untold.

Inside the house it was cold. Grandma had resisted all attempts to persuade her to have central heating installed. It was wasteful, she'd said, heating the whole house when you could be in only one room at a time. I turned the light on in the hall and went through to the front room to switch on the electric heater. I looked about to see if I could tell where the police had moved things. To be honest, it looked far neater than it had been. I smiled to myself as I imagined ringing the police and complaining about the tidiness they had left behind. Grandma wouldn't have liked it. She always used to say she had a place for everything: it was simply that she was the only person who knew where it was.

I walked back down the hall. I couldn't help thinking that any clues I was looking for weren't going to be hidden downstairs in the tangled mess of the final years of her life. They would be upstairs, in her bedroom, put away in boxes and shut off from view but not forgotten. Not by her, at least.

Grandma's bedroom was decorated in a pale lavender. For a moment, the colour tricked me into thinking the room smelt of lavender too, but it didn't. It smelt of dust and stale air, if anything. Time had stood still in this room. There had been no seventies floral carpet, no eighties makeover with Laura Ashley frills and co-ordinating accessories. The curtains were faded and plain. The dark wooden floorboards were covered with two large patterned rugs, one on either side of the brass bed. The wardrobes were big wooden ones: Grandma had never been impressed by MDF. She wanted solid and dependable. I suppose that was why she had married Grandad. I didn't remember seeing a loving glance pass between them, a twinkle of an eye or a quick smile. But he would never have gone off with anyone else. He was part of the furniture.

I opened the wardrobe in which I'd found the briefcase of documents and checked for anything else among the shoes and handbags but there was nothing. I stepped back and looked up. There was a shelf above the hanging rail at the top. I fetched a chair, climbed onto it and peered inside. There were several cardboard boxes, which looked as if they had been there for years. I took one from the left-hand side and lifted it down. It was heavier than I had expected. The word 'photos' was written on one side in blue biro.

I sat on the bed, brushed the dust off the box and opened the lid. There were piles of Kodak photo wallets inside. I pulled one out from the back of the middle row and opened it. It took me a moment or two to realise that the young girl I was looking at, wearing an orange polo-neck and short brown skirt, was Mum. She was grinning at the camera. Her whole face shone. I didn't think I could ever remember seeing her so happy. I turned the wallet over. It had '1971' written on it. She would have been about the same age as Ruby. I flicked through the other photos in the wallet. I wondered what had happened to that girl with the long legs and a ready smile.

She'd never spoken much about her childhood. I'd always imagined she must have been quite lonely, an only child on the edge of the village. She didn't look unhappy in the pictures, though. Quite the opposite.

I picked up another wallet from the front of the box, marked '1963'. The first picture in it was of Mum as a five-year-old, outside the back door, the same grin on her face. An older teenage boy was standing next to her, crouching to her height, with his hand on her shoulder. He had a mop of dark brown hair. I turned the photo over:, 'John and Irene' was written on the back in Grandma's hand. I flicked through the photos until I got to another with a woman, who looked very much like the boy's mum, standing behind them. The reverse of the photo said 'Olive, John and Irene'. I looked at Olive, trying to work out if there was any resemblance to Betty. The nose, maybe, and perhaps the jawline. There again, I wasn't much like Justin.

I put the wallet back and picked up another. John was in there again, this time with Mum as a toddler. There were more pictures of Olive with both of them and some with Grandma too. These were family photographs, I was sure of it. I picked out other wallets at random – John and Olive appeared to be around at all significant occasions, such as Christmas and birthdays. Eventually, I found one of John between Olive and a man with a moustache. I turned it over: 'Olive, Harold and John.'

I had a sudden recollection of a Christmas card that used to come every year when I was a child. It was signed from 'Auntie Olive, Uncle Harold and John'. I'd never thought to ask Mum who they were and why we didn't see them. But I knew now: they were family. Auntie Olive must have been Grandma's sister, the older one she'd fallen out with. I took out a later wallet marked '1974'. There was no sign of Olive, Harold or John. It was as if they had been air-brushed from Grandma's life. There were only photos of Mum as a sullen teenager, peering out from beneath a heavy fringe, the smile conspicuous by its absence.

Why had Grandma fallen out with Olive? Maybe she had known something about the babies. Had Grandma got pregnant in later life? Or had Olive threatened to reveal a secret from long ago?

I got out my phone and called Mum. She didn't answer. It was like *she* was trying to air-brush *me* from *her* life. Me and her only grandchildren.

I texted her: *This is stupid. There are things I need to know. Why won't you help me?* I pictured her staring at her phone, deciding whether or not to reply.

If you know what happened, please tell me. I just want the truth.

I waited. Nothing. I threw the phone on to the bed. I'd have to do this myself.

I went back to the photos and went through each wallet methodically, checking the reverse of every image. I'd been looking for a good half-hour when I found it: a photograph of Mum when she was tiny, being held by Olive, with John and Harold standing next to her. Written on the back was 'Irene with the Armitages'.

Bingo. I put the photo wallet into my bag, put the box back into the wardrobe and decided to leave the rest of the things I'd supposedly come to do. I wanted to go home. I wanted to try to track down my family.

I was so excited about what I'd found that I didn't notice the piece of paper on my windscreen until I sat in the driver's seat. It was flapping in the breeze. I got out and reached over to pull it out from under the wipers. My first thought was that it might be a rather strange sympathy note left by a neighbour. I held it up to the light from the lamppost. It was neatly typed in block capitals: CALL THE POLICE OFF BEFORE YOU REGRET IT. I heard my own sharp intake of breath and immediately looked across the street. It was dark. Nobody was around, not even any twitching of curtains from the houses opposite.

I got back into the car and locked the door. It was one of the neighbours. It had to be. It was clearly intended for me and they must have recognised my car from when I'd visited Grandma. Andrea had been right. People didn't want this sort of thing going on in the village. I wondered whether to knock in case she'd seen or heard anything but decided not to bother her. She was probably sick of the whole thing. Was that all it was, though? Someone not liking the unwanted media attention. Or did someone know something I didn't? Did they have something to hide?

I started the engine and took the handbrake off, aware that my heart was beating faster than usual. I needed to go home. I needed to think about what the hell I had opened up here.

James was in the front room watching the football with the sound turned down low.

'Hi,' he said, as I came in. 'Manage to get some stuff sorted?'

I took the note out of my pocket and handed it to him. I watched his face as he read it. Saw that tinge of reddish purple come to his cheeks.

'Where was this?' he asked.

'It was on my windscreen when I came out of Grandma's.'

'Fucking Little Britain, that village is.'

'Maybe someone knows something.'

'No. They just don't like having the TV cameras there, puts the village in a bad light. Probably worried that it'll affect their house prices.'

'I should give it to the police. There could be more to it than that.'

'Like what?'

'I don't know. Someone trying to hush up something that happened years ago.'

'More like Andrea next door having her nose put out of joint.'

'She wouldn't do that. She's always been dead nice.'

'Yeah, to your face. I can't imagine she's thrilled at having all that going on next door.'

'She still wouldn't do something like that.'

'Well, it'll be one of the others, then. Some old bloke too chicken to say it to your face.'

He handed the note back to me. He was probably right. It would just be some local busybody.

'So, what do you think I should do with it?'

'I wouldn't give them the satisfaction of handing it to the police. Ignore it. It's the best way to deal with people like that.'

I put the note back into my bag. 'I'll hang on to it for a bit. Wait and see if there are any others.'

'Anyway,' said James, getting to his feet. 'You look like you're in need of a glass of red.'

When he came back with two large glasses, I had the photo of John, Olive and Harold on the coffee-table.

'What's this?' he asked, sitting down next to me on the sofa.

'I think I've found Grandma's older sister and her family.' I explained about the photos I'd found. How it looked as if Grandma and John had practically grown up together.

'John's probably still alive,' I said, 'even if Olive and Harold are dead. He's Grandma's nephew. I should try to find him, let him know. He should have been at the funeral.'

'So why wasn't he?' asked James.

'I think Grandma had some big falling-out with Olive. I

remembered we used to get Christmas cards from them when I was little. I'm pretty sure I once caught Mum throwing one in the bin.'

'Well, she must know what went on.'

'I'm sure she does. She's not telling me, though. I tried calling, texting. She doesn't want to know.'

James blew out and shook his head.

'What?'

'It sounds like major family falling-out territory. I'm not sure you should get involved. It could make matters worse.'

'Worse than my grandma having two babies buried in her back garden and my mum having cut off all contact with me and my children, you mean?'

James smiled. 'Fair point. But I'm still not sure it's a good idea to go raking up old stuff.'

'I want answers. I want to know what happened.'

'So do the police. Leave it to them.'

'But Grandma didn't ask the police to look after her babies, did she? She asked me.'

James shrugged and went back to watching the football. I knew what he was thinking. That I was as stubborn as Mum and Grandma put together. I picked up my glass and took it through to the kitchen, getting my laptop off the dresser and setting it up on the table. It was probably a needle-in-a-hay-stack job, but there was no harm in looking.

John Armitage came up with tens of thousands of results: a hedge-fund manager, a professor of art, someone offering crystal healing and meditation. After half a dozen pages I clicked on images but soon realised I had no idea what I was looking for: the teenage boy in the photo would now be a grey-haired man.

I sighed and googled Olive Armitage, then scrolled down past a plethora of green wax jackets to a long list of Olives who clearly had nothing to do with Grandma's sister. I don't know why I bothered clicking through to the second page, when it seemed so hopeless, but as soon as I did, I saw it. The article from the *Halifax Courier*, only published in April. 'Olive celebrates her century' was the headline. My hand was shaking as I clicked on it. The photograph came up straight away: a frail lady with wisps of white hair, sitting in an armchair behind a little table with a cake, '100 Years Young' iced on the top.

It was her. It had to be. The caption underneath said: 'Olive Armitage celebrates her hundredth birthday at Rose Croft Nursing Home in Heptonstall.' My mouth fell open. You could see Heptonstall from Grandma's house: it was the village on the opposite side of the valley. I couldn't believe that the supposedly long-lost sister was so close. And still alive at a hundred, come to that. I picked up the laptop and went back into the living room.

The game had ended. The post-match analysis was in full-flow.

'I've found her,' I said, thrusting the screen in front of James. 'I've only bloody found Grandma's sister in Heptonstall.'

James looked at the screen and back at me. 'Jeez,' he said. 'What are the chances of that?'

'I should have dug around earlier. She could have come to the funeral.'

'Come on, Nic. They hadn't seen each other for years. She might not have wanted to come. Betty probably wouldn't have wanted her there either.'

'Well, it doesn't matter now, does it? The point is, I've found her. And if anyone's going to know what happened, it's her.'

It was only as I put my phone on to charge before I went to bed that I thought to check it for messages. There was only one. It was from Mum and it read: *Please leave it alone. You don't understand what you're dealing with.*

I couldn't make up my mind whether to go and meet him or not. I didn't even know if I'd enjoyed the kiss. It had felt quite nice but I'd been so shocked that he'd done it, and I knew it was wrong. I'd felt bad about it ever since. And I knew if I went to meet him now that he'd kissed me, it would be really wrong. Nice girls didn't do things like that. But if I didn't go as usual, he might come to find me. Knock on the door. Wake the whole place up. I couldn't let that happen. How would I explain what had been going on? I'd have to tell them everything and I'd be in such big trouble. It wasn't worth the risk. I would have to go as normal. Maybe he wouldn't do it again. Maybe I hadn't done it right and he'd tell me he didn't want to see me again. Perhaps he wouldn't even turn up. If he didn't, I could simply come back, no one would be any the wiser about what had gone on and that would be the end of it.

As I turned the corner I saw him standing by the gate. I wasn't sure what I was feeling but every muscle in my body clenched. I tried not to let him see that as I walked up to him.

'Told you you'd come back for more.' He grinned. I could barely climb over the gate, my legs were wobbling that much. As soon as I stepped over the top, I felt his hands on my hips and a second later he was lifting me down. When my feet touched the ground, he turned me around and started kissing me. Harder and more urgently this time. Like we had thirty seconds left on earth and he wanted to get this over with. I tried to pull my mouth away, but he wouldn't let me. I didn't like it. This wasn't what I wanted at all. His hand was on the back of my head and he was hurting my neck.

A second later his left hand went up my top and he was feeling my breasts, squeezing and grabbing them. I couldn't believe he was doing this to me. I knew I should push him away, but my hands stayed frozen to my sides. I couldn't shout out and, even if I could, there was no one around to hear, only a few sheep and they couldn't help me. And he was far too strong for me to fight him off. So I stood there and let him carry on, all the time feeling dirty and stupid inside. This wasn't how it was supposed to be. It was supposed to be romantic, us watching the sunrises together. I hadn't ever thought it would end up horrible and dirty like this. All I could think was that I was glad I didn't have a skirt on because if I had, he would have had his hands up there as well.

I could already feel him hard against me. I had to do something, but I wasn't sure what. He took his hands off me for a second to start undoing his trousers. In that split second, I ran. Without my head even thinking about it, my legs simply took off. Normally, he would have followed and caught up with me, but in the time he took to pull his trousers back up and fasten them, I was gone, over the gate and down the lane. I only stopped when I rounded the corner to home and glanced back to see that he wasn't behind me.

I closed the gate silently behind me and stood for a second, trying to catch my breath so it didn't wake anyone when I went inside. My body flooded with relief, so much so that my legs went a bit weak. But the relief was swiftly followed by the realisation that he wouldn't be happy about this. Not happy at all. And waiting for him to decide what to do about it would be the worst bit of all.

9

I lay in bed with my arm draped over James. It was one of my favourite times of the week, the Saturday lie-in. It wasn't even a lie-in, according to pre-children terms, but after a week of getting up at six thirty, it felt wonderfully luxurious to watch the clock edge slowly towards eight thirty. Maisie was already up: I'd heard her go downstairs half an hour ago. We had a deal at weekends: she could watch a DVD on her own as long as we were not disturbed before eight thirty. Ruby was still asleep, the teenage body-clock clearly kicking in. Not that we were complaining.

James stirred and turned to kiss me. 'Morning. You OK?' he asked.

I nodded.

'Is it tomorrow we get an extra hour or next weekend?'

'Next weekend.'

'Could we get away with telling Maisie it happens every Sunday?'

'Worth a try.' I smiled.

'So, what's the plan today?'

'Well, if you don't mind taking Maisie to her swimming lesson again, I want to go to the nursing home, see if I can talk to Olive.'

'Are you sure that's a good idea?'

'No, but I have to try.'

'They might not even let you in.'

'I'm family, aren't I? I'll take the photo to prove it.'

'She might not have all her marbles.'

'Like I said, I've got to give it a try. It's my best hope – pretty much my only hope.'

James sighed. A moment later Maisie burst into the room, like a crazed human alarm clock. 'Time to get up. I'm hungry and I want a puppy.'

'For breakfast? That's not very nice,' said James.

Maisie collapsed into fits of giggles and jumped on him. 'No, to take for walks and look after. Emily said she's going to get a puppy when she's nine.'

'Great. You can play with Emily's. I'm not going to get up at six thirty at the weekend to take the dog out.'

'I'll do it,' said Maisie.

'You'll have to pick up the puppy's poo in a plastic bag and bring it home with you.'

Maisie wrinkled her nose and made a disapproving noise, then disappeared out of the bedroom.

'Thanks,' I said. 'You're entirely wasted as a plumber, you know.'

'I know,' he replied. 'And you owe me big-time.'

*

I knew exactly where the nursing-home was. I'd driven past it several times over the years when I'd brought the girls to events in the village. I pulled into the car park at the back and took a moment to get myself together. I hadn't rung in advance: I'd decided the staff would find it harder to turn me away in person. I'd seen on their website that they had open visiting hours so thought I'd just turn up. All I needed to do was appear confident and matter-of-fact. And keep reminding myself that I had every right to be there.

I got out of the car and walked up the gravel path. If you had to go into a nursing-home, there'd be worse places than a beautiful Georgian building perched on the top of the hill, looking down over the valley. I imagined you'd have to pay extra for somewhere like that, mind. Or, rather, your children would. John must have had a good job to afford somewhere like this for his mother. I wondered if he had a family. I might have second cousins, or cousins once removed or whatever they would be to me.

I pressed the buzzer on the front door. A young woman, her dark hair tied back in a ponytail and wearing a navy uniform, opened it.

'Hi,' I said, 'my name's Nicola Hallstead. I've come to see Olive Armitage. She's my great-aunt.'

It was only as I said it that I realised Olive might have died since she'd turned a hundred. I remembered reading somewhere that a lot of people died shortly after reaching a landmark birthday. It was like they'd been hanging on for their big day and their will to live disappeared with the last of the cake.

'Have you been to see her before?' she asked, in an East European accent, frowning slightly as if she was trying to remember me.

'No. My grandma, her sister, died earlier this month. They'd lost touch years ago but we wanted to let her know.'

'You'd better come in,' she said, holding the door open for me. 'I'll get my supervisor.'

She walked off, leaving me in the foyer. At least Olive was still alive, that was the main thing.

The inside of the home was rather tired and faded. The walls were dotted with various framed certificates, hung so high up I couldn't read them properly.

'Hello,' came a voice from behind me. 'I'm Dawn, the duty manager. I understand you'd like to see Olive.'

I turned to find a large woman in her fifties smiling at me. 'Yes. I'm Nicola Hallstead, her great-niece. I've never met Olive before. We've only just tracked her down. My grandma, Betty, died earlier this month.'

'Betty?' she replied, frowning a little. I worried that she might have seen the news stories about the bones in the garden. I didn't want to put her off. 'She sometimes talks about a Betty.'

'Really?' I was unable to hide my delight.

'Betty and her little girl. Irene, was it?'

'That's my mum. I've got a photo of them all together,' I say, rummaging in my bag and handing it to her. 'There are lots of others at Grandma's house. I could bring them in to show her.'

'I'm sure she'd like that. She's got dementia, struggles to

remember anything that happened yesterday, but old photos
are a good way of getting her talking. John brings some in
with him sometimes,' she said, pointing at him in the photo.
'I nearly didn't recognise him with all that hair!'

I laughed along with her. I couldn't help feeling a fraud,
though, considering I'd never met him.

'Would it be possible for me to see her now? I won't stay
long.'

'Yes,' she said. 'She'll be delighted to have a visitor. I
wouldn't tell her about Betty dying, though. It might upset
her. Perhaps John could talk to her about it later.'

'That's fine. Whatever you think's best.'

'Follow me. She's in the day room.'

The day room was light and airy with a bay window looking
out over the gardens. Several residents were sitting on the
sofa and easy chairs clustered around the TV. Only one was
in an armchair in the window. I knew at once it was Olive
from the photo. She even appeared to have the same mauve
cardigan on.

'Olive, love, I've got a visitor for you,' said Dawn. Olive
turned her head. I was struck by her nose, which was very
similar to Grandma's.

'This is Nicola. She's Betty's granddaughter. You've talked
to me about Betty, haven't you?'

Olive frowned at me. For a moment I thought she was going
to send me away. Maybe whatever the family falling-out had
been about, she wasn't interested in making up. But then
something appeared to register on her face.

'Our Betty were always a good mum,' she said. 'Always looked after her own.'

Dawn pulled up a chair and gestured to me to sit down, then left us.

'Hello, Olive,' I said, sitting down and holding out my hand. 'It's lovely to meet you. I've never met anyone who's a hundred before. Congratulations.'

Olive clasped my hand. Her fingers were long and gnarled, blue veins standing out like motorways on a map. All I could think of was holding Grandma's hand as she took her final breath. Now I was holding hands with her older sister.

'Here,' I said, pulling the photo from my bag. 'This is you and Betty when you were younger, with John and my mum Irene.'

Olive stared at the photo for a long time without saying anything. Finally, she looked up at me and spoke. 'Like a little sister, she were to him.'

I smiled at her as I put the photo back into my bag. 'There are lots more photos of them at Betty's house. I could bring them in, if you'd like to see.'

She looked at me blankly. I wondered if she'd forgotten who I was.

'I'm Nicola. Irene's daughter. Betty was my grandma,' I said.

I realised as soon as I'd said it that I'd spoken of Grandma in the past tense. The last thing I needed was to upset Olive. 'Can I get you anything?' I asked, keen to distract her. 'A cup of tea or a biscuit?'

'Betty liked a custard cream,' Olive said.

I smiled. She was talking about her in the past tense too. I guessed, when you were a hundred, everything was in the past.

'Do you remember her biscuit barrel?' I asked. 'There was always a custard cream or two in there.'

'John preferred wafers,' she added, looking up at me. 'Is he here? Does he want a wafer?'

'It's just me, Nicola,' I reassured her.

'Is Betty here?'

'No, she's not.'

'She'll be busy in garden. She always kept that garden lovely. Hard to grow owt up there, mind. Always blowing a gale.'

This was my opportunity. I leant forward.

'Do you remember the fairy statues, Olive? The ones in Betty's garden?'

She looked intently into my eyes. She did remember, I was sure of it. She was there now in her mind.

'Pretty little things, they were.'

I swallowed, still not daring to say too much out loud. 'The statues?' I asked.

Olive fell silent.

'Can you remember when Betty got the statues? I wondered how long she'd had them.'

'They were there before Betty moved in,' Olive replied.

I stared at her. That didn't make sense. If the statues were there before Betty moved in, maybe the babies weren't hers. But, then, why would Betty have known about them?'

'Did she tell you about the babies?'

Olive looked past me out of the window. Her eyes had sadness in them. I was about to prompt her when I heard a cough behind me.

'Hello, Mam,' said a man's voice.

'Who's that?' asked Olive. 'Is it John? Does he want a wafer?'

I stood up and turned to face him. Dawn had been right: he did look different without a full head of hair. But there was enough in his features for me to see the boy in the photo. He was looking at me strangely, and I wasn't sure if Dawn would have told him who I was.

'Hello,' I said. 'You must be John. I'm Nicola, Irene's daughter.'

The colour drained from his face. He stared at me. Confusion was knitted into his brows. 'I don't understand. What are you doing here?' His voice was icy quiet. I stepped away from Olive.

'I'm sorry,' I said. 'I would have contacted you earlier, but I didn't have your details. Betty, my grandma, she died earlier this month.'

'I know,' he replied.

Of course he did. Her name had been all over the local TV news. He would have heard about it along with everyone else. He could have got in touch with us then. Could have put a card through Betty's door. Though maybe, understandably, he didn't want to get involved. I ushered him towards the far corner of the room.

'Look, we've got no idea what happened, with the bones and that, I mean. And we don't know anyone who has. I was clearing out her house and found some old photos. She'd written your names on the back. I tracked down your mum from the story about her birthday in the *Courier*.'

He continued staring at me. A line of moisture had formed on his top lip. I knew I'd probably said too much already, but my instinct in these situations was always to carry on talking to fill any awkward silences. I took the photograph from my bag and handed it to him.

'Dawn said I could show your mum the old photos. She said not to tell her about Betty dying, that I'd be better leaving that to you. I don't want to upset her, you see.'

John took the photo from me. His hand was shaking but his face seemed to soften. 'I'm sorry about your grandmother,' he said quietly.

'Thanks. And I'm sorry for turning up out of the blue like this. I know it must have come as a bit of a shock.'

He managed the first hint of a smile.

'Look, I've got no idea why Grandma and your mum had lost touch but I do hope we can start afresh. I'm simply trying to make sense of all this and I thought you might be able to shed some light on it.'

'Me?'

'You or your mum. I wondered if she'd ever mentioned anything to you. Or if my mum had ever said anything to you about it.'

He raised an eyebrow. 'Why don't you ask her?'

I didn't want to go into everything with someone I'd only just met, but if I was asking him to talk about things buried in the past, it was only right that I was open and honest with him. Besides, he was family. And I had precious little of that left.

'We've had a bit of a falling-out ourselves, actually,' I said. 'She didn't agree with me going to the police about the bones.'

'Oh, I see. So she hasn't talked to you about me or my mam?'

'She hasn't talked to me about anything, I'm afraid.'

'She always were a stubborn one,' said John. 'I take it she doesn't know you're here either.'

I shook my head. 'She never spoke about you. I didn't even know your names until I found the photos. Although I did remember afterwards that we used to get a Christmas card from Auntie Olive, Uncle Harold and John.'

He nodded slowly. He didn't seem to know what to say, so I continued. 'I was told there'd been some big falling-out years ago but that was all. Neither Grandma nor Mum ever talked about it, or any of you, for that matter.'

'I see,' he said.

'Do you have any family?' I asked.

'No. It's just us.' He turned to look at Olive, who had gone back to staring out of the window. 'How about you?'

'Two daughters,' I said. 'Eight and thirteen.'

'Lovely,' he replied. It struck me how lonely he must be, living on his own, his only relative having dementia.

'They'd love to meet you,' I said. 'I mean, they don't know about you yet, because I didn't want to jump the gun, but they'd be so interested to meet you and hear your stories about Mum and Grandma.'

He looked down at his feet and I wondered if I'd overstepped the mark. He might be one of those older men who preferred his own company. He might not even like children.

'That's nice of you to offer,' he said, 'but I wouldn't want to intrude.'

'It wouldn't be intruding. They've just lost their great-grandma and they're not seeing their grandma either. It would be lovely for them to have someone older to talk to. How about you come over Monday teatime? Have you got a car?'

'Aye, and I can still drive it.'

I smiled, appreciating the note of sarcasm. 'Well, we're only in Hebden. It would give us the chance to have a proper chat.'

'If you're sure, that would be grand. It's not easy to talk here. Mum gets confused and upset pretty easily.' He glanced at her again and lowered his voice. 'I know you wouldn't think it looking at her now, but she can get a bit aggressive when she can't remember things. That's why she's in here, you see. They provide the level of specialist care she needs.'

'Oh, I see. That must be so tough for both of you.'

'Where's John?' Olive called from her armchair. 'John's coming and I haven't got any wafers.'

John walked over to her. I followed a few paces behind. 'I'm here, Mam. And you don't need no wafers.'

'The new lady said Betty only had custard creams.'

'I'm sorry,' I whispered to John. 'I didn't mean to upset her.'

'I'll sit with her quietly for a bit. Try to calm her down.'

'Yes, of course.'

I took the piece of paper from my bag on which I'd written

my contact details, in case they hadn't let me in. 'Here's my address and phone number. Any time after four on Monday would be great. We're easy to find. Second road on the left when you come down from Heptonstall.'

He nodded, folded the piece of paper and put it into his jacket pocket.

I moved closer to Olive. 'It was lovely to meet you, Olive. I enjoyed our chat. I'm going now.'

'Tell Betty to get some wafers for when John visits. He'll be upset if she hasn't got any.'

I smiled and mouthed, 'Sorry,' to John on my way out.

19 June 1944

Dear Betty,

We can't go on like this, sneaking around and snatching precious moments together. I understand that you don't want to be seen with me. The last thing I want to do is to get you in trouble. But Betty, life is too short and I might burst if I have to wait any longer.

Meet me by the gate tomorrow morning at 5 a.m. If we get up real early before everyone else, we won't have to worry about being seen. I know somewhere we can be together without having to worry about anyone else seeing us. Please don't tell anyone. I want it to be our secret. If it was up to me, Betty, I'd take you to the swishest hotel in London or New York City or wherever you wanted to go. I'd buy you a pretty dress and you'd walk in and turn heads because you turn heads everywhere you go, even if you don't know it. But for now, we're going to have to make do with something a little less grand than that.

You don't need to bring anything. I'll be providing

everything we need. Just bring your smile and your sense of adventure. I can smell you already, Betty. The scent of you is still on my jacket, or maybe I just think it is. And tomorrow I will touch you and taste those lips again and everything will be fine. Don't be scared. I'm not going to hurt you. I would never do anything to hurt you. But it's time, Betty. Two of the guys from Thunderbird didn't make it back last night. We need to grab our moment while we can.

I love you, Betty Braithwaite. And I'm going to be counting down the minutes until we can be together alone.

Until tomorrow,

Yours always,

William

10

'Are you sure that's a good idea?' asked James.

'Are you sure you weren't sent by God to question everything I do?'

James pulled a face at me. 'I'm just trying to—'

'Protect me. I know. Only it's like you think the main person I need protecting from is myself.'

James sat down at the kitchen table and did his serious look. 'The police have just dug up two sets of bones in your grandma's back garden. And now you've invited around some long-lost relative to quiz him about it over afternoon tea with the girls.'

'I won't talk to him about it while they're in the room. I want them to meet him. He's one of the few relatives they've got left.'

James looked at me. An awkward silence descended on the kitchen. 'OK,' he said, 'but don't get your hopes up. He probably knows less than you do.'

'Olive said the statues had always been there. The babies might not be anything to do with Grandma.'

'So why did she call them her babies?'

'I don't know. That's what I'm hoping John can help me with.'

'I bet the poor sod had no idea what he's letting himself in for. Sounds more like an interrogation than afternoon tea.'

'It won't be like that. Anyway, I'm sure he'll enjoy meeting the girls. I felt sorry for him – Olive's all he's got and she won't be around for much longer.'

'Have you told your mum?'

'What do you think?'

'She is his cousin.'

'And I'm her daughter – she doesn't even want to know me any more.'

Ruby came into the kitchen. I wondered how much she'd heard.

'We've got a visitor for tea tonight,' I said quickly.

'Grandma?'

I tried not to be hurt by the note of excitement in her voice. 'No. It's her, erm, cousin, actually. A man called John.'

Ruby frowned at me. 'Have I met him before?'

'No. I've only just met him myself. Great-grandma and his mum lost touch years ago.'

Ruby shook her head. 'Why is everyone in this family always falling out?'

'What do you mean?'

'I'm not stupid. How come we haven't seen Grandma since the funeral?'

'We've been busy, love, that's all.'

'That's not true. It's because of this stuff with the bones, isn't it?'

'It's been a difficult time for her.'

'So why isn't she coming for tea this evening if her cousin is?'

'They lost touch too.'

'There you go. You all fall out with each other. We're not a proper family at all.'

'Come on, Ruby. That's not fair.'

'Yes, it is. Not only have I never met my father, I don't even know his name.'

The words stung as they slapped me around the face.

'Ruby, that was out of order.' James's tone was not one that any of us was used to hearing.

'So is not knowing who your father is.'

I looked down, unable and unwilling to see the hurt in her eyes. I heard the door bang and footsteps up the stairs. James came over and put his arms around me. 'Hey, come on. She didn't mean it. You know that.'

I let him hold me and tried to tell myself that he was right, while knowing she had meant every word.

'So, is he my real uncle?' asked Maisie, still clearly confused as she stared at the photo.

'No, love. It's all very complicated. I think he's my first cousin once removed so that probably makes him your second cousin, or first cousin twice removed or something. Which is why I said it's probably easier just to call him Uncle John.'

Maisie looked even more confused than when I had started. 'Why haven't I met him before?'

'Because I didn't know he existed. He's a long-lost relative.'

'Who lost him?'

I sighed. After a particularly stressful Monday at work, I was rapidly losing the will to continue the conversation. 'Like I said, it's complicated. But why don't you help me put some biscuits out and we can get the tea things ready?'

'Have we got cakes too?'

'Yes.'

'Is Uncle John coming every Monday?'

I smiled at Maisie as I handed her the plate. Ruby was still upstairs in her room. She had at least promised to come down when John arrived, though I suspected her welcome would be far from warm. We needed to talk about what she'd said this morning. We needed to talk about a lot of things. But now was not the time.

At five past four I heard a shout from Maisie, who had gone to look out of the front-room window. 'A bald man's got out of a blue car outside.'

'That's probably him. I'm on my way.'

'Ruby,' I called, as I passed the stairs. 'Can you come down, please?'

There was a polite knock on the door. Maisie flew to open it before I had the chance. John was standing there smiling, a bunch of flowers in his hand.

'Hello,' he said, looking at Maisie. 'I know I've got right house because you're so much like your grandmother.'

'But I haven't got grey hair,' cried Maisie, aghast. John laughed.

'He means when Grandma was little,' I said, ruffling her hair. 'Maisie, this is John. John, Maisie, my youngest.'

'Pleased to meet you,' said John.

'Can I call you Uncle John?' asked Maisie. 'Because Mummy said you're like an uncle even if you're not my real uncle.'

He seemed a bit uncertain and looked at me for reassurance. I nodded. 'Yes, of course,' he said, with a smile. 'And these are for you,' he added, holding out the flowers to me. 'Thanks for inviting me. It's right kind of you.'

'Thank you. They're lovely,' I said, feeling better about his visit with every moment. 'Come in out of the cold.'

He stepped inside, wiped his feet and immediately took his shoes off without being asked. Ruby appeared at the top of the stairs. Her long mousy hair covered one side of her face. She peered out from the other.

'This is Ruby, my eldest,' I said. 'Ruby, this is John.'

Ruby mumbled, 'Hello,' as she reached the bottom of the stairs.

'Hello, Ruby,' John said. 'My, you're tall like your mother, aren't you? Is your daddy tall too?'

Ruby looked at me, then straight down at the floor.

'Ruby hasn't got a daddy but she shares mine,' said Maisie.

Something twisted in my stomach as she said it. It would never go away, the feeling that I'd left her unprotected from innocent questions like that.

'Oh, I see,' said John, shuffling. 'Sorry, I didn't mean to—'

'It's fine,' I said, showing him through to the living room. 'Have a seat. Tea or coffee?'

'Tea would be grand,' he said. 'Yorkshire if you've got it.'

'Daddy drinks Yorkshire tea too,' said Maisie, as she plonked herself on to the sofa next to John.

'All the best people do,' John replied. 'I remember your great-grandma would drink nowt else.'

'You used to play in her garden, didn't you?' said Maisie. 'Mummy showed me the photo.'

'Aye, I did. I used to look after your grandma when she were playing out there when she were little.'

'Did she used to play with the fairy statues?' Maisie asked.

John frowned, then nodded. 'You're right, she did.'

Ruby was still hovering in the doorway. I gestured to her to come in. She perched on the armchair opposite him.

'Right there, Ruby. You must be at high school,' said John. 'Tell me what your least favourite subject is and let's see if we both hate maths.'

Ruby smiled. It was the first time I'd seen her smile that day. I went through to the kitchen and made up a tea tray. By the time I arrived back, John had both of them laughing.

'What am I missing?' I asked, as I put the tray on the coffee-table.

'Oh, just some of my tales from being a postie, most of them involving me getting chased by dogs.'

'How long did you do that for?' I asked, handing him his mug of tea.

'All my life, straight from school. It's what's kept me so

fit. Never been to gym in my life but used to walk ten miles before most people were up of a morning.'

'Good for you,' I said. 'I could never have hacked the early starts.'

'Best time of day,' said John. 'Right beautiful it is before folk come along and mess it up.'

I smiled at him and offered him the biscuits.

I was loading the tea things into the dishwasher later when John brought the empty biscuit plate out. 'They're lovely lasses,' he said, handing me the plate. 'You must be right proud.'

'I am, thanks. You're very good with them.'

John shrugged. 'It's nice being around kids again. They make you feel young.'

'Well, come as often as you like. I mean it. It's nice for them to have you around too.'

'Do they not see your mum at all now?'

I shook my head. 'Not since . . . you know.'

John walked towards the window and looked out at the backyard.

'I didn't recognise her,' I continued, 'from the stories you were telling the girls about Mum when she was little. I can't imagine her ever being that naughty.'

'It were a long time ago,' he said. 'None of us had a care in world.'

'Why did you lose touch?' I asked. 'Did my mum and yours fall out over something?'

'I think so,' said John, quietly. 'Mam never spoke about it, though. And in those days you didn't ask questions.'

'So I gather,' I said, shutting the door of the dishwasher. 'The fairy statues Maisie was talking about. Do you always remember them being in the garden?'

John nodded.

I wasn't sure whether to go on. I didn't want to grill him too much on his first visit. But I had to find out as much as I could. 'Your mum said she thought they were there when Betty moved in.'

John frowned. 'She told you that on Saturday?'

'Look, I'm sorry if I upset her, turning up like that. It's just that she's the only link with Grandma's past. I'm not going to bother her again, I don't want her getting in a state, but would you be able to ask her for me?'

John fixed me with what Maisie would have called a Paddington stare. 'Ask her what exactly?'

'If she knows any more about the statues. She's the only person alive who might be able to help.'

'I'll ask,' said John, 'but I'm not sure I'll get an answer. You saw how confused she gets.'

'Thanks. I just wonder if there's something I've been missing. Something that might help us solve what happened there.'

John came over and patted my hand. 'She were a good woman, your grandmother. I'm sure that, whatever happened, she didn't mean anyone any harm.'

I smiled at him, grateful for the reassurance. 'I'm so glad I found you,' I said.

'Me too,' he replied. 'Now, let me go and say goodbye to those two girls of yours before I get off.'

I lay in bed gripping the sheets and praying there wasn't a knock on the door. I wasn't going to meet him. I'd decided that straight after what happened last week. But I was terrified that if I didn't turn up he would come and knock on the door.

I watched as the hands on the clock edged their way to half past four, then headed up towards five. He would know by now that I wasn't coming. Somehow I didn't think he'd be in the mood to go and watch the sunrise by himself. He'd head straight back down the lane. I thought I heard his footsteps outside countless times. It was only when the hands made it to half past five that I decided he wasn't coming.

In a way, it was worse, though. It was simply prolonging the agony. Because he would come, I knew that. But maybe he was being clever, biding his time, waiting for his moment.

He waited until that afternoon. Till I was back in the house on my own. He would know that, of course. He knew all the comings and goings here. It was a couple of taps I heard at the back door. A cheery little rat-a-tat-tat that I hadn't been expecting. Maybe he wasn't annoyed at all. Maybe he'd come to apologise for what had happened the previous week. He must have realised that it was wrong. That it hadn't been what I'd wanted.

I crept downstairs and craned my neck to try to get a look through the kitchen window. It was him, all right. Only he had a bunch of flowers in his hand. He had come to apologise after all. I hesitated for a second before he knocked again. I hurried through to the kitchen to open the door. He was smiling at me. Smiling as if nothing had happened and this was all perfectly normal.

'I missed you this morning,' he said. 'Thought you might not be well, which is why I got you these.'

He handed the flowers to me. They were sweet peas. He'd obviously picked them himself and tied them with a piece of string, but it was still nice. No one had ever given me flowers before.

'Thanks,' I muttered. He stepped forward and put his foot in the way of the door. I knew as soon as he did it that he'd planned this. Got me the flowers so I would think he was simply being friendly. But I also knew there was nothing I could do about it now, so it was better to play along with his game.

'I had a stomach ache, a bad one.'

'You look right enough now, mind.'

'It went after a while.'

'Had a nice hot-water bottle, did you?'

I nodded.

'Me mam always swears by her hot-water bottle.'

He stepped inside and shut the door.

'Are you going to find summat for them?' he asked.

I nodded and picked up an empty jam-jar from the windowsill, *filled it with water and popped them in. They smelt nice. I would say I picked them myself. No one need know the truth.*

'May as well put the kettle on, while you're at it,' he said.

I did as I was told. The sound of the water hitting metal was cold and harsh. I took a match to light the hob, feeling his eyes watching my every move. It was like we were playing cat and mouse. He was going to pounce in a minute, I was sure of it. And when he did, I was aware that there was nowhere I could run to because I was already at home.

When the kettle started to whistle, I warmed the pot, as Mum had taught me to, then put in the tea leaves and poured the boiling water over them, feeling the steam bathe my face. It was the moment I put the cosy on that he chose. Almost as if he needed something to pass the time while the tea brewed. He came up behind me and rubbed himself against me.

'The thing is with you,' he said, breathing into my left ear, 'you want to be a big girl but when things get a bit steamy, you don't like it, do you? Go running home to Mummy. Only Mummy's not here now. It's just you and me. And you invited me in. I even brought you flowers. So, whatever you say, no one will believe you. They wouldn't believe you anyway, would they? Why would a good-looking fella like me want to knock around with a kid like you, eh? They'll know you were making it all up. They'll say you were being a silly little girl, telling stories.'

He reached his arms around me and slid one hand inside the waistband of my trousers. It went down inside my knickers. I froze. I could feel his breath hot against my neck. A moment later his finger was inside me. I screwed my eyes shut, wanting to make it go away. It didn't, though. He kept on.

'You're enjoying this,' he said. 'You wouldn't be wet if you weren't enjoying it. Not such a good little girl now, are you?'

He took his hand out with no warning and turned me round to face him, only I couldn't bring myself to look him in the eye.

'It won't be my finger, next time,' he said. 'I were trying you out for size. Reckon you're ripe for the picking, I do. The cherries taste best when they're straight off the tree, you see. Before anyone else has touched them. I'll be back the same time next week. Make sure you're here, mind. Because you wouldn't want people knowing what you've just done. And if you don't let me in, they'll find out, see? I'll tell them you were begging for it. Couldn't get your drawers off quick enough.'

He let go of me. Poured himself a cup of tea and sat down at the kitchen table to drink it. He took his time. And all the while I stood there, rooted to the spot. Unable to speak or move or think of anything, apart from how stupid I had been ever to want to go and see the sunrise with him.

11

We left for school on Wednesday morning in the usual rush, having been late to start off with, even before having to go back twice for things (reading book and PE kit) Maisie had forgotten. Ruby ran on ahead to make sure she caught her bus. I broke into what Maisie called my 'quick march', with her trotting alongside me to keep up. She was talking incessantly as usual and it was a wonder I noticed the piece of paper on my windscreen, especially as my car was parked three doors down from our house. But something registered in the corner of my eye, and when I looked, I knew what it was straight away. I attempted to reach over and take it off without Maisie noticing but I was stopped in my tracks by the scratches down the side of my car. Big, gouged-out lines, running the full length of both doors. Maisie saw them at the same time as I did.

'Mummy, what's happened to your car?' she said.

I tried to keep my voice calm. 'Looks like something's scraped against it,' I said.

'But they've spoilt it. They've ruined your car.'

I could tell by her voice that she was close to tears. And even though it was a battered ten-year-old Fiesta, I felt pretty much the same way. 'It's OK,' I said. 'I can take it to the garage and get it fixed.'

'But won't that cost a lot of money?'

'It's insured,' I said. 'That means I'll get the money back.'

'Why did they do that to your car?'

'It was probably an accident,' I said, trying to sound as if I believed it.

I tried to take the note while Maisie was distracted by the scratch but she was much too sharp for me to get away with it.

'What's that?' she asked.

'The person who did it probably left it,' I replied. I glanced down at the piece of paper, swallowed and put it straight into my pocket.

'What did it say?' asked Maisie.

'That they were sorry and they've left their phone number so we can get it sorted out with their insurance company.'

'That's good.'

'Yes,' I said, forcing a smile. 'Come on, we'd better hurry up. I'll ring the garage when we get to school.'

I took her hand and we went on down the road, the fingers of my other hand still touching the note in my pocket, my heart beating ridiculously fast, my eyes still seeing the words that had been written on the piece of paper in black marker pen: 'Secrets will destroy your family. Stop. Now.'

*

My hands were still shaking when I rang DI Freeman from school. I'd gone into the stationery cupboard in an effort to find some privacy.

'Hello,' I said, when he answered. 'It's Nicola Hallstead. Sorry to bother you but someone's left a threatening note on my windscreen this morning and they've scratched my car pretty badly as well.'

'What did the note say?'

'"Secrets will destroy your family. Stop. Now."'

'Right. Are you at work?'

'Yes. I'll be home by four.'

'OK. I'll ask one of the uniform guys to come over to you then and take a statement. Any idea who it was?'

'No,' I said. 'It's the second I've had. I didn't mention the first because it was left outside my grandma's house and I thought it was some NIMBY neighbour, who didn't like the media turning up there. But they know where I live now and I don't like that.'

'We'll get someone up to Pecket Well to do some door-knocking. Might be enough to put a stop to it. But do let me know if you get any more.'

'OK,' I said. 'Thanks.'

I put my phone back in my bag, conscious that I had only five minutes to get myself together before lessons started. Someone was trying to make me stop digging, yet the only people this was affecting was my family. Unless someone outside my family had something to hide.

*

I sat in the head's office at lunchtime and watched her mouth opening and closing but her words struggled to penetrate. I caught odd phrases such as 'more cuts', 'over-stretched budgets', 'impossible decisions' and 'going to have to let you go'. Even as I heard them, I reprimanded myself for not paying attention sooner. I had been so wrapped up in the discovery of the bones that the growing financial crisis at school had largely passed me by. I'd told myself the staffroom was always full of doom and gloom, that we were permanently short of money and somehow or other we would all survive.

Now, as I listened to the phrase, 'leaving us at Christmas', I realised that this was actually happening. To me. The head said some nice things too. There was mention of a 'glowing reference' and that she'd 'make enquiries with colleagues at other local schools'. It didn't matter, though. What mattered was that I had just been made redundant. And no amount of nice words could take that away.

I walked out of her office and into the staffroom, still in a daze. They all looked up and looked away again. I didn't have to say anything: my demeanour gave it away.

Fiona, predictably, was the first one brave enough to approach me. She raised an enquiring eyebrow. I nodded.

'Oh, Nic, I'm so sorry. This is outrageous. We'll get the union on to it, see if there's anything they can do.'

I gave a half-smile, though I knew it wouldn't do any good. The head had said it herself. She had done everything possible to avoid cuts to teaching staff. I wasn't the only one it was happening to either. The year-five teaching assistant had gone into the head's office after me. It had clearly been decided that the older kids would have to do without TAs to ensure the younger ones kept theirs.

'I don't blame her,' I said. 'She looked more wretched than me. It's not her fault there's no money.'

'Maybe when things ease a bit . . .'

I shook my head. Fiona was trying to be positive, but I wanted to be realistic. And realistically not only had I lost my job but I had no chance of getting it back.

'Maisie's going to be so upset,' I said. 'First Ruby leaving, now me.'

'I'll keep a special eye on her,' said Fiona, giving my shoulder a squeeze. 'You'll find something else soon, I'm sure.'

I smiled because it was the polite thing to do. The reality was rather more brutal. It was the only job I'd ever done. I wasn't qualified for anything else. And I was well aware that, having quit my degree course when I had Ruby, three A levels at B grade weren't exactly going to cut it in the jobs market these days. There'd be plenty of bright young things who were better qualified than I was, and older people with more experience.

I sat down, fighting back the tears that were elbowing their way to the surface. I was aware that about the only thing I had experience of and appeared to be particularly good at was screwing up my own life.

My text to James said simply, *Car vandalised this morning and now I've been made redundant – how's your day going?*

The phone rang straight away.

'Are you serious?' asked James.

'Yep. I'm leaving at Christmas. I suppose on the plus side I get to finish with the nativity rather than the decorated Easter egg competition or sports day.'

'Jesus, after all the work you've put in at that place.'

'It's not her fault. Bloody cut-backs, she's got no choice. Anyway, if you know anyone who needs a plumber's mate . . .'

'Don't be daft. Another school will snap you up.'

'They won't, James. No one's hiring and no one's leaving. I can't remember the last time I saw a TA job advertised.'

There was a silence at the other end of the line. James was pretty good at picking up the pieces of my life and putting them back together again, but even he sounded as if he was stumped on this one.

'What happened with the car?' he asked.

'Someone's scratched it all the way down the side. It was deliberate. There was another threatening note on the windscreen too.'

'Sorry,' said James. 'I shouldn't have told you to ignore the first. I didn't realise it would escalate like this. You need to let the police know – this is getting out of hand.'

'I have,' I said. 'They're sending someone round later to take a statement.'

'We'll talk when I get home,' he said. 'I'll try to finish early. Don't bother cooking. I'll pick up some pizzas on the way.'

'Thanks,' I said.

'We'll get something sorted.'

'Yeah,' I replied, though I had no idea how.

I managed to keep up the brave face almost all the way home with Maisie, mainly because she talked so much I didn't need to say anything. But as soon as I saw my car, the tears came.

'Don't worry, Mummy,' said Maisie, taking my hand. 'The garage will fix it.'

I smiled at her, not wanting to tell her the other reason for my tears – I couldn't bear the thought of having to explain it all again when Ruby got home. Fortunately, I didn't have to wait long.

'What's happened to your car?' she asked, as soon as she got in.

'Someone scratched it,' announced Maisie, 'but they've said sorry and the insurance is going to pay for it.'

Ruby looked at me.

I had no intention of worrying her by telling her the truth. 'The police are going to come soon and take a statement. I have to report it to them for the insurance, you see.' I couldn't work out whether she'd bought it or not but I decided to get the rest of it out in one go. 'I'm afraid I've had some other bad news today,' I said.

'Has someone else died?' asked Maisie.

'No, love,' I said. 'No one's died. I'm losing my job. They can't afford to have a teaching assistant in year six any more, so I'll be leaving at Christmas.'

The girls stared at me. It was Ruby who spoke first. 'But that's not fair.'

'I know, but life isn't always fair. The government haven't given the school enough money so they're going to have to lose people.'

'Who'll take me to school in the morning?' asked Maisie.

'I will. It's just that I won't be coming in with you because I won't work there any more.'

Maisie burst into tears. I went over and gave her a hug, smoothing her hair, which was always wild at the end of the school day. 'You'll still have loads of fun at school with Emily,' I said. 'And I'll come to all the parents' things.'

'I don't want you to leave,' she sobbed.

'I know,' I said, brushing away her tears. 'But these things happen. Mrs Atkins in year five is losing her job too.'

Maisie started shedding a fresh round of tears.

'Come on,' I said, conscious that the police would be arriving soon and I wanted the girls out of the way. 'I think we all need a film night. You go and get a DVD on. Daddy's bringing pizzas home for tea.'

Maisie's face brightened considerably and she ran into the living room. Ruby followed, rather less enthusiastically.

The policeman they sent was PC Hyde, the one who'd come to Grandma's house on the day I reported the bones.

'Hello again,' he said, taking his helmet off as he stepped into the kitchen. 'Nasty scratch on that car. I understand there was a note too.'

I handed him a plastic bag containing both notes I had received. 'The top one is today's. The other was left on my car outside my grandma's house last Wednesday.'

He read them both, then looked up at me. 'And you've no idea who's behind this?'

'No. Obviously it seems to be someone who doesn't want the police involved but other than that . . .' I shrugged as my voice trailed off.

'And is there anyone who's said that to your face?'

I immediately thought of Mum but that was ridiculous. However much she'd been against me going to the police, she was hardly going to trash my car. I wondered about mentioning Andrea but it seemed mean when she'd been so lovely to Grandma and I really didn't think it was her style. 'No,' I said.

'Well, we'll have a look at the notes and I'll take some photos of the damage to your car and see if your neighbours saw or heard anything. I'll let you know the crime number so you can report it to your insurance company and we'll be doing some house-to-house enquiries in Pecket Well later, see what we can find out.'

'Thanks,' I said, showing him to the door. All I could think was that there were an awful lot of people who didn't know anything. And one person who clearly did.

An hour later, James arrived home with the pizzas. The girls greeted him, then disappeared back into the living room with theirs to watch the end of the film.

'You OK?' James asked.

'Not really,' I replied. He came over and gave me a hug. 'What did the police say?'

'They asked if anyone had spoken to me about not involving the police.'

'I take it you didn't mention your mum?'

I shook my head. 'I've already got my grandmother being investigated for murder. I'm hardly going to turn my mum in for criminal damage, am I?'

'You don't think she—'

'Oh, come on, James. I know she's pissed off at me but she's not a car vandal, is she?'

'So it's some sad git from Pecket Well who's followed you down here?'

'Maybe. But I don't understand why. I don't get how it's anybody else's business.'

'There are always people who make things their business.'

'Yeah, well, perhaps the police knocking on their door tonight will be enough to get it to stop. Maisie was really upset by it. And me losing my job, of course.' The tears came as I finished the sentence.

'Come here,' James said, giving me another hug. 'You've had a pretty crap day by anyone's standards, on top of a few pretty crap weeks.'

I let him hold me, trying not to think about the fact that I had a feeling that worse was to come.

*

I sat on the end of the sofa eating pizza and staring blankly at the TV screen as Nicole Kidman got her comeuppance in *Paddington*. All I could think of was how the hell we were going to manage without my income after Christmas. The best I could hope for was probably a part-time job in a café or shop. And, as I didn't have any experience, even that was a long shot.

We were in the kitchen drinking coffee later when I decided to broach the subject.

'We're going to be skint after Christmas,' I said.

'You'll find something.'

'We don't know that. And even if I do, it's likely to be quite a bit less money than I'm on now.'

'We'll manage.'

'Will we, though? We're struggling as it is and you've already said your income's down on last year.'

'Things will pick up in the spring.'

'They might not. Anyway, we can't afford to wait that long.'

'So what's the alternative?'

I hesitated before I said it because I already knew what his reaction would be.

'How about we move to Grandma's house?'

James looked at me as if I'd just suggested we emigrate to the moon.

'It makes huge sense,' I continued. 'We don't know when or if I'm going to get another job. It'll be a huge strain keeping up with the mortgage payments and bloody stupid when we're struggling and we've got a big house sitting up there empty.'

'You're serious, aren't you?'

'Of course I am. We'd be mortgage-free and have some money in the bank to tide us over until I get something else.'

James sat down at the table with his head in his hands.

'Look,' I said, 'I know you don't want to move up there but what else can we do? We can't sell it.'

James pulled a face.

'What?'

'We could. I mean, there's nothing stopping us legally.'

'And I'm supposed to put her final wishes conveniently to one side, am I?'

'She's not around to know, is she?'

'Jesus, James. I can't believe you said that.'

'Look, I'm sorry but it's the truth. I'm simply saying there is another way. And, as far as I'm concerned, selling her house would be a much better option.'

'It's not even mine to sell. She wanted Ruby to have it. It belongs to her, really.'

'Well, you're welcome to sound her out but I can't see her going for the idea. There's no way she'll want to move there.'

James put his coffee mug down hard on the table and left the kitchen. I knew he was right but I also knew I had to respect Grandma's wishes. It was a no-win situation. And something had to give.

I waited until James had taken Maisie up for her bedtime story before I talked to Ruby. We let her stay up an hour later than Maisie on school nights. It was good to give them a bit of space at the end of the day.

Ruby was squashed into the beanbag in the living room, her head in a book. I knew disturbing her would get her hackles up, but I had no choice.

'Got a minute?' I asked.

'Do I have any choice?'

I smiled. 'Not really. We're trying to work out what to do for the best and I wanted to run something past you.'

Ruby put her book down.

'Great-grandma left her house to me in her will. But when I was with her just before she died, she said she'd like you to have it one day.'

She frowned at me. 'What about Maisie?'

It was typical of Ruby to ask that. She was such a stickler for fairness. It made me sad as well as proud: I realised how often what we did revolved around Maisie, not her.

'She wanted you to have it.'

'Why?'

'You were her first-born great-grandchild. You were special to her.'

Ruby's frown softened only slightly.

'The thing is,' I continued, 'we need to decide what to do with the house. We can't afford to keep it empty. And we'd wondered about renting it out but that'll be difficult at the moment.'

'Because of the bones?'

'Yes,' I said. 'But the thing is, now I'm losing my job, money's going to be very tight and one solution to that would be to sell this house and move up to Great-grandma's.'

The look Ruby gave me was not altogether different from James's. Except there was a bit more anger thrown in.

'No. I don't want to move. This is our home.'

'I know, love, but we can't afford to keep on two houses and we can't leave Great-grandma's place empty for too long or we'll get burst pipes and damp over winter.'

'Why don't you just get another job?'

'I'll try but it won't be easy. I'll probably have to do something completely different, like shop work or waitressing, and I'll have to work my hours around taking Maisie to and from school, so I'll not earn as much.'

'So sell Great-grandma's house.'

'I just told you, love. She wanted you to have it.'

'Well, I don't want it. The whole place creeps me out. The kids at school are saying the babies were murdered. They reckon Great-grandma did it. I don't want anything to do with that house and I certainly don't want to live in it.'

She got up and was about to storm off upstairs when she appeared to remember that Maisie would be having her bedtime story.

'Hey,' I said, stepping towards her but stopping short of touching her. 'Great-grandma would not have killed those babies. I told you that, didn't I? The bones have been taken away now and there's nothing there to be scared of. It's just a normal house.'

'Normal? There's nothing normal about that house, and there's no way I'm ever going to live there. If you want to go, it'll be without me.'

She stomped upstairs. I heard her lock the bathroom door behind her. She would stay in there until she was sure Maisie was asleep. I sank down on to the sofa and started to cry. It must have been about five minutes before I felt James's arms around me.

'I take it that didn't go too well?'

'You were right. It's a stupid idea.'

'No. I was being an arse. I'm sorry.'

'You were right, though.'

'What you said made complete sense. I just don't want to live in that house.'

'Neither does Ruby. I don't suppose Maisie will be too keen, either. It's a lot to throw at them, on top of everything else.'

'Let's not rush into anything. We'll sit down tomorrow and go through the finances. See if we can come up with any other options. I'm not ruling it out.'

'Well, Ruby is.'

'She'll come around.'

'You said that about Mum.'

James groaned. 'I really am just a total arse, aren't I? Maybe you should shoot me. That's what they do with old horses, isn't it?'

'Can't afford to,' I said. 'Not while you can still unblock a U-bend.'

*

The police called early the next morning before I'd even left for school.

'Is it a good time to talk?' asked DI Freeman.

'I've got ten minutes before I go to work.'

'We've got the DNA results back.'

'Oh.'

'Would you like me to go through them in person or is over the phone OK?'

'Now's fine,' I said, not wanting to prolong the agony.

'The DNA indicates that both babies were your grandmother's children.'

'Right.'

'However, paternally, they do not appear to be related to you.'

It took me a moment to work out what he was saying.

'You mean they weren't my grandfather's?'

'It seems not.'

The picture in my head of what might have happened immediately scrambled, like one of those little puzzles where you have to move the squares around. The babies weren't Grandad's yet they were buried in the garden of a house that Grandma had only moved to on the day she married him. I couldn't work out how to fit the pieces together.

'None of this makes sense.'

'I appreciate it must have come as a bit of a shock. The other thing you need to know is that our forensics team are satisfied that the babies were born at or very near full-term. What they aren't able to determine is whether they were stillborn or died shortly after birth.'

'So we're never going to know?'

'It makes the investigation very difficult because, without any other evidence, it's almost impossible to establish whether a crime was committed or not. They can't date the bones to a specific year, either. Their best estimate, due to their condition, is that they are between fifty and seventy-five years old.'

Grandma had got married in 1955, which was when they'd moved in. At some point after that, I still didn't know whether it was before or after Mum was born, she must have had the babies. Though I had no idea who the father would have been.

'So what happens now?' I asked. 'Are you going to carry on investigating?'

'We'll be having a case-review meeting to determine that, but I just wanted to pass on the information to you as soon as we had it.'

I could feel tears pricking at the corners of my eyes. It wasn't what I'd wanted to hear. I felt further away from the truth than ever. 'How will we clear her name, though? If you can't prove whether the babies were born alive or dead, there's always going to be this big question mark over her reputation, isn't there?'

'It's not our job to clear her name, I'm afraid. Our job is to find out if a crime was committed.'

The steeliness in his voice reminded me that, as far as the police were concerned, Grandma was still the prime suspect. 'Do you think she killed them?' I asked.

'That's not for me to say.'

'You must have a hunch, though?'

There was a pause at the other end of the line. I imagined DI Freeman rolling his eyes while he scrolled through the rest of the cases he had on the go.

'Look,' he said. 'Let us complete the case review next week and I'll speak to you then, before we make a statement to the media.'

That was it. There was no point in arguing any further. I was only going to end up pissing him off more than I already had done.

'OK,' I said. 'Thanks.'

I put the phone back into my bag and stood there, staring out of the window. They weren't Grandad's babies. Did she kill them because of that? Was that the great family secret? Or did he kill them because he'd found out? I needed answers, and if the police weren't going to provide them, I'd have to find them myself.

20 June 1944

Dear Betty,

Just to be alone with you today meant everything. You are so, so beautiful. I have never seen skin as pale as yours. You're a proper English rose, Betty. A thing of rare beauty. Only, unlike a rose, you're soft and sweet. You couldn't hurt anyone if you tried.

I told you I'd be gentle with you and I was. I promised it would just be kissing and touching but when I unbuttoned your shirt and saw you like that; ran my fingers down the curve of your back and stroked your breasts, it was all I could do to stop myself going any further. You nearly broke me, Betty. I've never wanted anyone as much as I want you. I know you want to wait but I'm not sure I can wait much longer. I can't get that image of you out of my head. I can taste you on my lips. Smell you on my skin. It's driving me wild just thinking about it. I can't concentrate. All I can think of is how much I want you.

You haven't got to worry about anything. I will treat

you better than any girl has ever been treated, give you everything you ever wanted.

Last night, when one of our planes didn't come back, I prayed that we'll have time, Betty. That I won't be taken before I've made love to you. I couldn't bear to be taken not knowing what it feels like to be inside you.

I hope you don't feel I'm putting you under too much pressure, because I sure don't mean to do that. I respect you more than anything but I also need you to understand that living for the moment is all I can do right now.

I can't wait until next week and there's no reason why we should. Meet me again on Friday. The same time and same place. Keep counting the planes out and counting them back in again but try not to worry because there's no way I'll be getting shot down until I've seen you again..

I meant what I said. I love you and I always will.

Yours always,

William

12

The house greeted me with an eerie silence and the slight smell of damp. As I stepped inside I realised I would never be its true owner and neither would Ruby. We would both be visitors, tiptoeing over the remnants of the life that had gone before. Perhaps it should be opened to the public as some kind of social-history museum. People could come and walk through Grandma's life, touch the wallpaper that went up in 1972, see the radiogram that was her social media and marvel at the hand-knitted tea-cosy.

Nobody's life would ever again be played out like hers. Sixty-two years she'd lived here. The current generation could only dream about being able to own a house in their mid-twenties. And people moved so often, these days, updating décor and contents so frequently. They passed through houses rather than leaving an imprint on them, as Grandma had.

I went to the living room. I still saw her lying there in bed, sipping her Ribena through a straw. Heard her humming to herself and reminding me to warm the pot before I made the tea. I switched on the heater, conscious that as the nights were getting colder we'd have to find a way to heat the house more regularly.

I left the door open and went back upstairs to her bedroom, switching on the heater in there too. I started going through the boxes of photographs in the top of the wardrobe, searching out the oldest ones, those before Mum had been born.

I came across the wedding photographs first. I had seen the one in the frame downstairs but had never thought to ask Grandma if she had any others. There were half a dozen black and white prints in an envelope. A tall, slim brunette with high cheekbones in a long dress with a tight-fitted bodice, standing next to a solidly built man in a sharp fifties suit, who looked like he couldn't believe his luck. I gazed at Grandad, wondering if he'd had any idea that the babies weren't his. Whether he'd mourned their loss or been responsible for it. Because if he had known they weren't his, he would have had the perfect motive to murder them at birth.

Was it possible Grandma had already been pregnant with another man's baby – or babies – when she got married? I stared hard at the photo for any sign of a baby bump, but the tight bodice suggested that was not the case. She might have been in the very early stages of pregnancy and tried to pass it off as Grandad's, until he'd found out somehow and taken revenge. What I hated about the revelation that the babies weren't Grandad's was that it made it much more likely that they had been killed. It was less likely now that this was a sad tale about stillborn babies. Suddenly there was a motive and a new prime suspect. My grandad, the murderer. How plausible was that?

I hadn't known him well enough to have a view on it. He'd died when I was sixteen, just one week into the new millennium, as if he'd given it a try but really didn't fancy being part of this new-fangled thing. I tried to think back to the sombre figure with the weak chest I remembered from my childhood. He'd been a man of few words, preferring to sit in his armchair and read the newspaper than converse with others. I didn't remember him playing games with me, or even laughing and joking. He was simply Grandad, who had sat in the corner after he retired from his job at the council and waited for death to come and get him. Except now he had blood dripping from his hands.

I sighed and moved on to the next box. A small one with a mixture of crumpled brown paper envelopes, rather than the Kodak wallets. I opened one at the back and took out the photos. Three young women in shirts and dungarees, their hair tied back with scarves. It took me a moment to see that Grandma was one of them. She looked very different from the wedding photo. Fresh-faced and natural, though still stunningly beautiful. She'd been a Land Girl towards the end of the war, somewhere in the countryside in North Yorkshire, which must have been quite a shock to her system, coming as she did from Leeds. She'd mentioned it to me once, fairly late on, when I'd been peeling potatoes in the kitchen. She'd told me it had been the Land Girls' job to grow and harvest the vegetables that were used at the air base next to the house where they lived.

I looked down at the photo. She seemed happy. Far happier

than she appeared in her wedding photo. I turned it over: 'Linton-on-Ouse 1944'. I got my phone out and googled it. Linton-on-Ouse had been home to several squadrons of the Royal Canadian Air Force during the Second World War. And she'd been living next door to them when she was, what, seventeen or eighteen?

I went back to the box and searched frantically through the photos. If she'd had a sweetheart in the air force, there might be a picture. There wasn't, though, not among all the envelopes I looked through. If there had been someone, he was so special she'd kept his photograph separately. Somewhere secret so that it wouldn't be found.

I climbed down and looked around the room. I went through the obvious places first: the chest of drawers, under her mattress, the bedside cabinet. Nothing. Maybe she wouldn't have hidden anything so personal in the room she shared with Grandad. I tried the back bedroom first, the one that used to be Mum's. But there was so much clutter in it, silly things like old laundry baskets and suitcases, that it was impossible to know where to begin. The other bedroom was no better, filled with carrier bags of old clothes and boxes of bric-à-brac that could have supplied three large jumble sales.

After half an hour of rummaging and finding absolutely nothing of interest, I sat down heavily on the floor. It would take me weeks to go through every bag and box in the house and I'd promised the girls I'd be back before bedtime. Besides, even if there had been a wartime sweetheart, he couldn't have been the father of the babies buried in Grandma's garden at

some point after 1955. Not unless the relationship had continued after she had married Grandad. But why would she
have married him and not her sweetheart? None of it made
sense.

I went back to Grandma's room and looked at the wedding
photograph I'd left on the bed. Grandma must have had a
secret lover and somehow Grandad had found out that the
babies were not his. If the babies had been killed, then one
or other of them must have been responsible. And my money
was on Grandad.

When I got home, James was watching the tail-end of *Finding
Dory* with the girls. He was sitting between them, one arm
around each. It was the only time Ruby still looked like a little
girl, when she was curled up on the sofa watching TV with
him. As soon as she unfurled those long limbs and stood up,
I would be reminded that she wasn't so little any more. But it
was nice that there were still moments when I could look at
my family and pretend everything was as it used to be.

I squeezed on to the end of the sofa next to Ruby. She
was so engrossed in the film that she let me take her hand
without protest.

'Hi,' I said. 'What bit are we up to?'

'Dory's just going to get flushed out into the sea,' said
Maisie, through a mouthful of popcorn.

James passed the bag to me, taking a handful as he did
so. 'I like sitting in the middle,' he whispered to me. 'Double
popcorn rations are always welcome.'

I took some, then offered the bag to Ruby, who shook her head and passed it back.

'She's going to follow the shells now,' said Maisie, who always kept up a running commentary on films we'd already watched. 'When we saw this at the cinema with Grandma, she started crying at this bit.'

I frowned. I hadn't remembered Mum had taken them.

'Well, there's no danger of you suffering from short-term memory loss, is there?' said James, as he ruffled her hair.

'When are we going to see Grandma again?' asked Maisie. 'We haven't seen her since the funeral.'

'We've all been a bit busy lately,' I said. 'I'm sure you'll get to see her at some point.'

James turned to look at me. I gave a little shrug. It was the best I could come up with.

'Can we see Uncle John again soon?' Maisie asked. 'Or is he busy too?'

'I'm sure we can arrange that. You liked him, didn't you?'

'He told good stories,' said Maisie. 'And he was funny.'

Dory started following the shells. I glanced down at Ruby, whose eyes were moist with tears. I gave her hand a squeeze.

'Has Grandma seen Uncle John yet?' asked Maisie. 'She was the one who lost him.'

'Not yet,' I said.

'She must be very busy.'

'Yeah, she is.'

Dory's parents swam through the murky waters at the bottom of the ocean to find Dory waiting there.

'And at this bit Grandma really, really cried,' said Maisie.

I heard a soft sniff next to me. I stroked Ruby's hair.

'They put the shells out for her,' said Maisie. 'That's how she found them. Why doesn't Ruby's daddy put shells out so she can find him? Or maybe we could put some out so he can find her.'

An anguished sob came from Ruby. She jumped up from the sofa and fled the room before I could say anything.

'Doesn't she want to see the end?' asked Maisie.

James looked at me but I shook my head. 'I'll go,' I said.

Ruby was face down on her bed, crying into her pillow. The knife twisted inside me. I'd done this to her and it never tired of reminding me.

'I'm sorry,' I said, sitting down next to her and putting my hand on her back. 'She's too young to understand how hurtful that was.'

'I'm not too young, though,' said Ruby, turning over to face me. 'And I want to know who my dad is.'

I swallowed and looked down at my other hand, fiddling with the cord of my hoodie. 'Oh, Ruby, we've been through all this.'

'No, we haven't. Not properly. Just some vague stuff about him not sticking around afterwards and never having been in touch.'

'That's all there is to know, sweetheart.'

'No, it's not. That's all you wanted to tell me. But I'm old enough now. I've got the right to know.'

Everything inside me squeezed tightly together. I feared

I might stop breathing. I also feared I might lose her trust entirely if I didn't tell her more than I had before.

'Look,' I said, 'I'm not proud of what happened. I'm pretty ashamed, to be honest. That's why I've never gone into too much detail. That and the fact that I didn't want to hurt you. That most of all.'

Ruby's eyes were fixed intently on my face. She needed more. But there was only so much more that I could give.

'It was only the once,' I said. 'I'd been to a party. I didn't really know what I was doing.'

'Were you drunk?' asked Ruby.

I screwed my eyes up and nodded.

'Did you love him?'

I shook my head.

'Does he even know I exist?'

'No,' I whispered.

'What was his name? I want to get in touch with him. I want him to know he's got a daughter. He might want to see me once he knows.'

I started crying. I could still hear Mum asking me the same questions. She'd said this would happen. She'd said I'd never be able to look her in the eye. And she'd been right.

'I don't know,' I said, my voice barely audible. 'I don't even know his name.'

Ruby burst into a fresh round of tears and flung herself face down on the pillow.

'I'm so sorry,' I said, leaning forward and attempting to put my hand on her again.

'Get off me,' she shouted, pushing it away. 'You don't even know the name of my dad. That's disgusting. I can't believe you'd do that to me.'

I stood up, not altogether sure that my legs would support me, and walked unsteadily out of the room, shutting the door behind me.

I was still sitting numbly at the kitchen table when James came down.

'Was Ruby asleep?' I asked. We'd let Maisie stay up a bit later than usual to give Ruby a chance to get to bed before she went into their room.

'No,' he replied. 'But she did a good job of pretending.'

'Oh, fuck,' I said, banging the palm of my hand against my head. 'She'll never forgive me.'

'What exactly did you say?' asked James.

'I basically told her it was a one-night stand. She said she wanted to know his name because she wanted to get in touch with him. It was when I told her I didn't know it that she lost it.'

James came over and put his hands on my shoulders. 'I'm sorry. We always knew this was going to happen at some point.'

'I'd hoped she'd be a bit older, more able to handle it.'

'So why did you tell her?'

I turned to face him. 'Look at the state the rest of my family are in. I didn't want us to be like me and Mum, or how Mum and Grandma used to be. I wanted to have a proper relationship with my daughter. Shame I've blown it.'

'She'll come—'

'Please don't say it.'

James sighed and looked up at the ceiling. 'How about I suggest adopting her?'

I frowned at him. 'I said you didn't need to do that.'

'Yeah, well. Things change, don't they? She wants a dad. If I adopted her, it would be official.'

'You already are her dad. She doesn't need a piece of paper telling her that.'

'Maybe she does. Pieces of paper can be important. One of these days she's going to ask to see her birth certificate.'

I bit my bottom lip. The sick feeling in the pit of my stomach started rising. I stood up and walked towards the window.

'Nic, sorry, I didn't mean—'

'No, you're right. It's not going to get any easier, is it? I'm so scared I'm going to lose her.'

James walked over and wrapped his arms around me. 'She's got the best mum in the world. She just doesn't realise it right now.'

'Maybe I've screwed up her entire life. Sometimes I wonder if it would have been better—'

James put his finger to my lips. 'Don't even go there,' he said.

I didn't bother to lock the door the following week. There was no point. If I didn't open it, he would simply knock louder and louder and someone would see or hear and then he would tell them all those things about me. And he was right: there was nothing I could say or do because no one would ever believe me. He had woven a web and I was trapped in it. It was my stupid fault for getting caught in the first place.

When the knock came, I walked to the door, opened it and let him in. He wasn't carrying flowers this time. There was no need for pretence. We both knew what he had come for. He shut the door behind him and sat himself down at the kitchen table.

'Best get the kettle on, lass,' he said.

I moved towards the sink, trying hard to disguise the fact that my hands were shaking. He was whistling, safe in the knowledge that he could get what he wanted at any point. There was no need to rush anything.

Maybe that was why he didn't make a move when I put the cosy on the teapot this time. He let me pour the tea and sat and drank his, then wiped his mouth with the back of his hand and smacked his lips.

'Right then,' he said. 'Better go upstairs, unless you want world and his wife watching.'

I sat, staring at the cup of tea in front of me. I don't know why I'd made myself one because I knew there was no way I could drink it. My hands were shaking too much to lift the cup and I knew I wouldn't be able to keep anything in my stomach, even if I could manage to swallow any.

A silent sigh seeped out of me. I didn't see what else I could do. If I ran out into the street, he would follow. If I shouted and screamed, he would tell everyone what had been going on. There was nothing I could do to stop this happening. It was better if I got it over with as quickly as possible. I simply wanted to get to the point where he was gone, and I could try to pretend it had never happened.

I stood up, pushing the chair back with my legs, all the time avoiding his eyes. I led the way upstairs, aware of them on my body, scanning every inch of me. I already felt naked in front of him. I went into my bedroom, trying not to look at any of my things, wanting to detach myself from what was about to happen.

As soon as he touched me, I shut my eyes. I didn't have to look at him: he couldn't make me do that. His hands were rough on me, his breath smelt stale. I'd put on a skirt because I'd thought I might be able to stay covered up. I didn't want to be any more exposed than I had to be. I squeezed my eyes shut harder as he put his hands up my skirt and roughly pulled down my knickers. I started crying as I waited for it to happen. Hot, silent tears that rolled down my cheeks. He pushed my legs apart, thrust himself into me. I winced and turned my head away. I thought I might actually split in half. I tried to think about other things, anything, to take me away from what was happening inside me. To block out the sound of him grunting and the pain searing through my body.

At some point I became aware that he had finished. I felt him removing himself from me. But even as he did so, I could still feel him inside me. And it was at that moment I knew I would always feel him there. That I would never be able to erase the imprint of him inside my body. I was marked, tainted for life.

I pulled my knickers back up, aware of the blood trickling down my leg.

'There,' he said, zipping up his flies. 'I've popped your cherry, for you. Said you were ripe for picking.'

He was smiling as if he somehow thought I had enjoyed it. That he had done me a favour.

'Same time next week, then,' he said. 'And if you tell anyone about this, I'll say it were all your doing. That you invited me in, begged me for it. You'll never live it down. You'll be an outcast. And you'll take that shame to your grave.'

13

John lived on the far side of Heptonstall in a small cottage tucked away down a cobbled side street, out of view from the main road. It was weird to think of how long he and Olive had lived on the opposite side of the valley from us, without us having any idea they were there.

I pulled up at the end of the road. Maisie got out first, babbling about how she'd quite like to live in Heptonstall but she'd get rid of the cobbles because they were too bumpy.

Ruby emerged from the car rather more reluctantly. She was still avoiding eye contact with me and was wearing the same scowl on her face she'd had since Thursday evening.

'Which one is it?' asked Maisie.

'Number eleven, at the end.'

Maisie ran up to the door and pressed the bell. When John opened it she threw her arms around him. He glanced up at me, almost as if he wasn't sure what to do.

'Hi, Uncle John,' she said. 'Can I come in and see your house, please?'

'Aye,' he said. 'That'd be grand. I'll give you guided tour, shall I?'

Maisie slipped her shoes off and disappeared inside.

'Hello, John,' I said, giving him a peck on the cheek. 'You may have noticed that she doesn't stand on ceremony.'

'No, and that's fine by me. Come on in, Ruby,' he said. 'Do you like birds? You might want to come and meet our budgie, Bert.'

Ruby followed him inside. The hallway was narrow and dark and the front room wasn't much brighter. As lovely as the mullion windows were to look at, I'd always thought I couldn't bear to lose all that light.

Maisie was standing in the far corner looking up at the blue budgie in the cage.

'That's our Bert,' said John. 'I bought him to keep Mum company when her last one died. She's always had budgies.'

'Isn't it cruel to keep it in a cage?' asked Maisie.

'I let him out to fly around in here every night,' John explained. 'But he's fine, just getting on a bit, like me.'

'Mummy said your mummy lives in a home for people who can't remember things,' said Maisie.

'Aye, that's right.'

'Do you take Bert to visit?'

'Afraid not, love. Pets aren't allowed.'

'When I'm old I'm going to have lots of pets.'

'Good for you,' John said. 'Do you want to give him some seeds?'

He picked up a bag from underneath the cage and handed it to Maisie. 'Put a handful in his feeder,' he said. 'He won't bite you. He's right gentle.'

Maisie did as she was told and smiled as Bert flew down off his perch to tuck in.

'Do you want to give him some, Ruby?' asked John. She shook her head.

'Right. Well, now Bert's sorted, I'll get us some drinks and that,' he said.

I left the girls watching Bert and followed John out to the kitchen. 'I'm afraid you won't get much out of Ruby, she's at that difficult age.'

'Oh, aye,' he said. 'She's all right. Don't need to say owt when you don't want to.' He filled the kettle, then got two mugs out from the cupboard and a couple of glasses for the girls.

'Is squash all right for them?' he asked.

'Yeah, that's great, thanks.'

'Bit of luck because I've got nowt else in. I've never been a fan of that fizzy pop they have.'

I smiled, warming to him all the time. 'How's your mum?' I asked.

'Not so good. Been in a bit of a state, last few days. They say it's only going to get worse.'

'That's tough on you. It must be hard to deal with that on your own.'

He shrugged. 'One of those things. It'll come to us all.'

It made me think. At least I'd have Ruby and Maisie to look after me. John had no one. I'd make sure he wasn't on his own. He was family now.

'How long have you lived here?' I asked, looking around the cramped kitchen.

'Oh, donkey's years. She loved it. Shame, really. Still, it got to point where it were too dangerous for her. She started wandering off to find me when I went out to shops.'

'It's lucky she had you to look after her, really. Not all sons would make the effort to do that.'

'Least I can do. You only have one mam, don't you?'

He looked at me, and I thought he must have realised what he'd said because the smile dropped from his face and he turned straight back to pour boiling water into the tea-pot.

'Did you, er, manage to speak to your mum at all?' I asked. 'About the statues?'

'Oh, aye, I did. She couldn't remember owt about them. She said house had been in family for years, mind.'

'Really?'

'It belonged to her great-aunt Aggie. She didn't have any children. Left it to Betty in her will. Six months later Betty got married and moved in.'

I frowned at him. 'Why Betty and not the older ones?'

'Who knows?'

'Is that what the big family falling-out was about?

John shrugged and poured the squash for the girls. 'Perhaps. Any road, that's as much as I could get out of Mam without upsetting her any further. I hope it helps.'

'Yes. Thank you. I'm sure it will, once I figure out everything else, that is.'

'Why, what's happened?'

I hesitated, unsure how much to reveal but I felt I could trust John with the information. 'The bones in the garden.

They were my grandmother's babies but they weren't my grandfather's.'

John said nothing, just nodded.

'You don't seem surprised.'

'There's nowt about folk surprises me.'

'You don't remember talk of her seeing anyone else, do you?'

'If there were, it wouldn't have been for my ears.'

'Your mum might have known, though, seeing as they were so close.'

'Do you want me to ask her?'

'If you wouldn't mind. As long as she's up to it. I wouldn't want to get her upset again.'

'I'll see what I can do.'

'Thanks. You and your mum are the only people who knew my grandparents back then. And I'm desperate to try to get to the truth. Even if it's not a very nice truth.'

'You think it might have been your grandfather that did it?'

'Maybe. He'd have had a reason, wouldn't he? I just don't know if he was capable of that.'

John was quiet as he poured the tea. Then he turned to me. 'I saw him kill a baby bird once.'

'I'm sorry?'

'Your grandfather. He found an injured baby bird in the garden that had fallen from its nest. Your mum were only little, said she wanted to take it indoors and try to make it better. He told her it were best to let nature take its course. Then, when she'd gone inside, he trod on it with his size nines.'

I stared at John, unable to disguise the horror I felt. 'Really? My grandfather did that?'

'Aye. I watched him. He told me it were best to put it out of its misery. That there were no use getting sentimental about nature. Survival of the fittest and all that.'

'God. I had no idea he was like that.'

Maisie ran into the kitchen. 'Come and see Bert. He's doing a little nodding dance with his head.'

I smiled and followed her.

'Maybe I should tell the police,' I said to James later, once the girls were in bed.

'Tell them what? That your grandfather killed a baby bird, so he probably killed the babies too?'

'Don't say it like that.'

'That's how they'd hear it.'

'It's not only that, is it? The fact that the house belonged to her great-aunt Aggie might be important. Maybe she had something to do with it.'

'You're sounding more like Miss Marple every day. You do know that?' said James, leaning forward to top up my glass of wine.

'I just want answers. The police might decide to close the case next week and then I'll never get any. This could change their minds. It's worth a try.'

'Can it wait till Monday? It would be nice to spend tomorrow together as a family. I think it would be good for all of us.'

'I don't think Ruby's going to forgive me because we spend the day together.'

'Maybe not but it's a start. We should go out somewhere nice for lunch. After we've told them about the house.'

I put my glass down and looked across at James. 'What do you mean?'

'I think you're right. We should put this house up for sale. It's the most sensible thing to do in the situation.'

I frowned at him. 'Really?'

'Yeah. Why put ourselves under massive financial pressure when there's a free house sitting up there waiting for us?'

'But you hated the idea of it.'

'I still do, long-term. But right now it makes sense. The money from this place will give us the cushion we need while you look for a job, and if you get one quickly and the whole thing with the police goes quiet, we can look at selling it in a year or two's time, once I've done it up.'

'I told you, we can't sell it.'

'You might feel differently in a couple of years. And, if not, we can at least rent it out then and find something else back down here when we're on a more stable financial footing.'

I didn't know what to say. He'd made it sound like a good business deal when it was Grandma's house we were talking about and I hated that. I also hated that, as I'd been the one who'd suggested it in the first place, I couldn't really say no.

'Are you sure?'

'Yep. I don't see how we can do anything else.'

'Ruby's going to hate me even more than she already does, if that's possible.'

'Then I'll tell her it was my idea.'

'Don't be daft. It's better that she hates one of us and still has the other one to talk to.'

'It's not fair on you, though.'

I made a little 'humph' sound. I didn't care whether or not anything was fair on me. The only person who mattered here was Ruby.

'We'll tell them together,' said James. 'Tomorrow morning. And then we'll take them out for lunch and to the pictures in the afternoon. We can forget all about it for a bit.'

I nodded but said nothing. Wished I had a fraction of his optimism.

We decided to strike straight after breakfast, the theory being that, fed and watered and still in their dressing-gowns, the conditions for open warfare were less favourable. I wasn't convinced but had decided to go along with it anyway.

'Your mum and I have got some news,' James began brightly. Maisie looked up from reading the smoothie carton for the seventy-third time. Ruby raised her head just enough for me to be able to see her eyes. It really should be me who told them, I thought.

'We're going to move to Grandma's house,' I blurted out. 'You're both going to be able to have your own bedroom and we'll have a garden. Maybe we can even get a puppy next spring.'

The last bit hadn't been planned. It had been prompted by the expression on Ruby's face as I'd delivered the first part. James looked at me. I shrugged. Maisie exploded in delight, jumping up and down. 'We're going to get a puppy,' she squealed. 'We're going to get a puppy.'

Ruby stared at me, her jaw set, a fierce darkness spreading over her eyes.

'Which one's going to be my bedroom?' shrieked Maisie. 'Will it be Grandma's old room or the other one? Can I have unicorn wallpaper?'

Ruby stood up and pushed her chair back with her knees. The legs scraped noisily against the terracotta-tiled floor.

'Are the fairy statues still there?' continued Maisie. 'Can I play with them? Can one of them be mine?' She looked at each of us in turn, desperate for answers, as she jigged around the kitchen.

Ruby took two steps towards me. 'I am not going,' she shouted.

Maisie froze in shock and stared at her.

'I am not going to live in that house. Whatever went on there, I don't want anything to do with it. I told you I didn't want to move and you haven't listened. You don't care about me. Everything's about her,' she yelled, jabbing her finger at Maisie. 'Just because she's your precious daughter and I'm some drunken mistake that you'd rather pretend hadn't happened.'

Maisie burst into tears.

'Ruby,' said James, sharply.

'Don't Ruby me! You're not my dad. I don't even know who my dad is, thanks to her.' Her finger pointed to me now. 'This whole family's a mess and I'm not going anywhere with you.'

I stepped towards her but it was too late: she rushed past me in a seething mass of hair and tears, slamming the kitchen door behind her.

'I'll go,' said James.

'No. Let her calm down first,' I said,

'Why is Ruby mad at me?' asked Maisie, running over and burying her head against James. 'Why is she mad at you? I wish you were her daddy. She wouldn't be like this if you were her daddy.'

I slumped on to the kitchen floor and started to cry.

23 June 1944

Dear Betty,

I don't regret what happened today for a moment and I hope you don't either. I'm in love with you and that's what two people do when they're in love.

I can still feel your body against mine, feel how soft and warm it was. I told you I'd be gentle and that it wouldn't hurt. I know you were frightened and I understand it's a big deal for a girl but, Betty, you were wonderful. I can't stop thinking about how special it felt to be inside you. I love you more than ever — and I didn't think that was possible. Whatever happens in the future, no one can ever take that away from us. Some of the boys lost their lives before they'd got to make love to their sweethearts but now that can't happen to us. And you know what, Betty? There's no way they're going to get me now.

We're over the worst, we have to be. So many more planes are coming back. When I think of all the boys we lost last year, it feels completely different when we go out now. We are starting to expect to come back instead of expecting to die.

I know I always rib Freddie that Goose have lost more planes than Thunderbird, but even the Goose guys are starting to look like they believe they might make it through. And when it's all over, Betty, I'm going to take you home to Winnipeg and my family are going to fall in love with you too. You're my girl forever now Betty, and don't you go forgetting it.

Yours always,

William

14

I looked at the text on my phone, which said, *The girls would like to see you this half-term.* Two months ago, I couldn't have foreseen a situation where I'd need to send it, let alone be worried that Mum might not respond. There again, two months ago I wouldn't have believed I'd be scouring the internet for jobs, getting the house ready for an estate agent's visit and praying my elder daughter would decide to speak to me at some point. Usually, half-term came as a welcome break. Not so this time.

I pressed the send button. I waited a minute or so. I was not expecting a reply but the silence still shocked me. She loved the girls. I had no doubt of that. And punishing them like this must be incredibly hard for her. The idea that her contempt for me was greater than her love for them was difficult for me to comprehend.

I put the phone back into the pocket of my hoodie. When it rang a few seconds later I physically jumped, like people do in cartoons. I grabbed it but, as I did so, I saw that it wasn't Mum. It was DI Freeman.

'Hello,' I said, trying not to sound disappointed.

'Hello, Miss Hallstead, I wanted to let you know before we release anything to the media that the case review has concluded that, as we can't ascertain whether a crime was committed and the potential suspects are deceased, there is no realistic prospect of us securing a conviction. We have therefore decided to close the investigation.'

'Oh,' I said. 'I was going to ring you later. I've discovered that the house belonged to my grandma's great-aunt, who left it to her in her will. I wasn't sure if that would make any difference to you.'

'I'm afraid not. And obviously as she's also deceased there really is nothing more we can do.'

It was everything I hadn't wanted to hear. There would be no answers. Not from the police, anyway. I wondered whether to tell him about Grandad and the baby bird but thought better of it. 'But what are people going to think?'

'As I said to you before, Miss Hallstead, it really isn't any of my business.'

'I think my grandad may have had something to do with it,' I blurted out.

'That's quite possible, but without him or your grand-mother being around, and with no conclusive forensics and no witnesses, there's really nothing more we can do.'

'What will you be telling the media?'

'Exactly what I've told you. We'll be making clear that as there is no way of proving if a crime took place there is nothing further we can do.'

'You won't tell them the babies were illegitimate, will you?'

'No. All we'll say is that we have been able to confirm that the babies were born to your grandmother.'

I sighed. Everyone would still think she'd killed them, I knew that. But I also knew there was no point in arguing any further. 'What will happen to the bones?'

'They will be given back to you in due course, so you can make arrangements for a proper burial.'

'Right.'

'We'll be in touch to arrange that but, in the meantime, I can only thank you for reporting the matter to us and for your cooperation with the inquiry.'

And that was it. I managed to say thank you and goodbye before putting the phone down and sitting there in silence. Grandma had left this with me. I believed she wanted me to know what had happened, which was why I'd gone to the police in the first place. But now I was going to have to try to find out on my own.

I stood up and walked towards the kitchen window, gazing out at the grey skies above. Mum had certainly been right about one thing: reporting this had, so far, only made things worse for our family. And now I had been left to clear up the mess I had created. I should tell Mum before she heard it on the news. Maybe then she might change her mind about speaking to me. After all, the police weren't involved any more. If she had something to say, she could say it to me. I still suspected she must know more than she was letting on. She wouldn't have reacted like she had otherwise. Maybe it was actually Grandad she was protecting. She'd always been closer to him than Grandma. Perhaps she knew he'd killed the babies and had been worried the police would find out.

I picked up the phone and texted, *The police are closing the case. They can't prove whether the babies were stillborn or died shortly after birth. If you know what happened, please tell me. I know the babies weren't Grandad's.* I sent it to Mum and waited. Again, nothing. I pressed the call button, determined to get some kind of response from her. She let it ring until it went to voice mail. It was a moment or two before I could compose myself enough to speak.

'Mum, I know you're there. Please talk to me. The police aren't involved any more but I still want answers. I need to know what happened. I need the truth.'

I sat and looked at the phone for a good five minutes, willing it to ring, before I put it back in my pocket and went downstairs.

I decided to tell Maisie first, mainly because she was the only other female member of my family who was on speaking terms with me.

She was in the living room playing with the flying fairy doll she'd got for her birthday, one of the rare things that had held her attention far beyond the usual two weeks. She'd got quite good at it, using her hand underneath to control it and bring it down a little when it looked like hitting the ceiling.

'Hi, love. Fairy Faye's very good at flying now, isn't she?'

'Yes. She does it all by herself. She doesn't need me at all.'

I wasn't sure that her lack of grasp on reality boded well for what I was about to tell her. 'You know I told you about the police finding the other bones in Great-grandma's garden?'

'Yes,' she said, still not taking her eyes off the fairy.

'Well, they've finished their investigation and they don't need to do any more digging.'

'Will I get my fairy bone back?' she asked, letting Faye fall to the floor and turning to look at me.

'Well, they're going to give us all the bones back but we have to bury them again. In a proper grave, like the one Great-grandma is in.'

She looked crestfallen. I hoped there wouldn't be more tears.

'We'll bury them next to Great-grandma and we can visit them.'

Maisie nodded solemnly. She picked up the fairy again and placed it on its stand. 'Whose bones are they?' she asked.

I hesitated, unsure how near the truth I should go. 'We think that, a long time ago, Grandma had two babies and they didn't survive so she buried them at the bottom of the garden.'

'Is she in trouble for doing that?'

'No,' I said. 'The police had to investigate but they aren't cross with her. We'll bury the bones and then we can all move on.'

'And then can we move to Great-grandma's house?'

'We've got to sell ours first,' I said. 'That's why the man I told you about is coming this morning to take the photos.'

'But then we can move?'

'Yes, hopefully.'

'And when will we get the puppy?'

'Let's wait and see,' I said. 'One thing at a time.'

I left her playing with the fairy and went upstairs to the girls' bedroom. I knew better than to go in without knocking. I also knew I was liable to get no reply from Ruby. After my second knock, a muffled 'What?' came from within.

'Can I come in?' I asked. 'I've got something to tell you about the police investigation.'

My calculation paid off that curiosity would get the better of her, and I got a grunted permission to enter. She was lying on her bed, reading. I smiled at her and shut the door behind me. 'The police have said they can't prove if the babies were stillborn or if they died shortly after birth, so that's the end of it. They're closing the investigation and they're going to give us the bones back.'

'So they don't think Great-grandma did it?'

'They can't say for certain but the fact that they're closing the investigation means they can't prove it.'

'Were they Great-grandma's babies?'

'Yes, love. They were.'

'That's so sad.'

'I know.'

'But everyone's still saying she was a murderer.'

'I'm sorry. I know it's been horrible for you but the police are going to put out a statement today saying there is no evidence that any crime took place so I hope that'll put a stop to it.'

'It doesn't mean it didn't happen, though, does it?'

I walked over and sat down on the end of her bed. 'We don't know what happened, love, and we might never get to the bottom of it, but I don't think for a moment that Great-grandma would have been capable of killing her babies, do you?'

Ruby shook her head slowly. I didn't want to complicate matters by mentioning her great-grandad when she'd never even known him. And I didn't really want to tell her they weren't his babies either. She'd had enough to deal with, without me adding to it unnecessarily.

'Well, then, that's all that matters.'

Ruby stared out of the bedroom window. 'What are they doing with the bones?'

'We're going to get them back to bury properly.'

'I don't want to be involved in that.'

'That's fine.'

'And are we still moving to her house?'

I looked up at the ceiling and sighed. 'Yeah,' I said. 'We haven't really got any option – financially, I mean.'

'Why can't you get another job?'

'I'm trying. There are no TA jobs available right now and I haven't got experience of doing anything else. It's tough out there at the moment, especially without a degree.'

Ruby looked down at her feet. I immediately wished I hadn't said that.

'I ruined everything for you, didn't I?'

'No,' I replied. 'I've never for a moment regretted having you, so don't start blaming yourself.'

'You're only saying that to make me feel better.'

'No,' I replied. 'I'm saying it because it's true.'

The estate agent arrived fifteen minutes early. I usually took an instant dislike to people who arrived early but, as he was kind enough to say the house looked very tidy when I apologised for the mess, I decided to make an exception.

'Are you the man who is going to sell our house?' asked Maisie, who was still wholeheartedly behind the idea.

'I am indeed,' he replied. 'Would you like to give me a tour? I'm going to take photographs in each room as we go.'

'OK,' she said. 'But you can't take a photo of my sister Ruby because she'll get really mad and she doesn't want to move anyway.'

The estate agent looked at me.

'Teenagers, eh?' I said, with a forced smile.

It was only when I thanked him as he left and he told me our house would be on Rightmove by the next day that it hit me. This was really happening, whether Ruby liked it or not. If we were lucky and it sold quickly, we'd be in Grandma's house in a matter of months. New beginnings and all that. Maybe everything would work out. Maybe the worst was behind us and we could all start to move on.

'Can we go and see Great-grandma's house tomorrow?' asked Maisie, when I'd shut the door. 'I want to go and play with the fairies and choose what bedroom I'm going to have, and then I want to dress up as a witch and go trick-or-treating with Emily.'

Ruby wouldn't want to go but we had to start making the plan a reality, and the sooner everyone got used to the idea, the better. 'We'll go after we get your hair cut. And then we'll come back and turn you into the Wicked Witch of the West.'

That night I watched the local news on TV. The same reporter was standing outside Grandma's house. The tone had changed, though. It was being portrayed as a sad story, rather than a breaking crime story. 'Police have announced they are closing the investigation into the discovery of bones belonging to two babies that were found at the home of a ninety-year-old woman who died earlier this month.

'Detectives confirmed that DNA tests have revealed the babies were born to Betty Pilling more than fifty years ago, but as there is no evidence a crime was committed, the bones will be returned to her family to allow for a lawful burial.'

They went back to the studio. A report about an open-air performance of *Macbeth* being staged for Halloween came on. That was it. The babies were old news. If people did believe Grandma killed them, this probably wouldn't have changed their minds. Maybe they would forget about it in time. We wouldn't, though. We had to live with it. And the idea that her reputation had been tarnished forever rankled with me. The police might have been willing to let it lie but I wasn't. I would get to the truth and somehow I would find a way to clear her name.

*

Maisie always wanted to go first at the hairdresser's. She sat in the chair, her feet swinging a few inches from the floor, and smiled at herself in the mirror. I could only imagine what it must be like to have the self-confidence to do that.

'Just a trim as usual, please,' I said to Gina, the hairdresser.

'Right you are,' she replied. 'Let's get these ends tidied up for you, Maisie. I don't know what your mummy's feeding you but it's certainly making your hair grow.'

Maisie giggled, then sat perfectly still as Gina snipped. Her hair looked no different by the time Gina had finished but she still admired it in the mirror as if it was a completely new look. 'Very nice, thank you,' she said to Gina, who smiled at me.

'Right, Ruby,' Gina said, as she put the gown on her, 'same for you, is it?'

'I want it cut short, please,' Ruby replied.

Gina turned to me. I shrugged – it had come as a surprise to me, too. But after all the things we'd argued about lately, the last thing I wanted was a fight with Ruby about the length of her hair.

'Oooh, feel like a change, do you? How about a nice long bob? Just touching your shoulders. Once you're used to it that length, you can go shorter next time.'

Ruby nodded. 'OK.'

Gina turned to me. 'That sounds great,' I said. 'We'll let you do your magic.'

Ruby didn't watch as Gina started cutting. She'd brought a book with her and sat there holding it high enough that she could keep her head up while avoiding her reflection in the mirror.

She didn't need to see it as Maisie kept up a running commentary of how much was being cut off. When Gina had finished and Ruby put the book down to look at herself, she couldn't hide how pleased she was with the result.

'Wow,' said Gina, 'don't you look grown-up!'

She did too. It scared me, but I smiled at her in the mirror. 'Thanks, Gina,' I said. 'She certainly does.'

'I'm going to have mine cut short next time,' said Maisie, as we walked back to the car. I glanced at Ruby. We both knew she wouldn't.

'What made you want to do that?' I asked Ruby.

'I didn't want to look like me any more,' she said.

Ruby sat silently in the back of the car on the way to Pecket Well. Her two best friends had gone away for half-term with their families, so she hadn't been able to come up with any suggestions as to where she might go instead of accompanying us. She was making no effort, though, to pretend she was a willing participant.

Fortunately, I could always rely on Maisie to compensate for any silence. Knowing she would get nothing out of Ruby, she'd brought her flying fairy with her and was busy explaining to her that she was going to meet some other fairies. I could see Ruby's eyes rolling in the rear-view mirror. My plan was to be as quick as possible at the house, get the heater on for a bit, collect a few bags and boxes I wanted to sort through at home, then head back.

When I got out of the car the sun was breaking through the clouds. It was so true that everything looked better when it was out. The house didn't seem anywhere near as forbidding. We could paint the door white, which would help to brighten up the dark stone. Maybe put up a couple of hanging baskets. A welcome mat – the girls could choose that. And James had already said he'd put in central heating and a new bathroom before we moved in. We could make it nice. We could make it feel like home. There was no reason we couldn't make it work.

I led the way down the side entrance. Maisie ran straight to the fairy statues. 'They've moved them, Mummy,' she said.

'Yes, I know. Just a little. We can move them back to how they were.'

'Now?'

'No. I've got to sort some bits out inside. We'll do it another time.'

'Look, Faye,' Maisie said, holding her doll out towards the statues, 'these are your new friends. You're going to come and live with them.'

I could sense that Ruby was liable to explode at any moment. 'Come and give me a hand inside,' I said quietly.

She followed me into the kitchen, turning her nose up. 'It smells in here,' she said.

'The whole house needs a good clean and a proper airing. But we'll get it nice, don't worry. We need to pop the heaters on while we're here. I don't want it getting damp. Can you go upstairs and do the one in Great-grandma's old bedroom for me?'

Ruby hesitated. I knew she wouldn't fancy going in there but it might help her to move on. She shrugged and walked slowly up the stairs. I went through and flicked the heater on in the front room next to Grandma's bed. Even being in there seemed easier today. I got the sense that Grandma was happy we'd be moving in: it was what she'd wanted.

'We're going to bury your babies,' I whispered. 'We're going to bring them next to you, where you can look after them.' I ran my fingers over the bedspread. If I could only find the answers, fill in the final gaps, then maybe I would be ready to move on too.

I went upstairs. Ruby was still standing in the doorway of Grandma's bedroom, seemingly afraid to enter. I put my hand on her shoulder.

'I still imagine her being here too,' I said.

Ruby was biting her bottom lip. 'It's so sad about her babies,' she said. 'She must have loved them so much she couldn't bear to part with them.'

I folded my arms around her as she started to cry. To my surprise, she didn't push me away.

'Come on,' I said, after a minute or two. 'Why don't you come and choose your bedroom?'

'Won't Maisie want to choose first?'

'The oldest gets first choice,' I said. 'Besides, Maisie will be happy with either of them.'

We walked through to Mum's old bedroom. It was the

biggest and looked over the garden at the back. Ruby shook her head. 'No,' she said. 'It doesn't feel right. I think I'd like the little one.'

'Are you sure?'

She nodded. We were on our way to have a look at it when Maisie hollered up the stairs: 'Mummy, Faye's flown over the wall into next door's garden.'

I groaned. 'I did tell you to be careful with that fairy.'

'Can I go and get her?'

'Not on your own. You can't just go running into someone's garden. Let me come with you. We'll have to ask Andrea first.'

I hurried downstairs and pulled my boots on.

'You can stay here, if you like,' I said to Ruby, but she put her shoes on too and we went across to Andrea's. There was a beautifully carved Halloween pumpkin outside her front door.

'Why doesn't ours look like that?' asked Maisie.

'Probably because Andrea's got more patience than me.'

Maisie reached up and rang the doorbell. I guessed Andrea would be off work because her two kids would be on half-term too. I heard footsteps coming towards the door.

'Hi,' she said, when she opened it. She looked a bit unsure. She would have seen the piece on the news last night too and be glad it was all over, but I wondered if she still had her suspicions about Grandma.

'Please can I get my flying fairy back? It's flown into your garden,' said Maisie.

Andrea smiled. 'Of course you can. I wish I'd had a flying fairy when I was your age. I don't even get to play with one now. It's only footballs that fly around in our garden. Go through and give me a shout if you can't find it.'

'Thanks,' I said. Maisie ran off. 'I'd better go with her,' I said. 'I don't want her trampling all over your garden.'

'Oh, there's nothing to spoil,' she said. 'Not at this time of year.'

Ruby and I headed down the side into the garden. I couldn't see Maisie at first. There was a tree and a shed at the bottom of the garden. She must be behind them, looking for the fairy. I hurried down after her. It was only as I got to the edge of the shed that I saw her clutching her doll and staring at the fairy statue in the corner. It was aged by the weather and had moss growing down one side.

'Look, Mummy,' she said. 'They've got one exactly the same as Great-grandma's.'

My punishment came every week, same time, same place. It was like an appointment with hell in my own home. And the days in between I spent hating myself for what I'd let him do to me and dreading his arrival the following week. My life as I knew it stopped. I didn't smile or laugh or sing any more. I occupied this cold, hard place and the cold, hard place occupied me. People thought it was my hormones. Said I'd become a mardy teenager. Always sullen and down in the mouth. Mum said that if I didn't cheer up soon, my face would be stuck like that forever. She didn't know, you see. I could hardly talk to her about it. She'd believe him, I knew she would. And it would break her heart to hear the things he'd say about me. So, I had to grin and bear it. Well, grimace and bear it, in my case.

I tried to tell myself that at least things couldn't get any worse. Until the Tuesday morning I woke up feeling sick and realised I hadn't been in hell at all, just standing in the waiting room above, about to fall through the trapdoor into it. I knew straight away. I'd missed my period, and although I'd tried to block it out and pretend to myself that it was the strain, I think I already knew.

I ran to the bathroom and retched over the toilet. I wanted to be sick. I wanted to get rid not only of the contents of my stomach but also the tiny baby inside me. He had put it there. I wanted nothing to do with it, and the idea that it was growing inside me, that part of him was growing inside me, made me want to vomit.

I couldn't bring anything up, though. I tried, but nothing came out. It was like even that was stuck in some horrible cesspit inside me. I felt dirty and wretched. I didn't know what to do. I couldn't tell anyone. I wanted to make it go away but I had no idea how you went about getting rid of a baby. Mum was on first-name terms with our doctor and I didn't know who else I could go to. I hoped I would lose it. I knew that happened sometimes. I wished I knew how you could make it happen because that was what I wanted more than anything else in the world. I wanted it out of my body.

By the time he was due to arrive later that day, I was in such a state. I was sure I was going to throw up all over him. I was worried he'd be able to tell. That although the baby was only tiny, he might somehow feel it inside me. I had no idea how he would react if he knew. Maybe he wouldn't want to do this to me any more. Maybe telling him would be the best way to get him to leave me alone. But if I told him, he might tell my mum. It would be all around the village by the following day and I couldn't bear that. Couldn't face people pointing and whispering, knowing I had let him do dirty things to me.

I had my back to the door when I heard him come in. My skin crawled as I smelt his now familiar sour sweat and cologne.

'Looks like I've got you well-trained,' he said, seeing the cup of tea on the kitchen table. I was simply trying to cut down the amount of time he spent in the house. To get it over with as quickly as possible.

I watched as he drank it and moved towards the stairs the second *he put the mug down. When we got to my bedroom the curtains were already drawn. He pushed me back onto the bed and held my arms down. I turned my head to one side and shut my eyes. I winced as I felt him enter me. Usually, I wished he wouldn't be so rough but today it occurred to me that it might be a good thing. That he might do it so hard I'd lose the baby. So that is what I thought as I lay there. Over and over again in my head, I said to myself, Please, please, hurt me so badly that I lose your baby.*

15

I stared at the statue, ice slithering slowly down my spine, the chill radiating through my whole body. The statue wasn't exactly the same but it was similar: a fairy asleep on a toadstool that stood on a square plinth, on which I could see some cursive writing. I squatted down to read it.

'What does it say, Mummy?' asked Maisie. 'I couldn't read the funny writing.'

'It says, "Tread quietly, so as not to awaken the faerie."' My voice caught at the end. I saw Ruby look at me, an uneasy expression on her face.

'Maybe Great-grandma gave it to Andrea because Andrea likes fairies,' said Maisie. 'She said she wished she'd had one like mine.'

I smiled and nodded at her. 'Tell you what,' I said, taking hold of her hand, 'you and Ruby pop back to Great-grandma's garden for a minute to see the other fairies. I'll just knock and say thank you to Andrea.'

Ruby gave me a look. I raised my eyebrows at her, acknowledging her concern but letting her know I couldn't say anything in front of Maisie. She followed her younger sister back to Grandma's garden.

I stood on Andrea's front step. Maybe I was being paranoid. Not every fairy statue in the country would have a baby buried under it but it was too much of a coincidence not to say anything. I gave the knocker a little tap – the bell seemed far too jovial on this occasion.

Andrea opened the door, 'Did she find it?' she asked.

'Yes, thanks,' I replied. I wanted to leave it at that, especially after all the grief we had been through. The easiest thing in the world would have been to say nothing and walk away. But I knew it would eat away at me forever if I did that.

'The, er, fairy statue in your garden, was it here when you moved in?'

'Yes,' said Andrea, frowning slightly. 'We didn't bother getting rid of it as it's tucked away there. Paul doesn't like it, says it's only one step removed from a gnome, but I don't mind it.'

'The thing is,' I said, 'there are two similar ones in Grandma's garden.'

'Do you want ours? You're very welcome if your little girl's taken a shine to it.'

'No,' I said, shuffling my feet, 'it's not that. It's that the bones which were found in my grandma's garden, they were buried under the fairy statues.'

I watched the colour drain from Andrea's face. 'You don't think . . .'

'I don't know what to think any more. It just seems a bit of a coincidence. Have you any idea how long it's been there?'

'No,' said Andrea. 'I think the people before us said they'd inherited it from the previous owners. I remember them pointing it out when they showed us around.'

I steeled myself to continue. 'Well, you probably saw what they said on the news last night.'

'I could hardly miss it,' she said. 'They filmed it outside our house.'

'I know, and I'm so sorry for what you've had to put up with these last few weeks. But I still want to get to the bottom of this, even though the police can't take it any further. And now I've seen your statue, I can't help wondering if it had something to do with it too. And maybe it might help us get some answers.'

Andrea stood there wringing her hands. I knew she didn't want to hear this. It had been a matter of days since the police had left and now I wanted to start it all up again.

'You think I should call the police?' she asked.

'I can do it for you. I've got the number of the detective in charge. They have one of these special scanner things. They won't even have to dig anything up if there's nothing under there.'

'I should probably check with Paul first,' she said.

'Yes, of course. I'll wait here.'

Andrea went back into her kitchen. I heard her voice on the phone, fast and low. I supposed her kids must be upstairs. Two boys, in the years above and below Ruby at school. It would be worse for them, if they did find anything. At least I'd been able to prevent Maisie and Ruby from seeing anything. They'd have the police digging up their own garden. Be able to see the white tent from the bedroom at night. It would probably give them nightmares.

Andrea returned a few minutes later. 'OK,' she said, her voice still sounding shaky. 'The police won't come straight away, will they? Only I need to explain what's happened to the boys.'

'Of course,' I said. 'I'll take my two home first and ring the police from there. Unless you'd like me to stay with you?'

'No, I'll be fine,' said Andrea. She didn't look fine. Not fine at all.

'I really do appreciate it,' I said. 'And I'm so sorry to do this to you after everything that's happened next door. I just felt I should tell you.'

'That's OK,' said Andrea. 'It'll probably be nothing anyway. Maybe Betty gave one as a present to whoever used to live here years ago. It's the sort of thing she would have done.'

'Yeah,' I said. 'I'm sure you're right. I expect I'm being a bit paranoid after everything that's happened.'

Andrea said goodbye and shut the door. I stood on the step for a moment, hating myself for doing this to her and wondering what I'd started this time. Because the truth was, I didn't think I was being paranoid at all. I thought the whole thing was about to get far, far worse.

Ruby waited until Maisie was watching TV at home before coming up to me in the kitchen. I still hadn't got used to her haircut – it was like I had a new daughter.

'Do you think there are bones under that statue too?' she asked.

I sighed and put down my mug of tea. 'I don't know, but I've called the police to tell them about it. That's what I was talking to Andrea about.'

'Are they going to dig up Andrea's garden?'

'Maybe. That's up to them.'

'But if the other babies were Great-grandma's, how come this one is buried next door?' Ruby looked as troubled as I felt.

'None of it makes sense to me, either,' I said. 'I guess we've got to let the police get on with their job and hope they come up with some answers. Thanks for not saying anything in front of Maisie.'

I went to give Ruby a hug but she stepped away. 'There's something wrong with this family,' she said. 'No one else has stuff like this going on.'

'I'm sure there's a perfectly innocent explanation.'

'Even if she didn't kill them, she still buried babies in back gardens. It's so creepy. There is no way I'm going to move there. She may have wanted me to have the house but I never want to set foot in that place again.' She walked out of the kitchen. The inevitable heavy footsteps on the stairs and the slamming of the bedroom door followed. It turned out I didn't have a new daughter at all. Simply one who'd had a haircut.

Maisie came into the kitchen. 'I don't ever want to be a teenager,' she said. 'Not if it makes me as grumpy as Ruby.'

*

I had just finished greenifying Maisie's face, ready for trick-or-treating, when the call came. As soon as I saw the name on the screen I jumped up and went into the front room, shutting the door behind me.

'Hello,' I said.

'Miss Hallstead, it's DI Freeman. I sent my scenes of crime officers up to the property next door to your grandmother's. After an initial investigation, I'm sorry to inform you they have found what appear to be bones belonging to a human infant under the statue.'

I screwed up my eyes, hoping the image in my head of the baby's skull I'd found would go away. It didn't: it grew even clearer.

'Right,' I said, in a barely audible whisper.

'I'm on my way up there now. Obviously, at this stage, we can't say whether there is any link with the other babies but we'll be testing the remains found and will keep you informed of the results.'

'Right,' I said again. It was all I could say. I was numb inside. I was too busy desperately trying to make sense of it all to be able to string sentences together.

'I appreciate this must have come as a shock, but if you have any questions later, please do let me know.'

'Thanks. Bye.'

I put the phone down. There were so many questions that I didn't know where to start. What the hell had happened up there? Why would another of Grandma's babies be buried next door? And if it wasn't Grandma's baby, whose was it?

I opened the door. Maisie was still admiring her witch's costume and green make-up in the hallway mirror. She turned around to face me. 'Pretend to throw water over me,' she said.

'Not now, Maisie.'

'Go on! I want to do my melting witch.'

'Maisie, I said not now.' The sharpness in my voice caught me by surprise, as much as it did her. She looked down at the floor forlornly. 'I'm sorry,' I said, mustering a smile. 'I've got a lot on my mind. Here you go, take that, you wicked witch.'

I threw a pretend bucket of water over Maisie, who dutifully melted onto the floor in a heap, just as James arrived home from work.

'You see,' he said, looking at Maisie, 'if I'd known, I could have rung the bell and come in singing, "Ding, dong, the witch it dead."'

'You're funny, Daddy,' said Maisie, jumping up and running to hug him.

'Hey, watch the green,' he said. 'These are my best plumbing clothes.'

Maisie laughed and threw herself at him regardless. James, aware that I wasn't laughing, looked at me.

I shook my head and gestured towards Maisie.

'Right, Witchy,' said James, taking hold of Maisie. 'Why don't you go and show off your outfit to that sister of yours and tell her it's time to get ready for trick-or-treating.'

'OK,' she said, 'Ruby's had all her hair cut off so she doesn't look like Ruby at all.'

James turned back to me. 'Has she really?'

'It's a long bob. She asked for it at the hairdresser's. I wasn't up to arguing with her about it.'

'What's happened?' he asked. 'Have you had another note?'

'No,' I said. 'Worse than that. They've found another baby's bones in Andrea's garden, next door to Grandma's.'

James stared at me. 'What? How? I don't understand.'

'We went to Grandma's house this morning. Maisie wanted to have a look around. Only her flying fairy thing flew into next door's garden, and when we went to get it, there was a fairy statue, very similar to Grandma's. I had a bad feeling about it so I told Andrea and persuaded her to let me call the police. They just rang me back to say they'd found another set of baby bones under it.'

'Fucking hell. Do you think it was hers?'

'Maybe, although I've no idea why it was next door. They're going to do DNA tests.'

'It'll be on the news again. I bet the media will be crawling all over the place. God knows what they'll make of this.'

'Ruby's already had one meltdown today, saying she never wants to live there, and I haven't even told her they've found more bones.'

Maisie came back downstairs. 'Ruby says she's not going and no one can make her because she's thirteen and she can do what she wants.'

I groaned.

'Right,' said James. 'Go back to your room and I'll be up in a minute to sort it out.'

Maisie did as she was told.

'I've got to go and warn Andrea before the media arrive. And I'm not leaving Ruby at home on her own, not with everything that's been going on.'

'I'll sort the girls and take them out. You go now.'

'But Ruby—'

'She'll be fine. I'll deal with it. Go.'

'Thanks.' I picked up my bag, took my coat from the peg in the hall and left before I changed my mind.

It was dark and drizzly as I drove up to Pecket Well. Every now and then my headlights picked out a little cluster of children walking along the pavement in an assortment of ghost, witch or zombie costumes. One or two were carrying pumpkin lanterns, another swirling a torch beam up into the night sky.

I pulled up outside Andrea's. There didn't appear to be any TV cameras or photographers, although I suspected it was just a matter of time before they arrived. I got out of the car. The familiar figure of PC Hyde was stationed outside Andrea's front door. The equally familiar police tape ran across her side entrance. Beyond it, I could see a white tent at the bottom of the garden. As I got out, two police officers emerged from the tent in hooded white overalls and walked up towards the tape. For a moment I pictured them knocking on the door and calling, 'Trick or treat!' But as much as I wished they were Halloween pranksters, there was nothing funny about this. Nothing funny at all.

I walked up the path. The pumpkin we had seen earlier on the doorstep was still there but it hadn't been lit. PC Hyde nodded at me.

'Is it possible for me to speak to Andrea?' I asked.

'Knock and see,' he said.

I heard footsteps coming towards the door, though they were more timid than they had been earlier. The door opened a fraction and Andrea's head appeared. Her face was pale and drawn.

'I'm so sorry,' I said. 'Is there anything I can do?'

She shook her head.

'I feel awful about this. I had no idea, not until I saw the statue. I wish . . .' I trailed off. I didn't know what I wished, other than that none of this had ever happened.

'I'd better go,' said Andrea. 'I don't want the kids—'

'No, of course. I understand. I'm so sorry.'

She shut the door. I turned away and saw several neighbours standing in their gardens or on the street, watching – the elderly man across the road, a couple of kids on bikes, who were in front of Grandma's house. I wanted to tell them all to piss off. That it was none of their bloody business. But it was: it was everybody's business. The whole village was involved.

'You'd better get going,' said PC Hyde, nodding across the road to where a Calendar TV van had just pulled up.

I hurried to my car, trying hard to ignore the staring faces. I got in, struggling to fasten the seatbelt because my hands were shaking so much. A group of little girls in Halloween costumes came around the corner. One of them screamed as she saw the men in white overalls. I started the engine as the mum with them took one look at the police van and shepherded them back in the direction they'd come from. I glanced across at Grandma's house, shrouded in the darkness. I had no idea who she was any more. Maybe she wasn't the person I'd thought I knew. Perhaps it was all an elaborate façade to cover up some horrible thing she'd been involved with.

'What happened, Grandma?' I whispered, as I pulled away. 'What the hell went on here?'

11 August 1944

Dear Betty,

Why didn't you come this morning? I waited for more than an hour and afterwards I went to look for you but I couldn't see you anywhere. I am hoping it was because of the King's visit, because you were too busy with the preparations. I didn't take my eyes off you during the parade, not even when the King and Queen walked right past me. I couldn't tell you what the Queen or Princess Elizabeth were wearing because I was too busy looking at you.

But you didn't look at me, Betty. Not once. It was as if you couldn't bear to lay eyes on me. If I've said or done something wrong, please tell me. You know how I feel about you. You're the one person who has kept me going through this war. I couldn't bear it if I've done something to upset you.

If someone's found out about us and you're in trouble, you must tell me. I don't want you to have to deal with anything on your own. And if they have found out, well, there's no law against doing what we've been doing, Betty. I love you and that's all there is to it.

Whatever has happened, I want to face it with you. I know I've told you this a thousand times but you must understand that this is a big deal for me too and I didn't enter into it lightly. I know you're only seventeen and, under different circumstances, maybe we would have dated for a couple of years and got married before anything happened between us. But these aren't normal circumstances. Every time I fly off on a raid, I don't know if I'll be coming back. So many guys haven't. I can't even remember all their names, there have been that many lost. So, yes, maybe we jumped the gun a little but, hell, when you don't know if you'll see the love of your life tomorrow, what's a guy supposed to do?

And that's what you are, Betty. The love of my life. As soon as this damn war is over, I'm going to tell the whole world about you and me.

But right now I need to see you. I need to know that you're OK and that everything's fine between us. Already, I can't bear the thought of flying off tonight not knowing. Meet me tomorrow morning Betty, the usual place and time. And if you can't make it please get a note to me and let me know what's going on.

I miss you so much. I miss stroking your soft skin, hearing your laughter, like a little tinkle of sunshine. I felt like shouting out to the King today as he walked past. I wanted to say, 'Look at my Betty! Isn't she beautiful?' I have seen a queen and a princess today and neither of them compares to you, my English rose. Please come to me tomorrow, Betty. I'll be waiting for you.

Yours always,

William

16

I lay in bed, waiting for it to get light and dreading what a new day would bring. I should have listened to my mum. As much as it pained me to think it, let alone utter it out loud, that was the only conclusion I could come to. I had meddled in something I didn't understand, something I understood less and less as time went on. I shouldn't have stuck my oar in. I should have let Maisie keep her bit of fairy bone and left it at that.

But then I would have been going against Grandma's wishes. And I was still sure she'd wanted this to come out. She wouldn't have said anything otherwise, wouldn't have wasted her last breath on something she could have kept to herself. Although whether she would have wanted her family to pay so heavy a price for it was another matter.

I swung my legs out of bed and sat on the edge. James was still asleep. He looked peaceful, and I envied him that. I couldn't imagine ever being able to sleep peacefully again. I padded silently across the floorboards, took my dressing-gown from the back of the door and left the room.

The bathroom was even colder than normal, the heating not on yet. I turned the radio on, aware that it was two minutes to seven but feeling the need to listen to the news. To know what everyone else would be waking up to. It was the lead item on BBC Radio Leeds. 'Police have discovered what are believed to be the remains of an infant in a back garden in Pecket Well, next door to the property where the remains of two babies were discovered three weeks ago. It is not known at this stage whether the two discoveries are linked.'

They went to a reporter outside Andrea's house: he talked about how the village was in shock. How the discovery of a third set of bones had left everyone reeling and people were now dreading what would be dug up next. They cut to an interview with DCI Langsdale. He was obviously taking it very seriously too, saying that the original investigation had been reopened and asking anyone with information to come forward. It felt surreal, like some kind of out-of-body experience. How could they be talking about Grandma? Yet they were.

I turned the radio off, crept downstairs, put the TV on and waited for the local news. I picked up my phone and went on to Twitter while I waited. I searched for Pecket Well: a stream of tweets came up. People were calling it the baby-killer village. Someone said Grandma must have been part of a cult, that something sinister had being going on and the babies must have been sacrificed.

I threw the phone on to the sofa as the local TV news came on. They had a reporter outside Andrea's house as well. I imagined her kids cowering in their bedrooms, afraid to open the curtains. Not only was our family's dirty linen being washed in public, it was now taking place in somebody else's back yard.

The reporter interviewed two neighbours, an elderly man and a middle-aged woman, both of whom I recognised, although I didn't know their names. They said the usual things: Grandma had seemed a lovely lady who had always smiled and said hello to them and they'd never thought anything like this would happen in their village. They clearly had her down as a mass-murderer now. It seemed wrong to hear Grandma spoken about like that when she wasn't there to defend herself. I should be on TV telling people not to believe any of it, protecting her reputation. I was pathetic, cowering at home behind the curtains instead of being out there, telling everyone it was all some dreadful misunderstanding.

My phone beeped with a text. I picked it up and saw straight away that it was from Mum. *I told you not to meddle.* I pressed the call button, hoping she'd be so annoyed that she would answer. She didn't. It went to voicemail. I left a message in the shakiest of voices.

'I didn't know it was going to lead to this, did I? And if you did, then you should have told me. If you know what happened, please tell me. I need to get to the truth.'

I waited for a few minutes in case she was composing a text. Nothing came through. She was a storm who had blown herself out.

I went back upstairs and crept into our bedroom, grabbing some knickers and a bra out of the chest of drawers and slipping them on. I opened the wardrobe and reached for my jeans but knocked a wooden coat hanger, sending it clattering to the floor. James stirred and squinted at me in the dark as I struggled into my jeans.

'What are you doing?'

'I'm going up to Grandma's. It's all over the news. They're making out she's some kind of serial killer.'

James sat up in bed and looked at the alarm clock. 'Jesus, Nic, it's ten past seven.'

'I don't care. Someone needs to go and defend her.'

'That's crazy! You don't want to go on TV.'

'She's being slagged off on social media. People are saying she was in a cult and all sorts of crap.'

'It doesn't matter what they say. You know the truth.'

'Do I? I don't know what I do know any more. I've got no idea what went on up there. But someone needs to stick up for her.'

I pulled on a jumper and headed for the door. I heard James scrambling out of bed behind me and following me down the stairs.

'Nic, you can't just go off like this. I've got to go to work at eight.'

'I'll be back by then.'

I reached the bottom of the stairs and pulled on my boots.

'You'll make it worse – the girls don't want this. All their friends at school will see it. Ruby will have a meltdown.'

'My family's reputation is being trashed. I'm not having it.'

'I'll go, then.'

'She's not your family, is she? She's got no one else to defend her. Mum's hardly going to come riding to her rescue.'

I yanked open the door, propelled by a combination of guilt and frustration. I couldn't move, though. The legs that had been about to storm out of the house were rendered useless by the sight that greeted me.

There was half a skull on the front doorstep. What looked like a pig's skull with one of the ears still attached. Pig rib bones had been arranged underneath it, with larger bones laid out to look like limbs. I screamed. James reached out and grabbed my elbow.

'It's OK,' he said.

'No, it's not. It's not fucking OK, is it?'

I pulled away and sank to the floor, sobbing. James crouched down to comfort me. I was crying big, noisy tears. Which was probably why neither of us heard Maisie approach. The first thing we heard was her scream.

'There's a head! There's a piggy head!'

James leapt up and shut the door, then grabbed her. 'Sorry, sweetheart, we didn't want you to see that.'

'Why is it there?'

'It's just some meat bones someone's left,' he said.

'Why did they do that?'

'I don't know. Probably some silly trick-or-treat thing.'

'But that's not how you do it.'

'I know,' he replied.

'So why is Mummy crying?' she asked.

Ruby appeared at the top of the stairs, her hair flattened

against her head. 'What's happened?' she said. 'Why is everyone screaming?'

James went to say something but I stopped him. This was my mess. I should be the one to clear it up. 'Someone's left some pig bones on our doorstep.'

'There's a skull,' said Maisie, her voice still high and frantic, 'half a piggy skull, and they've made the other bones look like a skeleton.'

'I want to see,' said Ruby.

'No,' said James.

'Let her,' I said, 'and then we'll all sit down and have a chat.'

I stood up and opened the door. Ruby came downstairs and stepped tentatively forward, peering outside, then wrinkling her face and turning away.

'I know,' I said. 'It's horrible. Now, I need to fill you both in on what's happened.'

I took them through to the living room and sat them down on the sofa. It didn't seem right, everyone still being in their pyjamas. It was a far too serious conversation to have in dressing-gowns.

'After we left Grandma's house yesterday I let the police know that there was a fairy statue in Andrea's garden. They went to look under it to see if there were any more bones buried there and I'm afraid there were.'

Ruby and Maisie stared at me. Neither of them said anything, so I carried on.

'The police have taken the bones away and they're going to find out if they had anything to do with our family or not. But it has been on the radio and television news, which means lots of people know about it and you need to know that, in case anyone says anything when you go back to school.'

'But why did someone put piggy bones on our step?' Maisie said.

'We don't know, love. They probably did it as a joke but it wasn't very funny, was it?'

Maisie shook her head.

'So in a minute I'm going to phone the police and let them come and investigate.'

Ruby was fiddling with the belt of her dressing-gown, well aware that it was more serious than I was letting on.

'The important thing to remember is that the police don't think Great-grandma has done anything wrong and these latest bones may be nothing to do with her at all.'

'What are you going to do with the piggy bones?' asked Maisie.

'I expect the police will take them away,' I said.

'Did the person who put the bones there kill the piggy?'

'No, love. They'll just have got them from the butcher's.'

'Now,' said James, 'how about you come and give me a hand with breakfast, as we're all up?'

Maisie jumped off the sofa and followed him through to the kitchen.

'Why are they trying to scare us?' said Ruby, still fiddling.

'I don't think the people in Pecket Well like all the attention they're getting on the news.'

'It's not our fault, though, is it?'

'Some people don't see it like that,' I said.

'It's like we're cursed,' said Ruby.

'Hey, come on. Don't say things like that.'

'Why not? That's what everyone else is saying.'

The police arrived as James was about to leave for work. Two uniformed officers I hadn't seen before. We'd told the girls to stay in their room so they wouldn't have to see or hear anything more that might upset them. The younger officer took photographs before picking up the bones with gloved hands and putting them into a large plastic bag.

'Any idea who's behind it?' the middle-aged officer asked.

'Presumably the same person who left the notes,' I replied. 'But it's been all over the news. It could be anyone.'

He took some more details while his colleague carried the bag back to the car.

'Why don't you go and see the butcher in town?' asked James. 'They might have got them from there.'

'Aye. We'll be making enquiries and we'll let you know when we've got any further information.'

They got back into their car and drove off.

'They're not taking this seriously, are they?' I said.

'It could have been kids this time. You said it yourself, it's been all over the news.'

'No. Someone's trying to get at me. Someone has something to hide.'

'Come on, Nic. Whatever went on up there happened sixty or seventy years ago.'

'Well, they could be trying to protect someone's reputation, like I'm trying to protect Grandma's. And whoever it is knows where we live.'

James hesitated on the doorstep. 'Look, do you want me to cancel this job? I don't mind staying home.'

'Don't be daft,' I said, aware he was putting in a new bathroom and that we needed the money. 'We'll be fine.'

It was half past nine when I got a call from the estate agent.

'Hi – Miss Hallstead? We've got a couple who are very keen to view your property. They'd like to come this afternoon.'

It was the one thing I hadn't been expecting. With everything going on, I'd completely forgotten it was on the market. But I did know Ruby would have a complete meltdown if she was here when someone came to look around. It needed to be at a time when I could get them out of the house.

'Oh, right. Er, this afternoon's a bit difficult with it being half-term. Could they make it early evening at all?'

'I'm afraid not. They're not from the area and are going back to London later. It would have to be early afternoon but they do seem very keen.'

I didn't know what to say. Moving to Grandma's was the last thing I wanted to think about right now but, having made the decision to sell, it seemed crazy to turn away a potential buyer. I'd simply have to find someone to take the girls at short notice. 'Shall we say two o'clock?'

'Great. I'll let them know. It's a Mr and Mrs Hargreaves.'

I put the phone down. Any other time I would have rung

Mum and asked if she'd have the girls. Clearly that was no longer an option. I tried to think who else I could ask. Ruby's two best friends were away and she wasn't close enough to anyone else for me to ask them. Besides, I didn't know many of the mums, these days. Things were so different at the high school.

The trouble was, she wouldn't want to go to Maisie's friend Emily's either. She'd say she was too old to hang out with little kids. And there was no way I was leaving Ruby at home on her own, not after what had just happened. I racked my brain and started scrolling through my phone, trying to find someone they'd both be happy to go to. The first name on my contact list was John's. They'd enjoyed themselves last time – even Ruby seemed to like him. And he'd made it clear he'd love to see them again. I pressed the call button, and he answered after a few rings.

'Hi, John, it's Nicola,' I said. 'I hope you don't mind me calling only I was wondering if you'd mind having the girls for an hour or so after lunch. I wouldn't normally ask but we've got someone coming to view the house at short notice and I'm a bit stuck, what with Mum not being an option.'

He said nothing for a moment or two. Clearly he wasn't used to being hired for baby-sitting duties. 'Oh, right . . . I haven't got owt in for them.'

'That's fine, they don't need anything. But if it's not convenient, please say.'

'No, it'd be grand.'

'Thank you so much. You're a life-saver.'

'I didn't know you were planning to move,' he said.

'Well, I've been left Grandma's house in the will.'

'You're moving there?' he asked.

'Yeah. You don't think it's a good idea, do you?'

'I think it's more trouble than it's worth. Have you not seen the news this morning? They've found more bones.'

'I know. It's horrible. But Grandma wanted the house kept in the family. She asked me to leave it to Ruby.'

'It's not up to her, though, is it? It's up to you do what's best for your family. What does your mam say about it?'

'She's dead against it. Well, she was the last time she spoke to me, anyway.'

'So you've got a choice of upsetting your grandma, who's no longer around, or your mam, who is.'

I hadn't thought about it like that. Maybe John had a point. 'I suppose, if you put it like that, it seems a bit daft.'

'I understand you wanting to respect the wishes of the dead,' he said, 'but you need to think about respecting the wishes of the living too.'

'You're right. Look, I'd better go and get the house tidied. It's too late to cancel this viewing but I promise I'll think about what you said. And thanks again. I'll drop the girls off about one o'clock, if that's OK.'

'Right you are.'

I put the phone down. I was glad I had John in my life. It was like finding a favourite uncle I'd never had, one who wasn't afraid to give it to me straight but whose opinion might be worth listening to.

*

We stood on John's doorstep as the church clock struck one. He did a double-take when he opened it and saw Ruby's hair.

'Thought I had wrong visitors for a moment,' he said. 'Makes you look right grown-up that hairdo does.'

Ruby smiled.

'I had mine cut too but you can't tell,' said Maisie.

'I hope they didn't charge,' said John. 'You should only have to pay for it if you can tell.'

I smiled at him. 'Thanks again, John. I'll text you when I'm on my way to pick them up.'

'No problem,' he said. 'We'll have a grand time, won't we?'

The girls followed him indoors.

Mr and Mrs Hargreaves were a nice couple, in their early thirties, no children, though I suspected from their questions about local schools that the plan was to start a family once they arrived. The path from Bohemian London coupledom to a stone-built family home in funky Hebden Bridge, within spitting distance of the Pennines, was a well-worn one.

I watched their expressions as they walked around the house, little sideways glances at each other, eyes full of excitement at the prospect of a new life together in an entirely different place. They didn't have to tell me they liked it: it was written all over their faces.

After they'd had a final look around, they thanked me profusely for the opportunity to view at such short notice and shook my hand. As I opened the door to let them out, I checked discreetly that nothing had been left on the doorstep while they'd been inside. Somehow I could still see a few marks from the bones, still detect a faint smell of them, though I'd scrubbed it twice before they'd arrived. Fortunately, they were so wrapped up in their excitement they didn't notice. I shut the door and leant back against it with my eyes closed.

It was all happening too quickly. After the events of yesterday and what John had said, I wasn't sure the move to Grandma's was right. I needed time to reconsider. To work out if this whole thing might be a huge mistake. And yet I had a horrible feeling the Hargreaveses were going to make an offer on the house, in which case we'd have to decide very quickly whether or not to accept it. And if we did, there would be no going back. We would be moving to Grandma's. And whatever secrets were buried there would become ours.

John opened the door with a grinning Maisie at his side.

'Hello,' I said, 'someone looks like they've had a good time.'

'Uncle John was telling me funny stories about Grandma being naughty when she was little,' said Maisie.

'Really?' I said, as I stepped inside. 'I can't imagine her ever being naughty.'

'She was a bit rude and a bit cheeky,' said Maisie. I looked at John.

'Aye, she was,' he said. 'Used to run Betty ragged, she did.'

'Maybe that's where you get it from,' I said, making a face at Maisie as I pulled up the scrunchie in her hair. 'Now, where's your sister?'

'She's in the living room, reading. I want to say goodbye to Bert.'

I had to think, then remembered the budgie. 'Right. Well, tell Ruby it's time to go and say goodbye to Bert while you're at it, please.'

Maisie ran off. I turned back to John. 'Thanks so much for having them,' I said.

'Any time. They're no trouble. How did it go?'

'I think they liked it. I'm a bit worried, to be honest. I've got a feeling they're going to make an offer and I think you might be right about it being a mistake. Please don't say anything to the girls, though. They don't know about the viewing.'

He nodded slowly. 'Ruby's already told me she doesn't want to move.'

'Has she?' I couldn't help feeling a bit put out that she had confided in him, though I supposed I should feel glad there was someone else in the family she could talk to. 'What did she say?'

'That you were doing it against her wishes and she thinks the house is creepy. She doesn't ever want to live there.'

'Oh. Didn't mince her words, then.'

'No. And I reckon she's right, too. All this business with the bones. I wouldn't want my children to live there. You'd never know what you were going to find next. Personally, I'd sell the house. Someone will still buy it. And it's not as if Betty will ever know. Mam always said—'

He was interrupted by Maisie and Ruby coming into the hallway.

'Hello, you two,' I said. 'What do you need to say to Uncle John?'

'Thank you,' they chorused, Maisie slightly more enthusiastically than Ruby, and they both gave him a hug. I said goodbye with a peck on the cheek and we all got into the car. It was still bothering me, though, what Olive used to say to John.

'Stay here,' I said to the girls. 'I've forgotten something.'

I slipped out of the car and hurried back up the path to where John was still standing in the doorway.

'What did your mum used to say?' I asked.

His eyes darkened a little. 'That it was a bad place. That bad things happened to those who lived there.'

'But she never said what things?'

'Just that they were too bad to talk about.'

My stomach clenched. I still had the sense that Olive knew more than she was letting on.

'You don't happen to remember who used to live next door to my grandma, do you? I was just wondering, you know, what with everything going on.'

John shook his head. 'I'm sure the police will find out soon enough.'

I didn't lose the baby. Not that day, or the week after, or the one after that. I wanted to. I willed it gone. I knew that if I didn't lose it in the first few months, I'd be stuck with it. I ran everywhere, carried heavy things, took hot baths, drank Dad's gin. Anything that might do the trick. At night I dreamt about it. Only I didn't see a tiny baby, I saw a big one, with his face, his eyes boring into me, his mouth smirking.

I hated it. Hated it more than I hated him. Because, as much as I dreaded his visits, he always left me afterwards. This – this thing was living inside me. Feeding off me, like a tapeworm. Growing and multiplying and embedding itself into my flesh. I tried to block it out the best I could, but it became harder every day.

I tried to hide it from others, as well as myself. I took to wearing baggy clothes, to turning away when I was undressing at school. I managed to fool a lot of people. But I always knew that the hardest person to fool would be him.

The week before, it hadn't shown. He hadn't suspected a thing, I was sure of it. But somehow, in seven short days, it had erupted out of me. And though I could still disguise it with clothes, I wasn't sure I could get away with it in the flesh.

When we got to my bedroom, I felt sick with fear. He might hit me when he found out – he might try to kill me. Although maybe that would be a blessing. I wondered if it would be better if I told him myself, rather than waited for him to find out. Instead of lying on the bed, I sat on the end of it as he took off his trousers. He looked at me. I opened my mouth to say something, but nothing came out. A smile spread across his face.

'You want it in there, do you? You really are a dirty little slut.' He dropped his trousers and moved towards me. I realised too late what he was going to do. He took hold of my head and forced himself inside my mouth and started thrusting back and forwards. I shut my eyes, but it didn't help. I hated it. Hated it even more than what he usually did. I wanted to bite him. More than anything in the world, I wanted to bite down hard and make him scream the way I was screaming inside. But my jaws, like the rest of me, were frozen in terror.

I was struggling to breathe, I thought I was going to black out or throw up. When I felt the warm liquid inside my mouth, I thought it was the sick rising up my throat at first. And then I tasted it. A taste I had never experienced before. One that truly did make me want to vomit. I pulled my head away, spat it out on the floor and ran next door to the bathroom, where I stuck my head under the tap, taking gulps of water and spitting it out. I knew I'd never get the taste out of my mouth. Not if I brushed my teeth a thousand times. It would still be there. Still remind me of him.

I heard the bedroom door open and him call out, 'See you next week,' before going downstairs. I waited to hear the back door shut behind him and collapsed in a sobbing heap on the bathroom floor. I wished him dead. Him and the baby. But, most of all, I wished I had never been born.

17

The estate agent's call came shortly before five o'clock that evening. Mr and Mrs Hargreaves had offered the asking price, as if determined to remove all scope for us to turn it down, or them to be outbid. I told the agent I'd have to talk to my husband. I think she thought I'd lost the plot. It was the only way I could think of stalling her until I'd had a chance to gather my thoughts.

They hadn't found the bones next door to Grandma's when we'd made the decision to put our home on the market. Maybe John was right. I certainly couldn't argue with Olive's statement that bad things had happened there. Three, at least. And what if there were more? What if we ended up living in one of those houses of horrors that featured on crime programmes on Channel Five?

If I hadn't been made redundant, I wouldn't have done it. It wasn't really a choice, more of a necessity. And as much as I would have liked to find another way out of the mess, I couldn't see there was one. No one would want to buy Grandma's house at the moment, even if we did decide to sell it against her wishes. It was like a family heirloom being passed down through the generations – only it currently appeared more of a curse.

I was sitting at the kitchen table with my head in my hands when James arrived home from work.

'What's up? Has something else happened?'

'We've had a viewing on the house and they've offered the asking price.'

'Jesus, that was quick,' said James.

'Couple from London. It's exactly what they were looking for, apparently.'

'Right. So we're moving.'

It was said as a statement, not a question. I was going to have to put him right.

'I haven't accepted yet,' I replied.

James frowned. 'Why? I thought this was what you wanted.'

'It was never what I wanted, only what I thought was the right thing to do. But I was talking to John today – I asked if he could have the girls while we had the viewing – and something he said made me think.'

'What do you mean?'

'He said it was more important to respect the wishes of the living than the dead.'

'It's a fair point, I guess.'

'Ruby's already told him she's not moving. She's having a tough time with everything that's been going on. This could push her over the edge.'

'I still think she'd come around,' said James. 'And we've

got so far down the line, it would seem pretty stupid to turn the offer down.'

'But you didn't want this in the first place.'

'I know, but I came to realise it made sense.'

'Does it?'

'Of course. We've got the chance of a quick sale, and when I've done your grandma's place up, we'll get a lot more for it than we would right now. And by that time all the fuss will have died down.'

'Will it? What if they find any more bones?'

'Come on, Nic, don't believe all that crap on social media.'

'So you've seen it too?'

'Yeah, but it's the usual suspects. All the nutters and trolls who come out of the woodwork anytime something bad happens.'

'Oh, God, I don't know. Something else John said threw me.'

'What?'

'It's almost like he thinks it's cursed. Olive told him it was a bad place and bad things happened there.'

'It's probably all superstitious crap and old wives' tales.'

'I don't know. I still think Olive knows what happened. I wish I could talk to her but John says her dementia's got worse lately.'

'Do you still think your grandad was involved?'

'I think if the babies were murdered, it would have been him. I mean, he had the motive, didn't he? If he found out they weren't his, he might well have wanted to get rid of them. And John's already said he was a nasty piece of work.'

'Doesn't explain the one next door, though.'

'Unless Grandad buried one under their statue without whoever lived there knowing.'

'Now you really have been watching too many crime dramas.'

I stood up and paced around the kitchen. The estate agent had asked me to confirm our acceptance as soon as possible. There was always a chance the Hargreaveses would get fed-up waiting and withdraw the offer.

'So are we moving there, or not?' I asked.

James shrugged. 'It makes complete sense financially. It takes all the pressure off you getting another job.'

'You don't think I'm going to find something, do you?'

'I didn't say that. What I actually think is that you shouldn't even try.'

I frowned at him. 'What do you mean?'

'How about you get your degree and a teaching qualification? Do the job you always dreamt of instead of slogging your guts out for crap pay in a café.'

For a minute, I was speechless. It was something I'd given up on long ago. To be honest, I'd never expected to get a second chance. 'Don't be daft. I'm the mother of two kids. I can't just drop everything and become a student.'

'You could. You could do it all in Leeds. You'd be home every night, unless you wanted to go to all the student parties.'

I smiled at him. 'And who would get Maisie to and from school? It's a nice thought but it's not going to happen. I had my chance. Blew it.'

'Hey, you mustn't talk like that. It wasn't your fault.'

I walked away a few paces. That was the trouble with James. He always saw the best in me. He hadn't known me back then, had never seen me off my face, like I had been that night. It was my fault and I'd had to live with the consequences. People like me didn't deserve second chances.

'Anyway,' I said, 'we need to make a decision.'

'What's your gut feeling?'

'It was that we should move to Grandma's. But that was before I talked to John.'

'I wouldn't put too much weight on that. You hardly know him and he certainly doesn't know us.'

'I feel like I've known him ages. He's family, almost the only family I've got that's actually talking to me at the moment.'

'What about me?' asked James.

'I'm worried you're only going along with it because it was my suggestion in the first place.'

'I thought you knew me better than that,' he said, with a smile. 'I'd tell you if I didn't think you were doing the right thing.' He walked over and took my hand.

'I hate this,' I said. 'I thought we had it all sorted out.'

'We did. This is simply a last-minute wobble on your part. You're getting cold feet because of what John said, but think how stupid you'd feel if we turned the offer down and didn't get another in the next six months. Then where would we be?'

'You're right,' I said, nodding vigorously, in an effort to make myself believe it. 'I'll call the estate agent and accept.

And we'll tell the girls after tea. I don't want them finding out when someone comes to put a sold sign outside.'

'Ruby's not going to be happy.'

'I'll handle her. You just try to stop me promising to get them anything more than the bloody puppy.'

As soon as I'd got the dishwasher loaded, we went into the living room. Ruby was on her tablet, Maisie was on her kiddie version, which I suspected wouldn't fend off much longer a request for a real one. They stopped what they were doing. Ours had become one of those homes where people expected bad news to be delivered with alarming regularity.

'We've found a buyer for our house,' I said, desperately trying for a positive, optimistic tone.

'But it's only just been put up for sale,' said Ruby.

'It was very quick. Someone came today and offered what we'd asked for.'

'Is that why we went to Uncle John's? Because you wanted us out of the way?'

I sighed. Nothing got past her. 'I didn't think you'd want to be here,' I said. 'Anyway, you both like going to see Uncle John.'

'Can we get the puppy now?' asked Maisie.

I smiled. 'We won't be moving for about three months. It takes that long for all the legal things to go through. We just wanted to let you know.'

'Well,' said Ruby, 'I told you, I'm not going.'

'Come on, love,' I said. 'I know you're not keen but you'll

have your own room and you can both invite friends around for sleepovers.'

'You really think any of my friends will want to sleep there?' said Ruby. 'Do you want me to show you what they're saying on WhatsApp and Snapchat? They're calling it a house of horrors. They reckon the whole street's full of dead babies. The running joke is that King Herod used to live there.'

'Ruby, that's enough,' I said, gesturing towards Maisie.

'She's going to get it at school too,' Ruby went on. 'Maybe not now but in a year or so. God knows what they'll have found by then.'

'Stop it now,' I said.

'Only if you say we're not moving there.'

'Well, we are,' I said. 'None of us wanted this. I didn't want to be made redundant but sometimes you don't get a choice in life.'

'Fine. You can go without me.'

Maisie started to cry. James went over and sat her on his lap.

'Now look what you've done,' I said.

'Oh, yeah, right, it's my fault. Everything's my fault. You're the one who was so drunk you can't even remember my dad's name. *You* move up there with your perfect daughter, the one who's got a dad whose name you do know, and I'll go and find mine. I'll get a DNA test done, and when I do find him, I'll go and live with him because I bet he loves me more than you do.'

'Ruby, that's enough,' said James.

'You're not my real dad,' she said, 'so don't pretend to be.'

She flew out of the room. Maisie broke into a howl and I

stood there, wishing I'd listened to Mum, to John and to every other person in my life who'd told me things I'd ignored.

The hush that eventually descended on the house wasn't an easy one. Maisie had been given special dispensation to sleep in our bed with James for the night because she was so upset and because I was scared of what Ruby would say to her if I left them in the same room.

I should have had Maisie's bed. That's what I'd told James I'd do. But the truth was, I was too ashamed to go in there and face her. Because she was right: it was all my fault. All the years I'd kidded myself that this would never be a problem and we could all play happy families together, I'd known deep down that wouldn't be the case and one day I'd have to face the consequences of being so bloody stupid.

And there was nothing I could say to her to make it right. No amount of apologising would make it go away or allow her to understand how bad I felt for my behaviour. The fact was, Ruby was wiser now than I had been when I was twenty. She would never get herself into a situation like that, never do something she would regret for the rest of her life. She was so, so much better than me. I was intensely proud of her for it, but it didn't make my own shame any easier to bear.

I got a sleeping bag and laid it on the sofa. It had been a tough day. We all needed time on our own and space apart. I went upstairs and pulled the light cord in the bathroom, wishing, as ever, that it wasn't so loud. I brushed my teeth with my eyes averted from the mirror, unable even to face myself. And when that was done, I took off my clothes and pulled on a baggy night-shirt. I took my dressing-gown from the back of the bathroom door, turned off the light and paused on the landing outside the girls' bedroom. I should go in and try to talk to Ruby, I knew that. I was failing her as a mother if I didn't. But I had failed her from the beginning. Why should that change now?

'Night. Love you,' I whispered through the door, then crept downstairs and zipped myself into the sleeping bag.

The next morning I woke early, surprised I'd slept at all. It took me a few moments to work out where I was before I stretched my aching back, sat up and unzipped the sleeping bag. I put my slippers on, went straight over to the window and pulled back the curtain. There was nothing on the door-step. My car, which still had the scratch prominently down one side, appeared to be otherwise unscathed, and there was no sign of a note. I sighed. This was what it had come to: being relieved that no one had vandalised my property or threatened my family during the night.

I busied myself getting out the breakfast things. There was no mention of the investigation on the local news. I guessed there wouldn't be now until there was a new development. It wouldn't stop people talking, though. I picked up my phone and searched again on Twitter. Someone was claiming the babies had been sacrificed in a Satanic ritual. This was what we were going to have to put up with unless someone could clear Grandma's name. I wondered how Andrea and her family were doing. I imagined she was glad it was half-term and her kids didn't have to face school. I should go up there and see her but I wasn't sure I'd be welcome. They must be ruing the day they'd moved in next door to Grandma.

I looked up as James came into the kitchen, closely followed by Maisie.

'Morning, sweetheart,' I said, giving Maisie a hug. 'Did you sleep OK?'

'Not really. Daddy's big and hairy and kept getting in the way.'

'Well, you can go back to your own bed tonight,' I said, smiling at James.

'Has Ruby stopped being mad at everyone?'

'She'll be fine,' I said. 'But we all need to give her a bit of time and space.'

'Are we still going to move?'

I glanced across at James. He gave a little nod.

'Yes,' I said.

'And we'll still get a puppy?'

'Yes, but it won't be straight away. We'll start looking for one that needs rehoming in the spring.'

'Will Ruby have to be rehomed too?'

I kissed the top of her head, unsure whether to laugh or cry. 'Ruby's not going to live with anyone else.'

'Why don't you know her daddy's name?'

I tried to think of an acceptable answer but nothing came.

'Tell you what,' said James. 'Why don't we let Mummy go and get a shower while we make a breakfast smoothie?'

'Yay,' said Maisie.

Ruby was at the table when I came down, though still avoiding eye contact and being decidedly uncommunicative.

'Morning,' I said, not expecting a response and not getting one. 'Wow, this smoothie looks good, Maisie.'

'There's a secret ingredient in it and you need to buy some more strawberry ice-cream.'

'Thanks for letting me know,' I said, with a smile.

Maybe we could find a way through somehow. It wasn't going to be easy or quick but at some point perhaps we would be sitting around the table in Grandma's house and everyone would be smiling.

The knock on the door brought me back to my senses. My first thought was that whoever was behind the threatening notes and the bones had finally plucked up the courage to threaten me face to face.

'I'll go,' I said. 'Probably the postman.'

I shut the kitchen door behind me, just in case. I opened the front door a crack and peered out. DI Freeman was standing on the step. 'Sorry to bother you so early,' he said. 'I did try calling but couldn't get a reply.'

I'd left my phone on silent last night. 'No problem,' I said. 'Come in.' I wondered if they'd found another body, whether everything was about to get even worse than it already was.

I showed him through to the living room. He sat on the edge of the sofa.

'We've had the DNA results back from the latest bones.'

'Oh,' I said. 'Is the baby Grandma's?'

'No,' he replied.

I shut my eyes. 'Thank God. I don't think I could have coped with another.'

DI Freeman's face was still grave.

'What is it?' I asked.

'The DNA doesn't match the father of the other two babies either. It had different parents from the first two but the maternal DNA is linked to your own.'

'I don't understand.'

'Obviously we can't say anything for certain at this stage but the baby appears to have had the same maternal DNA as you.'

I stared at him, unable to believe what I'd just heard. 'You're saying it's my mother's?'

DI Freeman looked down at his feet. 'The condition of the bones indicates that the baby was buried more recently than the first two, possibly forty to fifty years ago. There were fibres from a blanket which it was buried in too. Again, that points to a more recent burial.'

'No . . . There must have been a mistake.'

DI Freeman shook his head. 'I'm sorry. I appreciate this must have come as a shock. What we really need now is to get a DNA sample from your mother. I understand it's a sensitive situation, which is why I've come to see you. She's under no compulsion to give one unless we arrest her. Obviously, we don't want to do that, so I'd be very grateful if you could persuade her to do it voluntarily. We don't want to cause your family any more upset than you've already had.'

I sat there shaking, unable to process what I was hearing.

'All right,' I said. 'I'll go and see her now, although I don't know what shift she's on today. We haven't really . . .' I was struggling to hold myself together.

DI Freeman seemed even more uncomfortable than he had previously. He stood up. 'Thank you,' he said. 'I do appreciate it. Just let me know a convenient time for one of our officers to visit her.'

I nodded, although I still couldn't believe this was happening, and showed him to the door.

As I opened it, I asked, 'Do you think the baby was murdered?'

'It's too early to say,' he replied. 'But, as with the others, that has to be a possibility.'

12 August 1944

My Dearest Betty,

I wish I could dry those tears for you but please know that I meant every word I said today. I will stand by you. I will do more than that. I will marry you, and when this war is over, I will take you back to Winnipeg and we will set up home there and raise our baby together. Please don't think of this as the end, Betty. This could be the beginning of our life together. And I know you're young and I understand how scary this must be for you but I am going to do the right thing by you. Not because it's what I should do but because it's what I want to do.

I'm the one who got you pregnant and I'm going to take full responsibility for this. I will come with you to Leeds to tell your parents and I will make it very clear to them that I am not going anywhere. Maybe they won't react as badly as you think. I'll ask your father for permission to marry you and then they'll understand that this is serious. We can be married in a few weeks, Betty. How about that?

I know the others all laugh at me for being an optimist but I don't see any other way to be.

Those guys who didn't come back last month, Betty, mostly from Goose but Thunderbird too. Their lives are over but mine is not. How can I feel anything other than grateful for that? So dry your tears. We have nothing to cry about and plenty to celebrate. This time next year we will be married with a baby and living in Canada. I know you might think this is crazy but I'm excited. I can't wait for our baby to be born. I can't wait to spend the rest of my life with you. This is the beginning, Betty. It is not the end.

Yours always,

William

18

As soon as DI Freeman had left, I popped my head around the kitchen door. 'Have you got a minute?' I asked James, gesturing towards the hallway and trying to ignore the quizzical look on Ruby's face.

He came out and shut the door behind him.

'The police say the baby was Mum's,' I whispered.

He stared at me, his face screwing up in bewilderment. 'How could it be? That makes no sense.'

'I need to go and see her. The police want her to give a DNA sample and they might arrest her if she doesn't do it voluntarily.'

'Fucking hell,' said James, running his fingers through his hair. 'This goes from bad to worse.'

'She obviously hasn't been telling me the truth but I'm going to get it out of her. Can you hold the fort here? I'll be as quick as I can.'

'Fine. Go easy on her, mind. We don't know what's gone on here.'

I drove to Mum's on automatic pilot, still trying to process what I'd been told. One part of me was still in denial, convinced they'd made a mistake, got the results mixed up. But another part was starting to see that it made sense. It certainly went a long way to explaining why Mum had reacted in the way she did when I first called the police.

I still didn't understand why a baby had ended up buried in next door's garden, though.

I turned off the main road into the small terraced street that used to be my home. I started to do my usual thing of regressing into a teenager, then reminded myself that this time I was the one who had questions to ask of my parent and that she was the one with explaining to do.

Mum's car was parked outside her house. I pulled up right behind it. My way of saying that I knew she was at home and there was no point trying to pretend otherwise. I got out and approached the front door, trying to look more composed than I felt inside. I knocked: two single raps rather than a rat-a-tat-tat. The occasion appeared to call for some degree of solemnity. I waited. I wasn't sure whether Mum had looked out of the window and seen my car or adopted the policy of not opening the door to anyone.

I opened the letterbox and crouched to call through. 'It's me. Please let me in. I need to speak to you urgently.'

There was a brief pause before I heard footsteps coming towards the door and someone fumbling with the handle. The one thing I hadn't been prepared for was the sight that greeted me. Mum's face was gaunt and drawn and she appeared to have lost weight. There were grey shadows under her eyes and her face was devoid of make-up, even the usual slick of plum-coloured lipstick.

'Hi,' I said. 'Are you all right? You're not ill?'

She shook her head.

'Can I come in?' I asked.

She opened the door just wide enough for me to squeeze inside. We stood awkwardly in the hallway. It was hard to know how to start and I didn't want to scare her off straight away in case she threw me out.

'Are the girls all right?' she asked.

'A bit unsettled with everything that's going on, Ruby especially. We've accepted an offer on our house, so we'll be moving up to Grandma's in a few months.'

Mum stared at me. 'No,' she said. 'You can't do that.'

'We haven't got much choice. I'm being made redundant at Christmas. We can't afford to have two houses.'

'I'm sorry,' she said. 'About your job.'

'Least of my worries at the moment. What with everything that's happened.'

'I tried to warn you. You wouldn't listen. Not even when I—' She stopped abruptly, a mixture of guilt and frustration in her eyes.

'Was it you?' I asked. 'The notes?'

She fiddled with a button on her cardigan. 'I left a note on your windscreen, when your car was outside Mum's.'

'Jesus,' I said. 'That scared the life out of me.'

'I'm sorry,' she replied. 'I was just trying to make you stop.'

'What about the others? My car being vandalised? The bones?'

She frowned. 'No,' she said quickly. 'I didn't do anything else. What bones are you talking about?'

'Pig bones, left on our doorstep. The girls were completely freaked out by them.'

'That's horrible. I would never do that.'

'Well, maybe you know who might have, then. Because you clearly know more about this whole thing than you've been letting on.'

Mum was wringing her hands. Her body was contorted, as if some fierce battle was going on inside her. 'I've had photographers outside here, you know. I haven't been able to go to work for the past two days.'

'You should have told me. I could have asked the police to help.'

'They can't stop this, Nicola. Once you take the lid off something, you can't put it back on again.'

'You know what more there is to come out, don't you?'

It was a moment or two before she replied. 'I know that people have secrets and that sometimes it's better that those things remain a secret.'

'Did you know about Grandma's babies?'

'No.'

'But you suspected?'

There was a long pause before she answered. 'She told me once that she lived there before she got married.'

'Sorry?'

'The house belonged to her great-aunt Aggie.'

'Yes, I know. Aggie left it to Grandma in her will.'

'Well, Mum lived there for a while with her. Towards the end of the war.'

I stared at her. The puzzle had finally started to take shape. 'I thought she was a Land Girl.'

'She was. This was after that,' Mum continued. 'She never said why. She never spoke about what happened. But I do remember the way she talked to the fairy statues. She used to tell them everything.'

She'd had the babies there. She must have. She did have a wartime sweetheart after all. One who was the father of her babies. Babies that had brought so much shame on her family, she had been sent away. I needed to go back to Grandma's house. There would be something there, I was sure of it. Something to lead me to who he was. It would still be only one piece of the jigsaw, though. And having got Mum to open up this much, I now needed to ask her the most difficult thing. The reason I had come.

I walked to the end of the hall, so I wasn't facing her. 'The police came to see me earlier,' I said.

'I've told you, I don't know anything more. I don't want anything to do with it.'

'No, not about that. About the other baby.'

I turned.

Mum immediately averted her eyes and thrust one hand deep into her cardigan pocket. 'It's next door. It's nothing to do with your grandma.'

'No. It wasn't Grandma's baby. They've done DNA tests. It had a different mother and father from the other babies.'

Mum's entire face had turned a shade of grey. I could see her chest heaving under her cardigan. I had to go on, though. I had to get to the truth. 'They said it had the same mother as me.'

I saw Mum swallow. She grasped the banister with one hand. I took a few steps towards her and lowered my voice, not that anyone else could hear. 'They need you to give a DNA sample,' I said.

Mum shut her eyes and shook her head.

'If you don't do it voluntarily, they'll arrest you.'

'No,' she said. 'They've got it wrong. It's got nothing to do with me.'

'Whatever happened,' I said, 'it's going to come out. It's better that you're honest about it.'

'Nothing happened,' she shouted. Her hands were shaking. Even the one inside her cardigan pocket.

'It's OK,' I whispered. 'Whatever it is, you can tell me. We need to get this sorted.'

'You wouldn't listen, would you?' she said. 'So bloody head-strong. Just like I was.'

'If it was an accident, you need to say.'

'It wasn't an accident. I think you'd better go now.'

She started walking towards the door.

'Come on, Mum,' I said. 'Please help us out here. Ruby's getting grief at school about this. People are saying horrible stuff on social media. Poor Andrea's got the media camped outside her house.'

'How dare you?' she said. 'Trying to make out I've brought this on everyone. It's your fault. All of this is your fault. You're the one who had to stick your oar in.' She opened the door and stood there waiting.

'As horrible as all this is, I did the right thing,' I said, walking slowly towards her. 'And I think you know that.'

'Get out,' she screamed. 'And you can tell the police they're not welcome here and I will not be giving a DNA sample to anyone.'

I stepped down onto the pavement and she slammed the door behind me. All that anger. It scared me. Where had it come from?

I drove straight home, aware that James had to get to work. I wanted answers, though. And I needed someone to help me find them. James was loading his van as I pulled up outside.

'I'm sorry I took so long,' I said, as I clambered out of the car. 'Mum was hard work.'

'She's still not playing ball?'

'No. Told me to get out and leave her alone. She looked awful, though. She's lost weight. Said she hasn't been able to go to work because she's had photographers outside. Whatever it is she's hiding, it's eating away at her. She did tell me one thing, though. She said Grandma lived in the house with her great-aunt Aggie towards the end of the war. I think that was when she had the babies. She must have been sent away because she was pregnant.'

'How the hell are you going to prove that, though?'

'I'm going to call John. See if Olive can shed any light on it. And I'm going back to Grandma's house to have another dig around.'

'Ruby won't want to go.'

'Well, she'll have to. She can keep Maisie company in the garden.'

'But Maisie's got a play date with Emily this morning. She's been talking about it since you left.'

'Oh, shit, I forgot about that. Well, I'll sort something out, don't worry.'

'Are you going to be OK?' asked James.

'Yeah,' I replied. 'You go. It's not as if things can get any worse.'

The house was quiet. Maisie was in the front room watching TV and Ruby must have gone back up to her room. I wasn't going to leave Ruby on her own. What if whoever had left the bones came back? They might even be watching the house. I needed to know she would be safe. I went into the kitchen and shut the door before I got my phone out. It rang just once before he answered.

'Hi, John,' I said. 'How are you?'

'Not so bad, pet.'

'I'm sorry to bother you but I wondered if you'd be able to ask your mum another question for me.'

He was quiet for a moment. Then he said, 'She's been a bit chesty but she took a turn for the worst yesterday. She's in bed. They think she might have pneumonia.'

'Oh, John, I'm so sorry. Is there anything I can do to help?'

'No, thanks. Hopefully she'll pull through. She's a tough old bird, you know. I'm afraid she won't be up to answering any questions at the moment, mind.'

'No, of course not.'

'What were you going to ask?'

'It's just that I've found out Grandma lived at the house with her great-aunt Aggie for a while, towards the end of the war. I was going to ask your mum if she remembered her talking about it.'

'She's never said owt to me about it but I'll ask her – when she gets better, that is.'

'That would be great. But, really, don't worry about it right now.'

'You sound a bit stressed, pet. Has there been any more news from police? About the latest one, I mean.'

I didn't know what to say. I couldn't tell him about Mum. That wouldn't be fair to her. But I did want to talk to him. He was family, after all.

'It wasn't Grandma's baby, this one,' I said. 'Makes it all a bit more complicated than we thought.'

'And they don't know whose it were?'

'No. Although they do think it was buried more recently. Maybe forty or fifty years ago.'

There was silence at the other end of the line.

'I still think Grandma might have known about it. That would explain the statue. I reckon the answers are somewhere in the pile of stuff at Grandma's house. I'm desperate to get up there to have a rummage but Ruby's had a bit of a meltdown about moving there. You know what teenagers can be like.'

'Well, if you need a break she's always welcome to come here. They both are.'

'Oh, John, that's lovely of you but I couldn't, not at the moment. Not with your mum poorly.'

'Don't be daft. It'd give me summat to take my mind off it. Nowt I can do here except sit and twiddle my thumbs. She's sleeping most of the time, see. No point me sitting there all day when she's asleep.'

I hadn't wanted to ask, but as he was offering, maybe having Ruby around would help him.

'If you're sure, John. It would just be Ruby today. Maisie's got a play date with a friend.'

'That'd be fine. She'll perk me up a bit.'

'Thank you so much. I'll pop her up to you in about an hour.'

'Right you are, then.'

Maisie was singing in the back of the car. I hadn't told her I was taking Ruby to John's in case she complained about missing out, and I hadn't told Ruby where she was going in case she refused to go. That was how things had to be at the moment.

Maisie bounded out of the car and into Emily's house, like an excited puppy, without a backward glance.

I turned the car around and drove back in the direction I'd come, then up to Heptonstall.

'Where are we going?' Ruby asked.

'You're going to Uncle John's for the morning.'

'Why?'

'I've got stuff to do at Grandma's house.'

'What's going on?'

'Nothing.'

'So why did the police come this morning?'

'They were updating me about the investigation.'

'Have they found out more about Grandma's babies?'

'No. This was about the bones in Andrea's garden.'

'What's that got to do with us?'

I eyed her in the rear-view mirror. She wasn't going to let me get away with saying nothing. I had to give her some morsel to chew on.

'They were telling me the baby wasn't Grandma's but it might still be connected to our family.'

'How?'

'It could be a distant relative. They're going to do some more tests. Don't say anything to Uncle John, though.'

'Why not?'

'His mum's been taken ill. He's got enough on his plate to worry about. Anyway, it's all supposed to be secret at the moment.'

'So why did you tell me?'

'Because you're my daughter and you have a right to know what's going on.'

Ruby said nothing but I could see the slightest upturn to her mouth in the rear-view mirror.

*

When John opened the door he looked anxious. The worry about Olive was clearly taking its toll.

'Special delivery,' I said. 'She's come to cheer you up and take your mind off things.'

'Eh-up, Ruby,' he said.

Ruby gave a little smile. I knew she was only being polite and I was grateful to her for not complaining about being dumped like this.

'Be good,' I said. 'See you later.'

She nodded and walked into the house.

'Thanks again, John,' I said. 'And if you get a call from the home and have to go, ring me straight away and I'll come and get her.'

'Right you are.'

'I'll see you about one.'

'I'll have her all day if you want. She's no trouble.'

'Are you sure?'

'Yeah. I'm sure we can find summat to do. Is there owt on at the picture house?'

There was, although I suspected she might balk at the idea of going with John, in case other kids from school were there. But there again, it would be a long day for her otherwise.

'She wants to see *Murder on the Orient Express*. She's read the book, you see. Bit of an Agatha Christie fan.'

'I'll take her then. It'll make a change. Been years since I went to the pictures.'

'Here,' I said, fishing a twenty-pound note out of my purse and offering it to him.

'Don't be daft,' he replied, pushing my hand away.

'No, I insist,' I said, putting the note firmly into his hands. 'I'm not having you out of pocket. You can get her some popcorn, if you'd like to treat her, but nothing more.'

'Right you are,' he said. 'It'll be a nice trip out for us.'

I smiled and walked away, hoping I wouldn't get a mouthful from Ruby later.

I parked a couple of doors down from Grandma's so it wouldn't be too obvious that anyone was visiting. I didn't want to hand an open invitation to whoever was behind the threats and the bones on our doorstep. I glanced across at Andrea's house as I walked past. There was no sign of police activity and the tent had gone from the back garden. I should knock and ask how she was, but I suspected she was angry with me and I couldn't face that right now. Besides, I had things to get on with. Important things.

Grandma's house smelt damp as I stepped inside. James had said he ought to do the central heating in the next week or two, before winter set in. He was clearly right. It would make the world of difference too. The house seemed cold because it was cold. Once the heating was in, it would feel different. It would start to feel like a home. Our home, not Grandma's.

I went into the living room to flick the heater on. It would be so much more welcoming once we had a radiator in there. It was a decent-sized room, plenty of space for our sofa along the back wall. And with a coat of paint and maybe some laminate flooring, it would be unrecognisable. If our move was to work, we had to put our own stamp on the place. Make it different, so we weren't reminded of Grandma at every turn. It would be difficult, though, because so many memories were tied up in it.

I looked around the room, full of everything she had acquired over recent years. There were no secrets in here. I felt sure of it. I had to work out where she would have put something special when she'd first moved there. Something she wanted to keep safe but didn't want anyone to find, least of all Grandad.

I walked into the kitchen. This had always been her domain. Grandad had been of a generation of men who never stepped into the kitchen if they could help it. I wondered if she'd kept it in a bygone era because she wanted it that way. Somewhere time had stood still. Where she could be alone with her memories.

I opened each of the kitchen drawers in turn, riffling through the contents. I wasn't sure exactly what I was looking for, only that I would know when I found it.

An hour or so later, all cupboards and drawers searched, I turned my attention to the pantry. I remembered Grandma reaching up for her biscuit barrel in there. I lifted it down, holding it against my chest while carefully prising the lid open. There was a handful of biscuits at the bottom: a few fingers of shortbread, a couple of Bourbons and a stack of digestives. Grandma would have gone for a Bourbon. I picked one up, intending to do the same in her memory, when there was a knock at the door.

I sighed and put the barrel down. I wondered if Andrea had spotted my car and decided to find out if I'd heard anything more about the investigation. Or perhaps one of the other neighbours had arrived to vent their spleen at me.

When I opened the front door, I was surprised to find Mum standing there, looking even more dishevelled than when I had left her house. She stepped inside before I had the chance to say anything and shut the door behind her.

'How do you know about Great-aunt Aggie?' she asked breathlessly.

'Sorry?'

'You said you knew Mum had been left the house by her.'

'Yeah.'

'Well, I've never told you that. I'm sure of it.'

'No,' I said. 'Someone else did.'

'Who?'

I hesitated. I knew Mum wouldn't take kindly to discovering that I had meddled in a family falling-out, on top of everything else.

'Great-uncle John,' I said.

Mum's eye twitched. She was staring at me hard. 'What are you talking about? You don't have a great-uncle John.'

'Your cousin John, Olive's son. I tracked them down from the photos I found in Grandma's wardrobe. He only lives in Heptonstall. Olive's still alive. She's a hundred, living in a nursing-home there, although she's not very well at the moment.'

It was like a dark cloud had passed over Mum's face. Her eyes were wide and staring. She stood shaking her head, seemingly unable to say anything.

'What's the matter?' I asked.

'He's not my cousin,' she whispered.

'What do you mean?'

'He lived next door.'

'No,' I said. 'We've got crossed wires somewhere. Auntie Olive, Uncle Harold and John, we used to get Christmas cards from them.'

'They weren't my real aunt and uncle,' she said, her voice slow and shaky. 'They lived next door to us. I just called them aunt and uncle. They weren't related at all.'

I frowned at her. It didn't make sense. 'So John's not your cousin?'

She shook her head, tears forming in her eyes. Her hands were shaking. Somehow, I'd got this whole thing wrong. Very wrong indeed.

'But he said . . .' I realised he hadn't said anything. Not really. It was all me, putting two and two together and making eighty-four.

'Did you speak to him on the phone?' Mum asked.

'No, in person. I went to the home and saw Olive first. Then he arrived and it just sort of went from there. He came to ours for afternoon tea and we've been to his house a few times. The girls have really taken to him.'

Mum let out some kind of primitive howl and sank down on to her knees. My throat was dry, my head reeling.

'What is it?' I asked. 'What's the matter?'

'Have they been alone with him?' Mum whispered, unable

or unwilling to look at me.

'Only once, last week when we had the viewing. I had to ask John because it was short notice and, well, you weren't available.'

'Were they all right? Afterwards, I mean.'

'Yeah. As I said, they really like him. Ruby's with him now.'

'No!' Mum screamed. I flattened myself against the wall as she stood up and moved shakily towards me. My insides were twisted. I knew I'd done something awful but what?

'You need to go and get her now!' she shouted.

'Why? What's he done? Please tell me.'

Mum's face was contorted, her eyes laced with pain and fear. 'He did bad things to me,' she whispered. 'Things he shouldn't have done. When I was fourteen.'

I decided to tell him the following Tuesday. I knew he would notice and I didn't want him inside me when he found out. I'd had enough of him inside me.

I stood at the kitchen table and watched him drink his tea, waiting until he had a mouthful before I spoke.

'There's summat I need to tell you.' It was a whisper, barely audible above him slurping.

He put his mug down and his face darkened. I think he knew but said nothing. He was still going to make me spell it out.

'I'm pregnant,' the whisper came.

His eyebrows met and knotted in the middle, his face contorted into unimaginable rage. 'You filthy slag,' he spat. I stared at him, not daring to say anything more. 'Whose is it?' he barked.

'Yours,' I whispered.

'You think I were bloody born yesterday?'

'It's yours. I've never been with anyone else. You know that.'

'Aye, you hadn't. I bet you have now, though. Bet you've had all sorts going through your knickers.'

I started to cry.

'Get rid of it,' he said, standing up and walking towards me. 'Whoever's it is, you need to get rid of it.'

I cowered back against the wall. 'I think it might be too late,' I said.

He grabbed the collar of my shirt and pulled me towards him. 'I said, get rid of it. I don't care how. And you tell no one. If you do, I'll tell your mam and everyone in the fucking village what a dirty slut you are, how I've seen you up against the cowshed with half of the local lads. You'll have to leave. You'll have to go away somewhere. No one will ever want to see your face around here again.'

He pushed me back into the wall and walked towards the door, turning as he opened it.

'You were rubbish anyway, lying there like a piece of meat. A frozen one at that. Summat wrong with you, there is. Not that you should worry about it. No bloke will be interested in you now, not once I've told everyone what a whore you are.'

He slammed the door behind him. It was a long time before I moved. The first thing I did was go to the door and lock it, in case he tried to come back. And once I had locked it, I slid to the floor and cried. Cried with relief that he would never touch me again. That I would never have to shut my eyes and wish myself out of my own body. And cried with despair because I was still carrying his baby. There was still a part of him growing inside me. And I had no idea what I was going to do about it.

I didn't tell Mum. She came into the bathroom without knocking. I was standing there in my underwear, feeling the bump with my hands. She screamed. A proper terrified scream. All the colour drained from her face and she stared at me, her eyes wide and disbelieving.

I lowered my head. 'I'm sorry,' I whispered.

When I looked up she was still staring. Her hands were shaking.

'No,' she said finally, in a tiny voice. 'You can't do this to me.'

'I didn't have any choice,' I said, wiping the tears from my eyes. 'He made me do it.'

'Who did?'

The truth seemed so unbelievable, but I had to tell her, whether she believed me or not.

'John next door.'

She frowned. 'Don't be ridiculous.'

'I'm not. He came here every Tuesday when you were at work. He made me do it. I couldn't stop him.'

'John didn't do this to you. He's a lovely chap – he goes to church with his mother.'

'Well, he did. He forced me to do all of it. He said he'd tell on me if I breathed a word to anyone.'

She shook her head vehemently. 'Now listen here, young lady, you've got yourself into trouble and you are not getting out of it by blaming my best friend's son. He's twenty-five, for goodness' sake. What would he want with a little girl like you?'

'I don't know. I thought he were just being friendly. He took me up the ridge to watch the sunrise.'

'No, you're lying. You're making it up. Who are you protecting? Who is he? Some lad from school? Because whoever he is, he's going to be in big trouble when your father finds out.'

'I don't want you to tell Dad.'

'I've got to. Look at the state of you. You're not going to be able to

hide that for much longer, are you? How far gone are you? Three or four months?

'Five, I think.'

'Good grief. Why ever didn't you tell me before?'

'Because he told me not to. Said you wouldn't believe me.'

'Who did?'

'John.'

'Oh, for goodness' sake.'

She rolled her eyes and sighed deeply. John had been right. She didn't believe me. Dad wouldn't either. No one would.

'I don't want it,' I said, looking down at my bump. 'I want to get rid of it.'

She started crying this time. Her legs seemed to buckle underneath her. She sat down on the edge of the bath. When she looked up at me, her eyes were ablaze. 'You are not getting rid of a baby,' she screamed at me. 'That's killing, that is. It's against God's will. How dare you talk about killing a baby?' She was gasping for breath. I'd never seen her like that before. I'd known she would be angry, but nothing as bad as this.

'I can't have it. It'll always remind me of him. Of what he did to me.'

Mum swallowed. She appeared to be trying to compose herself. It was a moment or two before she spoke. When she did, her voice was quieter, more controlled.

'We'll give it up for adoption straight afterwards,' she said. 'Not official, like. Just someone who's desperate for a baby. And we'll keep you inside until then. It's a good place to hide here – we're out of the way enough. No one need ever know.'

She looked down as she said it. She appeared to be fighting back tears.

'What about school?' I asked.

'I'll make summat up. Tell them you've gone away to look after a poorly aunt. And as soon as it's born we'll get rid of it. And that will be the end of it. It will never be spoken of again.'

19

I screwed my eyes shut, not wanting to believe what I'd heard. 'Oh, God, I'm so sorry. What have I done?'

'You need to go and get her,' said Mum, who was now, oddly, the calmer of us.

'Yeah,' I said, trying to force my legs into action. 'I'll go and get her. Everything will be fine.'

'Where's Maisie?' asked Mum.

'She's at Emily's. It's only Ruby. But that means she's on her own with him.'

The legs that couldn't move a second ago suddenly broke into a run.

'Call me when you've got her,' Mum shouted after me.

I got into the car and set off before I'd even got my belt on. I'd never forgive myself if he'd done anything to her. Maybe he already had. I tried to remember how she'd seemed when I'd collected them yesterday. Maybe a bit quiet but I didn't think anything of it because she'd been quiet a lot lately. I hit the side of my own head as I drove. How could I have been so bloody stupid? Screwing up my own life was bad enough but now I'd put my daughters at risk.

I felt betrayed too. I'd trusted him, confided in him. He'd become one of the family. And all the time he must have been laughing behind my back at how gullible I'd been. I'd read about women like me. Women who hadn't known their daughters were being groomed online. Only I was worse than that. I'd introduced her to him, told her he was her uncle and left her alone with him. If I did get her back safely, she'd never forgive me for that. And nor did I deserve to be forgiven.

I drummed my fingers on the steering wheel as I waited at the traffic lights in town. Perhaps I should call the police. John might turn nasty when I got there. But there again, what would I tell them? That they should go and arrest a man in his seventies who I'd mistakenly believed was family, then given twenty pounds to so he could take my teenage daughter to the cinema?

I was unable to believe how stupid I'd been. As if I hadn't done Ruby enough harm already, I'd now delivered her into the hands of an abuser. I didn't know yet what he'd done to Mum but from the state of her it had been bad. Very bad indeed. And already in my head I had joined the dots. If it was Mum's baby they'd discovered next door, I now knew who the father was.

I felt as if I might throw up but I wasn't going to pull over. I wasn't going to waste a second more than I had to. I sped away from the traffic lights up the hill and turned left, trying to stop all the horrible thoughts that were going through my head. I pulled up twenty yards down the road from John's house and ran to the door.

It was only as I got there I remembered I hadn't thought what to say. Did I accuse him there and then or did I simply grab Ruby and go? I hammered on the door. There was no reply. I looked behind me and saw his car had gone. He'd taken her. He'd taken Ruby. I got my phone out, ready to call the police, then realised he might have taken her to the cinema. That had been the arrangement. I checked the time. The film would be about to start. That was where he was. He hadn't abducted her – although he would be sitting next to her in the dark. The idea of his hands wandering on to her thigh, or worse, came into my head.

I called Ruby. Her phone went to voicemail. She'd have turned it off before the film started. I left a garbled message for her anyway, telling her to meet me in the cinema foyer urgently. I texted it as well, just in case, then jumped back into the car and drove as fast as I could towards the cinema. We usually walked into Hebden from our house. I'd forgotten what a nightmare it was to find a parking space. After a fruitless circuit, I dumped the car on double yellows in Market Street.

I got out and ran towards the cinema, dodging a car as I crossed the road, slipping on the cinema steps as I sprinted up them. I burst through the front doors into the foyer. The woman in the kiosk looked up, startled.

'I need to get my daughter,' I said.

She frowned at me. I realised I was making no sense.

'My daughter. She's in there. Can I go in and get her?'

'You can do. The film's started, mind.'

'Right. Yes. Thanks.'

I went through the door. The first thing I saw was Kenneth Branagh, looming large on the screen, sporting a ridiculous moustache. I stood still while I waited for my eyes to adjust to the dark. I had no idea where they'd be sitting. It was going to be a nightmare trying to find her. I thought of calling her name but suspected she would simply sink into her seat in embarrassment if I did.

I walked down the aisle, looking backwards and squinting along each row in turn. It crossed my mind that I'd have to make up some excuse when I found her. She wouldn't under-stand what was going on. I'd need to say something to John too. I didn't want to accuse him of anything in front of Ruby. And I didn't want to alert him to the fact I'd spoken to Mum and knew what had happened. Maybe I could say I'd forgotten she had a dentist appointment. That was the sort of thing I'd do.

I reached the front of the cinema. There was no sign of them. I ducked down as I crossed the front row to go up the other aisle. A woman tutted. It was easier now to see people as I was facing them but I still had to wait for bright moments on the screen to illuminate them more clearly. I saw a couple of teenage girls with long hair and had to remind myself that I wasn't looking for someone with long hair since the haircut. Halfway up towards the back, I caught sight of a girl with hair the same length as Ruby's. I could just make out a parka hood on the seat behind her and, next to her, a man with a bald head. I stood at the end of the aisle and hissed, 'Ruby.' Her eyes were fixed on the screen. I'd have to go closer.

'Sorry,' I whispered to the woman at the end of the row. She stood up, as did the woman sitting next to her. Someone in the row behind tutted more loudly. I saw the girl glance across to see what the commotion was and, as she did so, realised it wasn't Ruby at all. And the man next to her was a lot younger than John. Someone behind us called out, 'Sit down.'

'Sorry,' I said. 'I thought it was my daughter.'

I shuffled back along the aisle, apologising as I went. I walked up past the last few rows. There was no sign of her. No sign at all.

I felt a tug on my jacket and jumped, looking down expecting to see Ruby. It wasn't, though. It was the mum of one of her friends from primary school. We always said it was impossible to go to the cinema in Hebden without seeing someone you knew.

'Hi. Are you looking for Ruby?' she whispered. 'Only I saw her outside with an elderly, bald chap, her grandad, was it?

'Yes,' I said. You didn't see where they sat?'

'They didn't come in. I waved hello and then I saw them walking away as we got to the top of the steps.'

'Oh, right. Thanks,' I whispered back. 'They must have changed their minds.'

I pushed my way out through the double doors at the back.

'Everything all right?'

It was only as I turned to see the blurred figure of the woman in the kiosk that I realised I was crying.

'Yes,' I said. 'Fine.'

I stumbled down the cinema steps and stood on the

pavement below, my body shaking. Maybe John had taken her away because they'd seen someone she knew. He must have been planning to do something to her. It wouldn't have bothered him otherwise. I got out my phone and tried Ruby again. It went to voicemail. I had to call it back three times before I could compose myself enough to leave another message.

'Please call me straight away,' I say. 'I need to know you're safe.'

I rang John's number too. My body went cold as I heard his voice on the message. I ended the call, unable to bring myself to speak to his voicemail. I texted him instead. Asked him to call me as soon as he got the message as I'd forgotten Ruby had a dental appointment.

I wanted to call the police but I still doubted they'd take me seriously. I'd sent Ruby off with him. I had no proof he'd done anything wrong or that she was in any danger. I called James, taking deep breaths as his phone rang in the hope that I'd be able to compose myself enough to speak if he answered. It went to voicemail too. He often turned it off when he was on jobs, so as not to get disturbed every five minutes.

'Please call me as soon as you get this,' I said, knowing that would freak him out but not being able to tell him not to worry when there was every reason to worry like hell.

I knew that standing there in a state of paralysis was not helping but I had no idea what to do. Somewhere from deep inside me, a calm voice told me to go back to John's. That they'd probably gone back there afterwards. Perhaps it was Ruby who hadn't wanted to be seen with John by people she knew.

I started running back to my car. When I got there, I noticed a parking ticket on the windscreen but I didn't even bother to take it off. I got straight in and drove back up to Heptonstall, trying hard to convince myself that Ruby would be sitting there reading and nothing would have happened.

John's car still wasn't there. I got out and knocked on the door again, though I knew I wouldn't get a reply. I remembered I'd told Mum I'd call her when I found Ruby. She must be worried sick by now.

I got my phone out again and rang her, relieved to hear an actual person at the other end of the line when she answered.

'They weren't there,' I said. 'Someone I knew from school said she'd seen them outside the cinema but they hadn't gone in.'

I heard what sounded like a whimper.

'I've come back to his house but they're not here. I don't know where he's taken her. Maybe I should call the police.'

'Come back here,' said Mum, her voice calmer than mine. 'I'm still at the house. I want to help look for her. '

I shut my eyes and nodded, even though I knew she couldn't see me. 'I'm on my way,' I said.

When I got there, Mum was standing in the back garden by the fairy statues. Her eyes were red-rimmed. Her face appeared to have aged since I'd seen her less than an hour ago.

'I should call the police,' I said. 'He could be doing something to her right now. I feel so stupid.'

'You weren't to know,' said Mum. 'No one knew.'

'I don't understand why he'd take her somewhere, though. I mean, he was alone at home with her. What did he want, somewhere with a better view?'

Mum didn't say anything, just started walking briskly, crossing the road and heading left up the path that hugged the dry-stone wall. She didn't say anything but I knew that she was going somewhere important and that I should follow her.

The earlier sunshine had disappeared behind a dark cloud, as if out of respect for the seriousness of the situation. We got to the gate at the far field. She turned to look at me.

'Over the gate and follow the path around to the top of the ridge,' she said. 'I can't come. I want to but I can't. I'll go back to the house and wait there.'

I climbed the gate, my legs wobbling as I jumped down the other side. He had a path, a well-worn route. How many times had he walked it over the years? What had he done to my mother when he'd got to the top? And what was he doing to my daughter right now?

I broke into a run. The sneakers I was wearing were covered in mud within seconds but I didn't care. I kept running, my feet ploughing through the mud. I heard my breathing get heavier with every stride up the hill. I wished, possibly for the first time in my life, that I'd bothered to keep myself in trim. Until that moment I'd never seen the point of going to the gym.

My nose was running. I wiped it with my jacket sleeve, all the time fighting to get rid of the images crowding my head. I kept peering into the distance, scouring the horizon for any sign of them. It started to rain. Big spots falling onto my face. Or maybe it was simply my tears, it was hard to tell. I had let her down. From before she was conceived I had let her down. Now I was being punished for it and deservedly so. I held my face up to the sky, keen to feel the full force of what I was owed. And then I rounded a corner and saw them, sitting on a picnic rug, a few feet back from the edge of the ridge, gathering up the things on it, laughing.

I ran up to them, barely able to speak by the time I got there. Ruby looked up with a start. I focused on her, unwilling and unable to meet John's gaze.

'We've got to go,' I said.

'Why?'

'You've got a dental appointment. I forgot. Sorry.'

Ruby glared at me. 'But we were having a picnic.'

'Yeah, well, it's raining now anyway.'

I took her arm. John was looking at me. I knew I had to try to conceal how I felt, as difficult as that might be. Our eyes met for a fraction of a second. It was long enough: he knew that I knew. He made no attempt to grab Ruby or make a run for it.

'Sorry,' I said. 'Forgot all about it.'

I dragged Ruby back towards the path. Her head was down, her hair hanging over her face. If she could have obliterated me from the planet at that moment, I was pretty sure she would have chosen to do so. But I had her. I had my baby. And I wasn't going to let him anywhere near her ever again.

She stalked down the ridge in front of me, propelled by

sheer fury. It was only when we got to the road below that she turned to face me, her eyes boring into me.

'I can't believe you did that to Uncle John. It was so rude, leaving him on his own like that. If I'd done that, you'd have had a right go at me.'

It was a moment before she seemed to register that I wasn't reacting in the way she expected. Then she noticed I was gulping air and tears, my whole body shaking, as I walked on, letting the rain beat down on me. It wasn't anywhere near hard enough.

'What is it?' she asked. 'What's going on?'

I shook my head. 'I'll tell you when we get back,' I said.

As we rounded the corner I could see Mum standing in the front garden. She cried out as soon as she saw us.

'What's Grandma doing here?' asked Ruby, increasingly frantic now.

'Just give her a hug,' I said. 'Tell her you're OK and we'll get in the car. Then I'll explain.'

Mum staggered towards us as we reached the garden, tears streaming down her face. I put an arm around her and pulled a bewildered Ruby between us. We held her so tightly she must have been struggling to breathe.

'Will someone please tell me what is going on?' Ruby asked, as she extricated herself.

'Thank you,' I said to Mum. 'Are you going to be all right?'

She nodded. 'I'll go home now.'

'Go and sit in your car a minute. I'll call you when we've had the chance to talk.'

She swallowed and nodded again, then gave Ruby a last hug. 'Your hair,' she said suddenly. 'It's very pretty. I used to have mine just like that.'

I led Ruby silently back to the car. Led, only in the sense that I knew where the car was and had retained a vague sense of direction. It was her arm around me. Her supporting me. Her taking me to a place of safety.

The parking ticket was still on the windscreen. I took it off and stuffed it into my pocket. 'It doesn't matter,' I said. 'It doesn't matter at all.'

We got into the car. I locked the doors from the inside. I turned to Ruby, brushed the damp hair from my face. 'I need to ask you a question,' I said. 'A few questions, actually. I'm sorry to have to ask you but I need to know.'

'You're scaring me,' she said.

'Has Uncle John ever touched you?' I asked. 'I mean in a way he shouldn't have. Has he said or done anything that's made you feel uncomfortable?'

She shook her head.

'If he had, it wouldn't be your fault. Do you understand that? He might have told you not to tell anyone but you can tell me, You're not going to get into trouble. '

'He never touched me,' she said. The expression on her face told me that she was speaking the truth. She clearly couldn't understand why I was even asking her these questions.

'And was he ever alone with Maisie?' I asked. 'Were you ever not in the room when they were together?'

'No,' she said softly.

I wiped the tears from my cheeks.

'Are you going to tell me what's happened?' she asked.

'When we get home,' I said.

I got my phone out and rang Mum. She answered instantly.

'She's fine,' I said. 'They're both fine.'

I heard her burst into tears. Saw her sitting in her car across the road, smiling through her own pain because her first-born grandchild was safe. I put the phone back into my pocket and drove my first-born home.

Ruby made the hot chocolate. It was like she knew she had to take over the parental thing for a bit. She was aware that I wasn't fit to look after myself, let alone anyone else. She put the mugs on the kitchen table, even remembering to use the coasters.

I sat there for a while, trying to form some coherent sentences in my head before I attempted to get them out into the world. Ruby waited patiently, seemingly understanding that an explanation would come.

'Grandma came to see me earlier,' I began eventually. 'I mentioned Uncle John to her and she told me that he wasn't her cousin at all. Olive and Harold weren't her real aunt and uncle. She simply called them that because they lived next door. Parents used to tell children to call adults they knew well "auntie" and "uncle". It was sort of a respect thing.'

What a horrible conceit that was. I paused while I waited for the next words to come. Ruby sat staring at me, her eyes searching my face for answers.

'You're not going to call John "uncle" any more because he isn't. He lived next door to Grandma when she was growing up. That's why he was in all those photographs with her.'

I paused again, trying to find the right words.

'The thing is, Grandma told me he did some horrible things to her. He touched her in places he shouldn't have. When she was fourteen years old.'

I watched the words land on Ruby, saw her try to deflect them and find they were too heavy. I was scared she'd buckle under the weight. She didn't, though. Her eyes sagged with tears but she tried bravely to bat them away. 'I'm sorry,' I said. 'It's not a nice thing for any of us to hear.'

'Poor Grandma,' Ruby said. 'Didn't she tell anyone?'

'I don't know. She certainly never told me.'

'Why not?'

I bit my lip. 'Sometimes, parents think it's best to protect their children from some of the bad things in the world, some of the hurt. It's like they don't want them to know what a scary place it can be.'

Ruby sat silently, still trying to take it all in. 'We won't ever have to see him again, will we?'

I shook my head.

'Are we going to tell Maisie about it?'

I hadn't thought that far ahead. 'We'll tell her we found out he wasn't Grandma's cousin after all. That he lied to us. We won't tell her what he did.' I put my arm around her, drew her close to me, the way I used to do. 'I'm sorry,' I said, my voice shaking. 'I'm really, really sorry for putting you at risk like that.'

'You didn't know, did you?'

'I still feel bad, though. It's like I said, parents always want to protect their kids.'

We sat in silence for a while. I took a sip of my hot chocolate.

'So he lived in Andrea's house where they found the other bones?' she asked.

The same cogs had been turning in her head as in mine. 'Yes,' I said. 'I think he did.'

I thought about ringing James but didn't see the need to worry him at work, now I knew the girls were safe. It would wait until he got home. Until I could tell him properly and he had the time and space he'd need to process it.

Ruby sat and read for a bit. She didn't go to her room, though, which she would usually have done when Maisie was out. She sat next to me on the sofa. She even let me stroke her hair. When the time came to collect Maisie, we got into the car together and drove silently to Emily's house.

'Are you going to tell her straight away?' Ruby asked.

'No,' I said. 'Let's wait until we get home.'

Maisie exploded into the car, full of chatter and tales of what she and Emily had got up to and how she'd been invited to her firework-party sleepover on Saturday. I glanced at Ruby. She had a smile on her face and tears in her eyes, like I did.

When we got home, I opened the door and the girls went straight through to the kitchen. It was only as I shut it and turned to hang my jacket up that I saw the brown envelope on the floor. I knew straight away who it was from. Who all the notes must have been from. My hands were trembling as I picked it up. I took out a piece of ruled notepaper. The spidery writing was now familiar.

Don't believe a word your mother says. She wanted it as much as I did. If you go to the police I will tell them that. They won't believe her. It will be her word against mine. She was very pretty when she was younger, you know. Just like your Ruby is now. And you won't always be around to protect her. Just you remember that.

I was gripping the envelope so hard that my knuckles were white. There was something else in it. I put in my fingers and pulled them out. Two photographs: one of Mum and one of Ruby. Taken on exactly the same spot at the top of the ridge. I cast my mind back, trying to remember if I'd seen a computer at his house. I hadn't, probably because it wasn't downstairs but in his bedroom. Bedrooms were a good place for secrets and it seemed there was a lot about John that I hadn't known.

15 September, 1944

Dear Betty,

I feel so stupid now for thinking your parents would approve of me, for believing they'd give us their blessing to get married. I know you said they were old-fashioned but I was not expecting that. Clearly, they don't see things the way we do. Please do not listen to them. You have not brought shame on anyone. This baby has been created by love and it will be loved more than any child has ever been. They may have the power to stop me marrying you now but they won't have next April.

Once our baby is born and you turn eighteen, no one will be able to stop us. The war will be over by then and I'll take you home to Canada to get married, so we can start our new life together. I know it's hard but we've got to be strong until that point.

You being sent away to your great-aunt's isn't the end, you must remember that. They might be able to stop me seeing you for now but it won't be forever. And every day, every week, every month we are apart, our love will grow stronger. They can punish us and hurt us but they cannot break us, Betty. I will not allow it to happen.

I will write to you and I will think about you every moment we are apart. And I will think of our baby, growing inside you, and how brave and strong you are being for carrying it, for not giving in to their demands. No one will touch our baby, Betty. You will keep it safe and it will be only a few weeks old when we get married. It will never know anything different than living with us as a family.

As far as I'm concerned, if your parents threaten to disown you, then they are not a family worth having. We are your family now Betty. Me and our baby. We don't need anyone else in the world. I will take care of you both and I will be counting down the days until we can all be together. We must never look back, Betty, only forwards.

I want to see you one more time before they send you away. I want to take you somewhere special and treat you like the lady you are.

Please meet me outside Bettys in York at twelve noon next Saturday. I am taking my girl out on a date. We're going to be in the tea rooms, not Bettys bar. I don't care who sees us, though. If some of the other boys are in the basement there I will smile and show you off and tell them you are my girl. We will find somewhere quiet to sit together and we will not talk about being apart. We will talk about when we are back together again. We will make plans for the future and I will tell our baby that it has the most beautiful mother in the world. We will make memories to keep us going while we are apart.

I love you, Betty Braithwaite, and even though I did not think it possible, I love you a little more now. I will see you at Bettys.

Yours always,

William

20

James sat at the kitchen table, his face, usually so amenable, struggling with emotions I had never seen on it before. My words still hung in the air; the noise of the TV show the girls were watching played out in the background. How could I have brought my family to its knees like this? Ruined the happiness of the people I loved most in the world. The word 'pig-headed' came to mind. Although even that had unsavoury connotations following recent events. I reached across the table and took his hand.

'I'm sorry,' I said. 'I am so, so sorry for putting them at risk like that.'

James shook his head. 'It wasn't your fault.'

'You've got to stop saying that,' I replied. 'Because sometimes it is.'

'You couldn't have known. Your mum hadn't told anyone.'

'But I could still have checked him out properly, couldn't I? I was that desperate to find a family member that I fucking invented one.'

'Are you sure Ruby was telling the truth?'

'Yeah. She's never been any good at lying to me.'

'To think that filthy bastard was going to lay a finger on her.' James brought his fist down hard on the table. 'I want to go up there now and see to him.'

The anger in his voice took me aback. He was the gentlest man I'd ever met, yet this was what he'd been reduced to.

'I get that, I really do, but it wouldn't do any good. It would simply mean you getting into trouble, instead of him. I'll go to the police tomorrow morning.'

'Why not now?'

'He's not going anywhere. Not with Olive being so poorly. That's why he threatened me. And I want to go and see Mum first. I want to try to persuade her to report what he did to her.'

'Do you think it was their baby?'

I shrugged. 'If you join the dots, that's what you get. But I don't want to rely on doing that. I don't want this to be guesswork. We need to get to the truth. And that needs to come direct from her.'

'Go now, then,' said James, pushing his chair back and standing up. 'I'll sort the girls out. I'm not leaving them until he's locked up, so it's best to get the ball rolling. I'll cancel my job tomorrow, so you can take your mum to the police station. And we'll get the bastard put away for good.'

When Mum answered the door she looked, if it were possible, even worse than she had that morning. All those years she had kept her secret and now it was out. She seemed to be unravelling from the inside. As if it was such an intrinsic part of her that to take the secret away meant taking part of her too.

I told her to go and sit down, made tea and carried it through to the living room where she was sitting on the sofa, staring vacantly at the wall. She took the cup and saucer from me, her hand shaking so much they vibrated noisily and she had to put them straight down.

'Thank you,' I said, after a moment. 'For telling me, I mean. I know it must have been difficult for you.'

She twisted her fingers together and broke them apart again. 'Are you sure he didn't touch her?' she asked.

'No. Ruby wouldn't lie to me about a thing like that.'

Mum gave a dismissive snort. 'He would have threatened her, would have told her she'd get in massive trouble.'

'And I made it clear to Ruby that if anything had happened, it would have been his fault, not hers. I told her I'd believe her. That no one would be cross with her.'

Mum nodded slowly and closed her eyes.

'Did Grandma not believe you?' I asked.

She shook her head.

'So it was never reported to the police?'

'No. You didn't speak about such things in those days.'

'People do now, though,' I said. 'All those cases on the news. It's not too late.'

'What, and have all that raked up in court? Have him leering at me and telling them filthy lies?'

'It wouldn't be like that,' I said. 'You wouldn't have to come face to face with him. And I'd be there to support you. You wouldn't be on your own.'

'No,' she said firmly. 'I won't give him the satisfaction of hurting me any more than he already has done.'

'What if he's abused other girls?' I asked. 'They might come forward too. That's often how it works now. He shouldn't be allowed to get away with it.'

'That's easy for you to say.'

I swallowed and looked up at the ceiling, struggling hard to compose myself. 'I get that this isn't easy,' I said. 'Believe me, I do. But he put a note through the door earlier, threatening to do the same to Ruby as he did to you. There were photos in with it too.'

I reached into my bag and produced them, laying them on the coffee-table.

Mum put a hand to her mouth to try to stifle the sound that came out. I went over and sat next to her, putting my arm around her. I could feel her entire body trembling.

'I'm taking them to the police tomorrow,' I said. 'I expect he was behind the other notes and the pig bones. But he won't get much of a sentence for that. He'd get a hell of a lot more for what he did to you.'

Mum sat forward, rocking back and forth. 'I want to,' she said, 'I really want to, but I'm so scared.'

'Then let me come with you and I'll hold your hand while you tell them everything. That way, you'll only have to tell it once.'

She nodded and wiped the tears from her face. I decided to go on while I appeared to be getting somewhere. 'And you can let them take a DNA sample, and they'll go and arrest him and take his. Then we can find out what really happened.'

I took her hand. She gripped it tightly, her fingernails cutting into my palm.

'He got you pregnant, didn't he?' I asked.

She bit down hard on her lip and screwed up her eyes, then gave an almost imperceptible nod.

'And did he kill your baby?'

'I don't know,' she whispered. 'I still don't know what happened to my baby.'

The next morning DI Freeman was waiting for us when we arrived at Halifax police station. I handed him the envelope with the note and photographs in. 'We've got CCTV pictures of a man fitting his description leaving Todmorden Market with a large bag on the evening before the bones were left outside your house,' he said.

'You're not bringing him here, are you?' asked Mum.

'Not while you're with us,' he replied. 'But we will do as soon as you've left. Someone's waiting outside his house just in case. Are you ready to make a start?'

I looked at Mum. 'Can Nicola come in with me?' she asked.

'Yes,' he replied. 'You're allowed to have an emotional supporter, so that's fine.'

DI Freeman led us through to an interview room, where a woman in her forties was sitting. 'This is DS Lockwood,' he said. 'She's a specially trained detective from our unit which deals with this type of offence.'

The woman stood up and came over to shake our hands. 'Hi, please call me Julia,' she said, smiling warmly. 'I'll be here for you all the way through this, and if you've got any questions, or there's anything you're not sure of, please let me know.'

Mum and I sat down and DI Freeman left the room. I took Mum's hand. All this time she'd had to deal with this on her own. All this time I'd had no idea what she'd been through. It was so stupid, so ridiculously stupid.

I was vaguely aware of Julia running through what would happen. All the time I was trying to steel myself for when Mum would start talking. I had to be strong for her, however difficult that would be. I hummed inside my head. The same made-up tune I'd hummed lots of times when I'd been trying to block things out.

I heard Julia tell us she was starting the recording, was aware of her giving the time and location of the interview, and the names of the people present. And then I heard it: Mum's voice, saying her name. Only it wasn't her voice as it was now. It was the voice of a fourteen-year-old girl. Scared and traumatised by what had happened to her. I squeezed her hand again and blinked back the tears as she spoke softly into the microphone. It was the spring of 1972. John Armitage, a local postman, lived next door to her with his parents, Olive and Harold. In the house where Andrea now lived.

*

We sat in the car, around the corner from the police station, for a long time afterwards, neither of us saying a word. Mum's eyes were red and puffy. I wiped my own eyes with my sleeve, the sodden tissue in my hand no longer capable of absorbing tears.

'That's why I never said anything,' Mum said finally. 'Because I fancied him. Because I was flattered when he asked me to go and see the sunrise with him. I led him on, you see. It was like he said, all my own doing.'

I shook my head repeatedly while I struggled to get the words out. 'You were fourteen,' I said. 'And he was, what, mid-twenties? You did nothing to make him do it and could have done nothing to make him stop.'

'They won't see it like that, though, will they?' she said. 'Not in a court of law. They'll try to twist it, make it look as if I came on to him.'

'You were fourteen,' I repeated. 'That is all anyone needs to know.'

He never spoke to me again. I saw him from the house sometimes, on his way to or from work. He never looked up to my bedroom. Not that I would have wanted him to. I felt sick just seeing him. And as my bump grew ever bigger, the shadow he had cast over my life was inescapable.

Mum never spoke to me about him again either. She had obviously decided that it was all made up on my part: he was in the clear and I was the guilty party. The one who had to be punished. It was a proper confinement: I didn't leave the house for four months and no one was allowed in. My condition was a shameful secret that no one spoke of. Mum had told Dad, but he never said a word to me about it. He didn't have to: his face said it all. He couldn't even bring himself to look at my bump. Mum wasn't much better. Baggy tops and large trousers with elasticated waists appeared on my bed without explanation. Clearly, proper maternity clothes were out of the question, in case anyone spotted her buying them, so I had to make do with clothes that were too big for me all over and too small in the one area that mattered.

Most of the time, I stayed in my room. It was, to all intents and purposes, a prison sentence, served in the place in which the crimes against me had been committed. I could still smell him, however much

I had the window open. I could hear his grunting, see that smirk on his face, feel his hands all over me. And if I managed to forget for just a second, the baby would kick, reminding me that I had been contaminated inside too.

The only thing I could do to pass the time was sleep, when the baby allowed it, at any rate. But when I did sleep, I had nightmares where I saw my baby for the first time and he was the spitting image of his father. In my dreams he was always a boy, and in my waking hours too. I couldn't bear the thought of seeing him in the flesh. I wondered if it would be possible to give birth without seeing him. To shut my eyes just as I'd shut them when he'd been created. And then hand him over without ever having to look at him.

Mum had told me she'd found someone to adopt the baby privately. I'd asked who it was, but she said I didn't need to concern myself with that. Once the baby was gone, I wanted to erase him from my mind. Pretend he had never existed, that the whole thing had never happened. Pretend I was the sort of girl whose idea of a bad day was when her socks fell down as she ran for the school bus.

All I had to do to get rid of him was give birth to him. I was scared, of course. Scared beyond belief. Especially the thought of doing it at home. I wished I could go to hospital and have him there, but Mum said that was out of the question: she didn't want the authorities involved. She'd told school I'd gone away to stay with an elderly aunt who needed looking after. Apparently, they had accepted that, although it meant I was skipping school. Maybe they had worked it out and didn't want to say anything, just like everyone else.

It was five past midnight when I woke up. I knew straight away. I'd been worrying that I wouldn't recognise a contraction for what it was, yet when it came, I knew it couldn't be anything else. I'd heard about contractions on TV. That was where most of my information about childbirth had come from. As far as I could gather, there was a lot of fetching towels, mopping brows, grimacing and screaming, but they never showed you what was happening at the other end. I could have asked Mum, I suppose, but we'd never talked about stuff like that. And, anyway, it was too late now.

I lay there on my own in the dark, gripping the sheets. Too scared to move or to go and wake Mum. The contractions hadn't hurt at first: it had simply felt like the baby was doing weird somersaults inside me. But by the time it started to get light, they were closer together and stronger. So strong that I knew I wouldn't be able to hide the fact that I was having them.

I didn't get up, I think because I was scared it might get suddenly worse. I didn't even call out for help. I simply carried on until my cries got so loud that Mum came in.

'Why on earth didn't you tell me?' she asked, immediately rushing out and coming back in with towels and a flannel to mop my brow. It seemed the TV programmes were true – so far, at least.

'I didn't want to bother you,' I said.

'You daft girl. It's not going to go away, is it? You're having a baby.'

Her words shattered the pretence I'd managed to build up that this wasn't actually happening to me. So much so, that I started crying.

'Come on,' she said. 'There's no need for that. Let's get this over with and then we can all get back to normal.'

It was a ridiculous thing to say, and I suspect she knew it as well as I did, but I decided not to take issue with it. She went off again and came back with a glass of water and two extra pillows.

'Where's Dad?' I asked.

'He's gone out for a bit.'

It wouldn't be a bit, I knew that. He'd stay out until this was all over. See no evil, hear no evil, speak no evil.

I let out the loudest cry I had yet, as a stronger contraction gripped me.

'What about next door?' I asked, once I'd recovered the ability to speak. 'They'll hear me.'

'No, they won't,' said Mum. 'Nothing gets through these walls.'

'They'll hear the baby crying when it's born.'

Mum swallowed and looked past me out of the window. 'Not all babies cry when they're born,' she said quietly.

After all the effort, all the pain and fear, the baby came quickly at the end, not long after Mum told me to start pushing. It wasn't only the baby I was pushing out, it was him as well. Finally expelling him from my body. Maybe that's why the baby came out so forcefully.

I heard him cry before Mum managed to say anything. And I did what I'd promised myself I wouldn't. I opened my eyes. He was lying on the towel on the bed, his body red and wrinkled, his face scrunched, his little arms and legs waving about. It was only when I looked at him more closely that I saw he was a baby girl. I gasped and sobbed at the same time. Mum was still sitting on the edge of the bed, tears pouring down her cheeks, seemingly unable to speak or move.

I reached down and touched the baby's hand. I didn't feel hate as I'd thought I would, or even indifference. I felt the one thing I hadn't expected at all. Pure, unadulterated love.

I struggled to stretch forward to pick her up. She was still attached to me but the cord was so much longer than I had imagined that I was able to pull her up to my chest. I didn't care about getting blood on my nightshirt. I didn't care about the blood all over the towels or about any of the other things I'd thought I would. All I cared about was my baby. The one I would soon be giving away.

Maybe it was seeing me holding her that released Mum from her stupor. Suddenly she got up and left the room, returning a few minutes later with her dressmaking scissors.

'No,' I said, shaking my head, 'please don't.'

'It doesn't hurt them,' she replied. 'And I've sterilised them in boiling water.'

It wasn't that I was bothered about, though. It was the fact that once the cord had been cut, I couldn't stop my baby being taken away from me. But before I could do anything, Mum took hold of the cord and cut it near to the baby. I waited for her to scream but she didn't, so I screamed for her. I screamed for both of us.

I pulled her back close to me again. The baby was grasping at my breasts through my nightshirt. I hadn't even thought about how I would feed it. The only mums I knew used a bottle. I'd never even seen anyone breastfeeding. But suddenly I felt the need to do what she wanted. To feed my baby.

I started to lift my nightshirt. I had no idea what to do but I wanted to try. Mum immediately took the baby from me.

'No,' she said. 'You mustn't.'

'Why not?'

'You'll get attached to it.'

'I was attached to it, for nine months, until you cut the cord. It's my baby.'

'You said you didn't want it.'

'I've changed my mind.'

'It's too late. All the arrangements have been made.'

'Well, you'll have to unmake them.'

'I can't. Anyway, you can't keep it. You're fourteen, for goodness' sake.'

'You could help me look after it. I'll learn what to do.'

'What on earth would people think, seeing you pushing a baby about in a pram?'

'I don't care what people think.'

'Well, your father does. He wouldn't stand for it.' She took a blanket from the chair and wrapped it around the baby. She started to walk towards the door.

'You're not taking her now?'

'I've got to. It's for the best.' Her voice cracked as she spoke. I saw tears welling in her eyes. I couldn't understand how she could do this to me.

'No, it isn't,' I shouted at her. 'You can't take her. I haven't even washed her yet. Let me clean her. Let me have her for one night.'

I could see Mum's body shaking. Tears were pouring down her cheeks.

'I promised your father it would be gone by the time he came home,' she said.

The baby started crying again, as if it knew what was happening. I tried to get out of bed, but my legs were weak and the umbilical cord was still hanging out of me.

'What do I do with this?' I shouted.

'It will come out soon. You have to sort of give birth to it.'

I collapsed back in a heap on the bed, sobbing uncontrollably.

'Give me my baby. Please don't take my baby.'

Mum let go of a noise so primeval that at first I didn't realise it had come from her, and then she ran, the baby hugged close to her, out of my bedroom and down the stairs.

I lay back on the bed and screamed, my fists beating the mattress, feeling worse now than when he'd done everything to me. I heard Mum pull the front door shut behind her. I would never see my baby again. For all those months I had hated it, wanted rid of it, wished it dead, yet the second I'd laid eyes on her, I'd known I would never love anything more than I loved that baby. The baby I would never see again.

I felt a clenching and cramping inside and realised I was about to give birth to the placenta. I struggled to the bathroom and sat down on the toilet, just in time. My body expelled the very last part of my baby from me. I sat there in tears, unable to stand up for fear of seeing what was there. In that instant I knew that, if my baby was gone, the only way I could survive this was to flush away every last trace of her. I reached up and pulled the chain. The water cascaded down beneath me. I waited until the cistern started refilling before I eased myself up to look in the toilet bowl. She was gone. It was like Mum said: it was as if she had never existed. And I knew she would never be spoken of again.

21

Mum didn't want to go home. She didn't want to be on her own. We went to a little café and sat at a table in a quiet corner, both of us seemingly lost in our own thoughts.

'I'm sorry,' she said eventually. 'For not telling you, I mean. I'd always hoped and prayed that one day I would see my baby again. And when you told me about Maisie finding that bone, I was so scared. So scared that it belonged to my baby.'

'And that's why you didn't want me to go to the police?'

'I didn't think I could live without hope. When I heard that baby were Mum's, that both of them were Mum's, I were so relieved, although I know that must sound awful. It meant I still had hope, you see. I thought that was the end of it. I was trying to gather the strength to get in touch with you to explain. I missed the girls so much.'

She started to cry again. I fished in my bag, found a clean tissue and handed it to her, staring straight ahead as she blew her nose.

'And then when they found the other bones, in his garden, well, I haven't really slept since.'

'I'm so sorry,' I said. 'I should have realised.'

'No,' she said. 'I hid it so deep that no one could have guessed.'

'Dad didn't know?'

She shook her head. 'It's not the sort of thing you tell a fella you've just met, is it? And there were never a right time to tell him, even after we got married. He offered to be there for your birth but I wouldn't let him because I didn't want him to find out you weren't my first baby. And after I gave birth to you, I cried and cried for days. The midwives thought I had post-natal depression. They didn't understand that I were crying because it had brought it all back. They thought I were tired because you were keeping me awake at night. That wasn't it, though. I was tired because I wouldn't allow myself to shut my eyes for one second in case someone took you away too.'

I reached for her hand. 'Thank you for telling me now,' I said. 'We're going to get through this together.'

'Yes,' she said, nodding. 'No more secrets.' I gave a little smile and looked down at the floor.

When she'd finished her tea, Mum popped to the Ladies to redo her make-up. I got my phone out. There was a message from DI Freeman. John had been arrested. He was in custody. I hoped he was sweating, hoped he was going to suffer in the way Mum had for all these years. And, most of all, I hoped he would provide some answers. For her and for everyone.

'He's in custody,' I said, when she finally emerged from the toilets, her glasses cleaned and a slick of lipstick freshly applied. 'How about coming back to ours to have tea with the girls?'

She smiled. The first smile I'd seen her give that day. 'I'd like that,' she said. 'I'd like that very much.'

'Grandma!' shouted Maisie, running to greet her with a hug as soon as we walked in. 'I'm getting a puppy and my own bedroom when we move to Great-grandma's house.'

'Are you now,' said Mum, glancing at me. 'Aren't you lucky?'

Maisie took her by the hand and led her into the living room. Ruby got up and went over to give her a hug. Mum hung on to her for an awfully long time. When she looked up, there were tears in her eyes and in Ruby's too.

'Right then,' I said. 'I believe Grandma's favourite is macaroni cheese. Why don't you all play a game together while I make tea?' Maisie gave a little cheer. I left them to it and went into the kitchen, where I stood silently, staring out of the window.

'Are you OK?' asked James, following me in and putting his hands on my shoulders.

'Yeah,' I replied. Even though I wasn't.

We lay in bed, James's arm draped over me. The streetlight outside was shining through the curtains. James had suggested getting blackout blinds a few times but I liked it as it was. I hadn't been able to tell him why, of course. I simply said I found it comforting.

I thought about what Mum had said earlier. How she'd

lain awake in hospital after she'd had me, too scared to close her eyes in case someone took her baby. I understood that. Understood it more than she would ever know. My terror had never subsided. Not at night when I lay there with my eyes open, not daring to close them for fear of what I might find when I woke. I had resigned myself long ago to the fact that it would always be like that. Some things you simply never got over. But that night all I could think about was what Mum had said. How she had never forgiven herself for something that was so clearly not her fault. The sea of shame had washed over her, leaving its debris on the shore. She had very nearly gone under. It had certainly dragged her down for most of her life, probably screwed up her marriage, although Dad had made a pretty good job of that from his end too. The years of suffering she had endured to get to today. The first time in her life when someone had believed her, had looked under the blanket of shame and seen she was drowning. That she had been drowning all those years but no one had noticed.

I hadn't realised I'd been crying until James brushed a tear from my shoulder.

'Hey,' he said. 'It's OK. It's over now.'

'It's not,' I said. 'It's never going to be over, that's the trouble.'

'The worst is over. We can get through the rest together. Everyone's going to be fine.'

The tears came faster. James pulled me into him. It hurt sometimes, how much he wanted to make things better for me. It was cruel to let him think the hurt inside me could be healed. Because he would go on trying to do so for the rest of his life, oblivious to the fact that it was like trying to mount a clean-up operation on a beach after an oil-slick. He needed to be told – needed to understand that sometimes the nasty stuff got so far into you that no one could get it out.

'I was asleep,' I blurted out.

'What – just now?'

'No. Back then. When it happened.'

'When what happened?'

'I woke up, you see. It was dark, pitch black. There wasn't even a window in the room. They seemed to think they could get away with that for student accommodation.'

James was listening now. I could hear him listening. Straining to make sure he didn't miss anything.

'My head was swimming. It was hardly surprising, given how much I'd had to drink that night. At first I thought I was actually swimming and the movement was me being buffeted by the waves. It took a few moments before I realised the movement was coming from inside me. And the weight on me wasn't the weight of the water at all.

'It was then I smelt him. Smelt him and felt him all at the same time. It was like an attack on the senses. I thought for a second I was going to throw up all over him. He didn't say anything. That was the one blessing. I never heard his voice, so I can't be haunted by that, as well. But maybe that was also why it didn't seem real. Maybe if he'd said something, it would have provoked a reaction. Woken me from my stupor. Only he didn't, so I thought it must be OK. Thought I must have wanted it. That we'd already done our introductions and I'd somehow nodded off in the middle of it.'

I paused. James was stroking my arm. He was here and I was safe now. Safe to go on.

'It wasn't like that, though. Maybe I'd talked to him at the party – I'd talked to a lot of people. But there were a lot of people I hadn't spoken to either. If he kept quiet, I wouldn't know either way, would I? And if I couldn't hear him and couldn't see him, there was no way I could identify him, was there?'

I felt one of James's own tears fall on to my shoulder. Soothing, healing, like antiseptic. Except this was a wound buried too far deep inside me to be able to get to.

'I didn't move,' I went on. 'I didn't hit or kick or bite. None of those things. And I didn't say a word either. Whatever had rendered my limbs useless also rendered me speechless. Because at some point I knew that, however drunk I was, I had not wanted it. Had not invited him into the room or into me. I was being violated and still I said nothing. Did nothing. It was as if I somehow thought that if I made no connection with him at all, didn't acknowledge his existence, he might not be real but just a figment of my imagination. I didn't want to make him real, so I told myself it wasn't happening. Even when it hurt and when he clawed at me and when he spat in my face before he left. I told myself it hadn't happened. That I'd imagined the whole thing. That something like that cannot happen to you one night when you go to a party with your mates.'

James was wiping the tears from my cheeks but no sooner had he done so than some fresh ones fell. The dam wall had been closed a long time: the pressure inside was immense.

'And at some point afterwards, I must have fallen back to sleep,' I went on. 'You wouldn't do that, would you? Not if a complete stranger had just violated you in that way. But I did. Because I woke up a second time and he wasn't there. And I thought at first I must have dreamt it but then I felt the burning pain down below and I reached between my legs and found all the evidence I needed.

'Do you know what I did with it, though? I got up, went to the toilet and wiped it away. I crept out of the house while everyone else was still asleep, and when I got back to my digs, I got into the shower and washed every last trace of it away. Well, I thought I did. It was only a few weeks later when my period didn't come that I discovered I hadn't managed to get to it all.

'And that was when I made up the story. The one about me shagging some guy at a party when I was pissed. And when you tell a story so many times, you start to believe it. And because it was an easier story to believe than the truth, I let it become my truth. Everyone else seemed to accept it, so why shouldn't I?

'I took all the crap that was thrown at me, heard all the comments about me being a slag, and when I had to quit the course because of the pregnancy, I got packed off home to a mother who bought it, who believed that was what her daughter had become. And I've spent my life struggling with the shame of what people thought of me and the shame of knowing what really happened. Until today, when I sat in a police interview room and heard my mother tell the very same story of blaming herself and letting it eat away at her for years, only she was fucking fourteen at the time. And all I know is that I cannot go on like this. Living a lie and hurting the people I love. I must not let it destroy me.'

I beat my fists against the mattress as the final part of the dam wall came away. James held me tightly, but not so tight that the tears couldn't find a way out. He stroked my hair, kissed my eyelids softly, and kept saying the same thing to me, over and over again. The same three words I had needed to hear for so long: 'I believe you.'

I don't know how long we lay there like that, just clinging to each other, as if we were on an upturned life raft being buffeted by the sea. But at some point, much later, when we had both stopped crying, James said something. The one thing I had not expected.

'I think you should tell Ruby.'

'No,' I said straight away.

'I understand why you haven't and why you don't want to now,' he said, 'but she needs you to be honest with her. I think that's what she wants more than anything else in the world.'

'What she wants more than anything else in the world is to have a father whose name she knows. A name that's written on her birth certificate. And that's the one thing I can't give her.'

'So give her this. Give her the truth. Because if you don't, she'll go on being angry with you, thinking you brought this on yourself, that you did this to her.'

'I did do it to her. I got drunk, didn't I? So drunk that I was practically comatose when a man started having sex with me.'

James turned my head to face his. 'He raped you, Nic. You have to call it what it was. You have to acknowledge it to yourself and to Ruby.'

'She's still too young. It's too much to ask of her to cope with that.'

'I don't think it is, not the way she reacted yesterday. She's wise beyond her years. She's tough too.'

'I want to,' I said. 'I had to sit there today and listen to Mum go into detail about what John did to her and how she kept it a secret all these years, and the truth is, I'm the one who persuaded her to tell the truth, who came out with all the it's-better-to-get-it-out-in-the-open stuff, and I'm such a hypocrite because I've been doing exactly the same thing. Only I've been doing it to protect Ruby. Because I cannot begin to imagine how horrible it would be to know that was how you came into the world.'

'I get that,' said James. 'Believe me, I want to protect her from it too. But I can also see how generations of your family have suffered because of the shame heaped on them and I don't want that to happen to Ruby. And if you keep it a secret, it becomes something shameful, something to hide from others. But if you call it out, speak it out loud, it's not a dirty secret any more. You'd be showing her that it was nothing to be ashamed of.'

I wondered how the man who always said he was no good with words had pulled that one out of nowhere. He was right, I knew. But that didn't make it any easier.

'I'm scared,' I said. 'Scared I'm going to make her hate me even more than she does already.'

'She doesn't hate you,' James said. 'She hates not knowing the truth.'

'But it's such a massive thing to put on her. It could screw her up for life.'

'I know. But so could the shame of having it kept a secret.'

I lay awake for a long time afterwards. James eventually dropped off, although even when he did so, his arm was still over me, protecting me. All I could do was lie there and try to work out what I would say to Ruby. There was no easy way to tell some stories. Especially when they'd been locked inside you for so long. They had a habit of rushing out in a torrent, mangling words and sentences, making no sense at all. Most of all, I wondered if Ruby would ever forgive me. I doubted it. But it was a price I had to pay to break the chain.

I waited until James took Maisie swimming the following morning. He'd drop her off at Emily's straight afterwards, ready for the firework party and sleepover. It would give Ruby space on her own to deal with it, and I'd have time to try to limit the fallout before Maisie returned.

I knocked on her bedroom door and went in when she answered. She was reading *The Secret Garden*. We'd first read it together years ago. It threw me, though, because she was mostly reading Young Adult books now. It reminded me that she was still a child, or at least in that awkward in-between phase. Maybe she wasn't ready to hear this. Maybe I was making a terrible mistake.

'That takes me back a bit,' I said.

'Yeah. Thought I'd read it again. It's sadder than I remember, Colin being locked away like that. All those secrets.'

I nodded, unable to speak, and sat on the edge of her bed. She put the book down, as if she knew what was to come.

'There's something I need to tell you,' I said. 'I don't know if it's the right time and it's going to be hard to hear. It'll make you angry and upset, so if you don't want me to tell you, or you want me to wait a bit longer, that's fine, just let me know. But I wanted to give you the choice.'

'It's about my father, isn't it?' she asked.

'Yes,' I replied.

'I want to hear it then,' she said.

I looked at the wall opposite. It was covered with pictures of puppies and unicorns, which seemed entirely inappropriate in the circumstances. But I knew that if I looked at Ruby, I would never be able to get the words out. I'd stop as soon as I saw the first signs of hurt on her face.

'Most of what I've told you is true,' I said. 'I was at a party in my second year at uni. I was drunk. I was twenty but I wasn't half as sensible as you are now.'

I paused, aware that Ruby was hanging on my every word. I was trying to sort out the jumble of things in my head so that the story came out as I wanted it to. It would be the truth. But I would spare her the full details.

'I fell asleep in my friend's bedroom. There was nobody else in there at the time. But when I woke up a few hours later, a man was in there. He was lying on top of me. He was inside me too. Although I hadn't said he could do that.'

I heard Ruby start to cry, I reached out for her hand, still afraid to look.

'I froze,' I said. 'I was scared, so scared and confused, and I didn't know what to do. I tried to move but I couldn't. He was a lot bigger than me and I was worried that he would hurt me, so I lay there until it was all over.'

I brushed away the tears that were coursing down my cheeks. 'The reason I don't know your father's name is because he never stopped to introduce himself. And when he was finished, he got up and left the room without a word and I never saw him again.'

Ruby let out a howl at almost exactly the same time as I did. I turned to her, seeing her wide, frightened eyes, the knowledge starting to seep through, the knowledge that would never leave her now. That she was the product of a rape.

'No,' she screamed.

'I'm so sorry,' I said. I tried to hug her but she pushed me away.

'It's not true,' she shouted. 'You're making it up so you don't look so bad.'

'I would never do that,' I said. 'I would never do anything to hurt you.'

'Well, you just have.'

'I wanted you to know the truth. I thought you deserved that.'

'If that's the truth, you should have got rid of me. You should never have let me be born.'

Her words slapped against me, stinging my face. 'I didn't get rid of you because the second I found out I was pregnant I knew I would love you more than anything else in the world. The most important thing you need to know is that the first time I saw you, when the midwife handed this little wrinkled, crying thing to me, I knew I was right, that you were the one good thing to come out of it. Every time I've looked at you since that's what I've thought too.'

'But don't I remind you of him?'

'No,' I said quickly. 'Because it was dark and I couldn't see him. I have no idea what he looked like, so I don't see him in you. All I see is a gorgeous girl who is turning into the incredible young woman I'm so proud of. And I don't want you to waste a single second of your precious life thinking about him because he isn't worth it, OK?'

'Does Grandma know?' she asked, between sobs.

'No,' I said. 'I couldn't bring myself to tell her. I knew how much it would hurt her, you see, and I didn't see the point of telling her because it wouldn't change anything. She was cross enough at me for getting pregnant and messing up my education. She didn't need to know any more.'

'But you let her be cross with you. You let everyone think you had sex with someone whose name you didn't know.'

'I didn't want them to treat you differently,' I said. 'I didn't want anyone to look at you and think about what had happened, and I knew that the best way to prevent that happening was not to tell them about it.'

'But you told James,' she said.

'Only last night. I had to tell him because not telling anyone was eating away at me, and I'd seen what that had done to Grandma. It was his idea to tell you. He said you were old enough to hear the truth.'

'Does he hate me now?'

'Hate you? God, he loves you more than I ever thought was possible. He's always been your father, you know. He's done more than lots of real dads ever do for their kids, and I don't want this to change things between you.'

'Well, it does!' she screamed. 'It changes everything. My father raped you. That's how I was created. How the hell am I supposed to live with that?'

'I don't know,' I said, 'but I'll help you if you'll let me. I know it's not going to be easy but you need to know I'll be here for you, and if you want to talk about it, that's fine, and if you don't want to talk about it, that's fine too.'

'Good. Because I don't want to talk about it, not now or ever again. I want you to get out of my room and stay out.' She hurled the copy of *The Secret Garden* at the wall.

I stood up and walked towards the door. 'I'm sorry,' I said. 'More sorry than you'll ever know.'

*

She didn't come out of her room for the rest of the day. I took a sandwich up to her at lunchtime. When I took her tea up later, the sandwich remained outside, untouched. When I went up to bed later, they were both still there, as if she was spelling out her hurt in food, outside her bedroom door.

'Can I come in to say goodnight?' I asked softly.

'No,' came the reply.

'Night,' I said, my voice cracking. 'I love you.'

There was no reply. I sat on the landing, my back against the wall, my head bowed, listening to fireworks going off outside and my elder daughter crying herself to sleep.

23 September 1944

Dear Betty,

You were so brave today, my darling. Walking away without shedding a tear. You kept your promise to me and I will keep my promise to you. The one that came with the engagement ring. On the day of your eighteenth birthday, I will come knocking on your great-aunt Aggie's door and whisk you away to get married. I might even do what you suggested and take you to Gretna Green, if we can't wait until we get to Canada. And there will be nothing your great aunt or your parents or anyone else can do to stop me.

I wish I could have bought you a ring with the biggest diamond in the world on it but I hope that little one did for you just fine. Every time I go in Bettys Bar I will see where we etched our names in the mirror with it, alongside all the other bomber boys' names. We are there now forever. No one can take that away. It is a public record of our love.

You looked so beautiful today, Betty. A proper English rose. Keep the Yorkshire one I gave you. Maybe you could press it. You can eat the butterscotch, though. I don't think that will save! I would have given you the world if I could, because that's what you've given me. And remember what I told you when you said you were sorry you hadn't bought me a gift. You are carrying the most precious gift in the world, Betty. It is everything I could have wanted and more. Take care of our baby for me. I will be counting down the days until I can hold it, can feel its little fingers gripping mine.

I'm excited now just thinking about the future. There is so much to look forward to. And when we are old, we will look back on this time apart as a tiny speck in our lives.

Remember that, Betty darling, and be strong for me. I will be thinking of you every second of every day and through the longest nights ahead.

Take care of our precious baby until we meet again.

Yours always,

William

22

The next morning Ruby's Coco Pops bowl was empty when I went back upstairs after we'd had our breakfast. It was a start, at least. I knocked on the door and heard a muffled 'Yeah.' I went in. She was sitting up on her bed reading *The Secret Garden*.

'Can I get you anything else?' I asked. 'Toast? Tea?'

'No, thanks,' she said.

'Did you manage to get any sleep?' I asked.

She shrugged.

'I meant what I said. I'm here for you any time you need to talk.'

She nodded, biting down hard on her lip.

'James has gone to get your sister from Emily's,' I said. 'Maybe see if you can come down for lunch, eh?'

She nodded again. I shut the door softly behind me.

Ten minutes later Maisie careered into the kitchen, shattering the quiet that still hung over the house. 'I'm home,' she shouted, bounding up to me and giving me a hug. 'Did you miss me?'

'We missed your noise,' I said, smiling at her.

'Hey, that's not fair,' Maisie said, grabbing James's hand as he followed her in and twirling around it as I tried to dodge between them to get to the fridge.

'Well, I hope you two didn't keep Emily's mum awake all night with your chatter.'

'Giggling,' said Maisie. 'She said we kept her awake with our giggling.'

'Well, we'd better have Emily sleeping over here next time, give her poor mum a break.'

'When we're living at Great-grandma's house?' she asked.

I realised for the first time that it would always be Great-grandma's house. Whatever we did to it – central heating, new bathroom, repainting the whole place – it would still never be our house. The imprint she had left on it was too deep. It couldn't be painted over or covered up. The stories the house had witnessed couldn't be untold. And the pain of one of those stories would be etched on Mum's face forever. It hadn't been a home for her. Not even a house. It was the scene of a crime.

'Let's wait and see,' I said.

'Where's Ruby?' Maisie asked.

'In your room. Leave her be, we need to give her a bit of space today.'

'Is she being a teenager again?' asked Maisie.

'Something like that.'

'How about I take you down the park for a bit?' James said to Maisie. 'Let off some of that pent-up energy.'

'Yay,' said Maisie, running to get her scooter from the back yard.

James came over to me and put his hands on my shoulders. 'Give her time,' he said.

I nodded, though I had no idea how much time she was going to need.

DI Freeman rang as I was emptying the dishwasher. I checked that the kitchen door was closed before I answered.

'Sorry to bother you on a Sunday,' he said. 'We've had some developments.'

'Go on.'

'We've got the DNA results back from your mother and from John Armitage. I'm afraid they do match the third set of bones.'

Even though I had been expecting it, hearing it confirmed still shook me. I sat down at the kitchen table.

'OK,' I said, trying to stop my voice cracking.

'Do you want to tell your mother, or would you like us to do it?'

'No, I'll tell her, thanks,' I said.

'Armitage remains in custody,' DI Freeman went on. 'We're going to be charging him with rape and indecent assault, as well as criminal damage and threatening behaviour against you. He'll appear in court tomorrow. I think it's highly unlikely he'll be given bail.'

'Right. It'll be on the news again, won't it?'

'Yes, but there are strict rules for the media once he's been charged. They won't be able to link him to your family because it would identify your mother. My colleague DS Lockwood will be in touch with her tomorrow but I thought you might like to speak to her first, reassure her that she will remain anonymous.'

'Thanks. Yes, I will. Has he admitted what he did?'

'He's claiming it was consensual. Let's see how that washes in court when the jury hears she was fourteen at the time.'

'But they still get off, don't they? People like him get off all the time.'

'They do, but we're going to be doing everything in our power to make sure he's not one of them. We've found other photos of girls at his house. Some printed out, some on his computer. We're going to try to trace as many as we can. I don't think for a minute that your mother was his only victim.'

'And what about her baby?' I asked. 'Has he admitted killing her baby?'

'He's denying all knowledge of it. Says he thought your mother had aborted the baby or it had been adopted.'

'But he can't. It was him. It had to be him.'

DI Freeman sighed. 'He was particularly vehement in his denial.'

'You believe him, don't you?'

'It is possible someone else was involved. Unfortunately, your grandmother may have been the only one who knew what really happened to that baby.'

'You don't think she did it?'

'No, but I think she may have known who did.'

I sat there afterwards, staring at my phone on the table. I'd thought this was all sewn up. Now everything was up in the air again. What if DI Freeman was right? What if John was telling the truth and Grandma was the only one who had known what had happened? Not just to her own two babies but to Mum's as well. How were we ever going to uncover the truth?

I couldn't bear to think she'd taken those secrets with her to the grave. That she hadn't left some clue, or there wasn't someone still alive who could shed some light. And then I remembered that there was. And that I needed to talk to her before it was too late.

I was standing in the doorway with my jacket on, ready to go, when James arrived back with Maisie.

'Have a good time?' I asked.

'Daddy says I could get an Olympic medal in scootering.'

'I'm sure you could. Go and put it in the back yard, please. I've got to pop out now but Daddy will make you something nice for lunch. Be extra kind to Ruby, all right?'

She nodded and carried her scooter outside.

'What's up?' James asked, as soon as she was out of earshot.

'The police have rung. The baby next door was Mum and John's. They're charging him and he'll be in court tomorrow. They say he had photos of other girls at his house.'

'Filthy old bastard. I hope he gets what's coming to him.'

'He's denying it, mind. Saying it was consensual. So Mum will have to go through a trial. He's also denying killing the baby. DI Freeman believes him on that one.'

'So who does he think did it?'

'I don't know, but I'm going to see Olive. She's the only one I can think of who might know.'

'Are you sure that's a good idea?' asked James. 'I thought you said she was ill.'

'She is, but I've no choice. I need to find out before it's too late. I'll go and see Mum afterwards, too. I said I'd tell her before the police call tomorrow. Can you sort lunch for the three of you? Something involving sausages. Ruby will be down. Just keep an eye on her for me. It's probably better I'm not there, to be honest.'

I drove up the hill to Heptonstall, passing the turning to John's house and trying not to think about whether anyone had fed Bert the budgie. I pulled into the little car park behind the nursing-home and stood on the step outside, remembering the first time I had done this and how long ago it seemed now, though it was only a matter of weeks.

Dawn, the duty manager I'd spoken to before, came to the door. She recognised me straight away. 'Hello,' she said. 'We've been expecting John. He hasn't been for a couple of days – it's not like him at all.'

'Is there somewhere private I can have a word, please?' I asked.

'Yes,' she said, her expression changing at once. 'Come through to the office.'

I followed her into a tiny room with beige walls, a sorry-looking pot plant and a stack of ring-binders on the desk. 'I'm afraid John's not going to be able to come for a while,' I said.

'Oh dear, is he ill?'

'No, he's er, been arrested. He'll be appearing in court tomorrow on some very serious charges. It's unlikely he'll be able to visit again.'

I watched Dawn's eyes widen, a frown crease her brow.

'Oh, goodness. That's come as a shock.'

'It's been a very difficult few days. I wondered if I could try to explain to Olive,' I said. 'I'll obviously spare her the details. I just want to try to get her to understand that he won't be visiting.'

'Right. Yes, of course.'

'How is she? John said she had pneumonia.'

Dawn's frown deepened. 'Not pneumonia, no. She's had a bad cold but she's a bit brighter this morning. She's in her room.'

Clearly John had been trying to put me off visiting.

'I see. Can I come through?'

Dawn led me out of the office and along the corridor to a door at the far end. She opened it and I stepped inside. Olive was sitting in her armchair next to the bed, wearing a cheerful yellow cardigan. I wished I'd stopped to buy some biscuits at the shop, anything that might help to break the ice and get her talking again.

'Hello, Olive, you've got a visitor,' said Dawn. 'Nicola, Betty's granddaughter. She came to see you before.'

Olive looked at me blankly, I wasn't sure if she remembered

at all. 'Is Betty here?' she said. 'There's some nice shortbread in the biscuit barrel.'

'No. Betty's not here.'

'Is John here, then? They've saved a wafer for him.'

I turned to Dawn, who gave me a little smile. 'Call me if you need me,' she whispered, and left the room.

'John couldn't make it today,' I said, sitting down on the bed.

'Is he playing out? I told him to make sure he got back for his tea.'

I sighed, unsure how to respond and whether I might be better off not saying any more. I had to tell her, though. It wasn't fair to deny her the truth, whether she could understand it or not.

'I'm afraid John won't be coming to visit for a long while,' I said. 'The police have found out, you see. Found out what he did to my mother, Irene.'

For a second, I thought there was a flicker of something on her face but it was gone before I could work out what it was.

'When we were chatting before,' I continued, 'you were telling me about the fairy statues in Betty's garden.'

'Oh, aye, pretty little things they were.'

'I didn't know you had one in your garden too.'

Olive looked at me for a moment, then the frown on her face cleared. 'Yes, I've had it years. Not as long as Betty's had hers, of course, but still a fair while.'

'Who gave it to you, Olive?'

'Would you like one, love? Betty'll get you one. She got that one for me.'

'So Betty gave it to you?'

'Yes, so it would match hers.'

I nodded slowly. I was frightened to go on but I knew I had to. 'Why did you need it, Olive? What was buried underneath it?'

I caught it this time. Her look of horror. She did understand and she knew exactly what I was talking about.

'It were just a garden ornament, same as hers.'

'Except it wasn't, was it, Olive? There was a baby buried underneath it, my mother Irene's baby. And your son John's.'

'No,' she said. 'John had nothing to do with it. He was always a good boy.'

She was scared, I could see that. Scared of what would happen to John, or maybe scared of what he would do to her, if she told me the truth.

'John can't do anything to you now, Olive. The police have arrested him. He's going to be charged and he'll be appearing in court tomorrow. They know he raped my mother but we need to know what happened to their baby.'

'Nurse,' she called.

'Please, Olive. Betty took her secret to the grave but you've still got time to tell me yours.'

She pressed the buzzer next to the bed. Dawn hurried in. 'I don't know this woman,' she said. 'I want her to go.'

I gave Dawn a shrug and stood up. 'I'm sorry to have upset you, Olive,' I said. 'I just thought you should know.'

I headed out of the door. Dawn shut it firmly behind us.

'Sorry,' I said. 'I hope I haven't upset her too much.'

'We'll keep a close eye on her. I think it will hit her hard, mind, John not coming any more. It's such a shame for her to have lost her son. To have no one there for her at the end of her life.'

'Look,' I said, taking out a scrap of paper and a pen from my bag. 'I'm aware John was the only person who visited her. If she changes her mind and would like me to visit again, here's my number. I'd be only too happy to help.'

Dawn took it. I walked back down the corridor, aware I was leaving behind any hope I had of getting to the truth.

Mum knew as soon as she opened the door and saw me standing there. 'It was my baby, wasn't it?' she whispered.

I stepped inside, closing the door behind me. 'I'm sorry,' I said, giving her a hug. 'The police said his DNA matched too. They're charging him with rape and indecent assault, and with criminal damage and threatening behaviour to me. He's appearing in court tomorrow. You haven't got to go but he is claiming it was consensual, so I'm afraid there will be a trial.'

Mum shook her head. 'He's going to drag my name through the mud,' she said. 'Like he always threatened to.'

'No. The media aren't allowed to identify you. It's him who will be on the stand, not you. The police say he won't be given bail. You don't need to worry about him. He can't get to you. He can't hurt you any more.'

Mum's face was ashen. 'Did he say he killed my baby?' she asked.

I took a deep breath. 'He told them he didn't do it. Said he knew nothing about it. The detective I spoke to said he was adamant about that.'

Mum broke down, sobbing. 'I need to know,' she said. 'I need to know who killed my baby.'

I took her arm and led her through to the front room. I lowered her onto the sofa and sat with her awhile before I went to make a cup of tea.

I was in the kitchen when my phone rang. A number I didn't recognise.

'Hello,' I said.

'Nicola, it's Dawn from the home. It's Olive. She's asking to see Irene.'

Not a day went by when I didn't think of her. Where she was, how she was doing, who she called Mummy. The house echoed with her absence, yet it was a silent echo. I slept in the room where she was both brutally created and cruelly snatched from me. It was like being in a prison cell for victims, where your assailant comes to laugh at you and poke a stick through the bars.

It wasn't only my bedroom: he had contaminated the whole house. I couldn't pick up the post from the mat because I knew he had touched it. I couldn't put the kettle on without hearing him whistling. I couldn't look out of the window for fear I would see him walking up the path.

The day he moved was the only bright spot in a sea of darkness. I listened to the van taking their things away, removing them from the house next door. Although I couldn't help wishing I could remove him so easily from ours.

And with every day that passed, I missed my daughter more. The fact that no one spoke of her again did not mean she had no presence. She was present in the silences at family mealtimes, the looks Mum and Dad exchanged, the laughter we never shared. The shadow she cast over the house was immense.

And if my parents had thought that getting rid of her would be the best thing for me, they couldn't have been more wrong. Without the determination to better myself so I could give her a good life, I lost all interest in learning. Without a daughter I wanted to be proud of me, I left school at the earliest opportunity without any exams and got a dead-end job in a shop. Without a reason for looking after myself and getting up in the mornings, I fell into depression.

It was not better for me to have her ripped away. I didn't forget what had happened to me simply because the result of that abuse had been removed from me. Instead I relived it every day as I went about my mundane, empty life, and every night as I lay in bed unable to sleep. Worrying about her, hoping she was living a better life than she would have had with me and hoping that when she grew up, whoever had given her a home would tell her the truth and she would come looking for me. If she didn't hate me too much for what I had done to her, that was.

Until then, I would continue to live in this prison that was home, surrounded by the sound of him, the smell of him and the taste of him in my mouth. It was punishment for my sin. For the shame I had brought on my family. For although nobody ever spoke of what had happened, an invisible film of shame coated me and the house. You could take the baby from the girl, but you could never take away the shame of what she had done.

23

We drove up to Heptonstall in silence. Mum had been adamant that she would come. She needed answers, I understood that. What worried me was whether she could cope with what she heard.

Dawn greeted us at the door. She led us down the corridor and stopped outside Irene's room.

'Do you want me to stay with you?' she asked.

'No, thanks,' I replied. 'I'll call if I need you, though.'

I opened the door and went in, Mum a few hesitant steps behind me. Olive was still sitting in the chair, as if she hadn't moved. She was squinting at Mum behind me. I turned and beckoned. Mum stepped forward and held out her hand. Olive grasped it – grasped it as if she would never let go.

'She were a pretty little thing,' Olive said.

'Who was?' I asked.

'The baby.'

'You saw my baby?' Mum asked, sitting down heavily on the bed.

'Betty asked me if I knew of anyone, see, after her Irene got herself in trouble.'

Mum turned to me, frowning. I shook my head, aware we needed to let her go on.

'I said my niece Jennifer would have it. She and her husband had been trying for years, poor mite. That's why she brought it to me after she were born. As soon as I looked at it, I knew.

'Even though it were a little girl, it were spitting image of our John. You never forget what your first-born looks like.'

'So did you say anything?' I asked. 'To Betty, I mean.'

'No. I think she knew too, mind. Just summat in the way she looked at me.'

We were interrupted by one of the care workers coming in to ask Olive if she'd like a drink.

'Cup of tea would be nice, lovey.'

The woman turned to ask if Mum and I wanted one. 'No thanks,' I said. I waited till she'd gone before prompting Olive to continue. 'So what happened to the baby?'

'Whose baby?'

Mum looked at me again, the hope fading from her face.

'Irene's,' I replied. 'You were telling me about Irene and John's baby.'

'That's right,' she said. 'Terrible business.'

'What was, Olive?'

'Harold were laid off from work. The factory gave a dozen of them their cards and sent them home at lunchtime. And I were sitting there, holding the baby, rocking it back and forth when he came in. I told him. I said it were our John's baby and he'd got Irene into trouble. He flew into a right rage. Said it were nowt to do with us and I were to get rid of it straight away, take it back to Betty's and let her deal with it.

'You didn't argue with Harold when he were in a mood like that. And he'd been in pub for a couple of swift halves on the way home. I handed the baby to him while I went to get my coat and shoes. Only when I came back into front room, the baby were just lying there on the settee. It had stopped breathing. Harold said he hadn't done owt but I could see the cushion behind her had been put back in a different place.'

I shut my eyes, wishing I could remove the image that was now in my head but knowing it would be there forever. I reached out to clasp Mum's hand. It was clammy and trembling.

'What did you do, Olive?'

'I panicked. Didn't know what to do. Our John were going to be home soon and I didn't want him to see it and get upset. So we buried it at bottom of garden. Harold dug the hole and I put it in there. Still wrapped up in her blanket, she were. Me own grandchild. Only one I ever had, as it turned out.'

Olive broke off as she started to cry. Beautiful, clear tears glistening down the paper-thin skin of her cheeks. I reached out my other hand and took hers. And I sat there, holding hands with the two women who had once held my half-sister.

'Why didn't you tell my mum?' I asked eventually.

Olive frowned.

'Irene. My mum. The lady here. She never knew what had happened to her baby.'

'No. I've never talked about it since, see. Well, only to Betty.

She came around the next day and asked how the baby were getting on at Jennifer's and I burst into tears. I only told her half the story, though I think she guessed the rest. She never spoke to Harold again.

'I asked her if she wanted the body moved to her garden but she said she didn't like to disturb her, just wanted grave marked.'

'And that's when she gave you the fairy statue?' I asked.

'That's right. She said not to tell Irene. Said it would break her heart. That she'd rather let her live with some hope of her daughter finding her one day.'

Mum let out an anguished cry. I squeezed her hand. The hand of a fourteen-year-old girl, who had just found out what had happened to her baby. And how her mum, who had lost two of her own, clearly hadn't wanted her to go through the same heartache.

'And John never knew?'

'No. Never asked owt about baby. We moved a few months afterwards. I thought it were best in the circumstances. And I were too scared to say owt. Scared of Harold and then scared of John. I knew what they were both capable of, see.'

The care worker came back with Olive's tea and popped it on the table next to her.

I stood up, aware from Mum's face that she needed to go.

'Thank you for telling us, Olive,' I said.

'That's all right, lovey,' she said. 'John will be here soon. They've saved a wafer for him.'

*

I sat with Mum for a long time when I got her home. She'd been silent on the drive back to Halifax. Even now, she looked like a dazed boxer who'd suffered a knock-out punch and was being counted out on the deck. I wasn't sure if she'd even be able to get up off the canvas, let alone go ten rounds with John in court when the time came. All the years of suffering, of not knowing, and when she finally got to the truth, it was so grim as to be unbearable.

'How could he do that?' she said eventually. 'Snuff out a little life like that with his big, dirty hands. She wasn't even an hour old. She didn't deserve to die like that.'

'I know,' I said. 'And I'm so sorry. It's such a horrible thing to find out.'

'Mum was right, though,' she said. 'I couldn't have coped with knowing, not back then. At least now I have a family of my own around me. I have something to live for.'

I thought of Grandma and what she must have gone through with the loss of her own babies – whatever had happened to them. And then I thought of the woman who had taken my mother's baby away when it was only a few minutes old and given it to the mother of the man who had raped her. It was difficult, nigh on impossible, to reconcile the two.

'I still don't understand how she could have taken your baby, though,' I said. 'Not after losing her own.'

'People react differently to loss, I suppose. And they were scared – so many women were scared of men, even the ones they were married to. It's like Olive said, they knew what they were capable of.'

I rang DI Freeman when I got home. Told him the whole story.

'And you think she was telling the truth?' he asked.

'I don't think she's capable of lying, not now.'

'We will need to interview her formally, but thank you, you've been a great help.'

'It's probably best if you send a woman,' I said. 'Preferably with some biscuits.'

I put down the phone and looked at James. 'That's it, then,' I said. 'At least we got an answer for Mum, as horrible as it was.'

'You mean you did,' said James.

'I just wish I could get some answers for Grandma. Well, not for her, she knew what happened, but to clear her name, at least. I want to go back to the house again. I still think it's my best chance of finding something.'

'I need to pop along sometime this week too,' he replied. 'Start measuring up for the central heating.'

I looked down at my hands and sighed.

'What?' asked James.

'I don't know any more,' I said. 'Whether we should move there, I mean.'

'It's a bit late for that. We've accepted the offer.'

'It's all the stuff about Mum and knowing what went on in that house. It feels like we'd be punishing her again by moving there. She won't come and visit us. She can't. It brings it all back for her.'

'But you didn't want to go against your grandma's wishes.'

'She was protecting the babies. She wanted someone to guard them. We don't have to do that now. They're not there.'

'You want us to turn down the offer?'

'I don't know what I want. But I do know it's not right for Mum, and I don't think it's right for Ruby, either. She knows too much about what happened there. I don't want either of the girls to have to sleep in that bedroom.'

'So what's the alternative?' asked James.

'I don't know,' I replied. 'But I'll find one.'

'Maybe we can drop the girls at your mum's after school and go over together to have a proper look around. If you're not too shattered after work, that is.'

'I'm not going to work tomorrow,' I said. 'I've already texted Fiona.'

'Good,' he replied. 'You've been through a hell of a lot. You need a day off.'

I shook my head. 'I'm going to court,' I said.

James frowned at me. 'You're not serious?'

'I am. And don't try to talk me out of it because my mind's made up. That man has caused pain and hurt to four generations of my family. Well, now it's my turn to see him suffer. And I'm going to sit there and stare at him, make sure he knows I'm not going to miss a moment of it.'

'Do you want me to come with you? I can take the morning off work if it helps.'

'No, thanks,' I said. 'This is something I've got to do on my own.'

'I've probably never told you this before,' he said, 'but I'm dead proud of you.'

The following morning, Maisie was already downstairs with James when I knocked on the girls' bedroom door. Ruby was brushing her hair, staring at the reflection of her new self in the mirror.

'How are you doing?' I asked.

'Fine.'

'Are you sure you're up to school today?' She had insisted on going, even when I'd told her I was taking the day off.

'Yeah.'

'Look, just so you know, it'll be on the news again later,' I said. 'He's going to appear in court today to be charged. They won't mention Grandma's name, though. So hopefully no one at school will know.'

'There were a few kids from school in the cinema,' she said. 'That's why I changed my mind about going. What if his photo's on the news or they show him going into court? They might recognise him.'

'Just say they're mistaken. Say it was your grandad. I don't suppose any of them looked that closely.'

She put the brush down and turned to me. 'It was their baby, wasn't it? The one they found in Andrea's garden. What happened to it?'

'It's a very sad story,' I said.

'Please tell me.'

'I'm not sure now's a good time.'

'It is,' she said.

I sighed. 'After it was born, Great-grandma took the baby from Grandma and gave it to Olive. She was going to give it to her married niece, let her adopt it. People did things like that in those days. Only it all went wrong when Olive realised it was John's baby. John's father came home and smothered it with a cushion.'

Ruby sat down on the end of her bed.

'Sorry,' I said. 'That's why I didn't want to tell you.'

Ruby sat there staring at the wall. I wondered if I had said too much.

'Grandma was only a year older than I am now,' she said, after a while. 'She must have been so scared, so upset.'

'It's horrible. The only little shred of comfort is the baby wouldn't have felt anything. She wouldn't have suffered at all.'

'Why did Great-grandma take the baby away?'

'Back in those days, it was a massive thing, love, an unmarried teenage girl getting pregnant. People said it brought shame on the family.'

'But he raped her. Like that man raped you. It wasn't your fault and it wasn't Grandma's fault.'

I shut my eyes. I hadn't expected that. My shoulders started to shake. 'Thank you,' I said, my head bowed so she wouldn't see the tears.

She reached out and took my hand. 'I'm sorry,' she whispered.

'What on earth for?'

'All that horrible stuff I said about you.'

'You had every right to be angry.'

'Not at you, though,' she said. 'You're the last person I should be mad at.'

We sat in silence for a moment or two.

'Are you going to report him?' she asked eventually.

'No,' I said. 'It's too late for that.'

'But it's not too late for Grandma. She's reported what he did to her.'

'I know, love. But that's because she knew his name and where he lived. I don't know anything about him at all.'

'Will you tell Grandma?' she asked.

'I think so. But not straight away. She's having to deal with so much right now and I don't want to throw something else in on top.'

'What about Maisie?' Ruby asked.

I shook my head. 'No, she's too young and she doesn't need to know. If you want to tell her one day when she's older, that's up to you.'

'OK,' she said. 'Maybe when she's much older. I'll see.' She fell silent again. 'You don't think I'm like him, do you?' she asked, after a minute or two. 'What if I've got something bad in me? What if I got it from him?'

I turned to face Ruby and put my arms round her. 'I don't think you've got an ounce of bad in you. I don't think I've ever met anyone who has more good in them than you do.'

She nodded, seemingly reassured, and picked up her school bag from the floor.

*

I sat in the public gallery; my hair tucked back neatly behind my ears, the collar of my freshly pressed shirt standing to attention. I wanted to show him that he couldn't break our family. He had hurt us, had taken a sick pleasure in tormenting us and making us suffer, but he was not going to get the satisfaction of thinking he'd broken us because he hadn't. We were still standing and he would not beat us.

A door opened and he came into the courtroom, escorted by two security guards, although they were hardly going to be needed. He cut a pathetic figure, standing there in his shabby brown jumper, his back stooped, suddenly looking every day of his seventy years.

He listened as the magistrate read out the charges and asked how he pleaded.

'Not guilty,' he said, in a shaky voice. His application for bail was refused, due to the seriousness of the charges. The magistrate told him that he would be remanded in custody until the trial. He started walking forlornly back towards the door, the guards at his side. He looked up for only a second as he passed me. It was long enough, though. Long enough to let him know I was there and I would not allow him to destroy my family.

Afterwards I drove straight to Grandma's house. As I pulled up outside I noticed that there was something on her doorstep. My first thought was that it would be bones, that somehow John had left them there before he was arrested. As I got nearer, I could see it wasn't bones. It was flowers, a bouquet of lilies and freesias. I picked them up. A small envelope was inside the cellophane, addressed to me. I took it out and read the message: 'To Nicola and family, sending love and thoughts, Andrea and family.'

I glanced over to her house in case she was watching from the window. I should go and knock, really, to say thank you. It was the least I could do with everything they'd been through.

She came to the door quickly and smiled as soon as she saw me standing there, the flowers in my hand. 'Thank you,' I said. 'They're much appreciated.'

'I'm glad you got them safely, I didn't have your address but hoped you might be over. They're for all of you.'

I imagined she must have worked out at least part of what had happened. 'Thanks,' I said.

'I was wondering if you'd like the fairy statue from our garden. It doesn't seem right for us to have it, in the circumstances.'

I was unsure whether Mum would want it, but decided to say yes. 'Thank you. That's very kind. Can I pick it up another time, please? I've got some things to sort in the house now.'

'Yes, of course. Whenever you're ready.'

I let myself into Grandma's house. There was an envelope on the mat. Again, my first thought was that it would be a threatening note of some kind. I opened it, edging the piece of paper from the envelope painfully slowly, until I could be sure there was nothing else inside. I unfolded it and started to read. It was from an elderly man in the village. He said he'd known Betty for years and was sad to hear of her passing. He then went on to ask if we were planning to sell her house, only his daughter and her husband were looking to move to be near him and he wondered if they might be able to have a look around.

I stared at it in disbelief. It was like being handed a get-out-of-jail-free card. This was a way out. Maybe we could still sell our house and find somewhere else in Hebden. Somewhere with three bedrooms and a little garden. Somewhere that wasn't here. A place we could all be happy.

I put the letter back into the envelope and slipped it inside my bag. I'd ring James later. See what he thought. I went through to the kitchen. It was exactly as I'd left it on Thursday when Mum had turned up unexpectedly. It was incredible to think that only four days had passed since then. So much had happened. So many secrets had come tumbling out. But there was still one left to be told.

I picked up the biscuit barrel from the floor and went to put it back on the shelf. Something had fallen down and was blocking it. I rummaged behind and felt it straight away: a rusty little tin. I lifted it down. Beneath the rust, it was dark green, with a little white rose on each end. On the lid it said 'Rowntrees Butterscotch' and there was a picture of York Minster. At either end there were two royal crests with 'By appointment to H.M. The King' written above and below them. I shook the tin gently. Something tinkled inside. I opened it. There was a ring. It looked like an engagement ring with a tiny diamond. I picked it up and held it up to the light. Grandma must have worn this. Grandma had planned to get married to somebody else entirely.

I put the ring back. Beneath it was the pressed head of a white rose. My breath quickened. They were from him, the father of her babies. They had to be. I shut the lid, feeling as if I'd just opened an Egyptian tomb and peered inside. Personal artefacts preserved for future generations to wonder at. I stepped back and looked up at the pantry, wondering if any other treasures were stored there. I fetched the stool from under the kitchen counter, the rickety one I'd always told Grandma wasn't safe to use. I put it down next to the pantry and climbed up to reach the top shelf. It was covered with what appeared to be a mixture of flour and dust. There were a few half-used packets of flour. Some jars of what looked like homemade jam, preserved in time. And a tin. A bigger one than the first. I reached up and dragged it forward to a point where I could pick it up. The one thing I knew straight away was that I'd never seen it before. That was what interested me most. That, and the fact that it was worn and rusty and had a distinctly wartime feel to it.

I climbed down and sat on the stool to open the lid. There were letters inside. Lots of them. Handwritten on pale blue Royal Canadian Air Force paper. My hands were trembling as I took out the bundle, which had been tied with a piece of blue ribbon. Tied by Betty, I had no doubt. A date was written in the right-hand corner of the top letter: 28 April 1944. I untied them and flicked through quickly to see if they were in order. They were. I started reading the first, immediately transported to a different time and place. I tried to imagine Betty as a shy Land Girl, left blushing by the young airman. It was signed 'William'. It was him, the father of her babies. It had to be.

I raced through the rest of the letters, struggling to comprehend that this was real, this was my grandmother's life, not some wartime love story I'd stumbled across in a magazine. I loved how William had stood by her when she got pregnant, loved his pure, boyish optimism about the future. Yet all the time I was reading, I was thinking, How does this end? How can something so beautiful end with two babies buried in a back garden? And then I got to the last letter, the one where he talked of their date at Bettys in York. How they'd etched their names in the mirror there with the diamond engagement ring he'd given her.

The letters appeared to end abruptly when she was sent away to her great-aunt Aggie. William had promised to write. Had he not kept that promise? Or had Aggie destroyed the letters before they'd ever got to Grandma?

I put the last letter down on my lap, frustrated to be left hanging like that. I folded them and tied the ribbon around them. Maybe that was as close to what happened as I was going to get. It was only as I went to put them back into the tin that I noticed the envelope at the bottom. It was addressed to William at Linton-on-Ouse. And it was in Grandma's handwriting. Stamped on the envelope was 'Return to Sender'. I picked it up. It had never been opened. I turned it over to find Grandma's address circled on the back.

I got up and took a knife from Grandma's cutlery drawer, carefully slitting the top, then taking out the letter and starting to read.

5 March 1945

Dear William,

I am so sorry. I hardly know how to begin this letter. I know I promised to look after your baby but I didn't, couldn't, and I'm so dreadfully sorry.

The baby was born sleeping and so was the other one. There were two of them, William. A boy and a girl. I was carrying twins, although I didn't know it up to the birth. My family had forbidden me to leave the house. I wasn't allowed to see a doctor or a midwife, so I'd had no idea, no idea at all.

I laboured on my own. Great-aunt Aggie provided hot towels and water but she has never had a child of her own so she didn't really know what to do.

It was hard, William. The hardest thing I have ever done in my life but I thought of you and everything you have been through in this war and that was how I kept going.

But when he finally came, there was no sound from

him, no intake of breath or heart-wrenching cry. He was silent and peaceful. He was perfect in every single way apart from the fact that he was not breathing. I held his little hands and imagined how it would feel to have his fingers grasp mine, and I cried because I knew that would never happen and because I'd broken my promise to you. I hadn't taken good enough care of our baby.

I was still crying when I felt something else inside me and I realised it wasn't over yet, that there was another one coming. And as I struggled with the pain, I dared to hope that it would be different, that this would be the baby we had dreamt of. But she wasn't. She too was born sleeping, although she was perfect in every other way. She had dark hair and rosebud lips and tiny, perfectly formed fingers. She was so very beautiful, William. You would have adored her.

I wanted to keep them and hold them for longer. To be honest, I wanted to keep them to show you when you came. But Great-aunt Aggie said we couldn't do that. Said we had to bury them right away. She dug the holes in the back garden. She's very strong, says it's from working in the mills all her life. And she came back and told me their graves were ready and I cried so hard. I couldn't bear to be parted from my babies. Great aunt Aggie told me to be quiet. That no one must hear. She said I had to bear my pain in silence and that it was God's will that my babies had been taken. That it was a blessing and I would now be able to forget all about them and get on with my life.

I screamed at her, William. I told her she was wrong, that God was wrong to have taken our babies and that I would never forget them, or forgive Him, until my dying day.

I wanted to climb into those holes with them and hold them and never let them go. To make up for being such a bad mother by being with them in death. The only thing that stopped me doing that was you. Because it would be too much for one person to bear to lose everything.

So I kissed my babies goodbye and I whispered to them that I loved them and that their daddy loved them and they were to sleep tightly forever until we could be with them again.

I am so sorry to have to write this letter to you, William. I feel awful for having let you down and I pray that you forgive me. All you asked of me was to look after our baby and I couldn't do it for you. I couldn't protect either of them.

When you come for me, William, when the war is over, we will lay flowers for them and mark their graves in some way. Until then I will stand watch over them. I will not fail them in death as I did in life.

Yours always,

Betty

24

I finished reading and brought the piece of paper to my face. It even smelt of Grandma. How could that be from so many years ago? I sat there, numb inside, holding the letter. And I whispered to her, in the vain hope that she could somehow hear. Whispered the words that three generations of my family had needed to hear. 'It wasn't your fault.'

I sat there for some time, rereading the letters, making sure I had taken in every single detail.

I suspected I already knew why Grandma's letter had been returned to her unopened but I still got my phone out and did a search of Linton-on-Ouse air base in the Second World War anyway. Just to see it for myself. To know for certain. A Wartime Memories Project website came up. They listed all the service personnel killed, who had flown out of the air base during the war. I scrolled through it. There were a lot of names, each one with a story attached to it, no doubt. A story of loss and heartache. I found the entry eventually. William Thomas Harrington (died 5 March 1945). I shut my eyes and held Grandma's letter tighter to me. He'd never read it because he'd died the day she'd written it. All I could think was that at least she'd had that tiny shred of comfort when the letter had been returned to her. That her William had gone to his death not knowing that she'd lost his baby. Still full of youthful optimism, of the hopes and dreams of the life they would build together when the war was over.

Further down there was a report of that final ill-fated mission. The three Halifax planes from Thunderbird squadron had taken off mid-afternoon for the long haul to Germany. They hadn't even managed to leave Yorkshire. Within minutes of taking off, they encountered severe icing in the fog. One collided with a plane from Goose Squadron, another came down in a nearby village. The third, the one that listed Flight Lieutenant William Harrington among the dead, broke up under the weight of ice and crashed into houses on the outskirts of York, killing all but one of the crew and several people on the ground.

I sat there, tears running down my cheeks and falling onto Grandma's letter. When life could be so cruel, perhaps it was no wonder that it could leave someone with a shard of ice in their heart.

My phone beeped as I was packing up to go home, the tin containing the bundle of letters tucked safely inside my bag. I got it out. It was from Ruby: *I'm on my way home. I'm OK but I got a bit upset earlier. They've said to take the afternoon off.*

She was getting off the bus at the end of our road as I turned into it. I pulled over and jumped out, running over to her. She let me fold my arms around her. Let me stroke her hair and kiss her.

'Are you OK?' I asked.

'Yeah. I guess I didn't realise how much it had all got to me.'

'I'll phone them this afternoon and explain,' I said. She pulled back, alarmed. 'Not everything,' I said. 'Just some of it. I'll tell them you need a bit of time off. They'll be fine. Come on. Let's have a hot chocolate without Maisie knowing.'

James came straight home from work when I messaged him, even though I told him he didn't need to.

'I do,' he said. 'I've got two of you to take care of.'

We went for a walk after lunch. Just the three of us, up to Gaddings Dam at the top of the moors. The last time we'd attempted it, Maisie had complained so much about her legs hurting on the steep climb to the top that we'd given up and turned back.

This time, Ruby set the pace, striding out in front of us and using her walking pole to steady herself on the steepest parts. We didn't say much, partly because it was such hard work we didn't have the breath to talk and partly because we didn't need to. It was enough that we were all together.

We paused at the top to look down across the valley to the Stoodley Pike monument on the hills beyond. The autumn colours were so rich and warm I wanted to wrap myself up in them against the cold, against everything our family had to deal with in the coming days, weeks and months.

James took my hand and gave it a squeeze.

'It's just the wind,' I said, brushing away the tears at the corners of my eyes. He squeezed my hand harder. He knew me too well.

'Can I climb along the rocks to the other side?' asked Ruby.

'Yeah,' I said. She set off.

'I'll go with her,' said James.

'No,' I replied, catching hold of his arm. 'Give her some time on her own. I think she needs it. She's got a lot to get her head around.'

We watched her pick her way carefully across the rocks to the far side. Saw her stand, silhouetted against the sun, pick up a handful of pebbles and throw them one by one into the dam. Waiting each time for the ripples from the one before to disperse before she flung the next.

'Do you think she's going to be OK?' James asked.

'Yeah, I do. I'm not saying it's going to be easy but she's strong. Way stronger than me. She'll come through it.'

'And what about you?' asked James.

'I'll be fine, once I stop beating myself up over everything I've done and shouldn't have done, and everything I should have done but didn't.'

'You're way too hard on yourself.'

'I don't know. Maybe I've got a lot to be hard on myself about.'

'Or maybe you don't get told often enough how amazing you are.'

'Don't go all soppy on me,' I said, nudging James in the ribs. 'You're a Yorkshireman, remember.'

I looked up and watched Ruby hurl a huge stone, more

like a rock, into the dam. We heard the sound of the roar she made as she did so, even from where we were. The ripples stretched out across the surface. Ruby stood staring into the freezing cold water below, before turning and starting to pick her way back across the rocks.

'Shall we tell him now?' I asked, when she got back to us.

Ruby nodded.

'Tell me what?' asked James.

'We had a chat earlier. Ruby would like you to be her father, officially, I mean. She wants to take up your offer to adopt her.'

James looked from Ruby's face to mine and back to Ruby's. They both burst into tears at exactly the same time, then stepped forward and embraced each other.

'Thank you,' James whispered into her hair.

'Come on, you two,' I said, when they finally separated. 'There's leftover pizza in the fridge to eat before Maisie gets back.'

James went to fetch Maisie from school.

'Why's Ruby home?' she asked, as soon as she got back. 'Why isn't she in her school uniform?'

'She got some time off for good behaviour,' I said. 'Anyway, we've some exciting news for you.'

'Am I getting the puppy now?' asked Maisie.

'No,' I said, with a smile. 'Daddy's going to adopt Ruby. It means he'll officially be her daddy too.'

'Yay,' said Maisie. 'So she won't be going to live with her other daddy?'

'I haven't got another dad any more,' said Ruby.

'Do you mind?' asked Maisie.

'No,' Ruby replied. 'I don't mind at all.'

'And the other news,' I said, looking at Ruby, 'is that we won't be moving to Great-grandma's house, after all. We've found somebody else to buy it. We think it will suit them better than us. And we're going to find somewhere new so you can still have your own rooms and a garden.'

Ruby smiled at me. I suspected she would have cried if she'd had any tears left.

'Will we still get the puppy?' Maisie asked.

'We will,' I said. 'But you might have to wait a little while longer until we get everything sorted.'

It was the ordinariness of everything the next morning that was so comforting. The walk to school, Maisie charging up to Emily as if she hadn't seen her for two weeks, not twenty-four hours, Reuben Johnson forgetting his PE kit, even the moaning and grumbling in the staffroom at break.

I'd decided not to tell Fiona everything now. For a start, fifteen minutes wasn't nearly long enough. But, more importantly, I wanted a day away from it, a day remembering what life had been like before all this had kicked off. I'd arrange a meet-up soon, one evening after school, when I could fill her in. For now, I wanted to return to some kind of normality before the next round of changes began.

'Had any luck with the job hunting?' she asked, putting a mug of coffee down in front of me.

'No,' I said. 'I haven't really had a chance and, to be honest, I think I might do something different.'

'Great,' she said. 'Like what?'

'Teaching,' I replied. 'I'm thinking of getting a degree and doing my teacher training. You have permission to tell me how stupid that is.'

'It's not stupid, it's brilliant,' she said. 'I've always told you you'd be an amazing teacher.'

'Thank you. It just had to be the right time for me, I guess.'

'Well, as you're wanting teaching experience, I think I've found just the right person to be in charge of the year-six Christmas show extravaganza.'

I smiled at her. 'I'm the sad Martin Freeman character in the remake of *Nativity*, aren't I?'

'Got it in one,' she said. 'And, no, you can't have real donkeys. This is Hebden Bridge. We'd have an animal-rights protest on our hands.'

I saw the text message from Dawn at the nursing home when I got home that afternoon. I rang her back as soon as Maisie had gone up to her room.

'Hello, Nicola,' she said. I knew straight away from her tone but let her go on anyway. 'I'm afraid Olive passed away this afternoon,' she said. 'It was very peaceful. She slipped away in her sleep.'

I thought of the lady in the yellow cardigan whose hand I had held two days ago. Who had asked me to bring Mum to her because she needed to tell her something. A secret she didn't want to take to the grave.

'Thank you,' I said. 'I think it's probably for the best. I think she was ready to go.'

EPILOGUE

I rang Mum's bell and she answered straight away. She was starting to look a little better. The plumpness had returned to her cheeks. Her lipstick was firmly in place.

'Hello,' she said, smiling at Ruby next to me. 'Come in a second before we go. I want to show Ruby where I've put it.'

We followed her through the house to the back door. It was only a small garden, not much more than a yard, really. But there was a little flower border along the back by the fence where we'd cleared a space for it. The fairy statue's face was turned towards the morning sun.

'I think it's a good spot for it, isn't it?' said Mum.

Ruby nodded. 'She looks happy here,' she said.

'Good,' Mum replied. 'I'm happy to have her too. You must bring Maisie to see her soon. She'll like that.'

'Are you ready?'

'Yes,' said Mum, taking a deep breath.

'Are you sure about this?' I asked Ruby. 'I can drop you back home with James and Maisie if you've changed your mind.'

'No,' said Ruby. 'I want to be there.'

We got into the car, Mum climbing into the back with Ruby.

'Who are they from?' asked Mum, spotting the two wreaths on the front passenger seat, beautiful hoops of delicate cream daisies.

'William's niece, Deirdre,' I said. 'She ordered them online from Winnipeg.'

She'd got in touch after I'd posted a message on the Wartime Memories Project website. She hadn't known about Betty. Although she had always wondered who the Land Army girl was in the photos that had been returned to William's family.

'That was nice of her,' said Mum.

'Great-grandma would have liked that, wouldn't she?' asked Ruby.

'Yes,' I said. 'She would.'

I turned into the gates of the cemetery and pulled up in one of the three spaces next to the chapel. They'd said I could park there because we were the only mourners. Mum had insisted it should be private and she was right. The public had had their turn to gawp and speculate. It was our chance for quiet, privacy and solitude. For closure.

The funeral car swung through the gates and parked in front of the chapel. I gripped Ruby's hand tightly on one side and Mum's even more tightly on the other, as the first of three tiny coffins was brought out, Mum's wreath of yellow roses sitting on top.

The other two followed. I stepped forward and placed the wreaths from William's family on each of them, alongside our own, and took a photograph of them, as I'd promised Deirdre I would.

The undertakers stood for a moment, then carried each coffin forward into the chapel. We followed, Mum dabbing at her eyes with a tissue, Ruby staring stoically straight ahead.

We sat in the front pew on the right-hand side. The young vicar nodded at us, gave a tentative smile. I don't suppose he'd ever had to conduct a funeral service like this one. He was probably more than a little nervous himself. I'd asked him to keep it short and simple but I think he understood how important it was that he spoke of these three babies. That in death, they were finally recognised.

'Today we gather to mourn the loss of William and Ruby, much-loved son and daughter of William and Betty, and of Joanne, much-loved daughter of Irene.'

I squeezed Mum's hand again. She'd said she hadn't thought about names when she was pregnant, mainly because she hadn't wanted to think about the baby growing inside her. But she'd thought about it afterwards, once she'd been taken from her, and that was what she would have liked to call her, had she ever been given a chance. We'd found the names William and Ruby scratched on to the bottom of the other two fairy statues, when we'd moved them to our back yard. I'd told Ruby her great grandma had suggested her name while I was pregnant. That was why she'd always been so special to her.

We stood for 'All Things Bright and Beautiful', which Ruby had chosen. Not that our voices could be heard above the organ. I could barely hear Mum's next to me. But we moved our lips and sang the odd word we could manage.

The vicar spoke of Betty's time in the Land Army and of William's service in the war. He spoke of their love and devotion to each other, of their hopes and dreams, of William's boundless optimism and a life cut cruelly short. And before I knew it we were standing again, singing a final hymn before walking out behind the coffins and following them down the path to the far side of the cemetery.

We passed Olive's grave on the way, though I didn't point it out. There was a bedraggled wreath of white carnations in the shape of the word 'Mam' still lying on top of it. I'd come afterwards, to pay my respects. To stand at her graveside and whisper a final thank-you.

The undertakers stopped and stood over the two graves that had been dug, one bigger than the other, just the other side of Grandma's grave. We'd all agreed she would have wanted the twins to be buried together.

They lowered Joanne into the little grave nearest us first. Mum clutched my arm but stared intently at the coffin. This was what she'd wanted, to see her daughter buried. We stood with our heads bowed as the vicar said a few words. Mum stepped forward shakily and bent to throw some earth into the grave, before turning back to me, her eyes moist with tears.

I grasped her hand and we all stood together, linking arms, as William and Ruby were lowered into the remaining grave. They were being buried for good this time, having finally given up their secrets.

I walked over to Grandma's grave and bent to lay the bunch of flowers I'd brought for her. 'Rest in peace,' I whispered. 'I'm glad you're with William again. And you've got your babies with you too.'

Afterwards we went straight to York. We all needed a lift, a reminder of happier times. I'd phoned Bettys and asked if it would be possible to view the mirror, the one on which hundreds of servicemen had etched their names during the war. They'd said we were very welcome. That although part of the mirror had been destroyed during a bombing raid, the majority of it remained.

I took Mum's hand as we entered the tearooms. It was hard to imagine it as it had been then. The boys from the Royal Canadian Air Force laughing and joking with each other, knowing that they might not survive the night.

We went straight over to a member of staff who led us downstairs to the basement.

'Take your time,' she said. 'There are a lot of names to get through.'

It was Ruby who found it, her eagle eyes able to pick out their names among all the others. She pointed, tugging my sleeve, and I crouched down to look.

'William and Betty forever', it read.

ACKNOWLEDGEMENTS

Huge thanks to the following people: my editor, Emily Yau, for her patience, encouragement and helping me to get so much more out of the characters and the story; Jon Butler, for coming up with the title (someone should give him a job in publishing!); and all at Quercus for their hard work and tireless championing of my books. My agent, Anthony Goff, for his ongoing support and invaluable advice and all at David Higham Associates.

My copyeditor, Hazel Orme, for her eagle-eyes and removing all the words you didn't need to read; Rebecca Bradley, for her excellent police fact-checking service; Blacksheep, for the cover design; Lance Little, for my website; Nansi Rosenberg, for her archeological wisdom and having some great bone photos on her phone; members of The Book Club on Facebook for their thoughts on the Yorkshire dialect (have gone for the middle option so as not to alienate our friends down south but feel free to Yorkshirefy it fully in your heads!).

The books *Yorkshire Airfields in the Second World War* by Patrick Otter and *Yorkshire Women at War* by Marion Jefferies were invaluable sources of research, as was The Wartime Memories Project website (www.wartimememoriesproject.com).

Thanks to my friends and family for their ongoing support, my husband Ian, who is now an old hand at the trials of living with an author but continues to bear it with good grace (while producing cracking book trailers for me!), and my wonderful son, Rohan, for being brutally honest on plot ideas and always seeing the potential for his future stage adaptations of my work.

A special thank you to the various tradesmen who, eventually, after months of our house being under dustsheets and me having to shift my laptop to every room of the house in turn, finished the rewiring/plastering/painting/flooring and left me alone to write. Thanks, as always, to the fantastic booksellers, librarians and book bloggers who do a wonderful job promoting books and reading and, most importantly, to my readers, for buying, borrowing, recommending and reviewing and whose lovely messages about previous books once again kept me going through the tough bits and the odd one-star review on Amazon. I hope you all enjoy the book!

Please do get in touch on Twitter: @LindaGreenisms, Facebook: Author Linda Green, or by email via my website www.linda-green.com. I look forward to hearing from you!

ABOUT THIS BOOK

WARNING: Spoiler Alert!

It was something which my nan said, shortly before she died a couple of years ago, which made me think about the secrets people take to their graves. Particularly women, who for so long have borne the shame that society has dealt them for their supposed 'transgressions' from what it deemed to be acceptable or simply for the workings of their own bodies. On so many occasions, when I told people what my next novel was about, they responded with stories about women in their own family who had harboured painful secrets for many years for fear of how they would be judged.

Over time, the things for which women have been made to feel shame may have changed but the one constant thing is that it is women who have been made to feel responsible for everything that have happened to them, even when criminal acts have been involved.

My hope in writing this novel is to spark conversations that encourage more women to share their secrets without fear of being judged and to inspire the next generation to ensure that women are freed from the shackles of shame to live their lives without judgement.

I'll be making donations from the royalties of this book to Rape Crisis www.rapecrisis.org.uk and the NSPCC www.nspcc.org.uk to help them continue the amazing work they do supporting women and children who have suffered rape or sexual abuse. If you're able to make a donation too, however small, I'd be hugely grateful. Thank you.

BOOK CLUB QUESTIONS

1. Why do you think Betty mentioned the babies to Nicola before she died?

2. What purpose did William's letters to Betty serve throughout the book?

3. How do you feel the nature of shame has changed over the decades?

4. Why does Nicola finally acknowledge to herself what happened at the party when she was 20?

5. What significance do the fairy statues have throughout the story?

6. How is the relationship between siblings with different fathers, living in the same family, explored?

Read on for an extract from
Linda Green's bestselling novel

After I've
GONE

Everybody loses their mum at some point. But your mother is supposed to be old when it happens; wrinkled and stooping and frail.

They are not supposed to be cut down in their prime. When they are still bleeding every month, haven't received any 'keep calm at forty' cards, or even started using anti-wrinkle moisturisers, for goodness sake.

When life ends so rudely, so prematurely, it makes no sense at all. The world stops turning. Your foundations have been removed. The floor beneath you could give way at any point. It's like playing one of those ball in the maze games and knowing that at any second you could fall down the hole.

Precarious. Life is precarious. And if people try to tell you otherwise, and say you are crazy for thinking that way, you have to remember that the crazy ones are those who deny it. Because the only thing which is certain in life is that we are all going to die one day. And that day could be sooner than we think.

PART ONE

JESS

Monday, 11 January 2016

I smell his bad breath a second or two before I feel his hand on my arse. That's the weird thing about public transport gropers, they always seem to have personal hygiene issues.

'What's your problem?' I shout, as I spin around to face him. Immediately, the crowd of people jostling around the ticket barriers parts. The one thing commuters hate even more than delays is a confrontation.

The guy with the dodgy breath and wandering hand obviously hadn't expected this. He looks to either side, desperate to pass the buck.

'Nope, it's definitely you, middle-aged man in the shiny grey suit. Get off on touching women's arses, do you?'

He shuffles his feet and looks at the ground then pushes his way towards the ticket barrier.

'That's it, you run along to work. I bet the women at your office can't wait to see you. Keep your mucky hands to yourself next time, OK?'

I glance behind to see Sadie looking at me with a raised eyebrow.

'What?' I say. 'He got off lightly if you ask me.'

There is now a clear path in front of me to the ticket barrier. I go straight through and wait for Sadie on the other side.

A young guy with dark hair stops in front of me. 'Nice takedown,' he says with a smile. 'Do you want me to go after him for you?'

He is wearing a plum-coloured jacket over a white T-shirt, like he's come in for dress-down Friday on a Monday by mistake.

'What I really want is for all members of the male species to go to hell and stop bothering me.'

The smile falls off his lips. 'Point taken,' he says, before walking off.

'What did you do that for?' asks Sadie, staring at me. 'He was only trying to be nice.'

'Yeah, well, it's difficult to tell sometimes.'

Sadie shakes her head. 'I don't get you. Is this national bite-someone's-head-off day or something?'

'PMT and hunger, always a bad combination. Come on, I need food.'

Breakfast (I hate the word 'brunch' so I refuse to call it that, even when it is after ten thirty) for me consists of a huge blueberry muffin (that I hope will count as one of my five a day) and a can of Tango (that possibly counts as another). Mum used to tell me that the day would come when I wouldn't be able to eat and drink all that crap without looking as if I did.

I'd taken it as a green light to have as much of it as possible while I could still get away with it.

I hear footsteps approaching as I stand waiting to pay. Sadie gives me a nudge. I look up. The guy who'd offered to go after the groper is standing there, bunch of flowers in hand. Actually, it isn't a bunch; it's a proper bouquet. Hand-tied, I think they call it, not that I've ever seen a machine tie flowers.

'An apology for earlier,' he says. 'On behalf of the male species. To show we're not all complete jerks.'

All conversation in the queue stops. I am aware my cheeks are turning the same colour as the roses in the bouquet.

'Thanks,' I say, taking them from him. 'You didn't have to do that.'

'I know, but I wanted to. I also want to ask you out to dinner but I'm not sure if that would be risking a massive public bawl-out so I've left my business card in there with the flowers. Call me if you'd like to take up the invite. And thanks for brightening my morning.'

He turns and walks away, one of those supremely confident walks that stops just short of being a full-blown swagger.

'I hate you,' says Sadie. 'I have no idea why I chose someone who strangers give flowers to as a best friend.'

'You didn't choose me,' I reply. 'I chose you, remember? Mainly because you had the best pencil case in reception.'

'Well, whatever. I still hate you. You don't even have to try. You wear a puffer jacket, leggings and DMs and you still get a gorgeous stranger asking you out.'

'I might not call him,' I say, lowering my voice, aware other people in the queue are listening.

'Then you're a bigger mug than I thought.'

'Well, I'm certainly not going to do it straight away.'

'Playing hard to get, are you?'

'No. I'm just starving and I'm not going to do anything until I've stuffed this blueberry muffin down my gob.'

Sadie smiles at me and looks down at the flowers. As well as the roses there are lilies and loads of other things I don't even know the names of. 'They must have cost him a packet,' she remarks.

'Shame he didn't know I'd have been happy with a blueberry muffin then,' I reply. She laughs. I hold the flowers a little tighter, despite myself.

Leeds city centre is its usual Monday morning self: grey, drizzly and slightly the worse for wear from the weekend. Someone presses a copy of a free magazine into my hand as I stand at the crossing. I take it, not because I want to read it but because I feel for anyone who has to get up at the crack of dawn to force magazines into the hands of grumpy commuters. I roll it up and wedge it into the side pocket of my backpack as I cross the road. The woman in front of me has her right arm turned out and a bulging tote bag hanging from it. I resist the temptation to tell her she looks like a Barbie doll that has had its arm twisted the wrong way by a little boy. I am convinced that if the female species carries on like this, baby girls will eventually be born with their right arms protruding at this weird angle, ready for the midwives to hang tote bags on them.

Sadie follows my gaze and smiles knowingly at me. We are both fully paid-up members of the backpack brigade.

'I wonder if they'll do something for Bowie at work,' Sadie says. 'Put *Labyrinth* and *Absolute Beginners* on, maybe.'

'Yeah,' I say. 'I bet a lot of people would come if they did.'

I decide not to tell Sadie, who has spent most of the train journey talking about David Bowie, that, actually, I am already fed up with it all. Every time I look at Facebook it's full of people posting tributes to him, all doing that RIP crap as if they'd actually known him, actually suffered some deep personal loss. Never stopping to think about what that must feel like to someone who had genuinely lost a loved one. The most important person in their life, even.

We turn off the road into the comparative warmth of the shopping centre. Someone had the bright idea of not putting any sides on the building, so people have to sit at the tables outside the restaurants with their coats and scarves on in winter, even though they are technically inside.

I follow Sadie up the escalator. The cinema is on the 'leisure' floor, with all the restaurants. It's a trendy independent one with squishy sofas and pizzas served in your seats. That's how I justify working there (well, that and the fact I don't have to start work before 11 a.m., even on an early shift). I could never work at a multiplex. It would be like letting the Dementors suck out your soul.

Nina, who's on a rare outing as duty manager, is on the

front desk. She looks down at my flowers and raises an eyebrow. 'I hope you're not thinking of starting a Bowie shrine here.'

'It's nothing to do with him. I was given them, actually.'

'What for?'

'Telling a guy he was an arsehole.'

'Very funny.'

'No, really,' I reply. 'Only the arsehole wasn't the guy who gave them to me.'

Nina shakes her head and sighs. 'So, basically, you bought yourself some flowers on the way into work to make it look like someone gave them to you.'

'Actually,' says Sadie, jumping in before I have the chance to say anything, 'she got them from a drop-dread gorgeous guy who came up to her in the station and asked her out. She's just too modest to admit it.'

'Oh yeah? What's his number then?' asks Nina.

I reach for the business card inside the cellophane and read it out to her. 'Call him if you like,' I say. 'I might not bother.'

Nina rolls her eyes and goes back to whatever it was she was doing on the screen. Sadie nods at me and we head off towards the staffroom. When we get there, I realise I still have the business card in my hand.

'What's his name?' asks Sadie, following my gaze.

'Lee Griffiths. It says he's an associate director at some PR firm in Leeds.'

'Woo. Big cheese. Call him.'

'Nah. It's probably a wind-up.'

'Well, if you don't want him, I'm very happy to take second-hand goods.'

I smile at her as we step back into the lobby to find Tariq and Adrian laying the new red carpet leading to screen one.

'Here you go, ladies,' says Adrian, 'just in time to try it out.'

'Me first!' cries Sadie. I laugh as she sashays up and down the red carpet, posing for imaginary photographs for the paparazzi.

'Hang on,' I say, throwing myself on the floor in front of her. 'Name the film premiere.'

'Suffragette,' she shrieks, before joining me, prostrate on the floor.

'What's all this noise?' asks Nina, sticking her head around the corner.

'Guess the film premiere!' I say. 'Do you want to have a go?'

'No. I want you two to stop treating this place like a soft-play centre and get to work.'

Sadie groans as Nina returns to the front desk. 'I bet Carey Mulligan never had to put up with this,' she says.

I wait until lunchtime to text Lee, when I am on my own in the staffroom. I want to be sure no one else is around in case the whole thing is a wind-up. I decide to keep it short and sweet.

Hi, thanks again for the flowers. Let me know a date and time to meet up. I finish work at 7pm until Wednesday, then I'm working late for a week. Jess.

I hesitate for a second, aware that I might be about to make myself look incredibly stupid, but then I decide to do it anyway. I exhale deeply and press send. It is only once I have done so that I realise how bothered I am about whether or not he responds. Fortunately, I have to wait less than thirty seconds before my phone beeps with a message. Clearly he is the sort of guy who doesn't have to worry about looking desperate.

Hi Jess. That's great. How about Wednesday @ 7.30pm, the Botanist?

The Botanist is an uber-trendy bar just along from the shopping centre. I have never been there, mainly on account of the fact that I am not uber-trendy and don't know anyone who is.

I text back to say that I'll see him there, as if it's a usual hangout of mine. He replies, Great, looking forward to it already.

I am still sitting there with a smug look on my face when Sadie comes in.

'You've called him, haven't you?' she says.

'Texted.'

'And you're going out with him.'

'Might be.'

'If you two get married, I'm going to hunt down the arse-groper guy and invite him to the wedding.'

'I don't think there's any danger of us getting married.'

'Why not?'

'Er, different leagues.'

'Bollocks. You're well up there with him.'

'I still reckon he did it for a dare. Anyway, you'll be on your own on the train home on Wednesday. Think of me surrounded by hipsters trying to order cocktails I've never heard of.'

Sadie snorts. 'I hope he's paying.'

'So do I. Otherwise we're going to Subway, I tell you.'

It's only as I'm walking home from Mytholmroyd station later that I realise Dad will ask about the flowers. I think for a second about chucking them over my head – bride-style – but a quick glance behind confirms that they are likely to be caught by a long-haired, overweight guy, who probably wouldn't appreciate it. I decide to tell Dad a censored version of what happened. He may be able to cope with a guy hitting on me but I'm pretty sure he would freak if I mentioned the arse groper.

I walk past the rows of little back-to-back terraces, lines of washing hanging across the backyards like something out of a bygone era. I bet the people down south watching the Boxing Day floods on the news couldn't believe that a place like Mytholmroyd even existed. It does my head in most of the time, the smallness and oldness of the place. Some people have lived here all their lives, have never even been to Leeds, let alone London. I think that's why I took the first job that came up in Leeds when I left college. No, it wasn't doing what I had planned to do, but at least it meant I could get out of Mytholmroyd.

Our front door opens straight onto the street and the back door onto our yard behind. If I can ever afford a flat in Leeds (which is doubtful), I've already decided I'll get one high up, so people walking past can't have a good gander inside when you open the door.

I go in the back way, as usual. Dad's in the kitchen, Monday being a rare evening off for him because the Italian restaurant where he works is closed.

'Smells good,' I say. Dad looks up from the pan he's stirring, his gaze immediately dropping from my face to the flowers.

'They're nice.'

'Yeah.' I put the flowers on the kitchen counter, knowing full well that I'm not going to get away with that answer.

'So, who are they from?' Dad is still stirring the vegetables on the back hob, trying to pretend he's not that interested.

'A guy I met at the station this morning.'

He nods slowly and puts the wooden spoon down on the chopping board.

'That was nice of him.' Dad's tone suggests he actually thinks the man in question is a serial killer. I decide to get it all out in one go.

'Yeah. I'm going for a meal with him on Wednesday.'

'Are you now?' Dad picks up the spoon again and stirs with an intensity that is entirely unnecessary.

'How old is he, this guy?'

'I'd say seventies, maybe eighty at a push.'

He turns to face me. I have the smile ready prepared for him.

'Very droll,' he says.

'Well, what do you expect? He looks like he's in his late twenties but I don't know. I'll take a questionnaire with me on Wednesday, if you like.'

'So you've never met him before?'

'Nope.'

'And he just walked up to you this morning and gave you flowers and asked you out?'

'Yep. That's pretty much how it was.'

'Doesn't that strike you as a bit weird?'

'Not really.' I was starting to think it would have been easier to tell him about the arse groper after all.

'It sounds a bit weird to me.'

'Look, you've got to let me do normal stuff like this.'

'It's not normal, though, is it? Giving flowers to someone you don't know. Maybe he does this all the time. Some kind of scam he pulls on pretty girls.'

'Dad, I can't win with you. You're the one who always used to tell me to get out more.'

'Yeah, I didn't mean with a stranger.'

'Well, he's not a stranger now, is he? He gave me flowers and asked me out. I said yes. I thought you'd be pleased.'

This is a lie. I knew he'd be exactly like this but I also know how to play him in an argument. He looks down at his feet.

'I'm happy for you. It's just that after last time I, you know, I don't want to see you get hurt.'

'Callum was an emotionally inadequate bastard.'

'Jess.'

'Well, he was! And I've grown up a lot since then – I'm not going to make the same mistake again, am I?'

'So how do you know this guy's not like that?'

'I don't yet, but he gave me flowers, which is a pretty good start, and if I don't like him on Wednesday I won't see him again. Simples.'

Dad nods. He is trying his best to be two parents rolled into one, I know that. But I still wish Mum was around to tell him to let me learn from my own mistakes.

'OK. I'll give him a chance. What's his name?'

'Voldemort.'

For the first time in the conversation, Dad manages a smile. 'Really?'

'His name is Lee and he's the associate director of a PR firm in Leeds and I don't know anything else about him – but if you submit your questions by midnight tomorrow, I'll be sure to put them to him over dinner, OK?'

I flounce out of the kitchen and up to my room. When I return ten minutes later, Dad has put the flowers in a vase. I smile at him. Sometimes he tries so hard it hurts.

Sadie Ward ▸ **Jess Mount**
2 mins

Your dad just told me. I can't believe you're gone. Can't believe you're never going to crack me up laughing again. I'm so, so sorry I couldn't save you. Love you forever. RIP Jess.

JESS

Monday, 11 January 2016

I'm in my room later when I see Sadie's post. It's the photo I see first, one of Sadie and I when we were at primary school. My socks are around my ankles and I have messy hair. We are both grinning inanely. I am about to message her when I read the words she has posted above it.

I read them again, twice more, sure I have missed something. I wait for another post to pop up from her saying it was a joke. It doesn't. I call her.

'Why did you just post that?'

'What?'

'That RIP thing on Facebook.'

'About Bowie?'

'No, about me.'

'I didn't post anything about you.'

'You did. To my timeline. Two minutes ago. A photo of us at primary school and stuff about how you can't believe that I'm gone and you're so sorry you couldn't save me. You basically said I was dead.'

'Why would I do that?'

'I don't know. That's why I called you.'

'I honestly haven't posted a thing.'

'Check Facebook now. You'll see it.'

'OK.' It goes quiet at the other end of the phone for a minute. 'There's nothing there,' she says. 'I haven't posted anything for hours and I've looked on your timeline and there's nothing there either.'

I look again at my phone and read the post out to her.

'That's really sick. I'd never do that. Not even as a joke.'

A comment comes up underneath Sadie's post from Adrian at work.

'Listen,' I say, 'Adrian's just posted this: "Oh Jess, so sad to lose you. Will miss your smile and the laughs we had together. RIP sweetie."'

'Maybe someone's hacked your account,' says Sadie. 'I wouldn't put it past Nina. She could have got hold of your phone or something.'

'But how come I can see it and you can't?'

'I dunno. Maybe there's some way you can do that.'

'Well, they must have hacked into yours as well because the post's from your account.'

'Change your password. I'll change mine too. That should put a stop to it.'

'OK. I'll call you back in a bit.'

I go into my account. I'm rubbish at remembering passwords

so I have to write down the new one as soon as I've changed it. I log out of Facebook then log in again and go back to my timeline. There are now eleven comments underneath Sadie's post, a couple of them from people I haven't seen since I left school and who I unfollowed on Facebook long ago. I have no idea how this is happening but I am going to put a stop to it straight away. I begin to type: *Ha, ha, very funny. It seems the news of my death has been greatly exaggerated* – which I seem to remember was a line from a book or a play or something. I post it. It doesn't appear. I post it again, twice more in fact. Still nothing. I don't get it. I don't get what's happening. I call Sadie back.

'I changed my password but it's still there. Lots of people have posted comments on it but I can't, it won't let me.'

'Maybe it's a virus or something.'

'And you're sure you can't see it?'

'Absolutely.'

'I don't understand how that's even possible.'

'It'll be some thirteen-year-old hacker who's bored stiff doing his maths homework and gets off on doing sick things like this.'

I sigh and shake my head.

'So what do you think I should do?'

'Do a virus scan. That should get rid of it. And if no one else can see it apart from you, there's no harm done, is there?'

'But what if the people who commented can see it? What if they think I'm actually dead?'

'Well, Adrian would have messaged me for a start, wouldn't he?'

'I guess so.' Adrian is lovely. I'm actually touched that he sounded so gutted in his comment. Which is really stupid, I know.

'But the things people have said in their comments,' I continue. 'They actually sound like the sort of thing they would say.'

'Well, nobody's going to say they're delighted you've popped your clogs, are they? Everyone says the same stuff when people die.'

'Adrian called me sweetie. How would they know he calls me sweetie?'

'Probably because he calls everybody sweetie on Facebook? There's probably some algorithm that tells you what words people use most.'

'What if you were right about Nina, though? Maybe she has got something to do with it.'

'She might have the motivation but I'm not sure she's actually bright enough to do it.'

'Well, who else hates me, then?'

'No one hates you, Jess.'

'What about Callum?'

'He's hardly super-brain league either, is he?'

'Why didn't you tell me that at the time?'

'Because you wouldn't have listened. Anyway, why don't you front Nina up in the morning and see what she says. And quit worrying. You're clearly alive. OK?'

'Yeah.'

There is a pause on the other end of the line. I have a feeling I know what Sadie is going to say next.

'You are OK, aren't you? I mean you'd say if . . .'

'I'm fine.'

'And you would tell me if you weren't?'

'You know I would.'

'Good. Now turn your phone off, do a virus scan on your laptop, zap anything that comes up and I bet when you look in the morning there'll be nothing there.'

'OK. Thanks. See you tomorrow.'

I put my phone down and open my laptop. Maybe I won't even be able to see it on there. It might only have been on my phone. I click on Facebook and scroll through everyone's posts from the past couple of hours. Nothing. The photo isn't there. I click on my timeline to double-check. Sadie's post comes up straight away. There are loads of comments now. People asking what happened. And others have started posting to my timeline. Jules from college and Tariq from work and a couple of Mum's friends. They all say the same: that they're in shock; they can't believe I've gone. That it's too much for one family to bear.

I brush the tears away from my cheeks and tell myself not to be so stupid. If it is a virus, the person who created it won't have stopped to think how upsetting it is for someone who has lost a loved one. Sadie's probably right – it'll be some kid who's bored out of his brain and thought it would be a laugh. I shouldn't take it so personally.

I can hear voices on the television drifting up from downstairs. It doesn't sound like football – maybe it's a cookery programme. They're about the only two things Dad watches.

I wonder for a moment about going down to join him, just to clear my head. Snuggling up on the sofa together like we used to do. He'd like it. He always says we don't spend enough time together. I decide against it, though. He'd probably ask me what was wrong. Either that or start quizzing me about Lee again.

I get my earphones, push them into my phone and play the first thing that comes up on the menu. But I can't stop thinking about the post. I suddenly remember the arse groper at the station. What if he's an IT nerd who has decided to get his own back on me for his public humiliation this morning? What if he's somehow managed to find my photo and track me down online?

I pull my earphones out and throw the phone across the bed. I get up, go over to the laptop and start a virus security scan. I'll leave it running overnight and by the morning the whole thing will be gone.

Joe Mount
12 July 2017 • Mytholmroyd, United Kingdom

I'm heartbroken to say that my beloved daughter Jess died yesterday following an accident. I've lost my little girl and I don't have the words to say what she meant to me. My only comfort is that she will at least be with her mum and that Deborah will take care of her for us. RIP beautiful girl.

JESS

Tuesday, 12 January 2016

I died in an accident. I screw my eyes up tight and then open them again, just to make sure that I am fully awake. The words in front of me remain the same. I go cold inside. The overnight laptop security scan came up clear. *No viruses found.* Probably the only time someone has been disappointed to hear that. Because, if it's not a virus, what the hell is it? I am about to phone Sadie when I realise there's no point – she won't be able to see it. I'll have to show her the posts on the train. That way she'll know I'm not making it up.

I read Dad's words again, tears pricking the corners of my eyes. They sound like the words he would use. I can see him sitting there, typing it with two fingers on his keyboard (he never does posts from his phone. He says his fingers are too big for the buttons and he doesn't get on with predictive text). His eyes are red. A scrunched-up tissue is poking out of the pocket of his favourite cardigan – the grey one Mum got him the Christmas before she died. This feels too real, far too real for my liking. It doesn't feel random. It doesn't feel like some hacker messing around. It feels like whoever is doing this is getting at me on purpose.

It is only when I go to read the post for a third time that I notice the date above it: 12 July 2017. I stare at it for a long time, my brain trying to process what my eyes are seeing. How can someone change the date on Facebook? That's eighteen months from now. Eighteen months exactly. I scroll down to last night's posts. At the time I read them, they just had *2 minutes ago* or *1 hour ago* above them. Now Sadie's says *11 July 2017*. My breaths are coming fast and shallow. I Google 'How to change the dates on Facebook'. There is a surge of relief when I see that you can. Apparently, you can change the dates of posts to as far back as 1 January 1905. But a second later I am reading that you can't change the dates of posts to the future. Can't. As in, impossible.

Someone is screwing with my mind. Maybe some kid I used to go to school with who knows what happened to me, who thinks it would be funny to freak me out like this. There are a few comments below Dad's post now. One from my cousin Connie in Italy. She's done a breaking-heart emoji at the end of it. And another from a chef at the restaurant where Dad works, saying how sorry he is for his loss.

Nobody has asked yet what kind of accident. I probably got run over by a bus. That's the sort of stupid thing a space cadet like me would do. Probably looking at my phone at the time. I find myself thinking that I hope it wasn't messy. That, however I died, people didn't have to scoop up parts of me from the road. I wouldn't like that. Wouldn't like it at all.

I'm not going to let them get to me like this. I'll report it to Facebook, let them find out who is doing it and have them blocked or whatever. They can get the police involved if they want, or at least threaten them with it. I just want it stopped.

I pull my dressing gown on. It's a huge purple fluffy thing; Sadie says it makes me look like an extra from *Monsters, Inc.* I pad across the landing to the bathroom. I can hear Dad downstairs in the kitchen. I try to get the image of him sitting at his laptop, crying, out of my head.

Usually, I turn the temperature in the shower down when I use it after Dad. He likes his showers hotter than me, like he drinks his tea hotter than me. But today I leave it where it is, welcoming anything that takes my mind off what is happening – even the scorching sensation as the water hits my body. My skin is decidedly pinker than usual by the time I step out. I grab my towel off the rail above the radiator and hug it around me. It's one of the things I always remember about Mum: her rubbing me dry after a bath when I was a kid and singing cheesy eighties' pop songs to me.

By the time I make it down to the kitchen, Dad is on what I suspect is his third coffee of the day. He smiles and comes over and kisses me on the forehead. Sometimes I pull away and remind him that I am no longer seven years old. Today I don't say anything, just give him a little smile back. I know he won't have checked Facebook yet. He doesn't even bother turning his phone on until he leaves for work some days. I'm pretty sure he won't be able to see the posts, though. And for that I am mightily relieved.

'You OK?' he asks.

'Yeah, not a great night's sleep, that's all.'

'Were you cold? I'll put an extra blanket in there for you if you want.'

'No. Just couldn't get to sleep for ages.'

He nods. I catch sight of the flowers, still in the same spot on the table as last night. I'd almost forgotten about Lee with everything that has been happening.

'Early night tonight then, before your big date,' Dad says, bringing over my mug and putting it down in front of me.

'It's not a big date,' I say.

'What is it then?'

'A meal. That's all.'

'Right,' he says with a wink. I look down; I can't even look him in the eye without thinking about it. What it would do to him if I died.

I meet Sadie on the platform as usual. We're not always on the same shifts, but if it's Chris or Liz doing the rota they try to make sure we are. People used to take the piss out of us at secondary school. My English teacher called us Jessadie because he said we were inseparable, like conjoined twins. I've always liked it though, having one best friend rather than being part of a big gaggle. Or a threesome. Threes were a nightmare at school because you never knew who to sit next to.

'They've done a post from my dad now,' I say, reaching

into my pocket to get my phone. 'Saying I died in an accident. And they've changed the date to make it seem like it's from next year.'

'How can they do that?' asks Sadie.

'You can't, according to Google,' I reply, clicking on Facebook and going to my timeline. 'Which is why it's freaking me out. The virus scan was clear too. Somebody's doing this on purpose.'

'Show me. I still can't see anything on mine.'

I don't respond because I'm staring at my timeline. It's back to normal. The posts aren't on there. I scroll up and down. Nothing. I look up at Sadie, phone in hand.

'They've gone.'

'Good. Maybe it just took that long for the password change to take effect.'

'But they were there just now, before I left the house. I checked again before I came out because I wanted to show you.'

Sadie looks at me. I can almost hear her choosing the right words in her head before she says anything.

'Well, at least they're gone, that's the main thing.'

'I wanted you to see them though!'

'I believe you, Jess. But it doesn't matter now, does it? They've gone and that's what you wanted.'

'Yeah. I suppose so.'

'You could always check with Facebook? Maybe they could tell you if your account was hacked.'

'But I haven't got any proof now, have I? It would just be

me saying there were some crank posts with nothing to back it up. They wouldn't bother looking into it.'

'I guess not. Anyway, like I said, it was probably some spotty thirteen-year-old lad in Hong Kong with nothing better to do.'

I hear the whistling on the tracks and a moment later see our train coming into view. Sadie's right. I should forget it, I know that. But there's a cold place deep inside me that can't. Somebody did that, knowing full well how upsetting it would be. And I can't let that go.

Nina is back with the rest of us plebs on the hosting team today. Hosting is a rather grand word for dashing in and out of different cinema screens with pizzas and burgers (posh ones that they can charge more for because they've got halloumi in). I suppose it's like the bin men now being called refuse collectors, and woodwork and metalwork being called resistant materials at school. Everyone and everything has to have a souped-up title these days.

'No flowers today then,' Nina says as I walk past her in the corridor. I turn and look at her, trying to work out if the smirk on her face is a guilty one.

'Have you been messing with my phone?' I ask.

'What kind of question is that?'

'One that I want answered. You were pretty interested in who gave me the flowers yesterday.'

'Do you honestly think I'm desperate enough to go trawling through your contacts for your supposed boyfriend?'

'Maybe you wanted to have a look at my Facebook.'

'Why would I do that?'

'I dunno. You tell me. Some people get off on that sort of thing.'

'Well, I'm not one of them. I have no interest in your private life. And I suggest,' she says, jabbing a finger towards my face, 'you don't go around making accusations like that.'

I look at her, trying to work out whether she's telling the truth. Her dyed blonde hair is scraped back into a ponytail. The whole of her face looks like it's been scraped back with it. She has one of those mean, vacant faces you see in mugshots. But, despite the smirk, I'm not sure Nina's capable of doing something as clever as hacking into my account.

'Fine. We'll leave it at that, then,' I say, walking off.

I hear a loud tut and muttered swearing behind me, but I choose to ignore it. I go to the staffroom to make myself a tea, swishing the kettle side to side to check there's enough water in it before I flick the switch. No one else is around. I know I shouldn't but I can't help myself. I get my phone out of my bag and go to my Facebook page.

The posts are back, with even more comments under them, dozens of them now. Sad emojis and RIPs by the bucketload. My fingers tense around the phone. I don't understand this. Has the hacker somehow discovered my new password? I go into my account and change it again. I check back but the posts are still there. And the dates on them are all from July next year.

The kettle has boiled, but I'm no longer bothered about the tea. I march out of the room to go and find Sadie.

'Look,' I say, hurrying into the kitchen, where I find her sorting out the ketchups and mustards. 'They're back again.'

I thrust the phone in her face. She takes a step back, stares at it then looks at me, a frown creasing her brow.

'Crazy, eh?' I say.

'There's nothing there,' she says softly. I turn the phone round to look at it. She's right. It's my usual timeline. No RIPs in sight.

'I don't understand!' I cry. 'They were there a minute ago in the staffroom. I just checked.'

Sadie gives me that look. The one she used to give me when it was at its worst. The one that says, *I really don't want to hurt your feelings but I think you should know you've lost the plot.*

'Maybe leave it for a bit, eh?'

'I know this doesn't make any sense, but it's like I'm the only one who can see them.'

Sadie nods slowly. 'Like I said, maybe stop checking all the time.'

'Yeah,' I say, putting the phone back in my pocket. 'You're right.'

She smiles at me, but even Sadie, who is experienced in these things, can't hide the concern behind her smile. She returns to organising the mustards.

'Here,' I say. 'I'll give you a hand. Pass me the ketchups.'